Matthew Gardner, N. (Nicholas) Summerbell

The Autobiography of Elder Matthew Gardner

A Minister in the Christian Church Sixty-three Years

Matthew Gardner, N. (Nicholas) Summerbell

The Autobiography of Elder Matthew Gardner
A Minister in the Christian Church Sixty-three Years

ISBN/EAN: 9783337031060

Printed in Europe, USA, Canada, Australia, Japan

Cover: Foto ©Raphael Reischuk / pixelio.de

More available books at **www.hansebooks.com**

THE

AUTOBIOGRAPHY

OF

ELDER MATTHEW GARDNER,

A MINISTER IN

THE CHRISTIAN CHURCH

SIXTY-THREE YEARS.

EDITED BY N. SUMMERBELL, D. D.

Pastor of the First Christian Church, Cincinnati, Ohio.

His last text, " *Preach unto it the preaching that I bid thee.*" *Jonah 3: 2*

————————◆————————

DAYTON, OHIO:
CHRISTIAN PUBLISHING ASSOCIATION.
1874.

INTRODUCTION BY THE AUTHOR.

To THE READER: Having kept no diary or journal of my life, the following pages, up to July 4, 1865, were written entirely from memory, with the help of a few papers and documents which had been preserved. Therefore, of course minute particulars of my life are not given; while all the principal matters and events thereof are plainly, honestly, and truthfully narrated and set forth.

The subject of writing my own life had for several years borne with a great deal of weight upon my mind, as a duty, but I put it off, sometimes thinking that I would do it, and then almost concluding never to undertake it, but to leave it for others to do, if it is ever done at all. Thus, after much consideration, for and against the undertaking, the idea came into my mind that I knew more about my own life than anybody else; and I consequently determined, if the Lord would continue my days in this world long enough, that I would leave my life, written, except the close, by myself. So, on the 1st day of May, 1864, the work was begun by me, when I was in the seventy-fourth year of my age. It was not long after having commenced, till I found that the labor would be far greater than I had expected. I therefore would have given it up, had it not been a rule of mine through life, not to undertake any thing without going through with it. So the labor was continued, in hope that the work might be useful to some of my fellow mortals, when this hand is cold and can write no more, and this tongue of mine is silent in death. It has taken all my time that could be spared from other engagements, from the 1st day of May, 1864, to the 4th day of July, 1865—one year, two months, and four days— to write my past life up to the latter date. May the Lord give me a tranquil hour in which to die. Farewell.

M. GARDNER.

I appoint Elder N. Summerbell to publish my life, as written by myself, which will be delivered to him at the proper time. I will leave the proper sum to pay for printing, etc., a stereotype edition of one thousand copies; two hundred of which he will see are delivered to my executors for my children and grandchildren; further than this, all profits then and forever after are to go to Union Christian College. In case he should fail, he may appoint another man to publish my life, or the President of Union Christian College shall do it, whoever he may be; always provided that the college continues to be owned and controled by the Christians, otherwise the profits of the book will revert to such benevolent cause as said Summerbell or his successor, as publisher, may select.

MATTHEW GARDNER.

Ripley, Ohio, July 21, 1865.

CINCINNATI, OHIO, August 6, 1874.

We, the undersigned, B. B. and John W. Gardner, approve of the continuation of the biography of our father, beyond the end of his own writing, by N. Summerbell, and the continuing of the narrative to the close of his life, bringing in whatever may properly belong to the book, or add to its interest, usefulness, and value. Also, as far as we have been able to examine the work, we approve of the pains which he has taken to supply deficiencies, and the faithfulness with which he has prepared the copy for the press.

B. B. GARDNER.
J. W. GARDNER.

P. S.—The following letters, in the autobiographer's own hand, give an exact view of his wishes concernig the preparation of his works for the press, and of his autography, the difference in appearance being merely that the autograph to the engraving was written with great care and a good pen, and the letters carelessly with an old pen.

N. S.

EDITOR'S PREFACE.

For publishing these pages no apology is required. It has the defects common to human productions, but the character is rich in originality and interesting in events; its historical treasures are valuable, and the life-lessons profitable. It has lessons on pioneer life, conversion and preaching, economy, law, and religion. It has sermons, discussions, prayers, and songs of devotion, with interesting narratives and remarkable adventures. If one desires dates concerning the early settlement of the State, or facts concerning the state of the country, incidents in pioneer life, or views of pioneer preaching, dates of the organization of churches and conferences, or names of early ministers, he will find them in this book. There are strong arguments against secret societies, but they can bear them; and hard reflections on Unitarians, but they deserve them. His words are pointed; his remarks are sharp; his meaning is plain, and his animadversions designed; and it is as well, that responsibility may rest where it belongs. That the autobiographer was a man about whom thousands had always something to say while living, is good evidence that his book will be interesting since he is dead. His opponents will concede that he was great in the things they dislike, and successful in the things which they disapprove; and his friends will indorse the rest. As the stones, clubs, husks, and shells mark the tree that has borne fruit, so the constant struggle marks the remarkable life; and without excusing his defects or magnifying his virtues, his friends contend that his life gives its own lessons, and that he was a great thinker, a great worker, a great economist, a great friend, a great antagonist, a great preacher, a great debater, a great farmer, great financier; great in will, great in wisdom, great in planning, great in executing, great in self-denial, great in self-government, great while living, and great in dying.

And it is published in the hope that it will be blessed of the Lord in winning the wayward from ruin, saving the sinful from sin, and comforting many hearts.

> "Lives of true men all remind us
> We can make our lives sublime;
> And, departing, leave behind us
> Footprints in the sands of time;
> Footprints which perhaps another,
> Sailing o'er life's stormy main,
> A forlorn and shipwrecked brother,
> Seeing, may take heart again."

Cincinnati, Ohio, August 10, 1874.   N. SUMMERBELL.

CONTENTS.

CHAPTER I.

A. D. 1790—DECEMBER 5.

CHAPTER II.

A. D. 1800—SECOND DECADE OF HIS LIFE.

CHAPTER III.

A. D. 1810—THIRD TEN YEARS OF HIS LIFE.

CHAPTER IV.

A. D. 1820 TO 1830—FOURTH DECADE.

CHAPTER V.

A. D. 1830—FIFTH TEN YEARS OF HIS LIFE.

CHAPTER VI.

A. D. 1840—SIXTH TEN YEARS OF HIS LIFE.

CHAPTER VII.

A. D. 1850—SEVENTH TEN YEARS OF HIS LIFE.

CHAPTER VIII.

A. D. 1860 TO 1870—EIGHTH TEN YEARS OF HIS LIFE.

CHAPTER IX.

A. D. 1870 TO 1873—NINTH DECADE.

LIFE OF
ELDER MATTHEW GARDNER.

CHAPTER I.

"MY PARENTAGE AND THE FIRST TEN YEARS OF MY LIFE."

MY DEAR CHILDREN:—I will give you a brief account of my parentage, as related to me by my father, and as I learned it during three visits to the place of my birth, after an absence of over half a century. I was born in Stephentown, New York, on the 5th of December, A. D. 1790. My father moved from there to Ohio, A. D. 1800, and I visited the place after that, first in May of 1851, and again in August of 1854, and in August of 1857; during which visits I made particular inquiries respecting the ancestors of our family. I will then give you a true narrative of my own eventful life. The Gardners who were our forefathers came from England to America, and settled in Rhode Island about 1685 or 1690. Being devoted adherents of the principles of George Fox, and of the religious denomination of Friends, commonly called Quakers, a people not tolerated by the Puritans, then settling Massachusetts and Connecticut, they settled in Rhode Island, where all forms of religious worship and all varieties of doctrines were tolerated. My own father was born in Rhode Island, on the 13th day of September, A. D. 1760. My mother was born in Connecticut, on the 29th day of September, A. D. 1762. Her maiden name was Lucy Hawks. She was my father's second wife. The Gardners, my ancestors, as far as I have seen or been able to learn, were large men, tall, stout, and of good constitution, and were generally farmers. When my father was but ten years old, which was about the year 1770, my grandfather Gardner moved to the State of New York, and settled near the line of Massachusetts, on the lands of the Rensselaer manor, now Rensselaer County. The manor of Rensselaer covered the whole county. When about seventeen, my father went into the revolutionary army. After independence was gained, and peace secured, he returned home, and settled on thirty acres of poor land. This land, as all the lands there, was not sold, but obtained by lease for a low rent. Being a house-carpenter by trade, he devoted little time to the cultivation of his land, but supported his family principally by his trade. There were ten children, of whom one sister and two brothers were older than I. When only eight years old, I was hired out. Two years after this, my father being about forty years old, and vigorous and strong, and having a large family, he determined to go West. The territory now called Ohio was first settled in 1788. At the close of the Revolution, 243 officers of the army, mostly New England men, solicited Congress, through General Washington, to secure lands for them between the Ohio River and Lake Erie. In 1783 General Putnam said "that the country between the Ohio and Lake Erie would be filled with inhabitants, and thereby free the western territory from falling under the dominion of a foreign power." This was desirable, for, having no strong general government, foreign commanders kept defiant possession of forts on the very soil now Ohio. The first settlers, formed under a grant of Congress, were led by General Rufus Putnam, from Massachusetts and Connecticut, and laid the foundation of the State of Ohio at the mouth of the Muskingum River, on the 7th of April, 1788. Cincinnati started in 1789—the same year that the Constitution of the United States was adopted. Then the lands from the Ohio River to the Pacific Ocean were inhabited by Indians and wild beasts, excepting a very few distant forts and French posts or settlements in the valley of the Mississippi. In 1800 my father sold his leasehold, and we all started for the north-western territory of Ohio. This was two years before Ohio became a state. It was on a beautiful morning on the first of September A. D. 1800 when we started. I was in my tenth year when we left Stephentown; and well do I remember those scenes of my childhood. It was a beautiful morning. Not only our relatives, but many of our neighbors and friends, came to bid us farewell, and to see us start. It was regarded by many as impossible to succeed in such a journey with such a large family of small children, especially with our limited means. We had but one small wagon, with three horses, and other means correspondingly limited. The country we had never seen. The route was new, and to us unknown until we approached it. There was then little communication with the wilderness west. Not only railroads and steam-boats, but even turnpikes, were unknown. Most of those who came to see us start, after bidding us farewell, stood looking after us with tearful eyes until we passed beyond their view, while others accompanied on horseback for miles before turning back. We then pursued our way patiently but perseveringly. The mountains were difficult to climb, the streams were dangerous to ford, the undertaking was hazardous, and the journey was long. The weather was pleasant, and the journey as prosperous as we could expect. We reached Pittsburg, on the Ohio River, by the first of October, just one month from the time of starting. Pittsburg was a small village. We waited two weeks before we found a boat going down the river. Then we embarked on a flat-boat—the boats then used—with four other families; furniture, wagons, horses, and all, crowded on one small flat-boat. The river was low: the progress was slow: sometimes we floated rapidly; and sometimes we were long aground. We were nearly four weeks coming down to Limestone—a little village on the Kentucky side of the river. It had but few houses then. Limestone is now called Maysville. Here Henry Hughs, a land-trader, came to the boat to sell us land in Ohio. Father went with him to see it. He liked it, and traded him two horses for one hundred acres. We then proceeded on with the boat down the river, about twelve miles, till we came opposite our land, at a landing two miles below where Ripley now stands. There we disembarked, and the boat and its other passengers went on down the river. There was no town then where Ripley now stands. We landed within a few miles of our land, and soon reached our future home, where every thing seemed new and strange. We were all in good health, except one brother and sister, who had slight attacks of fever and ague, which soon disappeared. It seems extraordinary that such a large family could thus journey so long and all be preserved from more serious sickness. My father rented a little cabin to move into, while he and my two older brothers built a cabin on our own land. It was now about the last of November—the most pleasant and delightful Autumn I have ever known before or since. This fine weather continued till after Christmas. So my father and brothers having completed our new house, we moved into it about the first of January, 1801. The fine weather continued that year all winter, there being no weather to prevent out-door work. Being ten years old on the 5th of December, 1800, the first ten years of my earthly life had now passed, no more to return.

CHAPTER II.

EVENTS OF THE SECOND TEN YEARS OF MY LIFE.

I HAD now entered upon my eleventh year, in what seemed like a new world. Oh, what a contrast between this and the same time the preceding year. Then we were in a thickly-set-

tled country, surrounded by friends; now we were in a dense
forest, with no human beings, except ourselves, within two or
more miles of us. Then we could hear the songs of devotion,
praise, and prayer; but now we listened to the hooting of owls,
the howling of wolves, and the screams of panthers. There
were but two cabins within some two or three miles of us.
There was no ground to rent. Provisions were scarce, and only
to be procured at any price, from a very great distance. Our
money was about all expended. Our land was covered with a
heavy forest, principally of beech and poplar, which must be
immediately cleared for crops, to prevent starvation the coming
year. All who were large enough commenced work. By
spring we had nearly five acres cleared, which we planted in
corn and potatoes, which sustained us the coming year. One
of our greatest difficulties was to procure those things which
the land would not produce. Salt cost from three to four dollars for a bushel of fifty pounds; and other merchandise was
proportionately high. We were forced to study economy, and
compelled to practice it. This impressed the lessons upon my
mind. It was difficult to procure money to purchase a little;
and we learned to make a little do. Wild beasts were plenty.
There were birds in abundance. Bears, deer, and wild turkeys
supplied our table with meat, till we reared domestic animals.
Sheep and wool were not to be had, so our clothing was of flax
and hemp. Suits of these served for all seasons, summer and
winter alike. Father and the boys prepared the material, and
my mother and sisters manufactured the cloth, and made the
garments. We wore no shoes but moccasins, made of dressed
deer-skins, for we could get no leather. The deer-skin being
spongy, absorbed the water from the ground and snow, so our
feet were often wet. Yet we were all stout and healthy. We
needed no doctors, which was well, as none were to be had.
Where doctors abound, sickness much more abounds. We did
not eat the wheat, because it was called "sick-wheat," making
those sick who ate it. Our swine refused it. We tried other
stock; but all the animals rejected it. We preferred the corn.
I regard the health which I now enjoy, at the age of seventy-
four, as the consequence of the plain diet of my early life being
continued to this time. We were able to work, and we were
willing. We went on clearing for crops, and in a few years the
heavy timber gave place to orchard-trees, and the wilderness to
fruitful fields. Then our wants for food and clothing were
plentifully supplied; but there were other wants. We had now
passed the crisis of want for food and raiment, but began to feel
sadly the want of schools and churches. There was no teaching,
no preaching, no schools, no gospel, no religious meetings. My
father and mother had united with the Freewill Baptist Church
in New York; but, on moving West, father neglected religion,

though mother retained her piety; so that, though we were without church or school, the children were encouraged by their mother's pious example.

My earliest religious impressions began in the State of New York, when I was hardly six years old. I then, influenced by the Holy Spirit, had my mind exercised with thoughts of a future state, and felt that I must be good here or I could not be happy there. I often shed tears over my faults, and resolved to do no wrong, and prayed for help to be good. But when among my playmates, my vows were easily forgotten as I took part in their amusements. After coming to Ohio, my employment led me to much meditation. Two brothers being older than I,—the youngest of the two being over three years older,—they were more able to do heavy work; therefore it fell to my lot to take care of the cattle. We had no fenced fields; and while they therefore roamed in the forest for food, it was my care to seek them, and keep them from straying far away and being lost. If I at any time failed to find them, I was severely reprimanded by my father. Sometimes in cloudy weather I would get lost, and finding the cattle by the tinkling of their bell, they would then pilot me home. Being much alone in the forest, I have since thought, begat within me a love for retirement and meditation. In these lonely hours the good Spirit often strove with me, and renewed the impressions of my earlier childhood. I had again seasons of weeping, and renewed my former resolutions. Sometimes I would keep my religious vows for several weeks, and then be thrown off my guard and break them. In the time of one of these vows, kept longer than any before, although I had said nothing about it, even to my mother, who was so kind to me that I told her nearly every thing, the family noticed the change in me, and my father seemed more religiously inclined than for years before. But this did not continue long.

Parental Control.—My father possessed many good traits of character He was frugal and industrious. He kept each tool and farming implement in its place. He was kind to strangers and to the poor. His intellectual capacity was above ordinary, and his memory was perfect. He was punctual and honest in business. Yet he was passionate, and often reproved and even punished his children when in anger, which parents should never do. If any thing went wrong on the farm, or a tool was broken, somebody must be blamed, and I thought the blame too generally fell upon me. The corrections of my father, the taunting of my older brothers, and the neglect of prayer, soon led to the full neglect of my vows, and I became more hardened than before. I lost the happiness which I experienced in forming those resolutions, and the peace which I enjoyed while I adhered to them. When laboring under conviction, my mind was impressed with the duty of preaching the gospel of Christ, which for me ever to do seemed impossible.

My First "Quarter."—When I was perhaps in my fourteenth year, during February or March, my older brothers concluded to improve their evenings by hunting raccoons, in order to sell the skins for the fur, and secure some money. I desired to share the peril and the profits, to which they would not consent. I then offered to go for the twentieth skin, to which they consented. We hunted, night after night, till we secured twenty-two skins. The twentieth one happened to be a large, fine one; and when the purchaser came, I showed it to him, and said, "What is this skin worth?" He answered, "A quarter of a dollar." This was the highest price for the very best skins. When I got the money I, of course, felt a little proud. It was more money than I remember having had at one time before in my life! What was I to buy with it? I could perhaps get a pocket-knife, which I needed very much. I stood in need of so many things, that it was hard to decide which of them all I should purchase. I finally decided.

A Fortune for a Spelling-book.—My father went, from time to time, to Limestone village, now Maysville, Kentucky, distant about sixteen miles, to purchase stores for the family. I sent my "quarter" with him, and bought "Webster's Spelling-book." The price of the book was twenty-five cents; so I gave all my newly-acquired fortune for a *book*. There being no schools where we lived, I had so far forgotten what I learned when six or seven years old, in New York, that I knew little more than the alphabet. I concluded, however, that education was worth more to me than any thing else; and I now think *that* the best purchase of my life. For that twenty-five cents has profited me more than a thousand dollars would have done, laid out in any other way, had I neglected my education. After this my spare hours at night were spent in study; and, by diligence, I soon learned to read. After some two years, an eastern man took board at our house during the winter, instructing us in the long evenings. At this night-school I learned to write, improving my hand afterwards by practice.

The Prodigal.—When I was about seventeen years old, the country having become much settled up, the young people would gather, for miles around, to frolicking and dancing parties. I am sorry to confess that my religious determinations were so far weakened that I fell in with these amusements, and tried in vain to find happiness in them. During the two years of this indulgence I became very wicked. I was profane in my language, and felt proud that in fist-cuff fights my adversaries were always worsted, for I was stout, and understood boxing very well! But with all these foolish vanities I was very unhappy. Death was an awful terror to me. My dreams troubled me. The Holy Spirit called me. Deep convictions seized me. During these times I read the parable of the prodigal son.—Luke xv. His resolution filled my soul with hope. I read the beautiful words, "I will arise and go to my father, and will say unto him, Father, I have sinned against heaven, and before thee, and am no more worthy to be called thy son; make me as one of thy hired servants." This melted my heart, and caused tears to flow, for I felt that, if possible, my state was even worse than his. But, alas! these feelings were of short duration, for I neither changed my company, nor prayed for mercy or grace, but continued to love and seek pleasure in sin. It was in the nineteenth year of my age that I became very restless and dissatisfied, as boys too frequently do at that age. I began to plan to leave my father. His government was too restrictive. Not being right myself, his bearing seemed unkind. There was no special falling out, but a general dissatisfaction. Every thing about the farm seemed hateful to my sight. My mind wandered far away, and I desired to get away. The only tie was my mother; she was always kind. To leave her was a great trial. I loved her dearly. I told her all my troubles, and she sympathized with me. If I left, it would grieve her; so I took time to consider, but finally concluded to leave—home, parents, brothers, sisters, and all. I kept my own counsel, without hinting it to any person. I gathered my clothes secretly, and on the fourteenth day of April, 1809, some time after midnight, while all were asleep, I arose and started on foot for Cincinnati, then a small village about fifty miles down the river, intending to go from there to New Orleans. I arrived at Cincinnati the following day at noon, walking the entire distance. Here I met Joseph Jenkins, with whom I hired as a hand on his flat-boat to New Orleans, to start in a day or two. So I wrote to my parents an account of my resolutions and prospects, and proceeded on my voyage.

Becomes a Universalist.—Mr. Jenkins was a kind and agreeable man, which made the trip quite pleasant, if I except two disagreeable storms on the Mississippi. There was much time for conversation, and sometimes religion was the subject. In these discussions Mr. Jenkins, the owner of the boat, defended the Universalist theory, that all will be saved. That was his faith; and as he was a man of mature years, and considerable intellectual strength, and I but a boy, unlearned in the Scriptures, I could not answer his arguments, but was brought over to his system, that God saves all alike, the good and the bad, the just and the unjust, the righteous and the wicked, and that after death all will be equally happy, irrespective of present character. The system seemed to suit my condition exactly, consequently I embraced it; and for a time it had a quieting influence on my conscience. True, I did not feel fully satisfied. Something within me continued to whisper, "All is not well." I was still thoughtful, however, and did not take part in extreme wickedness, though my new doctrine seemed to encourage it, in teaching that sin here will not prevent happiness hereafter.

Boating on the Mississippi in 1809.—With such thoughts we floated along on the bosom of the great Mississippi, which at that time flowed through an almost unbounded and unbroken wilderness. The few dilapidated French villages seemed to belong to other days; and the few cabins and beginnings of towns were far apart till we reached "Natchez under the Hill," as it was then called. Here we stopped for several days. A family had come down the river on our flat-boat, and landed here, and this gave us abundant opportunity to see the place. There were "under the hill" about forty houses, occupied principally by gamblers and lewd women. These houses were located on a narrow strip of bottom land; and there was no place spoken of as a greater sink of sin than "Natchez under the Hill." Some of our young men visited these houses of lewdness. I did not. To reach Natchez proper, we ascended the high bluff, where, nearly a mile from the river, the main town had a beautiful location. The owner of the boat having transacted his business, we left Natchez, and proceeded down the river. Soon after leaving, we fell into company with a boat, whose owner, a man named Tompkins, from Kentucky, was also a Universalist. So the two owners concluded to lash their boats together, for company. But a circumstance took place, which I will relate, and a remark made by him, which did not seem to me to harmonize with Universalism.

Manner of Whipping Negroes.—One morning as we were floating down along the coast, there was a whipping performance going on upon a sugar farm. It was then (and is yet, in 1862) the custom in the South to whip their negroes, after first firmly tying each hand and foot to a stake driven deep into the earth. The negro was thus tied down, with his breast and abdomen upon the ground, and the bare back up. The lash was about ten or twelve feet long, made of leather or raw hide, apparently nearly an inch in diameter in the largest part, with a handle about eighteen inches long. A man accustomed to it could swing this heavy lash over his head, and strike very hard, bringing the blood at every stroke, and the crack could be heard for half a mile. As I said, there was one of these whippings going on by the shore, in sight of us. We could hear the lash at every stroke. We could hear the poor Negro's every shriek; we could hear him scream and piteously beg; but still the lash went on. Oh! it was heart-sickening! Said Tomkins, "There ought to be a hell for that man," meaning the whipper of the Negro. Well, I thought, if Tomkins is right, that there ought to be a hell for the Negro-whipper. There may be some place besides heaven for other wicked men. If so, is Universalism true? But I had accepted the system, and desired it to be true; so the remark of Tomkins had very little weight upon my mind at that time. When approaching New Orleans, my health, which had heretofore been uniformly good, began to give way; and I became quite unwell with diarrhea, so that when we reached the city, about the last of May, 1809, I was so weak that I could scarcely walk; but having a good constitution, I refused to give up work. A gentleman who had a boat at the wharf, having become acquainted with me, and taking notice that I neither drank nor gambled, nor visited lewd houses, employed me to take care of his boat, while he attended to other business. For this easy work he gave me good wages; but I still grew weaker, and the vitality of my system became entirely exhausted. I at times became suddenly blind, for perhaps fifteen or twenty minutes, when the sight would return. It was a matter of great wonder to me what caused this blindness. I have since concluded that it was caused by my efforts to work during my extreme weakness. I remember one day becoming blind on the boat; next I found myself scarcely awake, and very sleepy, on a bed in a house. I continued in this half-sleeping and half-waking condition two or three days, scarcely knowing if I was awake at any time. I wondered how I got there. The owner of the boat had probably found me insensible, and had taken me there to be taken care of. My sleeping was the prelude to the great Southern fever, which is so generally fatal to the people coming there from the North. I awoke with a burning fever. I soon divided my money with the woman (a freed woman) of the house and the doctor. I gave them from thirty to forty dollars—all I had—and they were to nurse and doctor me till well, or till I died. They of course expected me to die soon, and acted accordingly, giving me little attention, as I thought. Perhaps I was wrong. There was no other sick person there, which made it better for me. The woman talked of her children, but I saw none, except a little girl ten or twelve years old, and but little of her. During the raging fever, oh! how I longed for cold water! But I could get none. Ice was even then shipped to New Orleans, but I knew of none, nor had I any money to buy it with. I only remember seeing the doctor once or twice. They proposed to move me to the hospital, but I objected, having heard that nearly all died who went there. If I died, my desire was to die where I was. Sleep had now forsaken me, and I passed the long dreary nights without comfort or company. It sometimes seemed as if light would never return. I was a stranger, and few called to see me or speak to me, or cared for me, except the poor black woman who had charge of me. Then I thought of my mother—more dear to

2

my heart than any other human being. I meditated upon her kindness to me; and oh! how I desired to see her! while I have no doubt she was praying for me. I grew worse. Death seemed very near. The feeble hope of recovery seemed nearly gone; the lamp of life seemed nearly extinguished. When composed I thought of my prospects after death. Should I find happiness or misery! I tried to trust in Universalism, but its hope vanished, and left me a helpless sinner, without a prop to lean upon when at the very verge, seemingly, of the spirit world. I then turned to Jesus. I remembered that he came into the world to save sinners; I was a sinner. I felt as if there was no greater sinner than I, why then may not I trust in Him who came to save sinners? In Him alone will I put my trust! I prayed night and day, when not deranged by fever. I renewed my broken vows. After many nights and days, spent almost sleepless, it seemed to me that my prayers were answered. I had hope. My weak faith trusted in and relied upon the promises of the God of mercy, and I resigned myself to his keeping in child-like, trusting faith. I said, "'Thy will be done,' whether I live or die." In this my troubled soul found a little peace, and I felt in a degree reconciled to die, but still prayed to live to see my mother. I remember feeling also troubled about being buried in the New Orleans cemetery, then called a swamp—a low, wet ground in which they buried strangers. I thought if my body could be buried at home, death would have less terror. After four or five weeks during the hot season of June and July in that hot climate, my body was a mere skeleton, and the bones seemed to protrude through the skin. But then I began to mend, and in a few days began to walk. I attribute my recovery to my trust in God, and the calmness of mind which I gained by this trust. I then believed, and have never since doubted, that it was by a special providence of the God of all grace that my life was preserved, otherwise I should have died in New Orleans in 1809. As I began to mend, the black woman began to ask for more money; but I had given all I had to her and the doctor, and had none for her.

The Black Woman's Words.—I remember her saying: "I would put you out of the house, and not let you stay here any longer, but I have children, and do not know where they may go to and be turned out of doors when sick!" Had she given me proper attention, her bargain would have been a hard one, for, according to the best of my recollection, I was at her house from four to six weeks. I remember the Fourth-of-July celebration while there in 1809. I was lying on the bed, helpless and weak. I had not yet begun to recover. It was the 15th of July when I was first able to walk the streets. While thankful to the Lord for returning health, new difficulties

arose. I was in a strange city, nearly fifteen hundred miles
from home, unable to work, without a dollar, and without an
earthly friend to ask help from. Of course as I was not yet
well, my contract continued with the colored landlady, whose
house was a *kind* of home for me for the present; but I could
not expect it to be so much longer. The gloomy question
arose, after leaving here, Who will take me in, as I am destitute
of money and friends? By what means can I return to my far-
off home? There were no steam-boats then. The only way
was to walk. How could I undertake this journey alone, four
or five hundred miles through dense forests, the home of Choc-
taw and Chickasaw Indians. I must pass through both their
villages. I have no money! Darkness rested on all the future!
but I trusted in the Lord. I desired to leave New Orleans, and
hoped that some way would open. My health so improved
that I was now able to walk two or three miles in the cool of
the day. So I went to the landing in search of work, with the
hope also of finding some one there from Ohio. There I found
Thomas Campbell, who had been at my father's house. He
owned a flat-boat. He willingly befriended me, lending me
thirty dollars, for which he took my note. This was about the
20th of July, 1809. I immediately prepared to start for home.
It was the custom of returning boatmen to form into com-
panies for mutual protection. I was too weak to keep up with
a company, nor did I wish to travel with them, but determined
to go as far as I could by myself. So I bade my colored landlady farewell, and started. It was called two hundred miles to
Natchez, by land; but to go that way we must cross Lake
Pontchartrain, the shore of which is three or four miles from
New Orleans. While on my way to a vessel, to cross this lake,
that night a heavy rain shower came upon me, and fearing a
return of sickness, I stepped into a liquor-shop, and purchased,
for six and a quarter cents, a dram of brandy, to prevent taking
cold. This is the only dram of any kind I have ever bought,
before or since. The vessel was propelled by sails or oars, and
we were out all night. I was very sea-sick. It was the only
time in my life that I have felt that sickness, though I have
been on the ocean since. We landed about nine the next morning. I was weak from vomiting, but the sickness soon ceased
after landing; and I started for Natchez—two hundred miles.
The way led through parts of Florida, then belonging to Spain,
and almost wholly wilderness. I was so feeble that I walked
but a short distance that day. The next day I traveled perhaps
ten miles, and some days fifteen miles, as my strength permitted. I carried no provisions, but ate such as I could procure of the few people along the road. This was an advantage
I had by being alone. They could spare something for one,
when they could not feed a large number. Much of the way

was through pine forests, where, when tired by walking, I could sit or lie down in the shade and listen to the moaning zephyrs of the wind in the tall pine tops, which seemed to harmonize with my inward spirit and soothe my mind. The few people whom I met treated me with marked kindness, and doubtless pitied me as a poor wandering, homeless boy. So I found shelter every night on the way, reaching Natchez about the 15th of August, 1809, tired and worn out. I obtained entertainment with the family we left at Natchez on the downward trip. Never having fully recovered from my first sickness, I desired to remain until able to travel; but if I remained there on expense, earning nothing, I would soon be without money, so I purchased water-melons by the load, and, by retailing them in the market, thus added a little to the few dollars in my possession. I avoided bad company, lewd women, and places of drinking, and all gambling, with one exception. There was to be a horse-race, and I heard some one say, "If the morning is cloudy, the dark horse will win." The morning was cloudy, so I bet five dollars on the brown horse. The money was staked, and the horses started. My heart fluttered with fear, for I had no money to lose. It was a close race, but the judges announced that the brown horse had won. I took the money; and as it was the first so it was the last bet that I ever made. I did it thoughtless of the evil; but it is a wonder that winning did not make a gambler of me. About the first of September, having purchased a mule, I prepared to continue my journey homeward, when I found a man who had purchased a large drove of cattle west of the Mississippi, and was driving them to Philadelphia or some eastern city. I engaged to accompany him to where our roads would part, which I hoped would take me at least half way through the Indian country. Just when ready to start, my clothes, except those I had on, were nearly all stolen. Misfortune never comes alone, so, on the day I left the drove, a villain who belonged to it took possession of my mule, and would neither return it or pay me for it. We were out of the jurisdiction of the United States. There was no law by which I could get justice. I applied to the United States Indian Agent, but he could do nothing for me, so I lost my mule. I was now again left very destitute, having little money, and being at the mercy of the wild sons of the forest. Yet the Indians were more honest than the white men who had wronged me. I started again on foot, alone, sick and weak. The Indians were kind. I ate what they ate. They always gave me a part of what they had, and permitted me to sleep in their wigwams. The food was generally parched corn, sometimes corn-bread. The best family government I ever witnessed was in the wigwams of these so-called savage people. The parents were promptly obeyed. There was no crying or freeting among the children. Once where I was lodging they had a dance—a common thing with them. I had some fear that when excited they might murder me for what little money I had. Neverthe-less, after observing the dance awhile, I fell asleep, and they danced on without molesting me. No squaws mingled in these dances, nor did I learn the object of the dances. Sometimes they adore the Great Spirit by these forms of amusement. I saw many white men among the Indians. Probably they were escaped criminals, who sought refuge there, taking squaws for wives. I had far more confidence in the Indians than I had in these white men. Sometimes I traveled for days without meet-ing a single person who could understand a word I said, neither could I understand them, and I longed to get among civilized people. At length I came into the State of Tennessee. Here I found a very kind, hospitable people, who made it seem like home, though yet hundreds of miles away from my mother. I tarried here several days, being so well pleased with the people, the country, and the climate, that I was almost persuaded to remain there. But my mind was not satisfied; so, after resting a few days, I started on again, though still ill of my first sick-ness, and very weak. I passed Nashville, then a small village, and next Lexington, Kentucky, then Maysville. Here I tarried all night, then crossed over to Ohio in the morning, and reached home—sixteen miles—the same day. The people all along through Tennessee and Kentucky were very kind. I arrived home on the twentieth day of October, 1809, having been ab-sent six months and four days. The family was not looking for me, and my sudden appearance was almost as of one who had been dead and was alive again. We could not restrain our tears! My mother afterwards told me that she had prayed to the Lord to give me no rest anywhere until I should return home. These prayers, I have always believed, were the cause of my restlessness and unsatisfied state of mind in Tennessee, where I so much desired to settle. My love for my mother seemed now greater than ever before; and my health improved rapidly, with a corresponding return of strength, consequently I was soon able to do light work. That winter, on the fifth day of December, I entered my twentieth year. I prevailed with my father to let me go to school.

The Old-fashioned School-house.—The school was two miles from our house. It was taught in an unhewed log cabin, the logs being covered with clapboards split from logs. The open-ings between the logs were filled with split blocks of wood, except four, which were left for windows, and these were cov-ered with greased paper to admit the light. The floor was of split logs, hewed on the upper side. One end of the house was cut through about five feet each way, for a fire-place. This was also built of logs, extending from the house outside, but connected with it by joining the ends of the logs which formed the chimney-jams in with the logs of the house which had been cut for the fire-place. The fire-place, thus built of logs, was faced inside with a thick wall of stone and clay, to prevent the logs burning. This work was carried five feet high. From there the chimney was built of long sticks two inches square, well daubed with clay plastering, first mixed with straw. It was carried up, independent of the house, in a sort of tower outside. If I remember rightly, our school-house chimney was not yet carried up to its proper hight, but terminated just above the five-feet-high fire-place. The teacher at our school-house had the reputation of being an excellent English scholar; but he would get drunk now and then. My trip to New Orleans had been a great lesson to me. It had taught me to endure suffering. I had learned to live among Indians. It had given me a knowledge of mankind in general, and of humanity. These lessons were useful in their place, but I felt the need of an education of a different character, therefore I went to school to learn.

Twenty-seven Days for Arithmetic.—I could read and I could write a little, but I knew nothing of arithmetic. I began with the beginning; and the teacher seeing my diligence, gave me all the assistance he could in justice to the other children. He even gave me instruction at noon-time, while the others were playing. I learned rapidly, passing from simple addition on till I soon was through the "rule of three" without difficulty, and found that I could do almost any practical sum in the arithmetic, including interest, tare and tret, mensuration, etc. In twenty-seven days I had acquired all the knowledge of arithmetic absolutely essential for ordinary business purposes. These twenty-seven days include all my school-house educational experience, except that received in New York, when I was six or seven years old. It was about the middle of February, in 1810, when my father desired me to quit school and go to work on the farm. My health was now fully restored. My younger brother, Seth, and I worked together as formerly, but I continued to improve my mind by study, as circumstances would permit.

The Christian Minister Comes.—There had been a general neglect of religion in our neighborhood until the summer of 1810. Then, in July or August, a Christian minister, Elder Archibald Alexander, from Kentucky, preached at my father's house, and quite a number embraced religion. I felt my own lost and miserable condition and a guilty conscience, which almost caused me to despair, for the vows which I had broken, especially those made when sick at New Orleans. But, after carefully counting the cost, I resolved, trusting in God's mercy, that through divine grace I would try once more, and that this

trial should last during my life. My broken vows were much
in my way. I sometimes feared that I had committed the un-
pardonable sin. But I determined to make a full surrender, an
unreserved sacrifice of all worldly pleasure and vain amusements, and to continue in prayer during my whole life; and if
lost, to perish praying. My mind continued under this dark
gloom for days, perhaps weeks. As I was alone in the field, at
evening, when the golden rays of the setting sun last rested
upon the tree-tops of the eastern hills, while contemplating the
glory and power of God in nature, my mind passed to the contemplation of the greater glory of his grace. "Jesus loved sinners, and died to save them. I am a sinner, therefore he died
to save me." The answer came: "He died to save you, and
will save you, if you will trust in him." Then I said, "O Lord,
I *will* trust in *thee!*" Quick as thought an unspeakable joy filled
my soul. All nature seemed to rejoice with me and smile approval. The departing rays of the setting sun appeared more
beautiful than ever before. Tears of joy filled my eyes. I was
filled with the love of God, and of his Son Jesus Christ, who
died for me. I was happy! Yet this continued but a short
time, for when I came to remember the words of others, relating their wonderful conversions, I began to doubt the reality
of mine. Then trouble and affliction of mind returned, with
darkness greater than before, for the darkness was more dense
from thoughts of the doctrine of unconditional election and
reprobation, as taught by Presbyterians and Baptists. If you
are to be saved, you will be saved. Why then this anxiety and
these efforts? Yet I continued to pray. At length the following thoughts relieved me: "If God from all eternity unchangeably ordained all things whatsoever comes to pass, and consequently predestinated a part of mankind to be eternally happy,
and doomed the remainder to eternal misery, why did he send
his beloved Son into the world to invite all to come to him and
be saved? Or, again, can it be possible that a kind heavenly
Father could, before any were born or had sinned, and when
all were equal in his sight, doom a part to eternal misery, and
afterwards mock them in his blessed Word, by directing them
what to *do* to be saved,' while he had bound them down by
immutable decrees, so that it was impossible for them to do
any thing to change their character or condition? My soul
replied, "It is not possible!" My mind was thus relieved from
this false philosophy; but I longed for plainer evidence of sins
forgiven and acceptance in Christ. How to obtain this was
beyond my comprehension. Still my fixed determination was
to continue a life of prayer, and to rely upon the testimony of
all the prophets. Acts x. 43: "Whosoever believeth in him
shall receive remission of sins." I hoped to be of that number,
being determined to believe God's word just as it stands in the

divine record. One afternoon, coming in from work a little before sundown, and entering the room when no one was there but myself, I opened the Testament and, seemingly accidentally, commenced reading in the tenth chapter of Romans, at verse nine: "That if thou shalt confess with thy mouth the Lord Jesus, and shalt believe in thine heart that God hath raised him from the dead, thou shalt be saved. For with the heart man believeth unto righteousness, and with the mouth confession is made unto salvation." I asked myself the question, "Do I believe this?" and answered, "I do; I believe it with all my heart!" Simultaneously with the answer inexpressible joy and gladness filled my soul! Every doubt vanished! I felt more than I had asked for, or could in anywise have expected. Oh! how precious was the name of Jesus from that moment! I loved God, and loved all his creatures. I desired that all would go to heaven with me. It seemed to me that I could plainly tell every one the way; and they would all surely come and be happy with me. I felt with the poet—

"Jesus, all the day long,
Was my joy and my song:
Oh that all his salvation might see!"

The fear of death, which had always before troubled me, was now gone. I felt willing to pass its dark valley to reach the mansions of glory, but like too many, I at first trusted entirely to my happy feelings. I soon found that I must adopt fixed principles, and that it was not safe to trust to feelings, which might vary with every circumstance. But, at the time, I was very happy, and—

"I could not believe
That I ever should grieve,
That I ever should suffer again."

It was perhaps past the middle of August, 1810, in the twentieth year of my age, when, through divine grace, I was brought to experience this happy change. My only sorrow was that I had not fully started years before, when my mind was so strongly impressed with duty, and that I had let so much precious time run to waste; for, had I then truly believed, without doubting, and truly repented, without falling back, and fully surrendered myself a living sacrifice, resolving to continue praying while life should last, as I now did, my happiness would have been as complete then as now. In view of the fullness in Christ, and his boundless love to lost sinners, I felt it my duty to proclaim the Savior's love, and to invite poor sinners to come unto him and be saved. It was a great cross for me to exhort my young companions to leave sin, and turn to God and seek salvation. I soon found that I had labored under a great mistake in supposing that because the enjoyment of religion was so great, and

the way so plain. I could persuade all to come to Jesus, and go
to heaven with me. To the heavy cross was added this great
disappointment. Yet I continued to exhort from a positive
sense of duty, fearing, if I refused to speak, it would grieve the
Holy Spirit, and cause it to forsake me. I had then very little
expectation of becoming a preacher, so great did the responsibility appear. I, however, resolved to discharge my duty as I
saw the way open, so far at least as to avoid falling under con-
demnation for disobedience. It was several weeks after I found
peace in believing before I united with any church. After examining the various systems, and the rules of the various
denominations, as far as my means permitted, I made choice of
the "Christians," on account of their liberality in fellowshiping all who love the Lord Jesus Christ, and their taking the
Scriptures for their only rule of faith and practice. I did not
know or care much for doctrines. There was no Christian
church near; but about the 1st of September of that year, 1810,
I, with many others of our neighborhood, attended a Christian
camp-meeting in Adams County, about ten miles south, near
the place now called Bentonville. Several ministers were there.
It was there that I first met and became acquainted with Elder
Barton W. Stone. The meeting opened on Friday. On Monday Elder Stone invited all who desired to confess Christ and
to unite with God's people to come forward. Many went forward, and among them myself; and there I publicly confessed
Christ, and took upon me the obligations of his holy religion.
I had not then been baptized, and do not remember having
thought of it. When I carefully examined the precepts of
Christ and his apostles, I was impelled to attend to this duty.
It was about the middle of October, 1810, when quite a number
went forward with me, and were baptized in the beautiful water
of the west fork of Eagle Creek, below the old state road to
Decatur, about two miles from my father's house, by Elder
Archibald Alexander, who shortly afterwards organized a Christian Church in the neighborhood, the meetings of which were
generally held at my father's house. Our meetings were interesting, for we seemed to love one another as the Savior directed.
Numbers were added, and the church grew rapidly. I took
part, praying and speaking publicly. I have always looked
at this time, the latter part of the summer of 1810, and the
autumn and following winter, as among the happiest days of
my life. On the 5th of December of that year I was twenty
years old. During these seasons of refreshing, we were invited
to hold meetings in different neighborhoods, and, through the
presence of the Holy Spirit, the meetings were attended with
much good. But where are those who labored with me then—
who sung and prayed and worshiped with me there? Gone!
gone! gone! no more to return.

CHAPTER III.

On the 5th of December, 1810, I entered my twenty-first
year, during which I was still subject to my father. My spare
moments, which were few, were devoted to the Bible, the study
of which at that time has since been of great advantage to me.
Our occupation was farming, in which my brother Seth and I
got along very agreeably, he having been baptized at the same
time that I was.

A Happy Family.—All of our family that were grown up had
professed religion, and was at this time, I think, trying to live
accordingly. This made home desirable. All being good singers, we enjoyed much happiness together. Labor did not seem
burdensome, but the time passed pleasantly.

The Young Preacher.—The only matter which caused me un-
easiness was the duty of calling sinners to repentance. The
church, without my requesting it, gave me their approbation,
and I exercised my gift in the regular social and prayer-meetings, and sometimes made distant appointments. Yet it seemed
to me that all I could say was of little account, and the people
would not continue to come to hear me, and if they did not
come to hear me, then I would be justified in ceasing to make
appointments. But the people continued to come in crowds.
I wondered what they came for, and was sorry to see them
there. The church to which we belonged, that is, my father,
mother, and several of the family besides myself, was organized
in the fall of 1810, and was one of the first Christian churches
in southern Ohio.

His Father Leaves the Church.—My father's intellect was of a
high order; and being a fair speaker, he generally opened and
led the meetings, which went on with harmony till the latter
part of the summer of 1811. Then a difficulty arose between
Elder Alexander (who organized the church) and my father.
The preacher did not like my father very well, for he was hard
to please, and often called in question things that Elder Alexander preached. The difficulty arose on the question of the
Sabbath. Elder Alexander's parents were Presbyterians. The
Presbyterians are particular to "remember the Sabbath-day to
keep it holy." As we made cheese, sometimes hours would be
spent at this on Sunday mornings, the same as on other days.
It was considered necessary to take care of the milk on Sunday.
Elder Alexander considered this a violation of the fourth

commandment, and considered my father responsible for it. It was of no use to urge that Elder Alexander had been brought up in Virginia, where they were inexperienced in this business, or that even Presbyterians, in dairy countries, sometimes do the same as we did. Elder Alexander laid the matter before the preachers at a grove camp-meeting, held near the large spring in my father's grove, in September, A. D. 1811. The result was very injurious to the church, for my father being, like too many others, very hasty, concluded that he was doing no wrong, and should not change his course. So, without waiting for a decision of the case, he withdrew from the church. I do not think that the preachers would have excluded him; and I thought then, and still think, that those designing to live religion should live in the church. If Jesus is with the church, to withdraw from it is to withdraw from him. This many do not think of when withdrawing from the church. I do not remember any person that I have known to withdraw from the church, without uniting with another, who has continued to live a true religious life. Although I did not approve of Elder Alexander's course, for no minister should become a party to accuse his members, yet I approved of his principles and did not leave the church. The church, also, had taken no part in the matter, for before it came before them my father withdrew. I also believed that the church-members, with few exceptions, were striving to live according to the gospel of peace; and I loved many of them as children of God near and dear to my heart. The consequence of this hasty movement of Elder Alexander was, that the church suffered a severe injury. My father being a man of determination, when he felt himself injured, manifested much resentment, and he soon became a great opposer of the church, and all who belonged to it. It wanted but three months of my birth-day, when I would become of age, and I did every thing I could to please him, except leaving the church, which I could not do, as I felt that it would offend the dear Savior. He was much displeased that I continued my membership, and would probably have ordered me away from home immediately had it not been for the press of work. There was much to do on the farm, and he needed me to assist in doing it.

Turned from Father's House.—I tried to bear all, and labored faithfully to have all the work done; but, a few days before my birth-day, which would come December 5th, 1811, my father, in a passion, told me to leave his house, not to return. My mother was always kind to me, and the opposition of father did not long continue. However, I gathered up my few clothes, and took them to David Devore's, a neighbor, the father of David G. Devore, of Georgetown, since so well known as an eminent lawyer. This family belonged to the church, and treated me kindly, for which I paid them, being very thankful to get a good home, even for pay. December the 5, 1811, I entered upon my twenty-second year, and was consequently free from the control of my father, or any other man, except by my own agreement. I at this time began the world properly for myself. I was a poor young man, having nothing to rely upon but health, strength, and a good constitution, and a pair of hands willing to work, and ability to use them. These will always procure a living, if prudently employed. My first work was chopping timber. My first wages went to procure a Bible. I chopped and split six hundred rails, at fifty cents per hundred. There was a neighbor who had bought a small pocket Bible for three dollars, the common price then. He found the print too small for family use, and offered it for sale. There being no book-store near. I was glad of the opportunity, and readily gave my first six days wages for a pocket Bible. I carried it with me as a constant companion, and when wearied with my daily toil, while resting, read its heavenly instructions. I have this Bible yet, nor will I willingly part with it.

Rules of Life.—I soon adopted the following rules to govern my life:

1. Attend to the demands of religion in preference to any thing else.

2. Never live a day without prayer.

3. Take no part in vain jesting or joking at home or abroad.

4. Do no manual labor on the Sabbath, or Lord's day, except in works of mercy or necessity.

5. Speak the truth, to the best of my knowledge, at all times, and under all circumstances.

6. Deal justly, doing to all as I would be done by.

7. When treated unkindly, or injured, I will bear no malice, nor seek revenge, but return good for evil.

8. Never occupy time except to the benefit of myself or others.

9. Never go security in a sum large enough to injure me, if I have it to pay.

10. Drink no ardent spirits, such as whisky, brandy, etc., as a beverage.

11. Punctually fulfill all contracts, promises, engagements, and appointments at the time set and understood.

12. Every night examine the transactions of the day, and, where I have erred, try to mend in the future.

His Trade.—My father being a carpenter by trade, I had acquired some knowledge of the business, and the use of tools, and now went to work at that occupation. When I could not command high wages, I took less, consequently found steady employment. Other carpenters agreed together to work only for a stipulated bill of prices, and urged me to unite with them;

but I preferred to make my own contracts, free from the control of others. It soon became known that where I undertook jobs, I fulfilled my contracts punctually and satisfactorily. When working by the day, I did nearly one half more than most other carpenters. Therefore, nearly all who wanted work called upon me, and I had abundance to do. I was never idle. While working at one dollar a day and board, which seemed to me then high wages, demanding faithful work, another carpenter hired by my employer seemed disposed to "nurse the job," that is, to keep it on hand as long as possible. He said to me, "Why do you work so hard? We will receive the same reward if we work slower." I answered, that when we agreed to do a day's work, it is not honest to do a half or two thirds of a day's work, and take pay for the whole day! I was then doing nearly double the work in a day that he was. He was displeased, and soon gathered up his tools, leaving me to finish the job. Though now such wages seem low, yet by close attention and constant employment, having little expense, and spending no money uselessly, and using strict economy, I was able to lay by some money. My father had not paid Thomas Campbell the thirty dollars which I borrowed of him in New Orleans. I was told that as the note was given before I was of lawful age, the law did not oblige me to pay it. But my decision was that honesty bound me to pay it; so the first money I could spare went to pay that thirty dollars and the interest for nearly three years, due on it when it was paid. The sense of duty to speak in the name of Jesus had not diminished, but increased, and I had appointments nearly every Lord's day, sometimes going on a trip with some of the Kentucky ministers into that state, by which I formed an intimate acquaintance with Elder Barton W. Stone, whose company was a great source of instruction to me. In September of 1812 the Kentucky Christian Conference met, fifteen or sixteen miles from us, in Bracken County, Kentucky, in the church where Elder Alexander, our minister, then lived; for Elder Alexander still had charge of the Christian church on the Ohio side of the river, of which I was a member. I attended this conference, and, on the recommendation of the church of which I was a member, I united with the conference, and received my first letter as a Christian preacher, dated September the 8, 1812, some two years after I had commenced public speaking, with the approbation of the church. I was, at the time of receiving this letter, in the twenty-second year of my life. In the latter part of this autumn, 1812, I started on a preaching tour with Elder David Kirkpatrick, and during some two months traveled through various counties in Kentucky, visiting on my way the eminent Christian minister, B. W. Stone. Elder Kirkpatrick was a pious man, and, having a tolerably good education, was an excellent preacher. My association with him and others at that time was very useful to me. On my return from this trip I went to work at my trade, but filled my appointments as before, speaking to the people with increasing confidence as my knowledge was increased.

His Marriage.—December the 5th, 1812, I entered upon my twenty-third year, and toward the spring of 1813, after carefully considering the matter, concluded to take to myself a companion for life. I had a fondness for female society, and had kept company with young women of respectable families, in good standing, always pursuing a course of virtue, for I regarded it sinful to trifle with the affections of the female heart, and make vain promises of marriage for wicked purposes, as too many young men are guilty of doing. I had kept company with a daughter of Jeptha and Sally Beasley for a year or more. Her name was Sally. She was of a very respectable family, and I concluded, if she would consent, to make her my wife. Being, however, determined to obey the call, as it seemed to me, of the Holy Spirit to preach, if the people would hear, I honestly told her that it was my expectation to preach during my life, and consequently she must expect to be poor in this world, and be left much of the time alone, if she married me. Being herself religious, she agreed to all this, and we then, in the presence of God, pledged ourselves to each other, and were married on the twentieth day of May, 1813. In two or three days after our marriage, I returned to my employment, while she remained at her father's house. The war with England at this time rendered it necessary to defend the northern frontier of Ohio, and a call for soldiers being made in the latter part of July, 1813, I obeyed the summons to arms. Yet, my religious sentiments and feelings, perhaps from my Quaker ancestors, were opposed to war. I might have been exempted also from ill health, being quite unwell. Yet, as my country needed my help, duty said, Go. We reached Upper Sandusky; but the victory of Commodore Perry on the lake rendered our services unnecessary, except perhaps one out of every four, who were drafted to remain forty days longer. The rest were discharged, and returned home. The lot fell upon me to remain; but being unwell, I hired a substitute, and returned with those going home. My custom, while a soldier, was to go out alone every night to some by-place inside of the pickets, and kneel before the Lord and pray for the help which he alone could give.

The Church at Home.—Quite a change had now taken place in the church to which I belonged. Near the close of 1812, Elder John Longley, of Kentucky, had preached for us; and being a fascinating speaker, notwithstanding his limited education, the people were much pleased with him, and chose him as their pastor; and he soon moved to Ohio, within the bounds of the church. Elder Alexander, the former pastor, was a man of learning, having been educated for a Presbyterian minister. On the change of pastors quite a revival took place, and many united with the church.

The First Church Built.—We soon built a good stone meeting-house. It was erected on the east bank of the west fork of Eagle Creek, just above the crossing of the old plank road. This was the first meeting-house erected by the Christians in southern Ohio. Though I had little means, it being soon after my marriage, I did nearly fifty dollars' worth of work on the house. The church now having a good house and an engaging speaker, prospered accordingly, until years after, when the preacher turned storekeeper; then got his brethren to indorse for him; then got in debt, got in jail, ruined his indorsers, lost his influence, changed his religion—joined the Campbellites, and left the country.

The First Farm.—In 1813, after returning from the army, as soon as my health permitted, I began to prepare for house-keeping. My wife still remained at her father's. We now had a little money; and we wanted a home of our own, if it were but a small one. Land could be entered in Indiana, not far distant, at a dollar and a quarter per acre, and I talked of going there. My wife's father did not wish her to go so far from them, and so offered to sell me one hundred acres of land joining their farm. He had offered it for six dollars an acre a few months before our marriage, which was about the price of such land when he offered it to me. He said that he considered the land worth ten dollars per acre; but he would give his daughter, my wife, four hundred dollars, and deduct it from the price of the land; and I could pay him the six hundred dollars from time to time, or year to year, as convenient. There being on the land a cabin to live in, into which we had previously made arrangements to move, and also a clearing of twelve or fifteen acres, his proposition was of course accepted, and I sowed a small piece of wheat, and did some work upon the land that fall, 1813. Having furnished a few things for housekeeping, we moved into our cabin on the first day of January, 1814. We felt at first strange, and as if not at home; but we still, after fifty years, live on the same place. Here, the first day we lived by ourselves, we erected the family altar, and here daily prayer and thanksgiving to God for all his mercies and goodness, have continued, with little exception, for upwards of fifty years, it being now 1865. Being now by ourselves, in a home of our own, I had greater opportunity for study, and feeling the need of more learning, I procured Lindley Murray's Grammar, the only one then published, determined to get some knowledge of its contents. After working hard all day, I frequently studied till twelve at night, and was soon able not only to speak, but to write the language so as to be understood. When able, I purchased other books, still adding to my little stock of knowledge, frequently being in company and traveling with Elder Barton W. Stone and William Kinkade. I improved these opportunities as a school to gain knowledge of almost every thing pertaining to the gospel ministry. These men were of much assistance to me; yet, I studied the Scriptures for myself, and formed my own views from them. The land we had purchased was heavily timbered. Even the clearing before mentioned, at least ten acres of it, had most of the timber yet on it. The small growth had been cleared off. The large trees were deadened and left standing, and many of them had fallen to the ground. This ground I cleared during the winter and spring, to plant with corn as our only resource for a crop. I worked almost day and night and had it cleared, and had nearly finished plowing, expecting to plant in a few days, when, about the 10th of May, 1814, there came a storm, which leveled to the ground nearly all the trees left standing. The field was nearly covered with the large trunks, limbs, and brush. It looked discouraging. It was then time for planting. I again went patiently to work, cleared it off the second time, and finished planting about the last of May, my labor resulting, by heaven's blessing, in a good crop of corn. Our cabin was quite an ordinary one—merely a shelter—hardly that. There was a place cut out for a chimney, and a fire-place built up of wood about five feet high, outside of the house, which I topped out with a chimney made of split sticks, daubed with clay in which straw was mixed. The roof leaked, but this I also repaired to make it answer present purposes till able to build. After my small crop was in I went out to work as a carpenter, until time for plowing, and then, by hiring a hand to assist me, I was soon through and at my trade again. I also attended my appointments every Lord's day, with few exceptions, and sometimes during the week. From time to time I went out on preaching tours, for several days at a time, but lost no time in any other way. I soon felt the need of a system to be guided by, and adopted the following rules, which I adhered to:

THE RULES ADOPTED.

1st. Set a time beforehand, if possible, for every particular work or business to be done, and arrange every thing preparatory to it; and do every thing at the time set, unless unavoidably prevented.

2d. Have a place for each tool of all kinds, and also for each kind of stock; and put every thing in its place, where it can always be found.

3d. Be particular in making contracts, and leave no room for any misunderstanding, so that if the opposite party tries to change it, he must do it knowingly, with the intention to defraud. If he does this, never do any more business with that man.

4th. Never hire a hand who will not promise to avoid profane language and getting drunk.

5th. Settle with a hand, and pay him before he leaves, and never let a hireling leave dissatisfied with his wages.

6th. Be careful. Save every thing; let nothing go to waste or be lost.

7th. If business becomes complicated and entangled, do not shun investigation, as too many do, but attend to it immediately, and never give up till it is corrected and made plain.

8th. Settle frequently. Never let an account run beyond one year.

The first of these rules I found very useful. By observing it, I could arrange my appointments and preaching tours to suit every work, so that they did not conflict. I generally set the day to plant my corn, perhaps two or three months before the time, and seldom failed to begin on the day appointed. I did likewise with all kinds of work. By keeping every thing in its place, and never permitting my business to become deranged, I saved much time that other men spent, without profit, in hunting tools, etc. I hired help; did some clearing; worked at my trade; and having also raised a good crop of wheat and corn in 1814, was able, in the spring of 1815, to make a small payment to my father-in-law on the land. Matters went on as usual until August, 1815, when the Kentucky Christian Conference met in Fleming County in that state, which I attended, and received my second letter of commendation as a minister of the gospel.

The object of the Christian ministers then seemed to be to travel and preach Christian union upon the Bible as the only rule of faith and practice, and to induce all denominations to thus unite in one brotherhood. To accomplish this I traveled much with Elder Barton W. Stone, and some with Elder William Kinkade. Elder Stone usually visited Ohio once a year, and I would have my matters arranged beforehand, and take the tour with him.

The Doctrine.—Having now entered more fully into the work of the ministry, I commenced a more careful examination of the doctrine of the gospel concerning the Father, Son, and the Holy Ghost than I had hitherto done. After examining the views of Elder Stone, and other leading Christian ministers, and the doctrines of the trinitarians, and comparing them with the Scriptures, I could not fully indorse either. And my examinations resulted in the opinion that all attempts to explain the origin of Christ, the Son of God, and his relation to and with God the Father and the Holy Spirit, are speculations calculated to bewilder rather than edify. If God had seen that a knowledge of these relations were needful, he would of course have

3

revealed them; but as he has not, we need not pry into them.
The following texts fully confirmed me in this view: "All
things are delivered unto me of my Father; and no man knoweth the Son, but the Father; neither knoweth any man the
Father, save the Son, and *he* to whomsoever the Son will reveal
him." Matt. XI. 27. Or, as worded by Saint Luke, "All things
are delivered to me of my Father: and no man knoweth who
the Son is, but the Father; and who the Father is, but the Son,
and *he* to whom the Son will reveal *him*." Luke X. 22.
Neither of these texts have I ever found quoted in either Unitarian or trinitarian writings. I also searched the Scriptures
in reference to the doctrine of atonement, and ascertained that
"vicarious atonement," as taught by some sects which style
themselves orthodox, is not in the Bible. The doctrine of the
atonement and the word atonement are in the Bible: but the
term, or word, "vicarious" is not in the divine oracles. The
meaning of "vicarious atonement" is, that "God poured out
his wrath upon his dear Son, and punished him in the room
and stead of sinners, to satisfy divine justice, and reconcile himself (God the Father) to the world." This doctrine seemed to
me to destroy at once grace, mercy, pardon, and justice. *Justice*—for how can it be just to punish the innocent instead of
the guilty? *Grace*—for how can there be grace where the favor
is purchased? *Pardon*—for how can there be pardon where
full payment is made? And *mercy*—for where is the mercy?
The punishment is inflicted. I learned that the primary scriptural meaning of atonement is the reconciliation of man to God,
not God to man; and to purge and cleanse the guilty conscience, heart and life, as taught by Saint Paul. "How much
more shall the blood of Christ, who, through the eternal Spirit,
offered himself without spot to God, purge your conscience
from dead works to serve the living God?" Heb. IX. 14.

Human Systems.—As I found no human system exactly suiting me, I adopted the following platform for myself: *I will use
no terms or language in explaining the personality, character, or relation of God and his Son, and the Holy Spirit, but such as are
contained in the Scriptures.* This being now the character of my
preaching, few were disposed to contradict me. Many of the
most talented Christian ministers traveled at large preaching
union, in the hope of bringing all the followers of Jesus into
union. Regarding this as their mission, some of the first and
most able and talented Christian ministers never organized a
single church, but seemed opposed to separate church organizations. I soon concluded that this would fail of accomplishing
much, as other denominations would organize, and if we did
not, we would soon lose our visibility as a people; therefore, a
change in our mode of ministerial labor seemed needful. Consequently, as I gave myself more and more to the work of the

gospel, I determined to organize churches in those neighborhoods where I was invited, where other Christian ministers had not preached. I sent appointments, and found large congregations assembled to hear the new preacher. I sometimes had a feeling like sorrow when I met these large congregations, for had the people not come out to hear, I might have felt justified in not going to preach; but the people came out, and by the help of the Lord, I preached to them. Every time before preaching I made special prayer to God to help me, and it was quite apparent that good impressions were made. I did not do as many others, preach once or twice. and leave no more appointments—the labor thus being lost—but I continued my appointments from month to month, and caused the people to understand my views of the gospel platform. The reader will keep in mind that at this time there was but one Christian church in southern Ohio, and Elder Longley was still its pastor. I was a member of it, and it was in a very low state, in consequence of the bad management of the pastor. There being no churches to sustain the preachers, I had to sustain myself and family by the labor of my hands. I had strong faith in God. I felt confident that by faithfully laboring with my hands one half the time, I could, by economy, procure a living for myself and my family.

The Covenant.—So I entered into a covenant with God, that if he blessed my labors in the ministry, I would devote half of the time of my life to preaching the gospel. I had inherited a good constitution. My hight was six feet and one inch, without shoes. My weight was from one hundred and ninety-six to two hundred and ten pounds. I had a strong, clear voice, which I took care not to injure by unnecessarily loud speaking, as too many do, my aim being to speak no louder than necessary to have the people distinctly understand me. With such a voice, there were few better singers; and I sang a great deal. At meetings in the woods, persons have said that they heard and knew my voice, and could distinguish the tune sometimes a mile and a half from the place. During the warm weather, we held meeting in the woods, for we had no meeting-houses, and the sects would not permit us to meet in theirs. The congregations were very large. Many embraced religion. Some of these united with the sects; but the greater number waited to be organized in true evangelical church order, on the Scriptures as their only rule of faith and practice. The requests for my labors were far more than I was able to comply with. Although I felt, "Woe is me, if I preach not the gospel!" and my heart and soul were fully devoted to the work of preaching Christ crucified, and the resurrection, I did not neglect my secular business. I had a set time beforehand in which every piece of work must be done, unless unavoidably prevented. Consequently when I returned from my appointments, my clothes were immediately changed, and I went right to work. Sometimes I rode home between midnight and daylight for this purpose. By diligence, I had in a few years paid for my land, and received a deed from my father-in-law, who received only $400 instead of the $600 first contracted; and I had a good orchard and plenty of fruit. I labored early and late clearing and improving our place.

Plan of Working.—Sometimes I would burn brush and logs, working by the light of their fire till midnight, and hoeing corn by starlight, to gain time to reach my appointments. I spent no time visiting, except to see the sick, and to visit my father and mother four miles away about once a year. I did not attend vendue sales and other gatherings, unless special business required it. I went to elections, but remained only to vote, then returned to my work. When business called me to town, or elsewhere, I remained no longer than was absolutely necessary. By this economy of time, I soon found that I worked as many hours in the week as other men, yet devoted one half of all my time to preaching. It is common for men to attend all sales and other gatherings in their neighborhood, and going to town of little errands, to spend the whole day, though two hours were sufficient, and to practice the same profligacy of time in paying visits and receiving calls. I continued to take jobs of carpenter work, as I could make as much at my trade in one day as would pay a farm-hand two or three days. Although poor, and limited in my means, and pressed by my work, I never failed to attend my appointments, except when sick, and then I have hired a man to go and inform the people.

The Sick Child.—I now well remember a time when Washington, our second son, was very sick. We had but little hope of his recovery. My appointments were out for a tour of preaching, of perhaps two weeks' duration, on the line of the Little Miami River. The conflict in my mind was great. Should I remain, and probably see my child die, and be at his burial, or should I go to my appointments. After prayer to God for direction, the thought came to my mind to leave it to the child. I went to his sick-bed and said, "Washington, you are very sick, and I will not leave you to go to my appointments, if you are not willing." He was in his right mind at the time, and after reflecting a moment, said, "Papa, I do not know that you can do me any good by remaining, so I am willing for you to go." I committed his case to God, and with a sad heart started, not expecting to see him alive on my return. All the time I kept praying in secret that, if it was the Lord's will, he might recover. I filled my appointments. I do not remember any other tour with so many manifestations of good being done. As I drew near our dwelling on my return, my heart trembled. I expected the sad word that our little boy was dead and buried.

Oh! how great the joy to learn that he had almost recovered! I thanked God, and praised him with my whole heart. That boy is now deacon of a Christian church. When I attended meetings of days, I arranged matters at home, so that I could remain through the meeting, but often met other ministers who would attend on Sunday and preach once, and receive an equal share of the collections; and then plead that having left their families without firewood, flour, or other necessaries, they must return.

Great Disappointment.—Numbers were now waiting for the organization of a Christian church, and for baptism. The church of which I was a member, and of which Elder Longley was pastor, having some knowledge of my labors, sent a special request in their letter to conference for my ordination. It was the Kentucky Conference, where I still belonged. It met in August, 1816. When my case came before the conference, I left the house, that being the custom then, which I think is not right, as things may be said in a man's absence which would not be uttered before his face. A man should hear all that is said of him. On my return I was informed that the request for my ordination was not granted. I was afterward informed that Elder Longley stated to the conference that there was no church requiring my labors; and but few of the church where he preached were present at the meeting when the request for my ordination was voted, and that the majority of the church did not desire it; but it was a long time after the conference before I learned these things. I did not become offended or discouraged, as too many do in such cases. I did not give up trying to preach, but continued to do what I felt to be my duty, as I must render account to Him that is greater than all conferences of poor fallible men. I continued my regular appointments in four neighborhoods, and occasionally complied with invitations to visit other places, as I had been doing. The congregations increased. When six or eight professed religion in a place, I advised them to have stated prayer-meetings, which they did. During the year 1817 several preachers from Kentucky came through, and labored some with me. Though I would preach often three times a day, and average as many sermons as there were days in the year, I continued to attend to my domestic duties; and as our cabin no longer sheltered us from the storm, I began to prepare materials for a new house.

Cabin, Cup, and Pail.—On one occasion, Elder William Kinkade having stopped with us for the night, he retired first to rest; but before we retired, there arose a heavy rain, and the water came through the roof upon his bed. "Give me a tin cup," he said. It was given him. "Give me a pail!" he cried. But so many streams through the roof could not be caught in cups and pails. So he arose; and we all smiled, notwithstanding the storm, as he sat his chair carefully over his boots to keep them dry. We saw that he was somewhat vexed, and said nothing; and the rain soon ceased, and we all retired to our beds and slept till morning. On the way to our appointments the next day, he said, "Brother Gardner, I thought last night that your house was little better than none, but, on reflection, acknowledge that you are better off than I am, as I have no house at all." I had neglected the roof since preparing to build. Kinkade was not then married. As the time approached for the meeting of the conference in 1817, the church of which I was a member, and one or two of the praying societies where I preached, prepared letters anew requesting my ordination. The conference met with a church near Lexington, Kentucky. It was far from our church, so as usual no messengers were sent, and Elder Longley and I alone went over to attend it. The conference met that year, I think, in September. In the course of business, my ordination again came up, and I withdrew as before. I was afterwards informed that Elder Longley renewed his former objections, especially insisting that no church needed my labors. This was in part true, though Elder Longley knew that he had gone with me, at my request, to baptize converts who had professed religion under my preaching, and that they preferred waiting for baptism until I could be ordained and attend to it. Yet as I belonged to the church of which he was the pastor, his objections had their influence; for the custom then prevailed, which is right, and calculated to prevent divisions, to receive no member into the church or conference, or for ordination, who is objected to by any member of the body. There were there, however, ministers who could not fail to discover in Elder Longley the spirit of jealousy below all his professed friendship. The conference, therefore, appointed a committee of judicious ministers to meet at the church in Ohio of which I was a member, and Longley pastor, and ordain me if they found no valid objections. The committee met on the second day of March, 1818, six months after their appointment. A few days previous to their meeting, Elder Longley told me that he had no objections to my ordination, but would favor it. There being, therefore, no objection I was, according to the order of the Kentucky Christian Conference, ordained to the work of the gospel ministry, by fasting, solemn prayer, and the laying on of hands, on the second day of March, 1818, as my credentials bear date. I then became a fellow-laborer in the vineyard of our Lord Jesus Christ, with Elders Barton W. Stone, William Kinkade, James Hughs, John Mouity, Nathan Worley, Reuben Dooley, David Kirkpatrick, and others of the same spirit, great ministers and able speakers, all now gone to the spirit world. I believe that these were

truly men of God, for certainly there never lived a more devoted, self-sacrificing class of men than the first ministers of
the Christian denomination. While there is no evidence that
Elder Longley's opposition to my ordination was prompted by
pure motives, have we not since been too hasty in ordaining
some men before they gave good proof of their calling, thus injuring the cause we desire to benefit? It was not long after my
ordination till Elder Longley moved to Indiana, and united
with the Disciples, commonly called Campbellites. He had
failed in business, and he left the church in a low condition. It
was before the war that he had started a store, and induced
some of his brethren to indorse for him. Barnet Restine was
an excellent man. Longley had baptized him, and he was a
member of the church. Longley persuaded Restine to indorse
for him. The war came. Hard times followed. Elder Longley could not pay his debts. Then there was imprisonment for
debt. So Longley was sued, and Restine was responsible; and
Longley went jail, and Restine was so injured as to be forced
to move farther west. Longley having ruined his own useful-
fulness, and broken down the church, moved to Indiana, and
united with the Disciples. He never organized a church in
southern Ohio; and I never heard of his doing any good after
he left there. Let this be a warning to ministers not to be entangled with the things of this world. When Longley left the
church in this low condition, they wanted me to preach for
them. But my time was all occupied. They settled a preacher
named David Hathaway. He preached a short time, and then
left. They obtained others, who did likewise, till finally the
Disciple sect, called Campbellites, arose, when their preachers
came along and began to preach there. Some of the members
united with them, and the rest were scattered. The Disciples
took possession of the house, and occupy it to this day.

The year 1818 was a year of hard labor for me. The calls for
my labors in the gospel abroad had increased, and proportion-
ally with them my duties at home. The cabin could not shelter
us from the storms of another winter; yet, to fill all the urgent
calls for preaching would have taken more than all my time.
I completed the organization of one or two churches only, while
in other sections where I had been preaching a year or two
they were equally anxious. I organized nowhere until satisfied of the stability of those going into the organization to sustain it. Having learned no particular mode of organization, I
was governed by common sense, as commended by Saint Paul
in other things.

Mode of Receiving Members.—At the close of preaching, I invited all who desired to profess religion to come forward.
When they came I took their profession, before all the congregation, of faith in Christ, and their determination to forsake all

wickedness and to follow Jesus. I then announced their names, and registered them myself.

Mode of Organizing a Church.—If there were twelve or more persons of stability in a place, desiring to be organized, and it seemed advisable, I appointed some future day. When the time came, after preaching on church organization and church order according to the New Testament, I invited to a front seat all who had previously professed religion, and were willing to give their names to the following:

The Statement.—We, whose names are hereunto subscribed, do agree to unite and walk in church order and fellowship, observing all the ordinances and commandments of our Lord Jesus Christ, and to watch over each other in love, taking the Scriptures of the Old and New Testaments as our only rule of faith and practice; to be known as the Church of ———, at ——— [naming the church, county, and state], organized in the presence of Elders A. B. and C. D., on the ——— day of ———, in the year of our Lord, 18—.

Then a clerk was elected to register the names and keep the records. Then the invitation was given to others desiring to unite with the church to come forward. These were received by a vote of the church, after which the church gave them the right hand of fellowship.

Ordination of Deacons.—Some time after the organization of a church, after some brethren were proved to possess the qualifications for deacons, as directed by Saint Paul, two or more were elected by the church, and ordained by the elder or elders, by prayer and laying on of hands. My manner was to appoint the election for a future day. All the members, both men and women—for all had a right to vote—were requested to consider until that time who were suitable to fill the place. On the day appointed, to prevent undue influence, no nominations were made, but the clerk being seated for that purpose, each member handed his vote to the minister or church clerk, and those having the largest number of votes were declared elected, and no others were named or publicly known as voted for. The elect deacons then came forward, and I read those Scriptures which directly allude to their office, especially the sixth chapter of the Acts of the Apostles, where they were to attend to any murmurings among the members of the church, that they might silence them; or, if any walked disorderly, to see and if possible restore them, or make the grievance known to the church. After this reading and charge, they were ordained by prayer and the laying on of hands.

Custom at Monthly Meetings.—It has ever been my custom, on the Saturday of the monthly meeting, or church meeting, to inquire, "Is there any business to come before the church?" This the deacons were expected to know, and to answer.

Unsectarian Mode.—I never labored to raise a church where there was already a church of any denomination, or very near another church, except in a village or city, as I had rather persuade sinners to embrace religion than to proselyte professors from their faith to mine, which frequently causes strife and division. Therefore, I labored mostly among non-professors, where they had been without preaching.

The First Church Organized.—The first church that, through divine grace, I organized was Union Church, in the western part of Brown County, two miles from Higginsport, on the Ohio River, and sixteen from my home. It was organized in 1818, soon after my ordination. The people were industrious, and able to sustain the cause; and few of them had been in any previous organization; therefore they were ready to receive the gospel. Sometimes there were thirty or forty baptized at one visit to the water. No other Christian minister had preached there, consequently they were unacquainted with our views previous to my preaching there. The additions were rapid. The preaching was in the woods in warm weather. The people came from far around, and the congregations were very large. The meetings at our seasons of communion would continue three or four days, and I seldom had help, but preached at least twice a day, with all the other labor. Such was my work in 1818, the first year of my ordination. I also made beginnings in some new places, and took some tours abroad to supply the numerous calls. Also, that year I hired help, and put up a house. By working night and day I got it under roof and inclosed, and had two rooms finished ready to move into by the last of December, 1818. We moved on the first day of January, 1819. Being now sheltered from the storms, I finished our house as time and circumstances permitted. During all this time, though my work was so urgent both on the house and farm, I attended all my appointments, giving to them from two to three days of a week besides Lord's day.

Prosperity of Union Church.—During the year 1819 my labors were abundantly blessed of the Lord, being crowned with great success. Union Church, the first church organized by me, received many additions, and soon numbered over two hundred members. I also began to preach this year once a month, in a neighborhood on Big Indian Creek, in Clermont County. I had visited there before, occasionally; but no other Christian minister had preached there. The people came out from far and near. The congregations were so large that no house could hold them. Many turned unto the Lord; and through divine grace I organized a church, which grew rapidly.

A New Preacher at Meeting.—One day, after I had preached to a very large congregation assembled in the forest, because no house could hold the people, I gave liberty for any one having

a word to say in the cause of religion to speak. A man arose
and walked directly into the stand, and without apology or explanation, said to the people that it had been reported of him
that he made his appointments on the days of the meetings
there to keep people away. This, he said, was not true. "I
am not like the 'dog in the manger,' that would not eat the hay
himself nor suffer the ox to eat it. If I can not do good myself,
I will not prevent others doing it who can." After he closed
his remarks I learned that this was Rev. William J. Thompson, the Methodist preacher, who lived some three or four miles
from the place of our meeting. This man had been a traveling
preacher. He was then perhaps near fifty years old. I was
not thirty. He was on a circuit after I became acquainted with
him, and was the strongest doctrinal preacher the Methodists
then had in southern Ohio. But they said hard things of him,
among others that he had made axes without putting steel on
them. I cared little for such stories; but having seen a pamphlet published by him, in which he, in an unchristian manner,
ridiculed the Baptists, I formed an unfavorable opinion of him,
which was confirmed by further acquaintance. It was said
that he still continued to make appointments on the days of
our meetings, to keep the people away; but we could not notice
that our congregations were any less on account of his appointments, and therefore thought little about them. Not long after
this, however, Mr. Thompson published a "Sketch," "designed
to show," as he said, "the difference between the Methodists
and the New Lights." By New Lights he meant the Christians. I paid little attention to this; barely stating to my congregation that Rev. William J. Thompson had misrepresented
our views, and thus passed his "Sketch" by. This displeased
him. He was probably disappointed that we were not more
troubled, and that his "Sketch" did not injure our congregations; but, instead of this, it increased them.

Another Church Organized.—During 1819 and 1820 I perceived, while occasionally preaching at Bethel, that there were
elements there for the formation of a church. I then gave
them regular monthly appointments. Bethel is in Clermont
County, thirty miles east of Cincinnati, on the old state road to
Portsmouth. No Christian minister had previously visited this
place. The congregations, large from the first, now rapidly increased, causing us to go to the woods for room. By the divine
aid many were brought to embrace religion, and I soon organized a church. Later in the year I formed a regular circuit in
parts of Brown and Clermont counties, with two appointments
for each day, several miles apart, which took me about two
weeks to get round.

Rev. Thompson on the Track.—At some of these meetings Mr.
Thompson was present; so, in passing the Indian Methodist

meeting-house in the summer of 1820, I stopped to hear him. He fixed his eyes on me; and pointed his finger at me; and, among other misrepresentations, said: "The New Lights deny repentance, and the operation of the Holy Spirit." After he closed I went up to him, and, before the people, told him that he had misrepresented me and the people with whom I stood connected, for we believed in repentance and the operation of the Holy Spirit as much as he did. After a short conversation he gave me his hand, saying, "Go on; preach repentance and the operation of the Holy Spirit. Do all the good you can. Bring your sheaves with you, and I will meet you in heaven."

Persecution Continues.—The following winter I preached at Neville, on the Ohio River, one of the points on my circuit. Rev. William J. Thompson was there. When I closed my discourse he arose, and taking from his pocket a paper which I was not permitted to read, commenced reading questions for me to answer in relation to the doctrine that Christ is the only self-existing and eternal God, etc., etc. I answered him as well as I could by the Scriptures; and when he was through, I asked him the following question, with others:

Gardner's Question.—"If Jesus Christ is the only self-existent and eternal God, and if he (that is, Christ) died to satisfy divine justice, and to reconcile his (that is, Christ's) Father to the world, as taught in the Discipline [and as I heard him preach], then are there not two eternal, self-existent Gods, one dying to reconcile the other?" He saw the dilemma, and did not dare to venture an answer, but had recourse to the following mode of extricating himself before the people. Said he, "You professed, the day you heard me, to believe the sermon which I preached on that subject." This I positively denied. While he pretended to affirm, he knew his statements were destitute of truth. He continued to affirm it, in order to get off probably, for he must have known his statement to be incorrect, as the only doctrines named that day were "repentance" and "the influence of the Holy Spirit." But why not answer my question? He could not without condemning his own theory, therefore he would not, but remarking, "There is not much difference between us," gave me his hand, saying, "Go on, and let us meet in heaven!" Had his views been sound, and had he not been fettered by his creed, he would have had a great advantage over me, as he was an able man. As it was, the weakness of his system was exposed, and he was put to shame, while Bible truth and pure Christian doctrine was established. Mr. Thompson feeling grieved by his failure to injure me, and desiring to recover himself, made a more unworthy effort to injure me, and the Christian cause through me. He wrote certificates, and persuaded the illiterate, uninformed members of his church to sign their names to them, stating that I agreed to all his sermon at the Indian meeting-house, the day that I heard him, and that I afterwards denied it at Neville. Such was the unrighteous conduct of this man in his efforts to destroy my usefulness among the people. Had he believed it himself, which he did not, he could not, without hypocrisy, have given me his hand there as he did, to meet him in heaven! But grieved at his failure on doctrine, he concluded to repair his loss by assailing my character; therefore he soon published a pamphlet containing these certificates. I went on with my work, however, trying to win souls to Christ, paying little attention to his pamphlet, which nobody seemed to care much about.

The Work of the Lord Goes On.—Notwithstanding all this persecution from Mr. Thompson and others of his caste, the cause of the dear Savior continued to advance, and the numbers added to the churches were many. I had no ministerial help, being almost alone in southern Ohio. I had a little assistance from Elder D. Kirkpatrick, a good man, and a good minister, who lived nearly forty miles distance from me, in Kentucky. He came over to Ohio and preached a few times. Elder D. Kirkpatrick and myself continued our connection with the Kentucky Conference until the Southern Ohio Christian Conference was organized in October, A. D. 1820.

The Slaveholder Rejected.—While I was a member of the Kentucky Conference, *Elder Joel Hayton,* a slaveholder, a very eloquent preacher, came forward to unite with the conference, at a session held in a church near Lexington.

Elder William Kinkade was present, and asked him if he owned slaves.

He answered that he did.

Kinkade then asked him if he intended to set them free.

Hayton replied that he did not think that his slaves were prepared for freedom; and he did not expect to set them free.

Elder Kinkade then objected to his reception!

Elder Barton W. Stone presided, I think.

He did not put the question, and the slaveholding preacher withdrew.

The Lesson.—In this two things were apparent: First, that the early Christian ministers, even in slave states, were generally antislavery men. The second was, that preachers could not be received into conference till all objections were removed. The reception, to prevent discord, required a unanimous vote, whether in conference or church.

Southern Ohio Conference Organized A. D. 1820.—Previous notice having been given, the elders and messengers from the churches met with the Christian Church at the forks of Brush Creek, in Adams County, about the middle of October, A. D. 1820, and there organized the *Southern Ohio Christian Conference.* I remember the following as elders present at the organization: Elders David Kirkpatrick, Robert McCoy, Cyrus Richards, Benjamin Van Pelt, and Matthew Gardner. There may have been others whom I do not now call to mind.

New Hymn-book.—There being no hymn-books of the Christian people in this part of the country, and as the churches were in great need of them, one part of the business of the first session of the Southern Ohio Christian Conference was to pass a resolution to compile and publish a Christian hymn-book. To do this there was a committee of three appointed, of which I was chairman. At the close of the business the conference adjourned to meet the following year; but very few of the ministers in this first session ever met with us again. Some of them moved away; and some even quit preaching. My associates on the hymn-book committee were favorable to my going forward with the book, but were unable to do any thing themselves, or to advance money and wait for the returns from sales, though one of them, a layman, who had the means, had at first promised to advance the money. As my means were too limited to commence such an undertaking alone, it seemed that the publication must be abandoned for the present at least.

Religion Still Advancing.—The cause of religion still advanced; and the calls for my feeble labors were such as would have more than required all my time, if I could have given it; yet my domestic cares absolutely required my whole attention. For a month or two I therefore did little more abroad than to fill my stated appointments, which took me two or three days of each week, and I devoted the rest of my time to home duties. I gathered the fall crops of corn, etc., prepared the pork for our meat the coming year, and closed the thirtieth year of my life, attending only my regular appointments.

CHAPTER IV.

THE FOURTH TEN YEARS OF MY LIFE—THE HYMN-BOOK—MINISTERS COMBINE FOR PERSECUTION—LAWSUITS—ORGANIZATION OF CHURCHES—GRACE SUFFICIENT.

On the 5th of December, 1820, I entered upon the thirty-first year of my life. In contemplating the past, it seemed to me that I had done but little compared with the much I should have done. I also noticed, with regret, my own failings, which, by divine grace, I resolved in the future to rectify. The first matter of public importance was the hymn-book, of which the churches stood in great need. A small book had been published some fifteen years before, which was now out of print, having involved its publishers in great loss. Yet, to supply the wants of the churches, as no one else seemed willing to take the responsibility, I determined, even with my limited means, to compile and have printed a new hymn-book, on my own responsibility. This I accomplished during the winter, in addition to my appointments and domestic duties, and got out an edition of one thousand hymn-books by the 1st of May, 1821, and the churches were soon supplied. By economy and care, I avoided loss, though some preachers neglected to pay for the books which they bought.

The Sudden Uproar.—While thus toiling to supply the churches and to do good, in the spring of 1821, as I went to one of my appointments, I found the whole country in an uproar. An old lady of the Presbyterian faith, having, in the bounds of the Union Church, attended an unfortunate girl in her sickness, fabricated a report prejudicial to my character. I was unacquainted with the party, but at once requested some of the members of the church to take her to a magistrate, or if she was unable to go, to take a magistrate to her, and obtain her sworn testimony. They did so; and she testified under oath that she never said so; that she had no cause to say so, and that the report was wholly false. This put to shame those who had been active in circulating the scandal. We regret that we too often see persons influenced by sectarianism acting upon the principles that "the end justifies the means," which means that falsehood and perjury are justifiable, if they sustain their creed, and hinder what those blinded by superstition call bad doctrines. The good work still continued, notwithstanding persecution, and in 1821 Union Church, which was the first which I organized, and which had become a very large church, built a substantial stone chapel, forty-four by sixty-four feet in size. Other churches which I had organized soon proceeded to build good houses of stone or brick for the worship of God.

Another New Preacher.—In the latter part of the summer or fall of 1821 a Presbyterian minister settled with the small church of that denomination at Augusta, on the Kentucky side of the river, within about three miles of the Union Church where I preached. The Presbyterians considered him a contentious man, which his subsequent course proved. There were one or two Presbyterian families in the neighborhood of Union Church, and so McCalla began to preach in the same school-house where I did, when it was too cold to hold meetings in the grove, before the church was built.

Trouble about Trinity.—The following winter, being in the neighborhood, I attended one of McCalla's meetings. After he closed his meeting he began to ask me questions on the trinity. I answered, and in turn asked him how he could reconcile the unscriptural absurdity of three infinite, self-existent, eternal Gods in one God, as stated in his creed. He replied; but he was angry, and said, "I will own you as the first-born child of the devil!" The people heard it, and in general attended his meetings no more. He continued his appointments, reading to his few friends the writings of the good Barton W. Stone, with unfriendly comments upon them, supposing of course that "the end justifies the means!"

The Rustic Pulpit.—In the early settlement of the country Christian Shinkle donated land for a church and for a schoolhouse. Before the church was built I preached in the schoolhouse. To accommodate the multitudes, the people built for me a stand in the grove, where I preached when the weather would permit. After we built Union Church, but before the inside was finished, they moved the stand from the woods into the church. The lines and landmarks in the woods not being well known, the stand had, by mistake, been set over the line, upon the land of John Clark a Presbyterian. When John discovered this, and that they had moved the stand, he, under the influence of McCalla, brought suit against about twenty of his neighbors for moving the stand. Clark admitted that the stand was not worth twenty-five cents to him; and all knew that none of the materials comprising it came from his land. McCalla now came in as the persecuted man. He circulated publications of his wrongs; represented himself as wickedly persecuted; claimed that the stand had been erected for him! said that it was destroyed to prevent his preaching there, and that Gardner helped to do it, though I was fifteen miles away at the time. I had been preaching in that stand more than two years before McCalla was known there. Notwithstanding all this, McCalla's story had its effect abroad, and securing two bigoted sectarians on the jury, these so managed the rest, that they returned a verdict in Clark's favor for one hundred dollars damages for moving the stand! Clark, all expectant, was pained to hear that the case was to be carried up to the Supreme Court. To avoid this, he, by his lawyer's advice, threw off all damages, and the defendants, for his sake, and for the sake of peace, paid the costs.

"The Measure Ye Mete," etc.—Clark's lawyer fees were fifty dollars. These he refused to pay; so his lawyer sued him; and he had to pay the fifty dollars, and nearly as much in costs. Thus by his preacher's bad counsel, he lost as much as he coveted, and lost also the good-will of his neighbors, and gained nothing, after all his trouble. What a lesson!

Trouble Increases.—I had received into the Union Church a sister Hughs, whose husband was an opposer. Rees Hughs,

her husband, sold me a horse; but he then thought he could do
better, and I let him keep it. When he afterward found that
he could not, he claimed that I should still take the horse, which
I refused, having learned that it was not as good as he had represented it to be. To avoid evil, I afterward paid Hughs the
full price for this horse, and got another man to take it of
Hughs. McCalla, in his publications, accused me of breaking
my contract with Hughs, of taking the stand from Clark, of
first confessing that I believed all Thompson's doctrine, and
then denying it, and other scandal, signed with a number of
names, and published over the *nom de plume*, "Rabbi Arhades."
McCalla had undoubtedly formed an alliance with Thompson,
to get me out of the way; and was zealously pursuing this method
by slandering me, to destroy the cause I advocated, on the
principle that "the end justifies the means!" On being charged
with being the author of these published statements of "Rabbi
Arhades," he confessed the truth, and dared me to sue him!
I now published a small pamphlet, giving a detailed account of
my conversations with Thompson, and the things of which
McCalla accused me, and hoped, as the people seemed satisfied,
that the persecution would end. But the pamphlets of McCalla
and Thompson were circulated far and wide by those in sympathy with them; and the two sects, at variance ever since the
days of Wesley, seemed to have formed an unnatural alliance
to destroy me. The Rev. McCalla continued to threaten, and
those who sympathized with him continued to repeat his words,
that he dared me to sue him. He boasted that he would come
over from Kentucky to Ohio and stand a trial, if Gardner dared
to prosecute him. I began to consider it my privilege as a citizen to claim the protection of the state, and my duty as a
Christian to vindicate my character as a minister of the gospel.
I had reason, however, to think that the Rev. Mr. Thompson,
and his partners in crime—the signers of the certificates—had
with McCalla united in a league to destroy me, and that these
signers and Thompson would go to all possible lengths to give
such testimony as McCalla might need to give him an advantage over me, as they now made common cause with him.

The Mistake of Going to Law.—I took legal counsel. I was
informed that neither Thompson, certificates, or signers would
be admitted to testify, but that McCalla would be compelled to
show that Thompson had proved his statements in a court of
justice, where I could appear to answer. Under these circumstances, I saw some little chance for justice, and considered it
my duty to vindicate the truth, as by leaving these men to pursue their disgraceful course was construed by them into an
admission of some truth for their wicked persecution. Consequently a suit was entered against William L. McCalla for libel,
in the Court of Common Pleas, Brown County, Ohio, A. D.

1822. The case came to trial in November, 1822. McCalla appeared, and with him ten or twelve other Presbyterian ministers. There was the far-famed orator, Rev. Mr. Edgar, of Maysville, Kentucky; Rev. John Rankin, of Ripley, Ohio; Rev. R. Moreland, of Cynthiana, Kentucky; and the Methodist, William J. Thompson; and other ministers whom I did not know. I was alone. Christian ministers who proposed to attend I had requested not to do so; that, if I fell, I might fall alone. Before court McCalla harrangued the people in the court-yard, on the justice of his cause and the bad doctrines of Gardner, and insisted that he should be put down. The case was called. Hon. John Thompson, the judge, was an elder in the Presbyterian Church, and accordingly decided every point in favor of McCalla, of which he previously assured McCalla, which accounted for his boldness. The charge was, that McCalla had falsely and maliciously published that Thompson had proved me a liar by scores of witnesses. As McCalla pleaded justification, my counsel insisted that the only evidence to be adduced on McCalla's part was such as showed his charge true. Not what I was; but if it could be proved, as McCalla published, was the point: namely, the charge that I had been proved a "liar" in a court of justice, or some tribunal where I could appear to defend myself. This the Presbyterian judge overruled, and decided that Thompson, and his friends—the certificate signers —his participants in crime, might be admitted to testify for themselves against me. The great advantage of belonging to a popular church was now very apparent. The judge permitted McCalla to try to do what he had published Thompson had already done, instead of compelling him to prove that Thompson had done it. So, by the ruling of the judge, I was tried instead of McCalla, and my enemies were permitted to testify against me. All McCalla's hopes depended on the judge's decision, and he was not deceived. Every indulgence was given for them to prove that I had agreed to Thompson's sermon at one time, and dissented from some things in it at another. If they could only do this, all these preachers thought themselves justified in publishing me before the world as a "liar!" The judge ruled to their mind. The witnesses testified as McCalla asked them to, but on the cross-examination, reluctantly admitted that at Neville, after all the admitting and denying he since charged me with, he had given me his hand, on our parting, to meet me in heaven, thus proving his subsequent charges to be malicious perversions, as it could not be consistent to pledge himself to meet me in heaven, and then, on some previous charge, publish me as a liar. The prospect for the success of the Thompson and McCalla combination now suddenly changed, as every impartial mind in the full court-house seemed fully satisfied that all that had been said against me was no

4

true, and invented by Thompson to turn the attention of the
people from the horns of the dilemma upon which I left him
impaled, when he failed to answer my question, "If Jesus Christ
be the self-existent and eternal God, and he died to reconcile
his Father, did not one eternal God die to reconcile the other?"
To cover this absurdity in his doctrine, he invented the story
which he published, to destroy me and my influence; and
McCalla entered into the combination for the same purpose.
After McCalla's witnesses were through, I introduced mine.
About twenty-five men of undoubted veracity, who were present at the meeting when I should have indorsed Thompson's
sermon, testified that I indorsed none of it except the doctrine
of "repentance," and "the operation of the Spirit;" and about
forty of my neighbors, who had been acquainted with me from
a boy of ten or twelve years old, testified to my moral character for truth and veracity. Against these irreproachable witnesses the others had none to testify. Three or four lawyers of
a side now commenced their work of pleading. The other side
pleaded that I had certainly at first agreed to all of Thompson's sermon, and afterwards disputed the doctrine; but still,
when they considered the many irreproachable witnesses to my
veracity, they dared not assail my character, and they were loth
to admit that Thompson knew that I was a liar while promising to meet me in heaven. My lawyers insisted that Thompson's own testimony was not true, for this reason, that if I was
guilty of lying, as he afterwards published, then he was one of
the foulest of hypocrites, when he pledged himself to meet me in
heaven. Therefore, they insisted that when he pledged himself
at Neville to meet me in heaven, he did not believe that I had
before lied to him about his sermon at the Indian meeting-
house, and they rationally concluded the slander an after-
thought, and that he got his witnesses to testify to that which
he did not believe himself. My counsel dwelt at length upon
the combination, headed by ministers of two of the leading
sects, to slander down the plaintiff, and thus break down a
young and feeble denomination, because they dared to believe
and teach a different doctrine. They referred to the persecutions of the rack in the dark ages, when men were tortured till
they would renounce their faith, or death relieved them, and
proved that these men, being actuated by the same spirit of
persecution, had tried to destroy my character, and would put
me to death if the law would permit. My attorney maintained
(how shameful the necessity of doing so) the right, under the
Constitution of the United States, of every man to teach any
religious sentiments he believed, "and," said he, "the State of
Ohio will protect him." The opposing lawyers made a labored
effort at the close, employing all their legal learning and skill;
but the evidence was unanswerable. The trial lasted four days.

The jury retired near night. It sat all night. About ten o'clock the next morning the members came in without a verdict. Two of McCalla's friends would agree to nothing against their preacher; the others would not clear him; and so his friends hung the jury. The others, of whom it is fair to say some were Methodists and Presbyterians, were in favor of a verdict of from $1,000 to $1.500 exemplary damages. Ten of them would have convicted him of libel. His two Presbyterian friends saved him. Informed by his friends how near he was to being convicted, he came directly into court and filed an affidavit for change of venue (See Appendix B). He realized now that his guilt was apparent to all, for he swore that such was the prejudice against him that he could not get a jury to do him justice in the county. But he knew, and all knew, that if I was as bad a man as he had represented me to be, and had every chance to prove me, I could not have so prejudiced a whole county of people who knew me, that he, a Presbyterian minister, with all his friends, could not get a jury to do him justice in the whole county. Judge Thompson, being unwilling to trust the trial out of his jurisdiction, appointed it in Highland County. My lawyers preferred Clermont, where the difficulty first originated with Rev. W. J. Thompson, so as at once to get it from under the jurisdiction of the Presbyterian judge, and to avoid the necessity of depositions. I was informed that there was an understanding between the attorneys on both sides, that McCalla would meet me there: so I drew the suit, and paid the costs, and entered it in Clermont County; but he did not keep his word, and I could not compel him to attend out of his state.

He Still Continues Preaching.—Although two or three years engaged in these perplexing litigations, yet, through divine grace, I retained a prayerful and devoted frame of mind, and the spirit and power of preaching. Much good was done, and many were added to the church. My domestic matters were not neglected. A barn and some smaller buildings were erected on my farm; the fences were kept up; weeds, briars, and grubs were not allowed to grow in the fence corners to rot down the fence. The children were sent to school, and were likewise taught business habits, industry, and economy—things too often neglected by ministers, especially teaching their children to work. While at home I was always closely employed.

Emancipation Baptists.—I was requested to send an appointment to the old stone meeting-house in Kentucky. This house was built by the emancipation or antislavery Baptists, who, about 1805, separated from the Regular Baptists on the question of slavery. They had now become extinct as a church, and their house was unoccupied. It was north-west from Maysville about five miles, and about three from the Ohio River, in

Mason County. I sent the appointment, and, on visiting there, the people received the Word with all readiness of mind, and urged me to visit them again. I did so, and continued preaching there till numbers embraced religion, and a Christian church was organized. Because my Sabbaths were occupied elsewhere, my visits were mostly during the week; but many were added to the church, which soon numbered nearly one hundred members.

Pay—Old-Lady Philosophy.—I labored there nearly four years, without receiving sufficient compensation to pay my ferriage across the Ohio River. One night an old Baptist gentleman and lady asked me to go and put up with them. I did so. During my visit the old lady said:

"What do they pay you for preaching to them here?"

"They do not pay me any thing except food for myself and horse," I replied.

"Then you had better leave them," she said, "for that which costs nothing they will value as worth nothing." I prepared to leave. Soon after this, an Elder Roberts, of Licken Knobs, came along. He was a Christian, of Campbellite sentiments. They insisted on my remaining pastor; but raised a good salary for him. He bought hymn-books of me to the amount of fifty dollars. He borrowed their money. One man visited him to collect a large sum, but, when he saw his family, had no heart to ask him to pay. I followed him to Licken Knobs with a like result. He was soon found to be untrustworthy, and the church broke up. Some went into Campbellism, and continued in the stone meeting-house; some went to the Methodists, who formed a class there after the Christian church ceased. Others stood alone. Rev. McCalla and his friends could not be still, but continued to defame me. He boasted that I had been glad to withdraw the suit and pay the costs. I now felt it my duty to follow him to Kentucky. I knew the power of the combination against me, and that Thompson and his signers would not stand for truth, in their efforts to save McCalla and injure me, so I consulted some of the best judges of the laws of Kentucky. They assured me that as McCalla had published that these things had been "proved by scores of witnesses," that this meant that it had been thus proved in court, or at least where I could appear to answer; and as he had pleaded justification, he would be bound to confine himself to evidence designed to prove this and nothing else. Being thus assured, I brought suit in Augusta, Kentucky, in August, A. D. 1823. The court-house was crowded with all ranks, and both sexes.

A Novel Court.—Old Dr. McCalla, a Presbyterian preacher, and his lady, the father and mother of Rev. William L. McCalla, were there from Lexington, Kentucky; and as a single judge forms a circuit court in Kentucky, they took their

seats on one side of the Court (Judge Beaty), on the bench with
him, and the noted orator, Rev. Mr. Edgar, a Presbyterian
preacher from Maysville, on the other side! Was there ever,
before or since, such a scene as this in a court pretending to
administer justice? Who will deny that Mr. McCalla's father
and mother, and his brother minister, Rev. Edgar, were indi-
rectly McCalla's judges? and so understood, and their influence
invited by this one-man court, when invited to take their seats
with the judge. But there was no help. The jury was summoned. I requested the sheriff to select none belonging to the
Methodist, Presbyterian, or Christian churches, and he said
that he would not. The judge gave liberty for objections. I
left this to my counsel, Mr. Marshall, as he lived in Augusta,
and was well acquainted there. He objected to one or two.
Mr. McCalla's lawyer objected to from twenty to thirty. It
seemed as though there could be no jury impanelled to whom
he would trust his cause. While the jury was being made up,
I was specially warned of a man who was received upon it,
named John Thompson. My informant said, "Thompson is a
Presbyterian, or holds that way, and will hang the jury." As
they had objected to so many, my counsel thought it best to let
the jury stand, and risk Thompson, hoping that he would not
let his sectarianism prevent his rendering a just and impartial
verdict. The witnesses were ready. I had twenty depositions
of respectable persons, who had known me from my boyhood,
to prove my moral character, and others present in person. I
had from thirty to forty witnesses and depositions to prove
that at the Indian meeting-house I agreed to none of Thompson's doctrine but those, namely: "Repentance" and "the influence of the Holy Spirit;" and these were not denied at
Neville. Our special count was that "William L. McCalla had
falsely and maliciously published in a pamphlet that William
J. Thompson had proved the plaintiff a liar by scores of witnesses." McCalla pleaded, as before, justification, because of
Thompson's certificates. My counsel argued that as the defendant pleaded justification, he must adduce evidence to show
that the plaintiff had been proved a liar in a court of justice, or
in some way where he could defend himself, and that the *ex
parte* certificates were not such proof. The counsel for the defense argued that McCalla had not said that it was in a court
of justice, and if confined to such evidence they must lose the
case, while they were ready to make good the assertion by the
certificates, etc. My counsel said that we had come into a court
of law and justice. The defendant had published that the
plaintiff had been proved a liar by scores of witnesses, and had
not named certificates; therefore, as the defendant pleads justification, he should not be permitted to put in certificates, but
be compelled to prove his charge, showing that the plaintiff

had been proved guilty by witnesses in that way which alone is
recognized by law and in 'courts of justice; and urged that
if *ex parte* certificates, got up in the heat of party zeal, signed
in the dark, behind the victim's back, and published in pamphlets to injure him, are to be considered as witnesses or evidence in a court of justice, justifying the publication that the
charge has been proved by scores of witnesses, then the best
man's character can be destroyed. The defendant's counsel replied, using about the same arguments as before, and left it to
the court. Judge Beaty, of course, decided that the certificates, and the signers, and Thompson's deposition, and all,
should go to the jury as evidence, going thus even beyond
Judge Thompson, of Ohio, who ruled the certificates out. As
Rev. W. J. Thompson knew that he and McCalla must now
stand or fall together, it was manifest that in his deposition he
went beyond the truth, and had his certificate men trained to
sustain his deposition, while he remained away to avoid being
exposed by cross examination. It was a long trial. The witnesses and depositions were near one hundred in all. Then
there were the cross examinations and pleadings. There were
four attorneys on each side.

The Lawyers.—The following gentlemen appeared for me:
Colonel Henry Brush, of Chillicothe, Ohio, who stood perhaps
at the head of the bar in that state; Mr. Martin Marshall, of
Augusta, who brought the suit; and two young lawyers—Mr.
Nicholas Cleman, of Cynthiana, Kentucky, and —— Brown, of
Kentucky, both of very fine talents. The defendant's counsel
were Mr. John Chambers, Mr. Walker Reed, Mr. —— Paxton,
and Mr. Haws, all of Maysville, Kentucky. The trial lasted
about four days. The court-house was constantly crowded
with both men and women, who listened very attentively.
From notes taken by me at the time, I will give a few items
from the lawyers' speeches, showing the sentiments entertained
by some people as late as A. D. 1823:

Mr. John Chambers said to the jury: "Any man propagating
a doctrine contrary to the commonly received opinions ought
to be put down."

Messrs. Reed and Haws seemed to feel that they were engaged in a bad cause, and said little.

Marshall replied to Chambers that we were in a free country,
where men have the right to believe and preach what they
please, and the Constitution of the United States and the laws
of Kentucky sustain this right. If they could put down the
people with whom the plaintiff stood connected, they would
then attempt to put down others, and so on till they had an
established religion.

Messrs. Brown and Cleman did not spare the Rev. Mr.
McCalla's feelings, but described to what a length his persecut-

ing spirit had led him, and showed him how far it was from the business of a gospel minister thus to unite in combination for calumny and defamation of the character of another minister.

Colonel Brush closed the argument for the plaintiff, and Mr. Paxton for the defendant.

Colonel Brush spoke nearly six hours. He showed what persecution had done in different ages, and proved that this attack was a deep-laid scheme on the part of Thompson and McCalla to destroy the character of the plaintiff. McCalla was to publish the calumny, and then Thompson was to come forward and swear to it. Thus two leading ministers in two popular sects united to crush one minister, thereby to stop the progress, if possible, of a young and rising denomination, because not of their own faith and order, and which they feared might yet be in their way. Colonel Brush animadverted severely upon Rev. Thompson's deposition; for therein he acknowledged that, at Neville, when he parted with me, he gave me his hand to meet me in heaven. Could a gospel minister expect to meet a liar in heaven? If what he afterward said were true, he should have said so at that time, and not have acted the hypocrite!

Rev. Mr. Thompson.—Thompson's character was indefensible. View him which way they would, his duplicity was apparent. If the plaintiff was untruthful, why promise to meet him in heaven? or if not, why the subsequent persecution? Who could believe a man guilty of such deception? His endeavors were evidently designed to make others believe what he did not believe himself. From this lamentable condition no friends could relieve him. Their kindest efforts only changed him from horn to horn of the dilemma upon which his own conduct had impaled him. Poor Thompson! I pitied him.

Mr. Paxton pleaded for McCalla with an interest bordering on agony. His eloquence was interesting. He pointed the jury to the aged parents of McCalla seated with Judge Beaty before them. It was as though they were on trial. Said the lawyer, If you convict the defendant, you "bring their gray hairs down with sorrow to the grave." He made a powerful appeal to the jury for sympathy for the aged parents, and they were affected with pity for the old people. The jury retired about noon, and continued out all night.

McCalla Convicted.—Notwithstanding the extraordinary efforts made to screen the reverend culprit, he was convicted at his own home, and among his own friends, as the author of a slanderous and malicious libel, and subjected to heavy costs. These costs his friend on the jury considered as part of the penalty, and hence argued its sufficiency, without exemplary damages. God has mercy on the penitent; but he was not penitent. Mercy without penitence encourages crime. McCalla was convicted, but not converted; and this ill-advised clemency became a license for continued calumny. My counsel foresaw this, and took a bill of exceptions against the ruling of Judge Beaty, and gave notice of an appeal. In Kentucky, the Court of Appeals decides law questions only. If the decision of a circuit judge is reversed, the case is sent back to the same court for a new trial. If confirmed, the case stands. After the appeal was taken, I had little hope of Judge Beaty's ruling being reversed, when I learned that part of the Court of Appeals belonged to the Presbyterian Church. I soon learned that the judgment was confirmed, without reasons being rendered, which is contrary to the custom of that court. The decision being the guide of the under court, the Court of Appeals gives the reasons for reversing a judgment. In confirming, it does the same. But the court gave no reason for confirming Judge Beaty's decision. I was now satisfied of what I should have known before, that, in the efforts by William L. McCalla and William J. Thompson, the two leading ministers in this country of the two prominent sects, they had this advantage over me in law, that sectarian prejudice goes onto the bench with the judge, enters the box with the jury, and reappears in the verdict they render. Dissatisfied with the decision of the court, he soon published a pamphlet. In this the convict tried the court; for he was witness, judge, and jury, and of course had his own way. So he cleared himself, and convicted the jury, saying that all except two of the jurors, who were my personal friends, were in his favor, but these two friends of mine caused the verdict to be against him. I then resolved to see the jurors myself. I visited Kentucky, and found all but two, who were dead, or had moved away.

Certificate of Nine Jurors.—"The undersigned jurors, who tried the case in the Bracken County Circuit Court, at the August term of 1823, wherein Matthew Gardner was plaintiff, and William L. McCalla defendant, do hereby certify that we believed, from the evidence before us as jurors, that William L. McCalla's publication, in which he said that William J. Thompson had proved Mr. Gardner a liar by scores of witnesses, is a slanderous and malicious libel. And we further certify that it was evident, from the testimony before us, that it was a spiteful, malicious scheme, laid between William J. Thompson and William L. McCalla, to destroy Mr. Gardner's character and influence. We, the undersigned, were therefore in favor of rendering a verdict against William L. McCalla for exemplary damages of perhaps twelve or fifteen hundred dollars; but finding that one or two were determined to hang the jury, so as to render no verdict at all rather than allow more than nominal damages, we thought it better to agree with them than for the jury to hang and render no verdict. We further state that every man on the jury agreed that Mr. Gardner's character was certainly proved to be good. Nor did any of us intend, or expect to be understood, that our verdict was the value or equivalent for Mr. Gardner's character, but intended to sustain the plaintiff's declaration, *to-wit:* William L. McCalla is the author of a slanderous and malicious libel against Matthew Gardner. And also to oblige William L. McCalla to pay all costs of that suit, amounting to quite a large sum; while we hoped that he would take warning thereby for the future. Given under our hands this fourteenth day of February, 1828. William Currence, Valentine Harmon, William Ambrose, Levi Waters, Daniel Keithler, Robert Power, Samuel Hamilton, Stanford C. Pinkard, William Norris."

John Thompson, the juror whom I was warned against, said that he did not belong to the Presbyterians, but held that way, and admitted that he was the principal one of the two jurors who prevented a verdict for exemplary damages.

John Thompson's Certificate.—"Being one of the jurors who tried the case of libel in the Bracken County Circuit Court, Kentucky, at the August term of 1823, wherein Matthew Gardner was plaintiff, and William L. McCalla defendant, I state that ten of the jury were in favor of finding a verdict for the plaintiff for exemplary damages; but I disagreed to it in consequence of a difference, as I thought, in the testimony, and so the verdict was rendered for nominal damages. I did not mean the verdict as an equivalent for Mr. Gardner's character, for his character was certainly proved to be good. I also believe that William J. Thompson took advantage of Mr. Gardner in one of the two conversations, either at Indian meeting-house or at Neville, or else some of Thompson's witnesses were mistaken. Given under my hand and seal this thirteenth day of February, 1828. Signed, John Thompson."

The McCalla sympathizers endeavored to make the impression that the low damages, instead of being measured by pity for the calumniator, were the measure of the value of my character; and when the certificates of the jurors came out, they hurried to the jurors to obtain counter, or modifying, certificates, which they refused. I then published in a pamphlet a concise history of the conduct of the Rev. William J. Thompson and the Rev. William L. McCalla, from the beginning, including the scandals of which they were the authors, the lawsuits in which they were exposed, the certificates of the jurors by whom they were convicted, certifying the twenty-four jurors who decided McCalla guilty, and the twenty who were in favor of punishing him by heavy damages of from one to two thousand dollars. This finally silenced their licentious talk; and not many years after, both Thompson and McCalla died. In the mean time, McCalla had sought a new home. The people at Augusta had heard the trial, and public opinion was aroused;

and McCalla, soon after the trial, moved, it was said, to the suburbs of Philadelphia, Pennsylvania. At any rate, there soon
turned up there a hero of the same name, as a champion against
the Christian faith. In a debate at Milford, New Jersey, with
William Lane, the young pastor of the Christian church,
McCalla suffered a defeat, exposing the errors of his faith as
plainly as the lawsuit had exposed the errors of his character.

Two Mistakes.—I must now record two mistakes for the good
of others: *First:* After seeing the spirit manifested by Rev.
William L. Thompson, in misrepresenting the Baptist Church,
I should have been on my guard, and had nothing to do with
him. It is a mistake to trust any minister whom you find to
be dishonest in his treatment of others. *Second:* I should not
have appealed to the law. They whom the Lord calls to preach
the gospel of peace must expect to be evil spoken of, as was
their Master. If the tongue does defame them, they should
not leave the Master's work, to which he has called them, to
attend vexatious lawsuits, which minister to the pleasure of
Satan and wicked men. He who is innocent, and has a clear
conscience, and goes right along, will be sustained, as a general
thing, by the unprejudiced and impartial public; if not at first,
he will certainly be in the end, after due consideration and
"the second, sober thought." But I was like most inexperienced men, in early life, who, being honest themselves, do not
suspect their fellow-men, and can not believe that men will
swear falsely. I had great confidence in preachers being what
they professed to be—honest, God-fearing men. I looked upon
a court of *justice* as almost perfect, and thought that these tribunals could not fail to administer equal and exact justice to
every man, under all circumstances. How greatly was I deceived! In my first suit I found a Presbyterian elder presid-
ing as judge, using his influence to shield his minister, and two
Presbyterian jurors preventing a verdict. In Kentucky there
was the preacher's father, a reverend doctor of divinity, and
his mother on one side of the judge, and a brother preacher on
the other, to influence the court, and a noted brother in the
faith to modify the verdict! I allude to these facts to warn
others, that no confidence can be placed in human tribunals,
where the officers are influenced by sectarian prejudice. Let
the reader suppose that I had slandered Rev. William L.
McCalla, as he did me, and that I had published that "*he had
been proved a liar by scores of witnesses!*" Does any one suppose that the courts so friendly to him would have permitted
me to put in, as my scores of witnesses, the list of names of
those who had, behind the curtain, in the dark, and without
his knowledge, propagated the very slanders, thus inviting injustice against him? No, no! no one believes it. Some will

say that I was too hasty; but they can not judge. Many a young minister has been destroyed by slander. It is of the Lord's mercy that I was not. In 1851 I visited, in the State of New York, Elder David Ford, formerly a talented, influential, and useful Christian minister, possessing an excellent voice, and good health; aged about fifty-five. I found him in the shop at work, making grain cradles. Why was he there? He had been driven from the pulpit by the slanderer; and the jury, through prejudice, or deceived by false swearing, gave their verdict against him. Thus his character was broken down, and he retired a disappointed man. Instead of appealing to the law, my proper course would have been to publish a correct version of the matter, stating plainly the untruths, and inviting the slanderer to call on me, and we would refer the whole matter to a committee mutually chosen, of neither church party, and abide their decision as final. If my opponent had refused to comply with this reasonable proposition, all honorable men would have considered him as the author of the libel, and all impartial minds would have been satisfied, and I would have been saved much trouble and expense.

Bethlehem Church to be.—After giving up preaching at the old stone meeting-house on Lawrence Creek, Kentucky, I began to preach once a month, on the Ohio side of the river, opposite Maysville, some twelve miles from my home. I had occasionally preached there on my way to the Lawrence Creek church. The neighborhood was famed for wickedness. Sabbath-breaking by horse-racing and gambling. Cock-fights and whisky-drinking were common. Immorality in rudeness was popular. I had a great desire to carry the gospel there. The love of Christ constrained me to pity the people.

Traveling Congregation.—There was no preaching on the Ohio side of the river within miles of them. A Methodist minister had sent an appointment; but when he arose to speak, the congregation in concert, as previously arranged, arose and left the house and empty benches for him to preach to. They needed salvation! Could I reach them? I would try. I appointed meetings in their dwellings or log-cabin school-houses; but the congregations soon became so large that, when the weather permitted, our meetings were in the woods.

The Fiddler.—The word of truth, attended by the Spirit and the power of God, reached the hearts of this wicked people, and scores of them soon turned from sin to righteousness. One who came out had been a leader. He had been a great violinist. One of his former comrades, a fellow-musician, seeing him pass, after the change, endeavored to decoy him by calling to him as he passed; but he went on. "Please to tune my fiddle for me," he cried. "Let every fiddler tune his own fiddle," he replied, and went on his way.

Bethlehem Church Organized.—A church was soon organized, composed of those who had been, but a little before, truly the "servants of sin." The revival continued. Many were added to the church; and in a few years Bethlehem church numbered over four hundred members. We soon built a good brick chapel, and the church prospered. If ever the power of the gospel was manifest to all, it was in that section of country.

Preachers Viewed from the Sinner's Point of View.—Before I began to preach there, the people were much prejudiced against all preachers. They looked upon them as a "lazy, trifling class of men, who preached for money, thereby to live without work." They regarded me in a different light. "for," said they, "we know him to be a hardworking man." And as I preached without charging them money for my labor as a minister, they believed that my motive was to do good among the people.

Georgetown.—About this time (1822 or 1823) I began to preach regularly in Georgetown, Ohio, the county seat of Brown County, about twelve miles from my home. This county was composed of parts of Adams and Clermont counties, and had been organized but a short time. The county seat had been located and the town laid out quite recently. The meetings were for some time held in a small school-house; but as this would not hold the people, as soon as the court-house was erected I preached in it.

Opposition.—There was much opposition from the Methodists and Presbyterians. They did not like to see the Christians taking a start with the town. But this did not prevent the people receiving that religion which has the Bible for its only rule of faith and practice, to the exclusion of all sectarian creeds.

Church Organized.—A church was soon organized, which grew rapidly. In a few years we erected a brick chapel. I was one of the largest subscribers, as I was generally to houses built by churches which, through divine grace, I had organized. I even went over and labored on the building. I assisted in putting on the roof, to secure the walls before winter came on. This church prospered for several years, increasing to the number of nearly two hundred members.

The Locality of Skeptics.—In 1824 I commenced preaching statedly once a month, five miles west of my home. It being on my way to and from the Union Church, I had frequently preached there; but there had been no stated preaching there, or near there, before this time. One or two of the leading men were infidels, who of course encouraged wickedness, and so sin and vanity did "much abound." The leading infidel had been a member of the legislature, which added to the importance of his influence against religion. With profane language, he represented that the object of the ministers was to get good living

without work, and be admired by the people. His opposition
did me little harm. I was known as well as he. My residence
being so near, it was almost as if I lived there; and the people
knew that his infidel reproaches and imputations, as far as I
was concerned, were untrue. The gospel was there, as everywhere, "the power of God unto salvation to every one that believeth," and many turned to the Lord.

The Pisgah Church Organized.—It was not long till a church
was organized, to be known by the name of "Pisgah Christian
Church." In one year after the organization, I wrote a subscription, and there was soon money enough signed to build
a brick chapel. Many were added to this church, and it
soon numbered over two hundred members. After about fifteen years or more, I attended a protracted meeting there, at
which there were between seventy and eighty added to the
church. The first chapel being too small to hold the people, I
drew up a second subscription; and a more eligible site being
selected near the first, the lot was purchased, and a chapel
built large enough to accommodate the people. The wife of
the infidel named soon became a worthy member of the church.

The Hymn-Book.—The first edition of the hymn-book having
been disposed of, there was a demand among the churches for
more books. Accordingly, in 1824, I published a second edition of three thousand copies. Being in great demand, they
were sent to different sections as soon as they were bound. My
mode of disposing of my books differed materially from that
pursued by others who have published Christian hymn-books
for the West. They let hymn-books go out of their possession
only to those who order; consequently they are not to be had
in book-stores; but the book-seller will tell those seeking them
that he has all other hymn-books; but there is no Christian
hymn-book in print to his knowledge. The books published
by me were sold at many book-stores, and by traveling book-
sellers, so that all who desired could get them at wholesale or
retail. Where book-stores would not buy, I left the books,
with instructions to send them out by their agents, for country
customers, as the people, as a general thing, who do not belong
to the sects, prefer our books. I never lost any thing by regular book-sellers. But the preachers seldom paid when they
purchased, but took the books to sell. I gave them every third
book for selling. The price was fifty cents. Some have never
paid me yet, and of course never will.

Labors On.—Publishing the hymn-books did not prevent my
preaching. I preached not only every Sabbath, but in various
places on week-days.

Overboard in the Ohio River.—Going to one of my week-day
appointments back of Augusta, in Bracken County, Kentucky,
where the Lord had abundantly blessed my labors, and many

were added to the Lord, I was crossing the river on the ferry-boat. perhaps in March, 1824. As I held my horse by the bridle, when the boat was well out in the river, they attempted to raise a sail. My horse sprang toward me, doubtless for pro-tection, which threw me overboard into the river. The horse jumping, came with his forefeet upon my breast. I shall never forget my prayer when sinking in the river, with the horse upon me, as I struggled in the water, expecting to be drowned. The prayer was, "O God, save me! save me!" I fell over the down-river side of the boat. The horse swam away from over me, and I came to the top of the water. No one on the boat had presence of mind to assist me, except a lad twelve or four-teen years old. He cried, "Throw the boat down stream, and save Mr. Gardner!" They then did so; and they pushed a pole out to me. I took hold of it, and with their assistance regained the boat, and was taken on board. I had on at the time a heavy overcoat, with a large cape, and wrappers round my legs, so that it would have been impossible to swim had I known how, which I did not. My horse swam back to the Ohio shore.

The Guardian Angel.—I have ever regarded that deliverance, with many others of my eventful life—for they have been many—owing to the special care of the guardian angel of the Lord, sent, as I firmly believe, to be always with me while I walk with God. Indeed every one who so walks is attended by a guardian angel; for He saith, "Are they not all minister-ing spirits, sent forth to minister for them who shall be heirs of salvation?" Heb. i. 14.

Special Providence.—I will mention another special provi-dence of God in saving my life: Once when returning to my home, I was riding a very skittish young mare. When a short distance from my residence, and was passing through a narrow lane, a man came riding quite rapidly after me, and when within a few rods of coming up with me, called. I stopped suddenly. Between us there was a small flock of sheep, which. becoming frightened at his rapid riding, passed me, jumping one after another, as sheep commonly do when frightened, and escaping by a narrow passage. My beast became frightened. She made a sudden spring and threw me off, hurting me badly, while my foot was fast in the stirrup. The beast stood still where I fell. She neither jumped, ran, or moved. The man approaching, released my foot, and assisted me to rise. Why did this skittish beast. that had frequently run away with the rider when approaching home, stand still at that time? She was frightened! She was approaching home! Why did she not run toward home? With my foot fast in the stirrup. she would have dragged me on and killed me. I never could ac-count for my preservation by reasoning from natural causes.

Therefore I gave thanks to God, and praised him for his special providence in saving me from an awful death.

The year 1825 was a year of great prosperity to the Christians. The churches in southern Ohio were blessed with many additions. Bible truth was received with favor by the people. Opposition did not seem so bitter as in former years.

Elder Alexander McClain.—About this time Elder Alexander McClain moved from Kentucky into southern Ohio. He was a very zealous man in religion. With moderate education, he was a good speaker. He read little except the Bible, and preached without much apparent system, but was a fine exhorter. He was very useful, and organized several churches.

Robert Patterson.—It was, I think, this year (1825) that Robert Patterson, of Kentucky, first visited Ohio. He was a young man of fine talents, good education, and remarkable piety. He was very useful, doing much good. He visited Ohio occasionally for several years, and assisted me in protracted meetings.

Elder Patterson's Death.—After a few years Elder Patterson married an excellent young lady. I knew her well, and have been at her father's house. She was a Christian. They both died of cholera in 1832, by which the churches suffered a great loss.

Elders Simonton and Walter.—There were a number of other able Christian ministers with whom I now exchanged, among whom were Elders Richard Simonton and Isaac N. Walter, whose labors were very useful in southern Ohio.

Young Ministers.—It was in 1825, I think, that four or five young men, who had begun to speak to the people on the subject of salvation, were recommended by the churches to the conference, and were received and recommended as ministers, and were heard from for good afterwards.

Cincinnati.—About this time I began to have frequent appointments in Cincinnati. Quite a number who had embraced religion under my preaching were living there, and others who had belonged to churches in various sections of the country. I preached in school-houses, and in a hall when we were able to obtain one. It was not long till a church was gathered, and arrangements made to purchase a lot and build a chapel. It is much more difficult to raise the means to build a church in the city than in the country. It requires much more time and attention. A subscription was started.

Jeptha D. Garrard.—A wealthy lawyer, who was of our views in religion, gave one thousand dollars. I perhaps signed as much as any one except Garrard. He was an excellent man. He died of lockjaw a few years afterwards, caused by the extraction of a tooth. His widow afterwards married Judge McLean, of the United States Supreme Court. To assist in the purchase of the lot and the building of the chapel, I borrowed, on my own responsibility, $700 or $800, and took a partial lien on the property for the amount. The house was built on Lawrence street, below Fourth, running through to Ludlow street, in the eastern part of the city.

Elder N. Summerbell.—After a few years they sold that house, being in debt, and built a frame house in the western part of the city. Then, after Elder N. Summerbell came to Cincinnati in 1850, they, through his influence, sold the last-mentioned house and lot, and by Elder Summerbell's enterprise and industry, purchased a lot, and built quite a large, respectable chapel on Longworth street, near the middle of the city. Having a great desire to secure a chapel for the Christians in Cincinnati, I have given first and last nearly $500 for that purpose. I may speak further of matters in the city, in their order, but must now return to the thread of my narrative—to A. D. 1825.

Visits Cane Ridge.—It was about August in 1825, while on a preaching tour in Kentucky, that I attended a large meeting at Cane Ridge, the place made memorable by the great revival in the beginning of this century. Having heard much about the great camp-meeting that was held there in August, 1801, it was very interesting to me to see the place—to stand upon the ground! Having been told, by those who were eye-witnesses, of the manifestations of the power of God at that great camp-meeting, it seemed to me holy ground. It was on these grounds on which I then stood that thousands met and camped, twenty-four years before, drawn together simultaneously from all parts of the country as by one accord, and one impulse to worship God and his Son Jesus Christ! It was here, at the same meeting, where many preachers of various evangelical denominations, with their people, labored and worshiped together in true Christian union! Sometimes six or eight ministers would be preaching at the same time in different parts of the encampment. Denominational distinctions disappeared. It was here that hundreds, if not thousands, found pardon and peace by and through Him who died but lives again. Many went there infidels, who, while lightly looking on or carelessly walking about, were stricken down to the ground, after a short time to rise and confess the Lord Jesus Christ, and exhort their companions to believe in him.

With one of those who thus fell I was intimately acquainted for many years. He was one of the best men I ever formed an acquaintance with.

The great revival commenced in 1800, in the State of Tennessee and southern Kentucky, in the Presbyterian Church, but was participated in by ministers of all denominations, and all shared its blessings. The great camp-meeting was in the parish of the Cane Ridge Presbyterian Church, of which Rev. Barton W. Stone was at that time pastor. The same Cane Ridge meeting-house, around which so many thousands met, was still standing when I was there in 1825, but was then a Christian church, for the church left the Presbyterian denomination when their pastor did. It is said that this great camp-meeting of 1801 was the origin of the camp-meetings of the United States.

Origin of the Christians in Kentucky.—When the great revival began to subside, many settled back in their old denominational creeds; others having learned the more excellent way, could not go back, but desired to be known simply as Christians, and resolved to take the Bible as their only rule of faith and practice. Thus the origin of the Christians was in a revival which began in the West, but existed soon in all parts of the United States.

In the West it was from the Presbyterians that a people came out taking the name Christian, and the Bible for their only rule of faith and practice.

In the South it was from the Methodists that a people came out taking the name Christian, and the Bible for their only rule of faith and practice.

In the East it was from the Baptists that a people came out taking the name Christian, and the Bible for their only rule of faith and practice.

These people in these distant sections of the country, and of different denominations, who, at the same time, took the same ground, knew nothing of each other, nor had they any correspondence till ten or twelve years subsequent to the time of their several organizations.

Christians always Opposed to Oppression.—It is worthy of remembrance that for several years during the revival spirit in Kentucky, those engaged in it were not drawn away into large speculations to make money, and that those who had slaves set them free. As the revival ceased, things changed. Professors of religion were soon found buying up hogs, to drive South for speculation, which was at that time a money-making business in that rich part of Kentucky. Then those who were able to purchase slaves began to argue themselves into the opinion that the poor Negro's condition is better in slavery than it would be if he were free.

Hewson Searching for his Mother.—I was told the following story, to illustrate the worldly spirit which succeeded the revival. Peter Hewson was a man of an eccentric mind. He had been converted during the great revival. He lamented the declension of religion in after years, and often made strange remarks illustrative of his feelings. One Sabbath, before service commenced, he was found wandering over the camp-ground about the church, as if anxiously searching for something. A friend said to him:

"Brother Hewson, what are you looking for?"

5

"I am looking for my mother," he replied.

"Your mother!" his friend exclaimed.

"Yes," he said, "the church that was once my mother."

"Why are you looking for her there?"

"She is dead, and they are embalming her body in hog's lard and Negro's wool."

The meeting which I attended there, like too many large meetings, was large in the number present, but small in the religious interest.

The Hymn-Book.—In 1826 the second edition of the hymn-book having sold rapidly, I published a third edition of three thousand. It was printed at Georgetown, twelve miles from my home, and sent to Cincinnati by the river, to be bound. It was not stereotyped, but each edition had to be reset, and the proof read, and corrections made. This did not prevent my preaching; and though it took much time, I did not neglect my domestic affairs.

Russellville Church Organized.—About this time I commenced preaching regularly at Russellville, a town on the Ripley and Hillsborough pike, about six miles from my home. A church was organized. I drew up a subscription, and a brick chapel was built.

Another Licken Knobs Preacher.—There being more churches than the preachers could supply, I invited Elder John T. Powell, of Licken Knobs, a very poor part of Kentucky, to move to Clermont County, Ohio, and take the pastoral care of several churches raised through divine grace by my labors. I had been acquainted with him for years, as he began to preach about the time I did, and knew him to be not only poor, but a poor manager, destitute of energy, having never raised a church, or had the care of one. Yet I hoped that a new field, where the churches were already raised, and the chapels built, and a tolerable salary for his support could be raised, would awake his dormant powers, and he would become useful. He consented to come, but, too poor to move, the brethren went with teams and moved him to the Salem church; and so much did the brethren sympathize with him, that they concluded to buy a small farm near the church for a parsonage. The church numbered near three hundred members, and was able. The question was, whether to make the deed to the church for its pastor, whoever that might be, or to Elder Powell, who was then their pastor. I, being perhaps as large a subscriber as any, and wishing to encourage him, advised them to make the deed to Elder Powell, and to Elder Powell it was made. Thus he had a good home given to him, containing nearly one hundred acres of good land. He took charge of two or three churches, which paid him a reasonable salary, but manifested his want of energy in neglecting other places near him, which

I had traveled nearly forty miles to preach to on week days. My hope that the various sections desiring Bible Christianity would be better supplied by this addition to the conference was disappointed. Little was done by Powell, except to preach to the churches that paid. He would take the young preachers with him to preach to the churches already organized, and in chapels already built, and where salary was paid, but neither he nor they raised a single church.

South of Covington.—I frequently visited Cincinnati, where my hymn-books were bound, to send them to different parts of the country. When there I preached, trying to advance the cause and assist the church in that city. During 1827 or 1828 I was conversing with a gentleman there, when, after we closed our conversation, a stranger, being much interested, asked my name, and requested me to send an appointment to his neighborhood. I did so, and this bystander, whose name was John Ellis, appointed for me to preach in the Dry Creek Baptist meeting-house, some seven miles south of Covington, Kentucky. I met a large congregation. The Lord blessed his word. My visits were repeated, and a church was organized. This man John Ellis became a preacher himself; and the church prospered till Campbellism came along under the Christian name, and church and preacher were carried away together by their dissimulation.

The Southern Ohio Conference was now prospering. Persecution had in a manner ceased, and we had peace and prosperity in the Lord. The third edition of the hymn-book could hardly supply the increasing demand, and was soon exhausted.

Hymn-Book—Fourth Edition.—Therefore, in 1829 I published the fourth edition, of three thousand, making in all ten thousand. I still kept them in the book-stores, and in the hands of traveling agents and ministers, and wherever I could supply the people with them. There was no loss in this. The book-sellers all paid. Some ministers sold my books, and used the money, and by them I lost, leaving me little profit; but I worked for the Lord. About a year after publishing the fourth edition, a minister in the Miami Conference, not actuated by the Spirit of Christ, offered the following resolution in that body. I was not there: "*Resolved,* That this conference does not approve of any man arrogating to himself the right to publish the Christian hymn-book." This was one of those acts of religious bodies wherein they frequently do individuals great injustice. The Miami Conference was older than ours; it had also more members. A hymn-book was greatly needed, and they had not enterprise enough to publish it; but when, by the appointment of the Southern Conference, I did it, at my personal risk, instead of encouraging me, they annoyed me, and talked of my "arrogating" to myself the right. And the more to oppose me, they appointed Elder Samuel Kile, one of their number, to publish a hymn-book, which he did, republishing mine with no material alteration. He published a small edition, and, probably finding it a losing business, published no more. So the churches were soon out of hymn-books again! The doctrine taught in the word of God as that preached by Christ and his apostles, was now being adopted by many people in southern Ohio.

Opposition in Doctrine.—In 1830 Rev. John Rankin, a Presbyterian minister in Ripley, Ohio, about five miles from my home, published a pamphlet to sustain the trinitarian doctrine, that—

I. The Father is God. The Son Jesus Christ is self-existent; co-equal God with the Father. And the Holy Ghost is self-existent; co-equal God with the Father and the Son; and these three are all co-essential, co-existent, and co-eternal—one God.

II. And the Son died to reconcile God his Father to sinful men.

As this system of trinitarianism seemed to be losing ground, so the Rev. John Rankin published the pamphlet to sustain it, in which he greatly misrepresented the Christian doctrine.

Christian Doctrine.—The doctrine which was spreading in southern Ohio was the Christian doctrine first preached by Christ and his apostles, viz.:

I. There is one God the Father, and one Lord Jesus Christ, the Son of God his Father, and one Holy Ghost the Comforter.

II. Christ died for all, to reconcile men to God, not God to men; and this salvation is free to all who will accept it.

These, with similar views on other points, were now being adopted by many people, to the exclusion of the unreasonable and unscriptural self-styled orthodox dogmas of trinitarians. When the Rev. Mr. Rankin's pamphlet appeared, I realized, as I had often felt before, the necessity of every minister being capable of plainly setting forth his views in writing, with arguments to answer objections, so as to have them printed to lay before the people. I felt thankful to God for the ability to do this, sufficiently at least for the people to understand me. So Mr. Rankin's publication had not been long before the people when a brief reply appeared by me, exposing his misrepresentations of the Christians, and illustrating the inconsistency and unscriptural character of his doctrine of trinitarianism. I also replied to all his arguments. This reply to Mr. Rankin greatly advanced Bible truth, and increased in many people their objections to trinitarianism. Mr. Rankin, knowing that my education was not acquired in a college, at first declared that some other man was the author, but soon confessed that it was my production. He had before treated me with disrespect, or as an inferior. Since then he uniformly treats me as his equal, and is friendly. During this ten years of my life, I had been three or four times sick, for several weeks at a time, of bilious fever, and ague and fever. At one time I seemed nigh unto death of bilious fever. I then chose the place to be buried. On reviewing my life, I saw many imperfections; but having full confidence in the Redeemer's pardoning love, my mind was composed. I had full assurance of salvation by and through Jesus Christ, the Son of God, who died for sinners. The grave looked dark and gloomy; but faith saw light beyond. The true value of religion can not be fully appreciated till we draw near to death. When only afflicted with ague and fever, I often rode thirty or forty miles to fill my appointments, while shaking with the ague every day. The ague was followed with a burning fever. My reply to Rev. John Rankin was near the close of the fourth ten years of my life, and the 5th of December, 1830, found me attending to my domestic duties, and filling my appointments as usual. I had then lived beyond my expectations when a boy. Then when I heard men say they were forty years old, I regarded them as old men, and did not suppose that I would ever live to that age.

CHAPTER V.

THE FIFTH TEN YEARS OF MY LIFE—CHRISTIAN MINISTERS DE-
CEIVED BY ALEXANDER CAMPBELL AND HIS SYSTEM—TWELVE
YEARS' OBSERVATIONS.

December 5, 1830, I entered upon the forty-first year of my life, with a family of eight children to educate and provide for. We kept them in school as much of the time as circumstances would justify, and also endeavored to teach them to work, and the importance of making their living by honest industry. Our oldest sons were able nearly to do the work of men. Our little farm—one hundred acres—not being large enough to afford them full employment, and having saved a little money, in March of 1831 I purchased another small farm of one hundred and thirty acres. It had been good land, but was a good deal worn, and much out of repair. In a year or two we had built new fences, subdued the briers, destroyed grubs, and built a barn to save the grain. This employed all the time which I could spare beyond my regular appointments, which took almost half my time.

His Aged Father.—In February of 1832 my father, now in his seventy-third year, sent for me to come immediately to see him on special business. I went, of course. The business was of the most unpleasant character possible. Some two years before, he had leased his farm of about two hundred acres, with abundant stock—horses, cattle, etc., to Benjamin, his youngest son and namesake, Benjamin agreeing to return it in good order to my father at the end of five years, when the lease would expire. Benjamin, like some other younger sons, not having earned by labor the large property put into his hands, knew not its real value, but squandered it rapidly. The consideration of the lease provided that he was to support father and mother, which it was claimed that he had not done. He had disposed of nearly all the stock; raised very little grain or other products; and I found my parents almost destitute of some of the necessaries of life. My father requested me to accept power of attorney, and repossess him of the farm by taking it out of Benjamin's possession.

My Father's Mistake.—My father made a mistake, as parents generally do, in putting his property out of his power. Also, he did not consider that Benjamin, having never accumulated property, his former history did not warrant the expectation that he would either preserve what was put into his possession, or acquire property to replace it at the end of the five years. The lease did not prohibit Benjamin disposing of the stock as he pleased; and it was gone, and he was unable to replace or pay for it. The lease contained no provision that it should be void if he failed to comply with its provisions. These were serious difficulties, which increased my objections to taking any part in the matter. But father and mother insisted; and from a sense of duty to my aged parents, I accepted the trust, and undertook the disagreeable task. My father advised immediate action by law, to dispossess Benjamin. I determined to have no lawsuit with my brother. I saw also that if I should go to law, he could keep possession during the five years, by the lease. A judgment for damages might be obtained, but he had nothing to pay the damages with. I finally persuaded him to leave the whole matter to arbitration. The result was that my father lost the stock, worth about $1,000; but father got possession of his farm again. Having straightened and arranged this business, I felt quite relieved, supposing that my attention there was no longer needed. Not so. Father and mother insisted that I should manage their business, renting the farm, and taking care of them. It seemed impossible. They were four or five miles from my home. It would require more time and attention than my own domestic cares. Besides, to please old people is sometimes difficult. The burden appeared too heavy for me; but, on consideration, I concluded that duty to parents is among the first religious requirements, and I complied with their request, taking upon me the care of them, and the management of all their affairs. This charge continued till father and mother both died, or about fourteen years from the time my father first sent for me to repossess him of his farm. In justice to myself, I must add that for all this labor and care I accepted no compensation from my father or the estate. My father appointed me the executor and administrator of his will. By divine grace I closed all the business without difficulty with any of the heirs, though there were then twelve children living.

A. D. 1832.—The summer after I was sent for to visit my father, in February, to repossess him of his farm, my wife and I were very sick. We were taken about the first of August with bilious fever, and, to all appearance, were brought very near to death.

Lessons on Visiting the Sick.—While sick I was impressed with what I had often been grieved with, and had too frequently seen the evil effects of in houses of sickness. Few persons can spare the time to visit the sick through the week, but on Sunday they rush in and almost fill the house. The sick are thus discommoded, the family is burdened with company, and, in addition to their sickness, are compelled to prepare meals for idle company. The conversation of such visitors is generally unprofitable, and often very disagreeable and annoying to the sick, and attended with great injury and no benefit. From these considerations, I have ever made it a rule to make my visits to sick families between meals, and to avoid eating or staying over night, so as to avoid increasing their trouble and care.

Kentucky Again.—In the spring of 1833 or 1834 a train of circumstances caused me to hold a protracted meeting in Millersburg, Bourbon County, Kentucky, on the turnpike from Maysville to Lexington, about forty miles from Maysville, and twenty from Lexington. The year previous I had attended the Kentucky Conference, some five miles from Millersburg. I preached at the conference by request. The word was accompanied with the Holy Spirit to the hearts of the people. By the urgent solicitation of the church, I afterwards preached there stately; and many of the most influential, wealthy, and respectable citizens embraced religion, and I baptized them. The people of Millersburg heard of the Lord's doings among the people, and came over in great numbers, as in ancient times. They requested me to come and preach in their town, and I went over there and preached.

The Revival.—The meeting in Millersburg was of ten or twelve days and nights' duration. The entire community seemed interested. Only part of the streets were paved, and rain made the ways quite muddy; but rain and mud did not prevent ladies and gentlemen of the first classes from coming out. It was said of some ladies, "Their fine shoes stuck in the deep mud and were pulled from their feet; but nowise discouraged, they grabbled them out with their delicate hands and came on to the meeting." Over one hundred embraced religion.

Duel Prevented.—One day at Millersburg I had preached to a large congregation. The word was attended by the Holy Spirit. Great good was effected. I noticed two intelligent-looking men starting from opposite corners of the house toward each other. They met near the center of the house. They threw their arms around each other's neck, and thus stood and wept. Then they clasped each other's right hand. The whole congregation was deeply moved, and wept. Tears flowed from almost every eye in the house. I saw, but understood not. Afterwards I learned that they had been at great enmity through malice and hatred, and had determined to settle all by a duel. The gospel of peace had now made them friends again—saved probably both their lives, and had made peace, and, we hope, had made new men of them. At this meeting I witnessed the most signal manifestations of the power of God that I ever beheld.

Church Organized.—By divine grace I organized a respectable church at Millersburg, though many united with other denominations of their choice. A few years afterward I met Elder Holady, a Baptist minister. who was converted at that meeting; but his family being Baptists, he united with the Baptist Church. There were additions to the Methodist and Presbyterian churches also from this meeting.

The Preachers.—A number of Christian ministers lived within a short distance of Millersburg; but they were not in the work, therefore, if they preached, they rather retarded than aided the cause. They attended, but not regularly. Two or three would attend one day and night, and two or three others the next, and so on. I found the reason to be that blind "jealousy," which Solomon says "is cruel as the grave!" I had been preaching twenty-five years, but never had reason to believe preachers possessed such a spirit of envy and jealousy before.

A New Sect.—About this time the religious views of Alexander Campbell began to be received by the Christian ministers and others in Kentucky. I will here mention a few things concerning Mr. Campbell and his so-called reformation. About the year 1815 Alexander Campbell and his father came to this country from Ireland or Scotland, when Alexander was a young man. Both were educated according to the Presbyterian Confession of Faith, and were members of that church. They became convinced that immersion was the ancient baptism, and both united with the Baptist Church. Alexander, by his writing and debates, soon became popular among the Baptists. About the year 1823 he commenced the publication of the periodical called the "Christian Baptist," in which he advocated the following doctrines:

I. The kingdom of heaven and of the Messiah was not set up till the day of Pentecost, and consequently Jesus was not a king while here on earth.

II. The keys of the kingdom were particularly delivered to Peter, and to no other apostle; and Peter used them in opening the door of faith to the Jews at Pentecost, and to the Gentiles at the house of Cornelius.

III. Gospel order. [I give this in Mr. Campbell's own words.] "Remission of sins is consequent on or through immersion. No prayers, songs of praise, no acts of devotion in the new economy, are enjoined on the unbaptized. Immersion next to faith is a *sine qui non*, without which nothing can be done acceptable to God," etc.

IV. "No church is in gospel order which does not meet every first day of the week to break bread," etc.

V. "The Holy Spirit has no direct influence in converting or regenerating mankind now, but conversion, or the new birth, consists in believing the gospel, repenting of sin, and being immersed."

VI. The gifts of the Holy Spirit are taken away from the church, therefore the Spirit does not qualify nor send any man to preach the gospel in our day; but preachers are to study the Scriptures, and preach what they learn, without looking for or asking aid of the Holy Spirit.

Of course the Baptist denomination could not embrace such novel views, consequently Mr. Campbell and his disciples were soon separated from that denomination, and went on to organize churches on his own system. While none were received except those who believed and practiced his new system, he professed to take the Scriptures as his only rule of faith and practice, to the exclusion of all men-made creeds, just as the Christian Church had been doing for a quarter of a century, which caused his views to be readily received by many Christian preachers in the West, especially in Kentucky.

Elder Stone.—After a time Elder Barton W. Stone, with others who were dear to my heart, received Mr. Campbell's views, with this exception,—Elder Stone would not make baptism a test of Christian fellowship. When these ministers embraced Mr. Campbell's system, it was one of the greatest trials of my life to part with them. Some of them were my companions in labor, with whom I had traveled, and with whom I had labored shoulder to shoulder and heart to heart in the ministry. We had preached together and prayed together, wept together and rejoiced together. I must do these ministers the justice to say that they did not all profess to change their views, but only to form a union. It was argued that as both took the Bible as their only rule, they ought to form a union, to give strength to the cause, and increase our influence. So, to bring about a union, one minister was chosen by each party, and these were to travel together preaching union to the churches in Kentucky. These ministers were Elder John Rogers, whom I had assisted to ordain, of the Christians, and Elder John Smith, of the Disciples, for Mr. Campbell called his people Disciples, that is, "Disciples of Christ." So the union was formed, which union consisted in our churches receiving the system of doctrine, and adopting the new practice, modes, and forms of the Disciples. Nor was there one case of union on any other ground. There were but few churches in Kentucky but what were deceived or coerced into this union. Those which were not were in the eastern and poorer part of the state, and those which loved the gospel more than they did popularity.

Desire for Union.—My great desire was to continue in union and fellowship with those ministers so dear to my heart; therefore, I strove to reconcile Mr. Campbell's system with the precepts and practice of Christ and his apostles. But the more I examined the Scriptures, the greater appeared the objections to Discipleism, and I was compelled to reject it. The ministers and churches which united retained the name Christians, which deceived the people.

Campbell in 1823.—Having heard Mr. Campbell preach in 1823, while he was yet in the Baptist denomination, I became a subscriber for the "Christian Baptist," the first periodical he published, and understood his theory of doctrine, and the arguments by which he sustained it. After twelve years' observation of its fruits and spirit, from 1823 to 1835, and seeing that nothing good could come of it, I published in 1835 an expose of the theory which has now in 1865 been before the people for thirty years, and no attempt has been made to deny its facts or to meet its arguments, except that, as soon as it appeared, they commenced a tirade of calumny and abuse of the author. Elder John Powell, whom I had found while he was living at Licken Knobs, Kentucky, and we had moved to Ohio to enter into the fruits of my labors, and take charge of churches which I had organized, now arranged himself as the leader to transport part of the preachers of his neighborhood over the watery way to Campbellism. These preachers were: Otho Perry, Alonzo Knowles, and George Fisher. I had given up to these men some of the churches which I had raised, and had extended my labors to new fields. When I heard the cry for union coming from these men, I knew the design was to break up the churches, or to carry them over to Discipleism. My publication, together with a few visits, prevented Powell and his three preachers taking the churches over, except a part of the church, which they divided, at Bethel, Clermont County. They also divided the church at Georgetown, and was thus the means of destroying it also.

His Error.—I now saw that the brethren who opposed making the deed of the parsonage farm to Elder Powell were right, and that I was wrong in causing the deed to be made to Powell, for he, having now abandoned the old Bible doctrine for the new system of Campbell, the church ceased to employ him, and lost the farm. He never gave up the property, though it justly belonged to the church. After his death it went to his heirs. My advice in that case was one of the mistakes of my life. I was the means of his getting the property into his possession, and obtaining influence; then he became my enemy; used it all to injure me. As he and those with him could not answer my arguments, they with one accord did all that they could to defame me.

What they Said.—They said: "Elder Gardner has done good. He has been a good pioneer; but the cause has outgrown him, and he now stands in the way in opposing the glorious reformation, and must be put down."

How they Talked.—One would invent or manufacture a slanderous report. He would then say to another: "Have you heard that report about Elder Gardner?" The person answers, "No; what is it?" "Oh," he replies, "I do not want to tell. I do feel so sorry." Being urged, he adds, "If you will promise not to mention it, I will tell you." The promise of secrecy is made, and the slander flies upon the wings of the wind. Elder Powell seemed to be silent until, feeling safe, he publicly announced to a congregation, "I can not publish Elder Gardner's appointments; his character is too bad." These new Disciples carried the thing so far that they would hold trials! Getting some half dozen Disciples together, they would make their own statements just as they pleased, without my knowledge, and then take a vote whether those present would fellowship such a man. This conduct was so frequent that it became a proverb of contempt—"They are trying Gardner again!" During all this time Powell and his three associates were still members of the Southern Ohio Christian Conference, and firmly declared that they had not changed their religious views, but believed just as they always had. It was only those things against Elder Gardner that they objected to. When the conference met in 1835, they presented a number of charges against me, of which they had given me no previous notice. On their way to conference they boastingly said, "We will have Gardner silenced and put down at this meeting." They of course came with their witnesses drilled for the occasion. Their charges were heard with patience. They were promptly proved futile and groundless. Truth was mighty, and did prevail. Powell tried to keep himself hid; but his participation in the unright-

cous persecution was plainly shown. Then, to save himself, he
offered me his hand, to live in peace and fellowship. "If he
repent, forgive him," said the Master; so I accepted his hand.
That covenant with Powell was made in the presence of hundreds of people, but broken by him soon after it was made.
They also continued to declare that they had not changed their
faith, but only objected to Gardner's wrong doings; that their
opposition to me was that the Christian church, which they
were in, might not be disgraced. This crafty mode of warfare
was to kill my influence, and thus destroy the effect of my publication before named. To this end they united all their efforts
during the year. Before the next conference, I caused notices
to be served upon Powell and his party, that I should present
against them the charge of "covenant-breaking." When conference met in 1836, they all appeared. But when the charges
were read, knowing their guilt, Powell declared that the conference (before which they had tried to condemn me) had no
authority to try ministers; the church to which they belonged
was the only tribunal to which ministers are responsible. They
refused to stand trial, and left. The conference heard the testimony, decided upon their guilt, and expelled them; and their
expulsion was published in the minutes of 1836. The conference also sent a committee to demand their credentials. This
committee, learning of the following meeting, attended it.

Ecclesiastical Trial Extraordinary.—The meeting was in this
wise. Powell and his faction having been condemned and excluded by conference, got up a meeting of their friends, about
a dozen in number, mostly their brothers and sisters in law, and
called these a church, and to them submitted their case; that is,
they appointed their own court, chose their own jury, told their
own story, prepared their own verdict, and chose their own
kindred to decide their case. Powell told this company, which he
styled a church, that charges had been brought against them at
conference, which was not the proper place to try preachers;
therefore, they had come before the church! He said nothing
of their attempts to try me before the conference. "But," said
he, "those in favor of acquitting us will rise up when each
charge is read." All were acquitted. So they refused to give
up their credentials.

The papers friendly to Campbell fanned the flame of discord,
and encouraged the factionists, and kept them in countenance,
by publishing their version of things and permitting no reply.
Campbell stooped to publish their calumny, but would admit
no reply in his paper! Why? Because these men were *reformers!* working for the glorious *reformation!* John L. Johnson had started a small paper in Georgetown, Kentucky. He
published their detraction against me, and then refused to admit my replies. Elder *Walter Scott* and *John Rogers* were in-

fluenced to traduce me. My only avenue of reply was in the "Christian Palladium," of New York, which few of the Disciples saw, so they had but one side of the story.

The Deacon Collars Him.—One of the Campbellite deacons, when I went to preach, came into the pulpit and called me a liar several times. When I was going out of the church, he met me in the aisle, and collared me, and would not let me go until the bystanders broke his hold. The civil law attended to him, causing him to pay a fine and a heavy bill of costs. Although such a combination seemed powerful enough to put down any man, yet, as the people knew the cause of the persecution, the aggressors were always confined to a small faction. The people knew me. I had labored with them from the commencement of my ministry, and the public decided the matter about right. All the abuse heaped upon me by the Campbellites did not diminish my congregations, but the cause of Christ still advanced. I continued to labor to win souls to Christ, and they continued to persecute me. Elder Powell and his three ordained (and, I think, one or two unordained) ministers, who went into Campbellism with him, soon lost most of their influence. They could get no churches to go with them, except the parts of the two which they divided, viz., at Georgetown and Bethel. Nor were they able to raise any churches. Elder Powell and two of the three did not live many years after these troubles. But the cause of Jesus continued to advance.

The Church in Cincinnati.—Being without a resident pastor, I preached and administered the ordinance for them there, once a month, except at various times, when they would have ministers residing for short times with them.

Frederick Miller.—At length, perhaps in the year 1835, I became acquainted with Elder Frederick Miller and his wife, both preachers, of the Central Ohio Christian Conference. Miller was a man of some education, and a good speaker. My anxiety for the church in Cincinnati caused me to introduce him there, and he became their pastor, and did well for a year or two; then he embraced Campbell's system. As the church in Cincinnati had been raised, and the chapel built, at least in part, by my feeble efforts, through grace, and I preached there yet occasionally, he could not get the church to go with him into Campbellism without first destroying my influence. Therefore, he commenced circulating defamatory untruths against me, carefully enjoining secrecy. This soon came to my ears, and, as he could not sustain his declarations against me, he was obliged to leave the city. I sent him word that I should present charges against him in the Central Conference, and at the end of the year met him there. To my astonishment, he had certificates from respectable persons to sustain his statements. One charged me with proposals to a young woman whom I scarcely knew, hav-

ing seen her perhaps but once, and not more than ten minutes,
in the presence of a family in Cincinnati, where I was invited
to dine. She did not eat at the table when I did, and I would
not have known her again. I had no rebutting testimony; so,
at my request, the case was adjourned to Liberty Chapel, where
our conference was to meet, three miles from my home. It was
to be decided by a committee of nine, four to be chosen by
Miller, four by me, and the chairman by the eight. The committee met at the same time and place of the annual session of
the Southern Ohio Christian Conference, September 27, 1836.
But Miller was not there. Not one of his committee was there.
Elder D. F. Ladley, of the Central Conference, was there, and
he was in possession of all Miller's testimony, having been on
the committee of that conference when it came up. It was
decided to choose four disinterested men for Miller. These,
with my part of the committee, chose Ladley, of his conference,
for the ninth. I simply proved by those whose certificates he
had presented, that they never gave any such certificates, or
authorized, or consented that their names should be put to
them. Thus Miller's testimony, being proved a forgery, the
case was decided against Miller. Signed: Elder D. F. Ladley,
chairman; Elder Alexander McClain, S. O. C. C.; Alvey Jaides,
J. B. Shinkle, J. Trees, deacons; J. R. Morris, conference clerk;
Elder Theobald Miller, Pennsylvania Conference; John T. Nixon,
of the Miami Conference; James Allen, Esq. This was the
same year and the same session of conference that excluded
Powell and his party for the same kind of slanders. The course
of Miller caused a small division in favor of Campbellism in the
Cincinnati church; but his influence soon ceased, and both
Miller and his wife died soon after leaving Cincinnati. Though
my mind was mostly employed in advancing the great and
glorious principles of gospel truth, I did not entirely neglect
the education of our children, or to prepare them to provide for
themselves in the future of their lives in this world. When
our children were yet small, I frequently talked to them,
and told them that ministers' children were generally said to
be leaders in wickedness above others, and kindly besought
them to be warned, so as to give no room for such talk. Our
older sons, having been early instructed, soon became able to
attend to the farming business in my absence, and, by industry
and economy, we accumulated nearly one thousand dollars a
year, above our expenses, although I preached without salary.
Honor and respectability are among the first things thought of
and desired by a child. These desires nearly all parents overlook,
instead of guiding them in the child for its improvement. Observe that little girl walk in her new dress; observe her desire
to be noticed and respected. See that little boy with his new
coat. He wants to be noticed and respected as equal to, if not su-

perior, to other boys. This ambition should be used to prompt the child to great and virtuous deeds. Some parents have a practice of saying, to persons who come in, "that is a bad girl," or "he is a bad boy." I early saw that this is wrong, and never practiced it. I never reproached our children. If they did wrong, I kindly told them of it, and taught them that it was dishonorable to do so, and instructed them how to be respectable, thus improving their natural desire for honor for their benefit. I also tried to teach our children that honesty, industry, and frugality never failed to make a person who practiced them honorable and respectable. Thus were our children brought up, and while they are not without reproach, they are doing better than some.

Four Hundred Acres.—Our two oldest sons, having become of age, needed homes of their own. So about the year 1835 I purchased nearly four hundred acres of excellent land, for which I paid, at that time, near five thousand dollars. A great part of the land was cleared and under cultivation. So I told my two oldest sons that if they would go on the land, and in their own time pay me back one half the purchase money, without interest, I would then make them deeds. In eight years they paid me, and got their deeds. I have pursued the same course with all our sons. They till the land and make a part of the value, or price of the farm, and pay it back to me before I make them a deed. I would do so, however able to give the property entire, because when a person has labored for and paid for property by his own industry, he better knows the value of it and how to take care of it. I never permitted my sons to do any work for me after they were twenty-one years of age without a contract; and I paid them accordingly. I was particular in this, from having heard many censorious remarks from sons; such as, "I worked so many months or years for my father, after I was of age, and got nothing for it; but my brother did not work for him after he was twenty-one, and he gave him as much as he gave me." My plan prevented censure and complaining by our children. None can justly say, "Father has wronged me."

Jamestown.—In the fall of 1835, perhaps, I commenced preaching in Jamestown, in Greene County. It was a small village in a wealthy section, not far from Xenia. The cause of my going there, as far as human agency was concerned, was as follows: A young woman, whose mother was a member of the Bethlehem Church, married and moved there. After being settled in life, perhaps remembering her early convictions, for she was not a member of the church, felt the need of peace and pardon through our Lord Jesus Christ; and so, with two or three others, sent a number of urgent requests for me to come and preach one discourse in Jamestown. An appointment was sent. I went and met a large congregation in the house of the Disciples; for so had my friends appointed. This house was the largest in town. It was built free for all to preach in, as I was told, who were willing that their sermons or doctrines should be investigated at the time preached, before the same congregation. In my first discourse I maintained the evangelical doctrine of the influence of the Holy Spirit upon the hearts of men in the new birth. This being denied by the Campbellites, M. Winans, M. D., who preached for them, rose up in the congregation and objected to the things preached by me. I replied briefly, showing the absurdity of his views to the satisfaction of all, except his Disciples. I continued my appointments several days and nights. Dr. Winans' objections caused large crowds to come out; so he did not offer any further objections, publicly, in the congregation. The preaching was not in vain, for many believed and turned to the Lord. Dr. Winans afterward wrote proposing a debate. But after a long correspondence, he seemed to fear the result, and entirely declined.

Jamestown Church Organized.—My visits to Jamestown continued from time to time, and in a few months, by divine grace, I organized a church there. A number of the members were of the most respectable citizens of Greene County. I continued my visits, assisted by other ministers, and the church grew in numbers and influence.

Lucas the Debater.—During one of my visits, while at the water baptizing, I stated, with other remarks, that Christ and his apostles did not teach that sins were to be remitted, after faith and repentance, by immersion in water. When I closed, a short, heavy-set man, with keen black eyes, spoke in the large congregation at the water, and challenged me to debate the next day with him on the subject on which I had been speaking. That man was John B. Lucas, a Disciple preacher, a great champion in debate for the defense of the new system. After I learned who he was, he boasted to me of having been in forty-five debates. I had never been in one. Whether Dr. Winans sent for him, I know not; but he was there, and I was challenged, and I accepted. We met the same afternoon, June 10, 1839, and chose the question, and settled the preliminaries.

The Question.—"Is it, or is it not, the order of God, according to the gospel of Christ, that baptism is to be added to faith and repentance in order to the remission of past sins, and admission into the kingdom of Christ?" J. B. Lucas affirms; M. Gardner denies. One of the rules was, that the Scriptures of divine truth are to be the only evidence offered by either party.

Elder Lucas, of course, had the advantage in the practice of debating, tact and skill, but I had the greater advantage of being fully acquainted with Mr. Campbell's theory and knowing its weak points. This he unwillingly learned during the discussion.

The Debate.—We met June 11, 1839, and Elder Lucas opened the discussion, affirming the kingdom of Christ was not set up till the day of Pentecost; the gospel was never preached till Peter preached it on that day.

Gardner's Reply.—First: Saint Mark says (I. 14), Jesus came "preaching the gospel of the kingdom of God." Luke IV. 18, and VII. 22. Second: Jesus spoke of the kingdom in the present tense, as then in existence, saying, "It *is* like good seed." "It *is* like leaven." "It *is* like a net cast into the sea," etc. Third: Jesus said (Luke 16), "The law and the prophets *were* until John: since that time the kingdom of God is preached, and every man presseth into it." How could men press into a kingdom which was not in existence or set up? Fourth: Jesus was anointed prophet, priest and king, immediately after John baptized him, and was proclaimed king by divine authority when he rode into Jerusalem. Matt. XXI. 5; Luke XIX. 37, 38; John XII. 13–15. Fifth: Is a person who does not love God a proper subject for baptism? Elder Lucas could not answer, he is. But every one that loveth is born of God. John III. 7-16. If born of God, their sins are remitted or pardoned before baptism. Sixth: No Scripture affirms baptism to be in order to remission of sins. Nor did Christ and his apostles ever so teach. Seventh: The order advocated by Mr. Lucas is too limited and circumscribed to be the one only order of an all-merciful God, as it is out of the power of many to comply with it. Again, if faith, repentance and immersion is God's only order for remission of sins, then many thousands of the best men that have blest the world have gone to eternal perdition, as they were never immersed in order to pardon or remission. Eighth: The one universal plan, or order of God, by which remission of sins can be obtained, as made known in God's word, is true belief and sincere repentance of past sins. Then God will pardon and restore the believer to favor; after which follows baptism and obedience to all God's commandments, as a child obeys his father; not to make him a child, but because he is a child. Baptism is a sign and a seal of remission of sins, and an emblem of the burial and resurrection of Christ, and for the confirmation of our faith therein.

Lucas relied principally upon Acts II. 38, "Repent and be baptized, every one of you, in the name of Jesus Christ, for the remission of sins," which he changed to mean, "in order to the remission of sins;" or to get their sins pardoned.

Gardner.—I showed that he had not given a correct explanation of the text, for they gladly received the word before they were baptized. Therefore, their sins were pardoned, or they would not all have been glad; therefore, they received pardon through faith and repentance before baptism, according to God's universal order. The word "for," in the above text

6

does not mean in order to, but because of; that is the reason why they were baptized, because their sins were remitted through faith and repentance. Said I, Take your choice. Accept this explanation, or try your own explanation; that is, take the sinner to the water, without his loving God, and baptize this sinner, who does not love God, in order to obtain pardon or remission of his sins. I asked him to show me one text in the Bible corresponding with his explanation of Acts II. 38, or to give one case where Christ or his apostles ever commanded a person to be baptized in order to remission. He could not. We had not spoken more than four or five times each—thirty minutes to each speech—till I felt certain of success. Elder Lucas tried every tact he so well understood, to evade the points; but I kept them before the people, showing that he had not answered my arguments, but only tried to evade them. He also tried sarcasm, in which he was well skilled. I disposed of that by asking the people to excuse me for not answering him, as I was not willing to lower the dignity of a gospel minister by replying to such things. He then desisted. I felt that his sarcasms and witty tacts were injuring him, and that the truth was on my side. This caused me to argue earnestly and solemn, as for eternity. The discussion lasted three days, I think, of six or eight hours each day. At the close it was proposed that the people should have the privilege of saying, by their vote, which side had been sustained. This Elder Lucas and some of his friends objected to. But the vote was taken. A few of the Disciples voted in favor of Elder Lucas, while the large congregation went overwhelmingly against him. From this time the Campbellite Church began to decline at Jamestown. In a few years it became extinct. Lucas, I think, never preached there again. The Christian Church at Jamestown continued to prosper. After Powell's expulsion, Elder McClain and myself being the principal ministers left in our conference, I sent, perhaps in 1837, an article to "The Christian Palladium," requesting ministers to come into southern Ohio.

John.—Six or seven months after that article appeared, I came home one cold evening, about sundown, in the latter part of December, and found a strange man and woman at our house. When I came into the room, the man arose and said, "My name is John." This was my first introduction to Elder John Phillips, afterwards known as "Antioch John," from his eagerness in inducing people to take scholarships in Antioch College. This man and his wife had come through from the State of New York, or perhaps farther east, in an almost worthless old one-horse wagon, with a horse almost as worthless. They had nothing with them except a few clothes; so they lived in our family, ate at our table, slept in our beds, and their horse was fed in our stable for about two months, or toward spring. Then they moved into the bounds of a church, which had been raised by my labors, and of which I was still pastor. The people assisted them, and they went to housekeeping that spring. John could preach, and the kind reception which he received impressed him favorably with the country and people, and he wrote back to Elder Charles Manchester, with whom he had been associated in the east; and about the first of May, 1838, Elder Manchester arrived. Elder Phillips soon proposed to organize one or two new churches. Had he gone into a new place, where there was no church, and preached there, and organized a church of those who embraced religion under his labors, it would have been praiseworthy. But he proposed to divide the large church where he lived, where he had been received so kindly, which had been gathered by my labors, and now numbered about three hundred members, and to organize out of it one or two smaller churches. This I could not approve of; but opposed and prevented, which caused him to entertain unkind feelings toward me. When conference met, in 1838, it was evident that Elder Alexander McClain was in sympathy with Elder John Phillips. On the first day of the conference, he offered a resolution, as follows: *Resolved,* That each and every church have the privilege of sending two messengers, and no more than two. This would make a church of ten members equal, in representation, to a church of three or four hundred members. This seemed to me both unwise and unjust; and while he supported it, I felt it my duty to oppose it. The conference adjourned before the vote was taken, to meet next morning at eight o'clock. The next morning, before the appointed time, indeed before I or nearly half the conference arrived, Elder McClain and those of his views had met and passed the resolution. I think that this was planned by Elder Phillips, so as to divide the large churches and make smaller ones, thus to outvote the large churches under my pastoral care, and carry such measure in conference as they might desire, though contrary to the wishes of the great majority of the people who were in the large churches, or under my care. This resolution, and the advantage taken to pass it, caused great dissatisfaction with more than two-thirds of the lay members; and a disagreeable state of feeling between Elder McClain and myself, the only two ordained ministers belonging to the conference who were preaching constantly: Elders Phillips and Manchester were not members. This disagreeable state of things continued and increased till the following April. Then Elder McClain and I met by agreement at the house of Deacon John B. Shinkle, in order to heal, if possible, the breach between us, and restore peace among the churches. Elder McClain, however, utterly refused to agree to any terms of reconciliation and peace other than that we should withdraw from the conference. This, it seemed to me, would dissolve the conference, as far as the eldership was concerned. Probably this was his intention, as preparatory to the forming of a new conference according to the plans of Elder Phillips. After considering his ultra proposal, that it might be better for the cause of religion for us both to be out of conference, and be in peace and harmony, than to be in it without fellowship or brotherly love, so, in the hope of the restoration of Christian fellowship, I agreed to his terms. We settled the matters of difference, and then and there gave each other our hands in Christian fellowship and union, and parted. The dissatisfaction in the churches and members then subsided, and union was restored. The conferences at this time contained about fifteen churches, with a membership of not far from fifteen hundred. Our leaving did not disorganize the conference, but the churches went on in harmony.

September, 1839.—As the time drew on for the next annual conference, the churches appointed their messengers to represent them, and conference was organized as usual, although I do not recollect of any ordained elder present belonging to it. There was a full representation from the churches by their messengers, one of whom was chosen moderator, while the former clerk still performed the duty of that office. The organization being completed, the usual invitation was given for members. Elder Charles S. Manchester and I presented ourselves for membership, and were received.

Doctor Dawson.—Elder Naaman Dawson was then preaching and doing good, but he did not unite with the conference till some time afterwards, when he came bringing with him churches and other ministers also. After this conference things went on in peace and prosperity till the following November, 1839, when Elder McClain was reported as saying to his congregation that Elder Matthew Gardner was an unfair man. This was without first informing me of any dissatisfaction since our covenant of peace at the house of Deacon B. Shinkle, on the 9th of April previous. The cause of his statement was not in any business transactions between Elder McClain and myself, but there was another man who had tried to defraud me in 1837, and the case had been in litigation nearly two years, and was then waiting a decision in the Supreme Court. This man had united with the church of which Elder McClain was pastor, and hence, no doubt through sympathy, he had heard that man's story, and made this public declaration while the suit was pending, and but a few months before the expected decision. The cause of litigation was this: Desiring to keep the teams and hands employed during the winter, and to make something when unable to work on the farm, I purchased a number of hay stacks to haul to market, including in the contract a calf of very fine stock. Having purchased hay of the same man the year before, in 1836, and done reasonably well with it, and having got along with him without much difficulty, I reasonably expected to again, and signed a contract written by himself. (See Appendix D.) There was some old timber remaining yet on the meadow, and when we began to haul the hay, we found it stacked up on large log heaps, large piles of brush, and old stumps, which reduced the hay very much in quantity from what it appeared. After removing six stacks, we examined the rest, and finding them in a similar condition, we ceased hauling, and I proposed to refer the matter for settlement to disinterested men, inasmuch as we could not agree. This he refused to do, saying, "I am a law-abiding man. When I go to law, I don't mind the cost." When I called upon him for the calf, he declared before witnesses that he never sold me a calf at all for that consideration, because the hay was mentioned in the contract as the consideration of the $193. The calf was valued at $12.50 when the contract was made, but the sum was not so written in the contract. He utterly refused all compromise other than for me to pay him $193 for what hay there was, and lose the calf. I tendered him $75 for the six stacks which I had taken, which he refused, and we parted. As soon as the time was up for payment, he sued me in the Court of Common Pleas, Brown County, Ohio. My witnesses not being there, and he having employed the Hon. Thomas L. Hamer, who controlled that court, he obtained a judgment against me. I then appealed the case to the Supreme Court. The trial came on in March, 1840. One witness testified that he heard him say, when having the hay thus stacked, that he intended to cheat Gardner with it. The case was now before a court that Hamer could not control; and I had for my lawyer Leonard, of Chillicothe.

Question on Words.—My lawyer said that the article called for fifteen hay stacks. The plaintiff piqued himself on his skill in writing an article, and his lawyer, as he supposed it to be his duty, sided with him. They contended that the words of the article—"*thirteen hay stacks, all in the large meadow, and the two choice in the new meadow*"—meant thirteen in all. My counsel claimed that thirteen and two make fifteen. I never supposed that he intended more than thirteen; nor did the difficulty arise about the number of stacks, but the manner of stacking. However, the contention became so earnest that the counsel on both sides made a written agreement, "that if the court decided that there were only thirteen stacks sold by the article, then the judgment in the lower court should stand against me; but if the court decided that there were fifteen stacks sold by the article, then he should take the $75 tendered him, and pay all costs."

The Decision.—The Supreme Court of Ohio, after hearing all the witnesses and the arguments on both sides, decided that thirteen and two, as per contract, made fifteen hay stacks, sold according to the article. So plaintiff took the $75 tendered, and paid the costs. After I discovered the manner of stacking, and he refused to come to any terms, I expected that the matter would go through a full course of litigation, which would take about three years; so I proposed to enter into a contract for one of us to sell the hay, the same not to effect the case on trial in court. This reasonable and just proposal he rejected, and the hay, standing so long, was, as I had forseen, almost an entire loss to him. After the case was decided, he still claimed that I had taken advantage of the contract (written by himself), and wronged him out of $193, though the court decided just as I had, for me to pay him $75, just what I at first decided to be right; and I had now paid him the $75 for six stacks, and he retained the calf and the remainder of the hay. He could not have effected much, as we were both well known; but his father and brothers belonged to the church of which Elder McClain was pastor, and they were wealthy and respectable people, and the man himself had professed religion and joined the same church; so Elder McClain readily credited his statements, and McClain's influence gave them currency. Elder McClain belonged to no conference, he not having joined again as I had, in 1839. Yet, as he was preaching in the bounds of our conference, to which the churches by which he was employed also belonged, by my request the moderator and clerk called an extra session to investigate his charges. Elder McClain having been duly notified, the conference met at Pisgah Chapel, on the 13th of April, 1840. Elder McClain appeared. Although he had offered a resolution, in 1838, that no church should have more than two messengers, there were now some twenty-six present from Russellville church, where he preached; and other places where he preached sent a like large representation. The rest of the churches sent the usual number, as, three or four from the larger churches and two from the smaller. Elder Charles Manchester proposed that the conference should be equalized, when it was agreed that all grievances should be submitted to a committee of fifteen, six of whom should be chosen by each party, and these twelve should choose three more, and that a majority of this committee should render a verdict which should be final. The week being far spent, the committee adjourned to meet on the 19th of May following. My grievances with Elder McClain were, first: That he had published me to be an unfair man. Second: That he had broken our covenant of friendship, made on the 9th of April, 1839, at the house of Deacon John B. Shinkle. As I had lived in the neighborhood from a boy of

ten years old, and they all knew me, I did not think that any
witnesses were needed to sustain me, and so took none. They
summoned many witnesses; even the plaintiff, who had failed
in his endeavor to get pay for his badly stacked hay, was permitted to testify against me. My trust was in God and justice.
I was among those who had always known me, even from a
boy.

The Decision.—The committee of fifteen decided that Elder
McClain had not sustained his charges, and was guilty of covenant-breaking. Elder McClain did not acknowledge to me,
but, without my knowledge, laid the matter before the church
at Russellville, and was there acquitted. This was a mistake,
and it was an injury to Elder McClain. The following August
or September, he went to the Miami Conference, some eighty
miles distant, and proposed to unite with it. That conference
sent a committee to the Russellville church, of which he was a
member, and where he lived, to investigate the matter and receive the minister and such churches as desired to go with him,
if the committee thought it advisable. Elder Manchester and
myself, having been notified of the meeting, attended, and protested against a committee of the Miami Conference having jurisdiction within the bounds of the Southern Ohio Christian
Conference, and also against any intermeddling in this case,
where the applicant for membership in their conference had
previously submitted his cause to a committee, and by a written
statement agreed that the decision of that committee should be
final. After we thus protested, we left. The committee, however, received Elder McClain and one or two churches into the
Miami Conference. This, however designed, was a wound to the
Redeemer's cause. So I attended the Miami Conference of the
following year, in September, A. D. 1841, to endeavor to get the
matter settled. At first I was coolly received; but a committee
was appointed, before which Elder McClain and I met. After
talking the matter over as Christians, and praying together, we
agreed to drop all past grievances, and work together in the
future, in union and brotherly love, to build up the Redeemer's
kingdom. To this we gave each other the hand of fellowship,
and returned home, traveling and preaching together. In a
year or so, Elder McClain, and all who went with him, returned
to the Southern Ohio Conference, and all worked together in
harmony again.

Elder McClain a Good Man.—Although Elder McClain had
his failings, and had been led to treat me unkindly, truth as
well as charity forbid me to view him as a hypocrite or a
wicked man. He loved to have the pre-eminence, and, like
others, perhaps, considered my influence too great with the
churches. Notwithstanding all the perplexity in conference
of the litigation concerning the hay, which the difficulty with

Elder McClain grew out of, yet I attended to my domestic business, and preached regularly to three or four churches, as usual,
and the cause of religion still advanced. After the two decisions
against him, one at the court and one at the church, in the Pisgah trial, almost any other man would have let the hay stacks rest.
Not so with the plaintiff. Talk against a minister of the gospel
is interesting to the hearers; and so he still kept talking. He
contended that by my lawyer taking advantage of the contract,
written by the plaintiff himself, I had defrauded him and his
family out of $193. This I bore some sixteen years, after which,
as the reader will see, we had another settlement. These
troubles did not hinder the work of the Lord where I labored.

Mount Pleasant Church Organized.—In 1839 or 1840, the door
was opened for the gospel in a wealthy neighborhood of farmers,
in Clermont County, between the town of Felicity and the
Ohio River. The word was readily received by this honest, industrious people; and after preaching there for a few months,
and visiting among them when in the neighborhood, I was able,
by divine grace, to organize a respectable and hopeful church.
It was at first called the "Olive Church," but having built a good
chapel, on a rising piece of ground, they changed the name to
"The Mount Pleasant Church."

Lucas Found Again.—In the autumn of 1840 I received a letter from a gentleman in Lebanon, Warren County, stating that
a Campbellite preacher by the name of John B. Lucas had been
preaching in Lebanon; and the writer desired to know if I was
willing to meet said Lucas in debate. I, of course, answered in
the affirmative, providing that we could agree on the question
to be discussed—the preliminaries, etc. After a few more com-
munications, the time was fixed to meet in the city of Lebanon
on the 20th of October, 1840. It had been but a little over a
year since I debated with the same man in Jamestown, in June
of 1839. We met as appointed in Lebanon, October 20, 1840.
Lucas at first seemed to refuse to discuss the question discussed
at Jamestown, and determined not to consent to any form of a
question which would expose Campbellism before the people.
But a number of intelligent gentlemen present, who had heard
him preach those views, expressed themselves so firmly, that he
agreed to the following, which differs but little from the question discussed at Jamestown.

Question.—"Is it, or is it not, the order of God, according to
the gospel of Christ, as taught by Christ and the apostles, that
baptism be added to faith and repentance in order to the remission of past sins and admission into the kingdom of Christ?"
Explanation by Lucas: "It is understood by past sins the sins
of an alien." *J. B. Lucas* takes the affirmative; *Matthew Gardner* takes the negative. Lebanon, October 20, 1840.

The discussion was opened by Elder Lucas, at eleven o'clock, in the large new Baptist church in Lebanon, of which Elder French was pastor. The speeches were to be thirty minutes each. I followed in the negative, making about the same points that I did at Jamestown. Elder Lucas had supposed that by the different phraseology of the question, and by his skillful *tact*, he could avoid or evade those points. But he failed entirely in this. When I made it plain to the people that he had neither met these points nor fairly replied to my arguments, he had recourse to his *irony* and *sarcasm*, in which he was quite expert. I, as before, requested the people to excuse me for omitting to reply to his ironical and sarcastic remarks, as I could not lower the dignity of a gospel minister by doing so; nor had I ridden sixty or seventy miles to that place to spend my time in that way. He saw and felt that the people in general disapproved of his course in this respect, and consequently he discontinued it. I requested Elder Lucas repeatedly to show one positive passage of Scripture that said "remission of sins is to be obtained, after faith and repentance, by immersion in water." I did not ask for his inference or mere opinion, but a "thus saith the Lord!" He, of course, could not do it, consequently I kept that request before the people. I made the people see how the system advocated by Elder Lucas doomed to *eternal perdition* the great majority of the best men who have ever lived, and whose labors have blessed the world—such men as Dr. Young, Dr. Watts, Isaac Newton, and William Penn, and all the Baxters and Wesleys, and hundreds of others—all lost, to save Mr. Campbell's new gospel. *This was a hard nut for Elder Lucas to crack.* He tried hard to get round this difficult and insurmountable objection to his theory, as follows:

What Lucas Said.—It is the kingdom of Christ upon earth, or in this world, that persons are to have their sins remitted and enter into by immersion, and which they can not enter into without, and not the kingdom above.

Gardner's Reply.—I, of course, denied his hypothesis, to-wit, that Christ has two kingdoms, one on earth and the other in heaven. The Scriptures speak of the kingdom of the Messiah as one—in the singular, not plural. It is not the kingdoms of Christ, but the kingdom. I made the people clearly see that there is but one kingdom, as there is but one king. I clearly showed that there are degrees of advancement in the Redeemer's kingdom. The first entrance is on earth, but not beyond the reach of any. We must be initiated into the kingdom in this world. This is by faith and repentance, and the power of the Holy Spirit, whereby we are brought to love God, and consequently are born of God; for the apostle saith, "Whosoever loveth is born of God." Thus we must enter in the first degree of this kingdom in this world, or we never can enter the exalted and glorious state of the kingdom in the world to come. So, if baptism (immersion) is the door into the kingdom, then all are out of the kingdom who are not immersed; are they not? I illustrated the absurdity of his theory, that those could enter the higher kingdom who could not enter the lower, by the similitude of a man endeavoring to master the Greek language, and to become a reader of the Greek classics, without learning the Greek alphabet. So it is as unscriptural and as absurd to speak of those entering the kingdom of glory above who can not enter the kingdom of grace below. I clearly showed the design of baptism in the New Testament economy, as preached by Christ and the apostles. It was not a procuring cause of remission, or door of entrance to the church, but the answer or illustration of a good conscience as a symbol of our faith in the burial and resurrection of Christ, and of our resurrection. I fully exposed the intolerance of the creed or system of Campbell, as advocated by the affirmative, and contrasted it with the blessed attributes of love and mercy in God. While I thus presented the subject, the people gave great attention, and there was much weeping in the congregation.

Elder Lucas failed on every position taken by him, while the points presented by me were invulnerable against all his efforts. It was evident to all that he felt that he had failed to sustain the affirmative of the proposition. The defeats at Jamestown and Lebanon were not chargeable to want of skill and ability, for he possessed both in a very superior degree. The simple truth is, that the *system* which he undertook to support can not be maintained against any man who understands it, and understands the Bible.

The Close.—The debate lasted three days. The attendance was quite large, comprising many of the most intelligent and respectable people in the city of Lebanon and the surrounding country. In the congregation were many ministers of the city and country. Among the noted men was the Hon. Thomas Corwin. At the close of the debate, Elder French, the minister in charge, went on with a protracted meeting. He afterwards told me that he received about sixty members.

Elder Lucas left, and never returned to preach in Lebanon. He did not live very long afterward. The debate at Lebanon took place near the close of the fiftieth year of my age.

December 5, 1840, still found me trying to advocate the cause of my Lord and Master, and in the arrangement of my domestic matters. I had now lived a full half century in this changing, flickering world of hopes and fears, where there are few hopes and many sorrows. Thirty years had been spent in trying to make the world better. I had been greatly deceived and betrayed by many men in whom I placed confidence. Yet I still believed that there were some good men. I could look back and see my own missteps and failings, and, as at all times, asked the Lord for his grace to save me.

> "Time, like an ever-rolling stream,
> Bears all its sons away;
> It flies forgotten as a dream—
> Dies at the opening day."—WATTS.

CHAPTER VI

THE SIXTH TEN YEARS OF MY LIFE—EDIT AND PUBLISH THE "CHRISTIAN UNION"—IT IS TRANSFERRED TO THE "GOSPEL HERALD"—DEBATE WITH A UNIVERSALIST—TROUBLES WITH MINISTERS OF SECRET SOCIETIES—FREEMASONS, ETC.

The fifty-first year of my life began (December 5, 1840), in good health, and a trust in the overruling providence and the guidance of his Holy Spirit, through Jesus Christ, and with a determination to do his will. The labors of the winter were as usual—traveling through mud to my several appointments, and attending to protracted meetings, etc. At that time the Christians had no paper in the west. Barton W. Stone had, for a number of years, edited the "Christian Messenger," which was published at Georgetown, Kentucky. But he had gone "over," in part, at least, to Mr. Alexander Campbell's system. He had taken John T. Johnson, a Disciple, as co-editor, consequently that paper had, for four or five years, advocated Campbellism; that is "remission of sins by immersion." Therefore, the churches in the west had been without a paper for four or five years. Many patronized the "Christian Palladium," published in the east. There had been, for two or three years, much talk about starting a paper, but the Christians in the east were so much opposed to it, that all seemed afraid to undertake it. Our brethren in the east insisted upon what they termed "general measures," which seemed to be that we of the west must take their paper and pay for it, while all who advocated starting a paper in the west were reproached as opposed to general measures, and favoring sectional interests. Under these circumstances there was not one minister or layman who heartily concurred in the undertaking, so far as to bear a part of the expense of starting a paper. There were two or three ministers, and many brethren, who had no objection to our having a western paper, provided that there was nothing more asked of them than to say "yes." Great as were these discouragements, yet, seeing and feeling the importance of having a paper to advocate our views, I resolved to shoulder the whole burden of the expense and labor myself. Notice was given for a mass convention, to meet at Pisgah Chapel, Brown County, Ohio, to form a "Western Christian Association." The convention met the 15th of April, 1841, and the "Western Christian Association" was then organized. I was chosen editor; Elder Naaman Dawson, M. D., assistant editor. The name of Dr. Alexander Campbell, a physician of Ripley, a great and good man, stood at the head of the editorial council. This was the first publishing association formed by the Christians in the west. It was not large at first, for there were few, if any, in it except those belonging to the Southern Ohio Christian Conference. All others seemed to stand aloof, fearing the reproach and opposition of the eastern brethren.

"Christian Union."—The name of the new paper was "The Christian Union." The first number was issued about the 15th of May, 1841. It was a monthly periodical, in magazine form. In the second number, I published an editorial on the subject of "general measures," so strongly urged by some of our eastern brethren; after which opposition measurably ceased. I sent the "magazine" gratuitously to many Christian ministers, both west and east, so that it might be fully known that there was a paper in the west. The whole pecuniary responsibility was borne by me. By means of this periodical, the sentiment gained ground among ministers and people that we should have a paper. I attended the next annual session of the Miami Conference, in September, 1841, and laid the matter of a paper in the west before that body, and proposed to transfer the subscribers, who were taking the "Christian Union," to any paper started on principles in which we could unite. The proposition was unanimously accepted. Steps were taken immediately for a new paper, to start soon after the close of the first volume of the "Christian Union." An association was organized, and subscribers were obtained, and the "Gospel Herald" was started accordingly, A. D. 1844.

Higginsport Church Organized.—In 1839, Elder John Phillips organized a church in Higginsport, on the Ohio River, about three miles from the "Union Church" Chapel. Some of the members of "Union Church," of which I was pastor, went into the Higginsport church. But Phillips made no effort to build a Christian chapel; and, when he went east, the organization went down, and the members from "Union Church" returned to it. In the year 1841, or the last of 1840, I, through divine grace, organized a church in Higginsport. Soon after the organization, I, as usual with me, got up a subscription and erected a chapel, to which I was about as large a subscriber as any. That church grew rapidly, and is yet doing reasonably well, in 1865.

Mistaken Principle.—The chapel in Higginsport was built upon the mistaken principle that too many of our houses of worship have been erected upon; that is, free for all who preach the gospel, when not occupied by us. Thus all who wish may claim the right to use the chapels built by us. *Thomas Gilmer*, a Universalist, came to Higginsport in 1842; there being one or two of that order who had subscribed small sums for the building, they insisted that he should preach in it. This I felt in duty bound to oppose, and publicly stated to the people my objection to that doctrine. At the same time, I perhaps declared that Universalism was not the gospel of Christ, therefore could not be preached there on any claim, according to the terms upon which that house had been built. This caused Mr. Gilmer to send me a challenge, which I accepted. I was aware that Mr. Gilmer was considered a great man and a successful debater among the Universalists. He had been engaged in many contests, and was a man of fine education, as I found on personal acquaintance. When we met to choose the question, he insisted upon the one which Universalists had been accustomed to have inconsiderate men meet them on; that is, "*Do the Scriptures teach that all men will be finally holy and happy?*" I told him plainly that he could not get me to debate on a question which permitted him to occupy either the ground of a Universalist or a Restorationist, at pleasure. If I debated, the question must define clearly one system or the other; he might take his choice. He accepted the following:

The Question.—"Do Christ and his apostles teach that all punishment, torment, sorrow, and death, for, and in consequence of sin, and rebellion against God, is endured and experienced by the wicked in this world, in this state of existence, in this body, in this life, and here only?" Gilmer affirms; Gardner denies. Mr. Gilmer had a great advantage to begin with. The debate was to be in our chapel, where we had a large Christian Church, while there were comparatively few Universalists in the town, or neighborhood; so I had little to gain and he nothing to lose. But I preferred to allow him this advantage, rather than to have him go on preaching Universalism without being exposed.

The Debate on Universalism.—The usual rules, and the choice of moderators having been agreed upon, we met in the Christian chapel at Higginsport on the 15th day of August, 1842, at 10 o'clock for discussion. The speeches were to be alternate, and thirty minutes each.

In Mr. Gilmer's first speech, he seemed to honestly commit himself, and take the broad ground of Universalism, teaching that "God unconditionally fore-ordained whatsoever comes to pass," therefore there could be no future torment for the wicked to endure, consequently all punishment for sin is in its commission in this world; that is, the evil attending sin is the legitimate punishment of sin, the punishment being in doing the wrong.

Gardner's Reply.—If, as the affirmative says, God has, by immutable decrees, fore-ordained all things whatsoever comes to pass, then all the acts of men take place according to his will, and men are compelled, by God's decree, to act just as they do. They have no choice what they will or will not do. If this be so, then why did God give us his holy Word, the Bible, to teach us what is right in his sight, and what is wrong, and how to avoid evil, while he had *predetermined* every choice of the heart, and every act of every human being for every moment of his life? If the affirmative be correct, is the Bible not a farce, a burlesque, and imposition upon the credulity of man?

The Two Gates.—Second: The Lord of glory taught the people that there are two gates and two ways. One is the strait gate of the narrow way which leads to life. The other is the wide gate of the broad way that leads to destruction. Matt. VII. 13; Luke XIII. 24. Universalists say that there is only one gate and one way, or both lead to one place, and both are right.

Third: The affirmative says that God has fore-ordained all the acts of men; yet God punishes men in this life for their evil acts. Thus God punishes men for doing the very things that he (God) predetermined they should do.

Fourth: If the punishment for every sin takes place at the time of doing the wrong act, as Mr. Gilmer affirms, will he explain to the audience how the sin of adultery is punished, which Jesus condemns so plainly?

Fifth: The history of the world proves that the best men who have ever lived have suffered more than the wicked.

Sixth: While God says, "Without holiness no man shall see the Lord," or be eternally happy, Mr. Gilmer affirms that all liars, drunkards, blasphemers, thieves, robbers, murderers, whoremongers, adulterers, fornicators, and all the abominably wicked, spoken of in God's word, are as sure of heaven and eternal glory as were the holy prophets and apostles. These points and arguments seemed to take Mr. Gilmer by surprise, as he could not, as he had done before with the ministers of different denominations, who did not oblige him to commit himself—he could not now avail himself of future punishment and final restoration, but had to meet *Universalism as it is.*

Gilmer did not try to evade the arguments by tact or sarcasm, but labored hard to sustain his position by fair arguments, though it was evident that he felt it to be "an uphill business."

The points made by me he could not answer. I kept them before the people. In my following speeches I showed *the gospel of Universalism to be*, that all liars, drunkards, thieves, robbers, blasphemers, murderers, and like characters, are on their way to glory, there being no future retribution nor any hell for such to go to. Therefore, all these wicked characters are on their way to peace, eternal happiness; and that they should rejoice, for "great is your (their) reward in heaven!"

Mr. Gilmer.—This appeared to entirely unman Mr. Gilmer. His energy withered, and he failed after this to get the attention of the people.

Universalists Through.—Consequently, on the second day, Mr. Gilmer and his friends proposed that the discussion close that afternoon. It was his privilege to close when he pleased, as he held the affirmative. So the debate lasted two days, viz: the 15th and 16th of August, 1842. Mr. Gilmer had been always victorious before, as his friends claimed, no doubt, because he could, when need be, step on the platform of restorationism, which teaches that the wicked will go into future torment (hell) till they suffer the penalty of their sins, and are reformed; after which the wicked will come out of hell and go to heaven. But pure Universalism denies any future retribution, or hell, and promises heaven and happiness to all without respect of character. On Mr. Gilmer's return to Higginsport, after the debate, to fill an appointment, he met a very small congregation—some four Universalists and a few stragglers. That was his last appointment in Higginsport. He soon quit preaching, and the discussion greatly benefited the Christian cause, as it was the means of many renouncing Universalism and joining the Christian Church. It is now (1865) nearly twenty years since that discussion, and Universalism has never yet been able to hold up its head in Higginsport. This year (1842), through divine grace, the churches were increased in numbers, and the Southern Ohio Conference was greatly strengthened.

Millerism.—In the latter part of 1842, the excitement about Millerism, or rather *Forty-three-ism*, began to spread all over the country. *William Miller*, a lay member of the Baptist Church in the east, a man of limited education, had so contrived his calculations on prophecies, as to make them seem to bear him out in his declaring, with much assurance, that "*the world must end in* 1843." The doctrine spread over the country like wild-fire. Many preachers of various denominations favored it to alarm sinners. Nearly all the "Disciples," in the bounds of my knowledge, were Millerites. They preached Millerism to alarm sinners, and get them to be immersed in order to the remission of their sins, or to obtain pardon, so as to be ready. Few ministers of any denomination came out boldly against *Forty-three-ism*. I regarded Mr. Mil-

ler's calculations to be positively false, and the whole thing a
farce and delusion, calculated to injure religion by its re-action.
I foresaw that it would also put a new weapon into the hands
of infidels when the time passed, and 1843 would be gone, and no
second coming of Christ or end of the world had taken place.
In view of these considerations, I felt it my duty to take a decided
stand in opposition to "Millerism." The words of the Savior
himself was my platform: "Of that day and *that* hour knoweth no man, no, not the angels which are in heaven, neither
the Son, but the Father;" "Be ye therefore ready also: for the Son
of man cometh at an hour when ye think not." Mark XIII. 32;
Luke XII. 40. I illustrated by ecclesiastical history, showing
how many *times* had been set, and gave the names of those
who fix these times for the world to end. Time had proved
their hopes all false delusions; and time would prove Millerism
so now. As 1843 drew on, the Miller excitement increased,
producing divisions in the churches of all denominations,
especially the Baptist and Christian churches in the east,
where Elder John Phillips was now carried away with it. In
the west it did harm, by creating discord. It divided the Christian Church in Cincinnati, and greatly injured it. The fanatical
proclaimers insisted that all who believed that Christ would come
in 1843 must "come out of Babylon;" that is, leave the church
organizations and be all united on the true faith of the coming
of Christ in 1843, otherwise they would be destroyed. The
Millerites were "come-outers." Many ministers, who had used
it to alarm sinners and get them into their churches, could not
now oppose it, and reaped their reward. My firm stand against
it, by divine grace, saved the churches of the Southern Ohio
Conference. At length 1843 came. As its days, weeks, and
months passed, the excitement increased. Many of its devotees
became monomaniacs; some became lunatics; merchants in the
cities quit their business; many gave away their property;
others cared little or nothing for the things of this world.
Some designated a certain day in September or October, when
the Savior would come with ten thousand angels. Many, having quit all business, prepared white robes in which to ascend
to meet the Lord at his coming. They looked! They watched!
They waited! But the day passed as other days had before.
There were no signs that the Lord of glory had left his abode,
in his own serene heaven, though he doubtless looked with
pity upon their folly. When 1843 had fully passed, and 1844
had come, and no Christ had made his appearance, the disappointment of the "Adventists," as they now called themselves, was intense beyond description. Some renounced
Millerism; others held on, saying there had been a small
mistake in the calculation, but Christ would come shortly; so
some held on! The great dearth in religion which followed

was felt all over the United States. Thousands who had been deceived by the ministers, to unite with the church, now back-slid. Infidelity was encouraged, and the paralyzing effects of that delusion were visible for ten or fifteen years afterwards.

C. B. Thorp, the Universalist.—In the year 1844, while preach-ing at Boat Run, a small town on the Ohio River, near Point Pleasant, in Clermont County, C. B. Thorp, a Universalist, who was preaching at Point Pleasant, where I also sometimes preached, attended one of my meetings. Hearing me object to the doctrine of Universalism, he sent me a challenge to meet him in debate. I declined, unless the editor of the "Star of the West," their paper, published in Cincinnati, would indorse him as to ability. I was aware that he had been in a number of discussions, and was regarded by Universalists as a "smart" debater, though not equal to Gilmer. I wished him indorsed, be-cause, if vanquished, as I felt certain that he would be, my knowl-edge of mankind made me foresee that they would say. "Ah! who is Thorp? We don't consider him one of our strong men at all. We have no confidence in his ability." Before I left, he came to a personal interview with me, and, referring to several men of ability of various denominations, with whom he had debated, he asked me why I required him to be indorsed, as this had not been done by any other man. I thus replied: "*I am not willing to load a six-pounder to shoot a tom-tit.*" He and his friends being very anxious for a debate, he positively asserted that he could and would be indorsed; so we proceeded to choose the question. Mr. Thorp insisted on my accepting the question proposed by Gilmer, and which others, for want of discriminating minds, have discussed with them, to-wit: "Do the Scriptures teach that all men will be finally holy and happy?" I stated that I could not discuss a question which would permit him to occupy at pleasure, or as necessity may drive him to, in the same debate, either Universalism or Restor-ationism. He finally accepted the question discussed with Gil-mer, viz: "Do the Scriptures teach that all the torment or punishment, for, and in consequence of sin and rebellion against God, is suffered and endured by the wicked in this world, and here only?" C. B. Thorp affirms; M. Gardner denies. We appointed the discussion to commence June 4, 1844.

Debate at Point Pleasant, Ohio.—We met accordingly at Point Pleasant June 4th, at 9 o'clock. Mr. Thorp was fully indorsed by their paper, the "Star of the West."

C. B. Thorp made the opening speech. He took no definite position, but pursued a random course, talking about God be-ing too merciful to punish the wicked, etc.

Gardner.—In reply I showed that the punishment of the wicked was not directly from God, but the consequence of their own actions. There are two roads or ways; the broad way,

7

which leads to destruction, and the narrow way, which leads to peace and happiness, and man has his choice which one he will take. This he could neither deny or get out of his way. I kept it before the people. I also presented the other points which I made with Mr. Gilmer. But I could not get Mr. Thorp to define his position till the second day.

Thorp the Second Day.—Then he said: "Man has not the power to choose and voluntarially do what he will. All things are fore-ordained of God."

Gardner's Reply.—That admission was all that I wanted or desired. I presented the same argument that I did with Gilmer, showing that if the ground taken by the affirmative be correct, then the Bible is a useless book. Worse than that, it teaches a man what he shall do and shall not do, while God had fore-ordained unchangeably all the acts of mankind. On his theory, there can be no proper punishment, either in this world or the next, as men do nothing else but that which God predetermined and fore-ordained they should do.

C. B. Thorp was a trickish, quibbling, quirking, dishonest man, and a very difficult man to get along with in a discussion.

Gardner.—In one speech I exposed the gospel of Universalism, by supposing it true, as follows: The most wicked and abominable of human beings are requested to hear the glorious gospel of Universalism, and to rejoice and be exceedingly glad, for there is no future retribution or punishment to await them. All their midnight crimes were ordained of God, and consequently were according to his divine will; therefore, all such characters ought to greatly rejoice and be exceeding glad, for great is their reward in heaven. This was too much of their own theory. I still further remarked that thousands and tens of thousands in every age of the world, who had lived lives of prayer and strove to be holy, in order to gain heaven and happiness, were all foolishly deluded (if Universalism be right), for they were just as surely on the road to glory and eternal peace, without thus striving to live righteous, as with it.

Thorp.—Mr. Thorp could make no consistent reply, consequently, on the second day, he and his friends proposed for the debate to close that afternoon, and it did close. It had continued two days, the 4th and 5th of June, 1844. He had an appointment, not long after, in Point Pleasant, but few came out, and he came no more. That discussion, like the one with Mr. Gilmer, was a great help to vital Christianity. Many renounced Universalism, and united with the evangelical churches. It is now 1865, that is, more than twenty-one years since that debate, and its effects are yet visible in Point Pleasant. Few in the country there pretend to advocate Universalism, nor is any preacher of that faith sustained there. The years 1843, 1844, and 1845, were three years of peace and prosperity of the churches of the Southern Ohio Conference. There were many additions. The conference was strengthened by quite a number of young men entering the ministry. The Disciples endeavored to disturb some of the churches, but the two defeats of John B. Lucas kept them at a distance. He was doubtless as great a debater as they had among them, not excepting Alexander Campbell himself. They still endeavored to defame me; but it seemed understood by the people generally that it was the business of the preachers and members of that faith to slander me. I did not reply.

Freemasons.—The Southern Ohio Conference having become somewhat popular, in the spring or summer of 1846 one or more of the elders united with secret societies, and some ministers who were Freemasons proposed to unite with the conference. This was a new state of things. From its organization till then there had not been in it one minister who belonged to a secret society, but all were supposed to be opposed to all secret combinations. From my earliest convictions of right and wrong, I entertained religious objections to secret conclaves. Soon after I entered the ministry, Freemasons held out strong inducements for me to unite with them.

What a Mason Said.—Said a Freemason to me, "Were you a Free and Accepted Mason, it would be of great advantage to you. When you visit a strange town to preach, a gentleman would arise in the congregation and propose a collection for you. You can become a Freemason without it costing you any thing. Ministers are received without charge." This, with perhaps other inducements, had some influence upon my mind. The Christians were at that time weak and persecuted. I had, from honest motives, become a minister of that denomination; and being quite poor as to the wealth of this world, and preaching without earthly reward, I was obliged to labor with my hands to support my family. Would it not then be right to become a Mason, and secure their friendship and assistance? These advantages seemed inviting from a worldly view. But I had put my trust in God for all things, and had so professed, and that trust I could not betray by going into a secret combination for the purpose of support, instead of relying upon God! Nor were these the only objections. It seemed to be constantly ringing in my mind, *Be careful that you do not take a leap in the dark, of which you may repent in the uncertain hour of death.* Not only so, I saw that the profane and infidels were Free and Accepted Masons; consequently I finally concluded that secret affiliated societies were not proper places for ministers of the gospel, but that they should obey the words of the Apostle Paul, "Come out from among them, and be ye separate, saith the Lord."

Sons of Temperance.—In 1846 Elder Alexander McClain

united with the Sons of Temperance, and marched in their processions, which wounded numbers of the members of the church. I attended a communion with him at the church in Bentonville, in Adams County. He was pastor. There I learned that quite a number of the members were so dissatisfied that they did not commune. This disaffection continued. A number ceased to attend upon his ministry, and he soon discontinued preaching there. Nor were the objections in that church alone, but in all the churches where he labored. As he had been useful in his preaching, his example had its influence, and not long after his taking that step other preachers joined the Freemasons. Although Elder McClain and I labored together, yet my known opposition to secret societies diminished our union, and love for each other's society. In that year, at the conference of 1846, in Higginsport, I was one of the movers of a resolution advising ministers and others to be contented in the church of God, and to refrain from uniting with secret societies and worldly combinations. We soon found that the ministers in favor of these secret conclaves were more in number than had been expected; so, after being debated, the motion was laid on the table. Matters went on as usual, till the conference at Ripley, in 1847. Then this resolution was taken up, and, after much discussion, it passed almost unanimously.

Another Debate.—In the summer of 1846, C. B. Thorp began to preach at Aberdeen, Ohio, a town opposite Maysville, Kentucky. As the Bethlehem church, of which I was pastor, and which numbered nearly four hundred members, was but about a mile beyond the suburbs of Aberdeen, many of our members resided there. Thorp, being a fluent speaker, drew large congregations, and was producing a favorable impression for Universalism. I, of course, presented to the people my objections to the doctrines. The Universalists there, having come to consider Mr. Thorp as invincible, supposed that a debate with me would destroy the Bethlehem church, and build up a Universalist Church. I soon received a note from Dr. Thomas Moore, the leader of the Universalists of that section, a man of wealth and influence, desiring to know if I would meet Mr. C. B. Thorp in discussion. I answered in the affirmative. After some further correspondence the time was set, and Mr. Thorp and I agreed to meet at Dr. Moore's house to frame the question. When we met, Thorp insisted upon their old favorite question, viz: "Do the Scriptures teach that all men will be finally holy and happy?" I refused to accept a question which would permit him to occupy the double grounds of Universalism or restorationism at pleasure. The question must clearly state one system or the other, and he might take his choice. After he utterly refused to accept any question but the one named, and it appearing that we could not get him to agree on any one, by Dr.

Moore urging him, he accepted the following, which placed me on the affirmative, to-wit:

The Question.—"Do the Scriptures teach that the future happiness and eternal salvation of mankind are to be obtained on the conditions of man's believing the gospel, repenting of his sins, and living righteous and holy in this life?" M. Gardner affirms; C. B. Thorp denies. Having arranged the preliminaries and chosen three moderators, we met in the Methodist Episcopal Church in Aberdeen, October 20, 1846.

Elder Gardner's Speech.—I first took the positive declaration of Christ and his apostles, namely, "He that believeth on the Son, hath everlasting life: and he that believeth not the Son, shall not see life; but the wrath of God abideth on him."

Thorp's Reply.—Mr. Thorp took the ground that salvation is the gift of God without any conditions of faith, repentance, or good works, or a holy life.

Gardner.—I showed that according to Universalism there is no such thing as salvation; for, according to that system, there never was any danger, there being no hell for the wicked to go to, and no one could be lost.

Thorp, seeing the dilemma that he was in, tried to sustain himself by planting himself upon the so-called orthodox doctrine of vicarious atonement; that is, that Jesus Christ become the surety to God the Father for all mankind, and satisfied the law of divine justice by his death, he dying "in the law-room and stead" of sinners; therefore, he argued, the whole debt being paid for all, all *must* be saved; nor is there any need of good works by men in order to salvation; for the debt being fully paid, and Christ's righteousness being imputed to all mankind, there can be no further demand against any of the human family. With Christ's death the law is satisfied, and with Christ's holiness imputed to us, heaven must be satisfied; therefore, all must be saved.

Gardner's Reply.—The affirmative denied there being any Scripture to sustain such doctrine. I showed the inconsistency of that doctrine with the character of God, and presented the true scriptural view of the atonement; that is, to purify, and reconcile, etc. I also proclaimed the gospel, according to Universalism, to be as follows: The abominably wicked, having their hands stained with innocent blood, in order to be saved, need not believe on the Lord Jesus Christ, nor even repent of their sins; but may go on their way cursing God and rejoicing, for there is an exceeding great reward awaiting them in heaven.

Thorp.—Mr. Thorp attempted to extricate himself, but he became confused, and finally took the ground that God fore-ordained every thing, and all is going on according to God's will; therefore, there can be no future punishment.

Gardner.—I was determined to illustrate the unrighteousness

of Universalism, and make it clearly manifest to the people.
How can a theory be true which can fill the hearts of the worst
men without causing them to repent, with equal or superior
joy, to that enjoyed by the very best? If Universalism be true,
the most depraved characters can glory over the most holy.

> " For Judas, that perfidious wretch,
>   Though by his Lord accursed,
> He, with a cord, outwent his Lord,
>   And got to heaven first.
> Bless, O my soul, the very rope,
>   On which old Judas died;
> It served for him instead of hope,
>   When he his Lord denied."

As I held the affirmative, I was not disposed to close till Mr.
Thorp and his friends got enough—until they had debated to
their heart's content; so we continued three days and three
evenings, viz: the 20th, 21st, and 22d days of October, 1846.
Dr. Moore, after inducing Rev. Mr. Thorp to go into the debate,
seeing, in the first forenoon, that Mr. Thorp could not succeed,
left him and never returned during the debate. This he did,
that when spoken to about it, he could say, I was not there,
and thus appear not to have been interested in it. Before the
discussion, the doctor had been ever ready in thrusting his Universalist opinions forward; even when called into a family on
professional duty, he took great delight in continually endeavoring to perplex the elderly ladies with questions on Universalism. After the debate, the mention of Thorp had the effect of
producing profound silence with the doctor.

Thorp Renounces Universalism.—Mr. Thorp once returned to
preach in Aberdeen. Very few assembled to hear him. This
was perhaps the last time he tried to preach Universalism.
About a month after the debate, he published a pamphlet renouncing the doctrine.

The Reason Why.—One of the reasons which he gave for renouncing it was, that he had preached Universalism for, perhaps, fifteen years, and had never seen any good attending it,
or any person made better by it. One reason why the
discussions held by me were not as tedious as such debates
usually are was, that in every case I had the rule inserted " that
the Scriptures, in the common version, should be the only evidence offered." This prevented quibbling about the translation,
and bringing many books written by men. It is now 1865,
over eighteen years since the last debate with Mr. Thorp, and
no Universalist preacher has yet come to renew their cause in
Aberdeen. Neither "Disciples" or Universalists manifest any
desire to support their systems with me by discussion. The
Universalists are more honorable than those who advocate Mr.

Campbell's system, for they seem to admit that they can not sustain their system; while others pretend that they can, but practice dishonorable defamation.

Some oppose debating religious subjects. Such persons should carefully examine the practice of Christ and his apostles. Jesus and the apostles seldom spoke publicly without being interrupted and contradicted. Such was the custom then. Consequently they were almost perpetually arguing and debating with the opposers of Christianity, as will be admitted by all who have examined the subject. While this is true, we admit that there are debates which have no good moral influence, in consequence of their being conducted in a light, trifling spirit. A minister, in debating, should prayerfully watch against a trifling spirit. In all my debates, my accountability to God was felt by me the same as when preaching, though my opponents appeared to be influenced by the spirit before referred to. Good has attended the cause I advocated in every debate. During the year 1848 there was peace in our conference, and reasonable prosperity in the churches. The resolution passed in 1847, advising ministers and others " not to unite with secret societies, and those already members to leave them," was not regarded. At the conference session in 1848 nothing was said about secret societies; but Jacob F. Crist, a Master Mason, united with the conference. It was understood that he intended to leave the Masons; but he did not.

Masonry.—Having carefully examined Masonry, Odd-Fellowship, etc., and made myself acquainted with them as far as possible without initiation, I ascertained that they had a form of worship, with a hierarchy and prayers and songs of devotion; while the members say to the world that they are *not* religious institutions. Is not then the pretended devotion sacrilege? My examinations forced me to this conclusion. I was also convinced that the name of our Lord Jesus Christ, though found in some of their songs, and mentioned by some of their writers, is not in the foundation or any component part of the system of Freemasonry or Odd-Fellowship, etc.

Creed of Masons.—The "Freemason Monitor" says, "To believe in one God is the religion of a Free and Accepted Mason." I observed that deists, and every grade of infidels, belonged to these secret combinations; consequently my decision was and is, that if the apparent religious devotion of those secret conclaves is not real, it is sacrilege; is it not? Therefore, those belonging to these institutions ought not to be admitted into the church of God. Or, if they are truly religious institutions, Masons should be contented with their own forms of worship, and cease to seek admission to the church. I, therefore, objected to admitting such. To prevent others following into these societies, it seemed to me best to let the preachers and people see the truth in relation to the subject, that those disposed to go into these conclaves might not do so *mentally* "blindfolded!"

Anti-Masonic Convention.—I have in my possession the proceedings of the United States Anti-Masonic Convention held in Philadelphia, September 11, 1830, as published by the authority of the convention. This work contains a history of the origin of Masonry, the mode of initiation, the revelation of the degrees, the obligations, oaths, and grips, etc., from the Entered Apprentice up to the Royal-Arch Mason, Knighthood, etc. There has probably never been a more respectable and talented body of men assembled in this nation than were found in this Anti-Masonic Convention. It was composed of one hundred and eleven members from different states of the Union.

Names of Members.—Hon. Francis Granger, of New York, President of the Convention, Ex-Postmaster General, and Ex-Member of Congress. Hon. William H. Seward, Ex-Governor of New York, now Secretary of State in the Cabinet of President Lincoln. Hon. Thadeus Stevens, now (1865) Representative in Congress from Pennsylvania. Hon. Joseph Ritner, Ex-Governor of Pennsylvania. Hon. Charles Ogle, Member of Congress from Pennsylvania. Hon. Harmer Denny, Ex-Member of Congress from Pennsylvania. Hon. William Slade, Member of Congress from Vermont, afterwards Governor. Added to these were a number of ministers of the gospel, who had renounced Masonry.

How it was Exposed.—It was by eleven seceding Masons, members of that convention, that Freemasonry was exposed to public view. Some of the eleven were ministers of the gospel. One was Elder David Barnard, a noted Baptist minister. He, with others, saw the wrong, renounced the craft, and exposed the evil. These proceedings contain a full account of the abduction and murder of William Morgan by the Freemasons. The unanimous testimony of such men as composed that convention convinced me that their testimony could be relied upon as correct and really true. So, also, some Masons told me that these disclosures were accurate. With this assurance, seeing that there was need of light on the subject, I, from a sense of duty, decided to republish the before-named expose of Masonry; and having, early in 1849, made arrangements for the printing in Cincinnati, the work was published.

The result of publishing the expose of Masonry was a flood of defamation and persecution from the craft. The "Freemasons' Monitor," page 4, expresses the sentiment that the efforts of those who expose Masonry "end in their own disgrace." This prediction they aimed to prove true. I had read how they slandered and persecuted Professor Robinson, Rev. Dr. Morse, Rev. Moses Thacker, Elder David Barnard, and others, who, in the cause of religion and morality, exposed their secret combinations. But charity led me to think that Freemasons now did not practice such proscription. I was wrong. I found that all secret conclaves act in concert against any man daring to oppose any one of them.

The Terrible Warning.—While the work was in press I received a letter, dated Cincinnati, April 2, 1849. In this letter the writer stated, in a friendly manner, that he had heard me preach a short time before, and was well pleased. But he had since learned that I was about to publish an expose of Masonry, which, if I did, they would punish me, by getting a woman to accuse me and to swear against me, and thus destroy my character.

He Determines to go on.—Feeling justified in the sight of God, I determined to use my privilege as a free citizen. So I completed the publication, considering our pretended rights of free speech a mere mockery, and our boasted civil and religious liberty an empty boast, if we can be driven from duty by the fear of slander and violence. Indeed I did not, I could not, believe that men were wicked enough to carry out such fiendly threats. But I was mistaken. They did as they said they would.

The Woman Whom they Used.—On a farm joining mine there lived a woman whom I had reproved for her conduct. Her husband had died in 1847, leaving a family of small children. Her character was not above reproach; and, soon after her husband's death, her house was used for fiddling and dancing frolics, contrary to the custom of the neighborhood. About one and a half or two miles distant lived a Freemason whose wife was very sick. Shortly after she died he began to visit and dance at this woman's house. Their fandangoes being noisy, we, the neighbors, could hear them at our houses. Their intimacy being apparent, was talked of among the people. I talked to them both separately about it; but learning that they were offended, I and my neighbors concluded to let them alone. Five or six months passed; and, except once, when she called at a house where I was, I had not seen her to speak to her. About six months after I had reproved this man and woman, my book came out.

The Plot Thickens.—I had returned from some appointments, and was on my way to Ripley, when I met a craftsman, who told me that this woman had filed an affidavit against me, and he kindly intimated that I had better run away! I thought that they had better all run away (from their lodges), and keep on "running away." I put my trust in the living God, and proceeded on my way to Ripley, to the office of the magistrate, and asked him for that affidavit. He said that it was not in his possession. But I learned from him that a Freemason lawyer from Georgetown, the county seat, had attended to the taking of it, and had taken it away with him. I also learned that the Freemason man who danced at her frolics was in attendance at the taking of the affidavit, and I inferred that others of the craft were present.

Another Letter.—While at Ripley that day, or shortly after, I received a letter from the post-office, dated "Georgetown, June 16, 1849." To which there were twenty-one names, most of whom I knew to be Masons. This letter proposed that I should deliver up all those books to the Freemasons at cost, or my throat would be cut from ear to ear, my body quartered and burned to ashes, etc. One man, whose name was to that letter, was then a member of the Christian Church in Ripley, since deceased. He was a man of property and respectability, whom I had baptized years before he became a Mason. I immediately called to see this man. I showed him the letter with his name. He denied authorizing his name being put there; but told me I should not have published the book, and need not expect any sympathy from the Masons! I answered that I looked for none; I asked for none; for nothing more than justice. I was a free man, and demanded only the legal rights of a common citizen. Of course, all denied authorizing their names being put to the cut-throat letter. They said, "The author is not a Mason; but Gardner or some of his friends wrote it." Consider how vicious were such intimations, while they knew the contrary! Whether they did or did not authorize the signing of their names to that letter, they willingly suffered it, and their conduct, both before and after, in trying to prevent the book being read by the people, and to destroy the influence of the book, was little better. I did not give up the books to the Masons at cost! Who was the author of the letter? Did they carry out the threat of the Cincinnati letter? After the Masons got the woman to make her affidavit, the word was spread all over the country "that Gardner was in jail," or "soon would be," and would go from there to "the penitentiary!" The people where I preached were informed that they need not go to meeting, as I would not be there. It was said, "Gardner is done preaching," and they were "very sorry," "very sorry!" I kept right along, attending all my appointments as usual, and, the people understanding the matter, came out as usual, or in greater numbers. *The sheriff did not come to take me to jail!!* Desiring to know more about that affidavit, and the author of the *cut-throat letter,* I went to Georgetown and called on a lawyer who did not belong to the craft. We sent to the "clerk's office" and procured samples of the handwriting of different men, and, on comparison, found the cut-throat letter to be in the handwriting of another Freemason lawyer. We then sent for the Freemason lawyer No. 1, which had the affidavit in keeping. I asked him to let me see it. He refused. He said that he, as counsel, was not at liberty to show the affidavit to me. I told him that he, as counsel, as a matter of law, ought to show it to me, as it was my right. I had paid my tax, and did not think that the law should be used as an engine to injure me. I told him of the statements, which I could prove, that he and other Masons had made about me in relation to it. I demanded to know why he did not prosecute it. But he could not be induced to show it. Nor have I ever seen it to this day. It was taken for the express purpose of slander, and no one dared to bring it to light or prosecute on it. I procured the writing corresponding to the cut-throat letter, which neither lawyer No. 2 or his brethren of the craft could deny. The Masons, when shown the two, admitted that the same hand wrote both, and that their brother of the craft, lawyer No. 2, wrote their names after they had said that my friends wrote it. Did the Masons expel lawyer No. 2? No! Did they even call him to account for forgery? No! Comment is needless. Is it not clear that they were willing to have their names used? They did not venture to deny the handwriting, public indignation being too strong against them.

Freemasons at Work in the Church.—This year, 1849, the conference met in Russellville. As the time drew on, preparations began, and the Masons were busy. Early in the fall, some weeks before conference, one day, about one o'clock, my son was at work, in a field joining the affidavit woman's place. He saw two men, with horses, come through our cornfield, not far from the house, and cross a piece of woodland pasture, and tie their horses to the line fence inside of our inclosure, and go to the woman's house. My son came and told me. I went to where he was at work and waited for them. They remained there till late in the afternoon, and we met them when they returned to their horses. It was the Master Mason and the Master Mason's pastor. It was that Master Mason which had joined conference with the privilege of preaching, and that pastor who was acquitted by his church after the Pisgah trial. When they came for their horses and found us there, they looked confused and ashamed. I felt sorry for them, and kindly said, "I would not have gone through your cornfield, but passed your house and stopped, as brethren should." I invited them to come to the house and to stop, and to go out at the gate to the road, which they did. As we came across the farm, I said to J. F. Crist, the Master Mason, in an indifferent manner, "Did she tell you why she said and did what she did?" He answered, as if before he thought, "She says it was because you talked about her and that man." Then, said I, emphatically, "Do not forget that! Now, be sure not to forget that!" The Master Mason's pastor also witnessed that she said that. This was enough to satisfy any impartial mind. I told them that if any thing was to be brought before conference, I desired to know it beforehand, for

I was of the opinion that they were there on that errand. Elder McClain answered, "If there is any thing going to be brought up there, you shall have timely notice." Conference met. No notice of accusations had been given. I had been appointed to deliver the opening address, and did so. It was noticed that again, as in former years, nearly all the visiting preachers were craftsmen. One of these said on his way, "*I am going to help put the old man down.*" The affidavit woman was there, and the man who danced with her was there. The Master Mason lived there and his pastor lived there. So the pastor, as perhaps he had promised at the time of the visit through my cornfield, took the woman to his house. Elder John Ellis was there, and reported to have said, "All would go well enough, if one old man was in Texas." Perhaps he did not say it. It was evident that trouble was coming. I put my trust in the God of all grace. Now a charge was read that I had made "indecent proposals to that woman." Elder Ellis wrote the charge, and Elder McClain presented it, without the notice, previously promised at my house. I insisted upon an immediate investigation, and an open trial, but was prevailed upon to let it come before a committee of five ministers. The committee was organized; and the woman who had suffered herself to be used to fix her deadly fangs of slander into my heart was brought forward. I felt sorry for her. Her statements were confused and contradictory in themselves, and she got into a passion and would not answer the questions put to her, and so withdrew. The committee were ready to make their report then, but were detained to look for other testimony against me. I called upon the elder, at whose house she put up, to state what she told him at the time they went through my cornfield to her house. He was a man of truth, and reluctantly stated that she told them that she "said those things about me because I talked about her and the Freemason man who danced with her at her frolics." Had he stated this to the conference at first, the whole matter would have been stopped at the threshold. This was sufficient to satisfy any impartial mind that it was the work of a designing woman, directed by wicked men. One of the committee was a Freemason, but such was the testimony that he could not condemn me. Elder Alexander McClain being the last witness, the committee at once agreed, and came in with a report of my acquittal. Such was the testimony, they could not do otherwise. After the decision a resolution was offered opposed to Freemason preachers, etc., becoming members of conference; but owing to the influence of Freemason preachers in attendance from other conferences it did not pass. The book was now in great demand. Persecution from the *craft* was silenced, and religion increased in prosperity.

The Woman!—What became of the woman? Her husband,

at his death, was worth about eight thousand dollars, in a farm of nearly two hundred acres, and other property. She commenced her frolicking course about a year after he died. About two years after his death, when two daughters were of age, the farm was sold by a petition for partition, and bought by three adjoining neighbors, who deeded her about sixty acres for her right of dower. After she had been used against me by the craft, there came along a stranger—a strolling youth of about twenty-one years of age—whom she hired to work, courted, and married. She was about forty! Their affairs soon caused them to sell their home. They afterward moved to Illinois. There he left her, with little or nothing wherewith to help herself. The way of sin is the road to sorrow! A few years after this she died.

The Design.—The designs of the craft in procuring the poor woman was twofold: First, to save their fellow-craftsman, the frolicking Mason; and, second, to fix the disgrace on me, and destroy the influence of the book.

The Preachers.—The ministers of the conference understood the design, and, with few exceptions, sustained me like good brethren. Elder Z. M. Lansdown was one of those who were bold and true. Since then he became discouraged, and has since gone into the practice of medicine, and now preaches little or none. *The Presbyterians,* who are my nearest neighbors, upheld me as a denomination, and from the beginning sustained me. For this I shall ever esteem them. *The Methodist preachers* nearly all belonged to the craft, and said little. *The Campbellites,* of course, were loquacious, repeating every thing against me, with additions, but had no influence, as the people knew them. No doubt, many opposers of the faith honestly desired to put me down, but they were disappointed. Religion, all the time of the persecution, advanced under my ministry, as usual. *In* 1850 *the conference* met in Fincastle, Brown County. This was the first Southern Ohio Conference attended by Elder N. Summerbell, of Cincinnati. A number of visiting craftsmen preachers were there. A resolution was again offered, disapproving of preachers joining secret societies. It was opposed, but passed almost unanimously. Elder McClain moved, the same year, to central Ohio, and settled with the Shiloh Spring church, near the city of Dayton. He was deceived, and treated me unkindly, and we never preached together afterward. But he was not a wicked or a bad man. During all these difficulties, I attended regularly to my ministerial labors, and gave enough attention to my domestic affairs to keep matters straight, and so, by the blessing of God, continued to prosper. Our condition, for some few years, was such that my wife had not so great a burden to bear in my absence, as when she was obliged, even in the winter time, to take her small children with her and go out to feed the stock. On the 5th of December, after these trials in 1850, I was sixty years old, and ten more years of my life had passed. In some things I had erred, which, seeing, caused repentance, though I had not erred intentionally.

> My life has been checkered with darkness and light,
> But the sweet star of hope was forever in sight,
> Though oft I have erred (I confess it with tears),
> Sustained by God's grace, I have reached sixty years.

CHAPTER VII.

SEVENTH TEN YEARS OF MY LIFE—CAN NOT CO-OPERATE FOR ANTIOCH COLLEGE—THREE VISITS EAST—SKETCH OF THE CONFER-ENCE—PERSECUTIONS PUBLISHED IN 1852—SECRET SOCIETIES—IN 1860 PUBLISHED A PAMPHLET ON MINISTERIAL WRONG-DOINGS—ACCUSED IN CONFERENCE—LABORS IN THE MINISTRY.

A. D. 1850, on the 5th of December, I entered upon the sixty-first year of my life, with full trust in God's grace and protecting care through the Lord Jesus Christ. My health was good, for a man of my age. My voice was but little impaired. The winter was employed in attention to my domestic affairs, which I never neglected, and in preaching and pastoral duties. *Elder John Phillips*, who had, some years before, returned from the east, had now been appointed agent to sell stock for Antioch College. We met in Cincinnati, at a committee meeting, where he asked me to co-operate with him. I refused to do so, telling him plainly that the plan upon which they had started would never succeed. In the spring of this year (1851) I had made arrangements to visit the place of my birth, in New York. I also desired to spend some time in various eastern cities, and to visit some other places of interest. I started soon after the middle of May.

Journey East.—I went to Cincinnati by boat; from Cincinnati to Cleveland by railroad; from there over Lake Erie, to Buffalo, New York, by steam-boat; then took the cars to Albany; and from there went by stage-coach to Stephentown, the place of my birth. Though only nine years and not quite nine months old when my father moved from Stephentown, and I had not seen the place for over fifty years, when I saw it every thing pertaining to the face of the country appeared familiar as when we left there. The mountains and valleys, the brooks, roads, and pathways, looked as they did when seen in my childhood. The houses looked time-worn. I went to the house which we moved out of on the first day of September, A. D. 1800, which brought sweet memories of days long, long gone by, when I loved to be with my mother. How mournfully dear to my heart the recollection! There was a great change observable in the people we left there in 1800, and those I found there in 1851. Very few of those we left could be found. Death had called away many, and others had moved to other parts. I found many relations (the Gardners), but only two or three of those we left remained. The nearest relations I found were cousins and second cousins. All my uncles and aunts were gone. I tarried at Stephentown a short time. I preached a few times near the place where I was born. The Christians have a good chapel there, but I was sorry to find the church in a low state, with little interest. From Stephentown I went to Boston by railroad. My stay in Boston was long enough to visit Bunker Hill and other places of interest. On the way from Boston to Plymouth I passed the house of the late Hon. John Quincy Adams. It is a small white frame cottage. We were soon at Plymouth, and I was disappointed to find it a place of no larger size. It is not a seaport town. I went to see the "Plymouth Rock" upon which the "May Flower" landed her "Pilgrim Puritans," after their tedious voyage in December, 1620. These people, persecuted in England for "non-conformity" to the established church, sought a home in the forests of America. I went to see the "Rock," and found the place. It was once a very large Rock, but fragments were continually broken off for keepsakes, till its upper surface was below the level of the ground. The taking away of any more is forbidden. I saw the Rock and the place where the Pilgrims first set foot on the land of the New World. I then visited the Antiquarian Hall, a large building, where I saw much of interest relating to the Indians. There were implements, and instruments, and costumes; drawings representing Indian customs, and their kindness to the Puritans. One drawing represented Elder Brewster, the Puritan preacher, with his little flock of Pilgrims kneeling upon the sea-shore to thank God for his goodness and protection through their long and perilous voyage and safe arrival in the country for which they started. There was Elder Brewster's chair, too, a large, rough piece of workmanship. Near this hall is a large fragment of Plymouth Rock, inclosed by an iron railing to preserve it from being carried away. On the railing are the names of the principal men who arrived on the "May Flower." I paid the keeper of the hall a quarter of a dollar for going in. There was once a large Christian Church at Plymouth, but divided by the preacher and deluded by Millerism, there is little left. Christ did not come in 1843, but many still hold on to the de-

lusion. I preached there a few times, and then left by the cars
for New Bedford, where I arrived the second week in June,
1851. New Bedford was long the principal city in the United
States, engaged in the whale fishery. It was noted for the
number of its ships, the enterprise of its sailors, its extensive
trade in oil, and for the wealth of its merchants. Here I found
three Christian churches; two large, prosperous churches, with
resident pastors and large Sunday-schools, and one colored
Christian Church. All the churches have good congregations.
I preached in both the churches first named, and had good attention. I am more pleased with New Bedford than with any
other town or city I have ever seen. It has an easy and beautiful ascent from the sea-shore, a beautiful harbor, and a delightful country back of it. It seemed pleasant and healthy. It is
the only city I have ever seen in which I thought I would be
willing to reside. After spending a few days in New Bedford,
I went on to Fall River. This is a thriving manufacturing
city. Here I found a large, prosperous Christian Church, with
a good pastor. I preached on the Lord's-day, and a number of
times before leaving. I was kindly received, and was pleased
with my visit. I now left Massachusetts for Rhode Island, the
first home in America of my forefathers. In Providence, Rhode
Island, there are two Christian churches. To one of them I
preached twice, at night, as I could not tarry over the Lord's-
day.

Spirit-Rapping.—It was during my stay in the city of Providence that I became fully satisfied of the wickedness of the
delusion of "spirit-rapping;" that is, of departed spirits returning to communicate to the living in this world, by raps on
a table, things pertaining to the spirit world, or the future
things of this world. This delusion started in Rochester, New
York, about 1850, by two or three girls, by the family name of
Fox, of uncertain character. It spread rapidly over the
country.

Story of the Girl.—A young woman in Providence, aged, perhaps, fifteen or sixteen years, was told, as she said, by the spirits
to kill her brother, some nine or ten years old, with a butcher-
knife. This she did. She was in jail for murder when I was
there. She was acquitted on the ground of insanity. That delusion, from the prince of darkness, has caused much crime and
driven many to insanity. From Providence I proceeded to
Stonington, Connecticut, where I took an ocean steamer for
New York City. We had a stormy night, but morning brought
us safely to New York a few days before the fourth Lord's-day
in June, 1850. I remained in New York over Lord's-day, and
preached for the Christian Church there twice. During my
stay, I visited many places of interest; but my stay was too
short to afford me opportunity to visit the larger number of

places of interest. Leaving New York, I went to the wharf to take a steam-boat up the Hudson River to Albany. The two boats were on a race, and left that morning a little before I got there. I then took the cars, and arrived in Albany at four P. M. I remained in Albany one day, and, having visited the Legislature of the State of New York, then in extra session, I took the cars on the New York Central Railroad, for Buffalo; then the lake steamer to Cleveland, Ohio, and from Cleveland the cars to Cincinnati, and then our own Ohio steam-boat to Ripley, within five miles of home, where I arrived early in July, after an absence of about two months. I was in reasonable health for a man of my age when I started; but on my return the debility of age was apparently gone, and my vigor and vitality seemed the same on my return, as when I was twenty-five or thirty years old.

Antioch John.—At the church-meeting at Bethlehem, on Saturday, I learned that Elder John Phillips was in the neighborhood, and designed to use the pulpit and my appointment for the next day, and the congregation, to lecture on Antioch College and sell stock. I spoke of this in the church-meeting. There was no formal vote taken, but a general expression that the meeting on the Lord's-day should not be diverted from its original design. I had, previously to going east, told him that I could not co-operate with him, as the plan upon which they had started must fail. It now seemed as though he had made his appointment upon the same day of mine to compel me to co-operate, or make a diversion in his favor to destroy me. For Antioch was then very popular with the Christians, and not to favor it was construed as opposition to education. I not only objected to the ineffectual plans of the college promoters, but I disapproved of Elder Phillips' practice of —— exaggeration to induce sales of stock.

What Phillips Said.—Phillips would say to the people, "These very scholarships which I offer you to-day for one hundred dollars, will, in less than two years, be worth two hundred dollars, and be sought after, and can not be obtained." In this way he deceived the people, and sold scholarships to many poor men, telling them that they would never have to pay any thing but the interest; and these men were afterwards sued for the money and nearly broken up, and the college was a failure. These things I understood; consequently my conscience forbid my taking any part in such doings. When Lord's-day morning came, as I had been absent two months and it was a large church, there was a very large congregation. Elder Phillips was there, and before all the people insisted upon the right to set forth the claims of Antioch College. I told him that the appointment was not made for that purpose, and the people had not come with such an expectation, and the church, the day before, had objected to it,

8

and that I myself was not willing to change the appointment; still, I asked him to preach. This was contrary to my custom. I am not accustomed to ask any man to fill my appointment. He declined preaching, remarking that his business now was to act as agent for the college. I told him that, as the days were long, he could make his appointment for the afternoon, and those who were interested would come to hear him. He said, "I must hasten; I can not tarry." I then invited him into the pulpit. As he had declined, I preached. After I closed, he arose and said, "I came here to present to this church and the people of this country the claims of Antioch College; but Elder Gardner objects to my doing so, and says that the church, at their meeting yesterday, decided that I should not speak on the subject in this house; therefore, I shall leave this afternoon, and you will not have another opportunity," etc. These statements caused a sensation. Indeed, his words astonished me. I did not think that a man could make such a perversion of what I said. I arose and calmly told the people just what I did say. Elder Phillips said he could not stay, and so no appointment was made for him. However, he went home with a member of the church, to whom he sold a scholarship, and so was persuaded to remain several days, selling to others. He did very well, as he got his six dollars cash for every share he sold, whether the college ever got any thing or not. He trusted the hundred forever, only requiring his part, the six dollars, in advance. Thus he did very well, whatever became of the college or the signers. It was soon reported that Elder Phillips said that "the reason he did not preach in the afternoon, was that I turned round to him in the pulpit and forbid him." But in the following conference Elder J. P. Daugherty, who was present in the pulpit, testified before a committee, appointed to hear the case, that he neither heard or saw any thing of the kind. The case was not pressed, as Phillips said that any injury to him would injure the college, and the committee, being all firm friends of the college, returned a verdict of "no cause of action." I reproved them pretty plainly. Phillips afterward explained, and the matter was dropped. But I could not approve of his course, either before or after, though others might.

Death of a Son.—In July, 1851, shortly after my return, our fourth son, James Alexander Gardner, died of "bloody-flux." This was the first death in my family. I attribute his death to the unskillful treatment of the doctors. They gave him calomel, which is almost certain to produce death in this disease. He was almost twenty-one years of age. He lived some five miles from us, and left a wife and one child. He was a young man of excellent constitution. I had baptized him and his wife a few months previous to his death. Shortly before he died he said, "The spring of life is the time to prepare for death. I shall soon be among the angels in heaven, praising God and the Lamb." His mother was constantly with him through his sickness. His loss we deeply felt, yet we were comforted by his words. His mother and widow and infant son all took the same complaint. Indeed all our family, four or five in number, seemed afflicted with the same. But I did not send for the doctors, as so many had died whom they attended, for the disease prevailed that year. I administered to them myself, and by the blessing of God they all recovered.

Secret Societies.—The resolution passed by conference in 1850, disapproving of ministers uniting with secret societies, should have prevented ministers belonging to these secret conclaves presenting themselves for membership; but it did not.

The Three Masons.—At the conference of 1851 three Freemasons came forward for membership. I asked them if they were Freemasons. They answered that they were. I asked them if they intended to continue so. They answered that they did. Then myself and others felt it our duty, in behalf of our Savior and his holy religion, to object to their reception. This should have ended the matter; but our moderator, being a friend of the craft, ruled me out of order. I appealed to the house, and was permitted to speak fifteen minutes; but the applicants and their friends were permitted the same time, each, thus giving them an hour. There was of course an unpleasant state of feeling, for which they were responsible, as they knew that they would disturb the peace of conference by applying for membership. If they had withdrawn their application when the objections were raised, harmony might have been restored. As Masons, they knew that no person could enter their lodge if one black ball (the vote of one) was against them; but here were many. It was apparent that it had been predetermined to force these three Masons into the conference. Elder P. M. Devore, a man born and brought up in the bounds of this conference, whom I had myself baptized, a man of large influence, and a useful minister, rose and said, "If these men are received, I shall leave." The moderator, contrary to good order and former usage, called for the vote, and declared them elected. They were received. Elder P. M. Devore withdrew, and their names were placed on the conference record on a party majority vote. They were, of course, preaching to churches formerly raised by the labors of others. One of them, preaching to a church which I had organized, soon sent, by the orders of his church, for me to come and attend a monthly meeting with them in February. I went, not supposing that he would be there, or expect me to associate in the meeting with him. But he was there. I soon let both him and the people know that I objected to uniting my labors with lodge-going Freemason preachers, who had united with the conference on a party vote, and would thus cause division. I preached a discourse, proving that those secret societies were unauthorized by the gospel, and consequently unrighteous, and left. After two or three months, a notice appeared, calling a convention of delegates, that is, lay-members of the churches.

The Laity Convention.—On this call, representatives from less than half the churches met at Russellville, on the 4th of June, 1852, and passed a resolution, perhaps at the instigation of two Freemason preachers, no other preachers being present, that any member of conference who objects to the reception of a man for political opinions, or because of membership in the order of Freemasons, Odd-Fellows, etc., "*shall be deemed guilty of disorganization, and be dealt with as unruly members.*" The last lines are designated by quotation marks as the exact language of the resolution. What a resolution! What a penalty for objecting to the amalgamation of the church of God with Masonry! Of course this was aimed against me. The doings of that convention had not been long before the world till they were followed by a publication by me, showing that it was contrary to the usage of the Christians, from their origin, to receive members into church or conference by a party majority vote, and that those thus uniting were not members according to the gospel, being received, not by the whole, but a part, a part only fellowshiping them! Therefore, these three Freemasons were not members according to the New Testament. This was proved by St. Paul, who commands the church to be of "one mind," without "divisions," and says, "Mark them that cause divisions, and avoid them." I proved that these three Masons had caused division, and were therefore the characters which the apostle commands us to avoid. I also proved, by the standard works of the Masons, that a man could not become a member of their lodge if there was one "black ball," as that showed that there was *one* objector. Yet these Freemason preachers forced themselves into conference, where there were many objections. I made it known that Masonry has its own worship, altars, priesthood, prayers, and songs of praise, and is consequently a system either religious or sacreligious. Therefore, their members are not proper persons to become members, and especially ministers, in the church of Christ while they hold their membership in their own former religious or sacreligious society sacred. Having a priesthood, if they are not sacreligious, then they are a religious sect; and it would be just as consistent for a Methodist preacher to apply for membership, and be received while retaining his membership in the Methodist Church, as for a Freemason to be received into the Christian denomination while determined to remain a member of the secret Masonic sect or denomination. Also, I urged in defense against the unrighteous resolution of the lay convention, that none of our early ministers in the west belonged to the Freemasons, or any other secret conclave. I also referred to a case where I was present at the Deer Creek Christian Conference when they expelled a preacher for having united with the Masons. Therefore, said I, "The resolution to restrain our objections against Masons is a departure from former usage, and an infringement of the liberty of speech." The former threats of the craft, their letters, their combination, the lawyer intrigues, their endeavor to use the poor woman, and their failure, to which I called attention, were still fresh in the minds of the people, so that before the regular conference of 1852 the people had all the facts and arguments before them, to examine for themselves, that the regular representatives of the churches might be prepared to vote, to approve or reject the doings of the lay convention. The conference of 1852 met. The three Masons took their seats. The usual business of opening was transacted. Then it was moved to approve the action of the lay convention of June the 4th, at Russellville. Elder Devore having withdrawn from the conference the former year, I was left comparatively alone, only one or two being with me to oppose the action. The debate was prolonged through two days. I had been very sick, and being yet quite unwell, was very feeble. The three Masons led the affirmative. They were above ordinary men in ability, well informed, of good character, fluent in speech, ready in argument, and withal men of influence. They made their cause look quite plausible to superficial observers.

The Arguments.—They urged the liberal principles of the Christians. They insisted that as we take the Holy Scriptures as our *only* rule of faith and practice, ministers have the *right* to belong to Freemasons, or any other secret society, and, while they do not violate any precept of the Lord, should not be objected to. It was evident that opposition to the adoption of the action of the convention rested principally upon me. I was physically feeble, but replied about as follows:

Elder Gardner's Argument.—The resolution you desire to adopt prohibits the freedom of speech, and is in violation of our legal and religious rights of conscience. These secret societies have their own forms of worship and religion, and therefore their members have no right to seek admission into other religious denominations while they continue their devotions in their own. Several branches of the Presbyterian Church refuse to receive those connected with these secret conclaves. This is also true of the Associate Reformed Church and many of the Baptist churches. Nor do the United Brethren or the Friends permit their members to be connected with these secret worldly combinations. Shall we, then, adopt a resolution depriving a member of the freedom of speech? Shall a Christian conference stifle free discussion? Shall we deprive a man of the privilege of objecting to the amalgamation of these secret conclaves with the church of the Redeemer, and brand the minister or brother who dares to object as "guilty of disorganization," etc., as the obnoxious resolution read? Shall we do it? The discussion closed; the vote was taken; the result was announced; the resolution was lost. The Masons were disappointed and discouraged.

End of the Three Masons.—So the three Masons, being unable to muzzle the conference, proposed to leave it; and they left. One or two others followed them, after which the conference existed as it did in the beginning, in 1820, without any ordained preacher in it belonging to secret conclaves. Peace and harmony was now restored. As the three Masons were gone, Elder Peter M. Devore returned. As he went out when they came in, so he came in when they went out; and the ministers all labored together in love and union to build up the Redeemer's kingdom. The churches were greatly prospered for several years in succession. Elder C. C. Phillips united with the conference in 1852, but finding the conference firm in its own understanding of things, he left it in 1853, soon quit preaching, and became interested in politics. He was a man of respectable talent, a tolerably good speaker, and, with piety and devotion, would have been a useful man. He had trouble with one or two churches. He and Elder John Phillips proposed to divide the conference. I said nothing in public about it. They failed, and the effort did little harm. Elder John Phillips continued to sell his scholarships, and I said nothing against it. I knew that the people were deceived; but they knew my opinion, and where they did not seek my advice I left them to be their own judges. I took no part in it, so they could not blame me. I did not publicly oppose him, so he was unable to make any capital in that way. This Antioch agent was the only ordained minister in the conference who favored division. All the ministers laboring in conference seemed united in peace and love.

Second Visit East.—My health being now improved, I made arrangements to visit Stephentown, New York, the place of my birth, again. I engaged an excellent good brother to preach for the churches of my charges during my absence. My will had been written by myself and legally signed and witnessed several years before. Some changes having taken place in the family, likewise in the property, required corresponding changes in the will. These, and some smaller matters having been attended to, I started in the latter part of August, 1854. I traveled the same route which I did in 1851, and reached Stephentown, New York, the last of August or first of September, 1854. My first visit was so hurried that I had not visited the spot of ground on which the old school-house stood, where I went to school when not more than five or six years old, and other places dear to memory, as scenes of my childhood walks and rambles. I now proposed to go no further, but take my time to visit these places. A new school-house having been built at a distance from the old site, the old house was abandoned and had been removed, and was yet in existence in 1854, degraded to a shelter for swine. For two or three weeks I rambled over places familiar in former years. I climbed the mountains; I roamed through the valleys; I wandered by the brooks, recognizing many a loved spot "to memory dear," as expressed in the following lines:

LAND OF MY BIRTH.

Oh! land of my birth! I once more behold thee;
  Thy mountains and valleys and brooks still the same;
Though fifty-four years, I passed far away from thee,
  Each scene is familiar, and cherished each name.

I gaze on the house of my father with sadness;
  I think of my mother, who used to be there;
To her, in my childhood, I told all my troubles,
  She soothed me, and cheered me, and wiped every tear.

The first of September, the year eighteen hundred,
  These dear parents left for a home in the west,
On the beautiful shore of the River Ohio
  They found us a home, and now lie there at rest.

Oh, where are the friends and relations and neighbors
  Who came on that morning to bid us farewell?
Some are gone to far countries, but most I remember
  Are gone to the tomb, where their bodies now dwell.

It was here, while a child, that my Savior first called me
  To give him my heart, and his service begin;
Though many long years passed before I obeyed him,
  I found him still willing to save me from sin.

Now forty-four years I have published his goodness,
  And pointed poor sinners to Him who was slain
To give them repentance, and ask him for pardon,
  That they in his kingdom forever may reign.

In age I walk over the play-grounds of childhood;
  I think of comrades left in my tenth year;
Oh, where are my schoolmates, my once happy playmates?
  All gone! and I lonely am lingering here.

Oh, land of my birth! again I must leave thee,
  And part with the few I have found here once more;
Oh, help us, dear Savior, to pray for each other,
  And meet in thy kingdom where partings are o'er!

United States Convention.—The general convention was to meet in October, in 1854, in the Christian church in Cincinnati, of which Elder N. Summerbell was pastor. I was a delegate from our conference to that convention. So after visiting about

four weeks, and preaching several times, my health, through
divine grace, having improved, I bid farewell to my friends and
relatives in Stephentown the last of September, 1854, and returned in time to meet with the convention. The convention was
quite large, being composed of ministers and delegates from almost all parts of the United States and Canada. Among the
prominent members and speakers were the Hon. Horace Mann,
then President of Antioch College. Among the resolutions
passed, there was one disapproving of American slavery. This
was strongly opposed by Elder W. B. Wellons, of Virginia, editor
of "The Christian Sun," and a few others. The "Christian Sun"
was our paper published in the South. When the resolution
finally passed, Elder Wellons, in tears, left the convention. So
from that time (1854) to this time (1865) there has been a division in the Christian denomination between the North and the
South. Perhaps we may soon be united again, as slavery is
now dead and the rebellion is put down, and peace will soon be
restored. Elder Wellons preached once during the convention
before he left. The sermon was very interesting, and manifested good education, sound culture, refined taste, and talents
of a high order. Though I have ever been, was then, and still
am opposed to slavery, yet it was my opinion that Elder Wellons was honest in his convictions, and believed, like many
southern men do believe, that God had ordained that "peculiar
institution" as the proper condition of the Negro race.

Southern Ohio Christian Conference of 1854.—A week or so
after the general convention of 1854, I attended a very pleasant
and harmonious session of the Southern Ohio Conference. From
conference I went in November, as previously requested, to
Mount Joy, a place near the line of Scioto and Pike counties,
to preach a funeral. Elder P. M. Devore accompanied me.
The deceased was a member of a family who were members
of the Bethlehem church, of which I was, and still am pastor at the present time, 1865. The family had moved to
this place, distant fifty or sixty miles. When we reached the
place, we found it to be a newly-settled section of country,
where the land was not very rich. The place was called Mount
Joy on account of its elevation. The appointment was for the
Lord's-day. The congregation was large for the circumstances.
The Lord assisted me in preaching, and many "received the
Word with gladness." The people were anxious to hear, and
we continued the meeting several days. About thirty professed faith in the Lord Jesus Christ. By the peoples' request,
before we left, we organized them into a church, after which
still others united, increasing the church to nearly forty members. When about to depart, the people urged us so pressingly
that they constrained us to leave appointments and return in
about four weeks, or the begining of winter. We returned

accordingly. The weather was unpleasant, but the people attended, and many turned to the Lord.

Warned Not to Call!—During these visits we called on a number of families. Some well-disposed persons warned us not to visit a certain large family in the neighborhood, as they were accustomed to having dancing frolics at their house, and they were tolerably well off, and would insult us. I desired to go there, as, to our knowledge, none of them had attended meeting. I asked Brother Devore to go with me, but he declined. So one cold, disagreeable afternoon I went through the snow to the house of Mr. Jones, by myself. I had never been introduced to him, but found him chopping wood at the door, and spoke to him in a kind and friendly manner. He invited me to walk into the house. The subject of religion was immediately introduced by me. The family seemed quite reasonable in their views. After having presented the plan of salvation, through our Lord Jesus Christ, I asked the privilege of leading in prayer, which was granted. While I was praying, and calling upon the Lord, nearly the whole family were in tears. That night nearly all came to meeting, and the mother and two or three of the grown children united with the church. Mr. Jones himself, and most of the family, united before we left. By visiting and preaching in that section, from time to time for a year or so, with the Lord's blessing upon my labors, I baptized many; the church grew rapidly, and soon numbered nearly one hundred members.

The Two Bad Preachers.—It was, of course, unreasonable to expect me to travel so far and preach regularly, or take the pastoral charge of the church; so they employed a pastor, whom some soon accused of wicked conduct. Then another preacher came who was not much better than the first. The second opposed the first, who had the pastoral charge. Each had his friends, and each his foes. So they divided the church, as is too often the case, and ruin was the consequence. There are yet, in 1865, a good many in that section who still continue in the Christian faith, and are trying to keep up their prayer-meetings and live Christian lives, which is praiseworthy. But they are like sheep without a shepherd. I have often been urgently requested, and even within a few days, to visit them once more. But the distance and my age seem to forbid it. During the year 1855 general prosperity attended the churches.

Antioch College.—The condition of Antioch College being made known caused general sorrow in all who loved truth and gospel liberty. The school had been ably conducted for two or three years by its worthy president, Hon. Horace Mann, and the learned professors. The trustees had in the mean time been borrowing money to pay for the building, and to pay the president, and to pay the professors, and to pay interest, and to pay current expenses, and now startled the public by announcing a debt of $40,000. Then special agents were sent out to raise the amount. Elder N. Summerbell came to consult me. He thought that if a few men would give $1,000 each, the whole debt could be raised. I took a short time to consider the matter. There had been great mismanagement by those who controlled its business. Believing that nearly all the managers aimed to make money for themselves, and though I had sacrificed more than forty years of my life in raising churches and laboring for the Lord in the Christian denomination, yet feeling a great desire and faint hope that Antioch would be saved for the Christians, I subscribed $1,000 of the means that the Lord had blessed me with; and he immediately proceeded to E. W. Devore, my neighbor, who signed another $1,000. But the word soon came that the debt was $60,000, or probably more, and Elder Summerbell became discouraged, and ceased his efforts. The conditions of my subscription provided that if there was enough money pledged by a certain day six months from date, to free the college from debt, I was then bound to pay $1,000; if not, my subscription would be null and void. I prepared to have the money in readiness, expecting that the whole sum would be raised, but was mistaken. The failure was evident. I requested Elder N. Summerbell to return my subscription, and it was returned. He was not a paid agent of the college, but only a friend. The principal agent, Elder John Phillips, was much displeased toward me because I did not sign unconditionally, and pay the $1,000. If I had done so, it would have been lost, as so many other thousands of dollars have been lost on that college. The conference met in October, 1855. The reports of the churches were generally favorable. The ministers were laboring in harmony, which always results in good. It was a yearly meeting of ministers and brethren, and all were glad to be there. My health being reasonably good, I was able to preach regularly, and as usual attended to my domestic matters, not permitting them to become confused and entangled, as too many preachers do. According to a fixed rule of mine, my debts must always be paid punctually to a day, according to promise.

The Hay Stacks Again.—Sixteen years had passed since the Supreme Court had decided the case of the hay stacks, and the decision had been confirmed by the conference. Many had now forgotten the facts. Also, another generation had grown up, which had never heard them. Under these circumstances, I found that some began to believe the plaintiff's version of the story, viz., that as the Supreme Court had decided that the article written by the plaintiff himself bound him for fifteen stacks, while he had but thirteen, I had taken all the thirteen, and paid him nothing for them. Perhaps he had come to believe it this way himself, as he still continued to talk about my wronging him. So I concluded, if opportunity offered, to have another settlement in order to satisfy him! I was soon after transacting some business with three or four gentlemen, wherein he was concerned, when he told me in their presence that I had wronged him and his family out of $193. This was in January, A. D. 1856. I immediately proposed to go into an arbitration bond with him. I would leave all the dealings that had ever transpired between us, including the hay and the calf, to three disinterested men; and if they decided that I had, contrary to justice and equity and the gospel of Christ, defrauded him, I would pay him fourfold, that is, four dollars for every dollar that they decided that I had defrauded him out of. And if he failed to sustain his accusations against me, he should confess to the Christian Church in Ripley, of which he was a member, that he had wronged me. I also consented for him to give his own testimony, with all other evidence he desired to bring in, and the referees should give it such credit as they considered it to deserve. The three magistrates of Union Township, Brown County, Ohio, were agreed upon by us for the referees, a majority of whom should render a verdict, which decision should be final, and all former differences be forever settled. The trial commenced on the 22d of January, 1856, and lasted three days. On the 25th the decision was rendered, which was, that the plaintiff "*has not sustained his accusation against Matthew Gardner,*" etc. So judgment was entered against him for all the costs, which amounted to a little over sixty dollars! What a lesson! The investigation took place openly, in the town of Ripley, in the presence and hearing of many people. This silenced the plaintiff, at least for a time, but he did not make the confession as he agreed to in the bond, which is a pity. As I now regard this matter, although it would have been a loss to me of nearly $100 perhaps, yet in view of the trouble and perplexity of litigation, it had been better if I had borne it. His father was wealthy, and had been an early friend of mine. A brother was a lawyer of much influence in our county, while the family in general were respectable, and in tolerable circumstances as to this world, and all of them had been friendly to me; but in this lawsuit *nearly* all of them took sides with him. In the conference of 1856 the churches continued to report the same prosperity as in 1855, and for several years previous. The ministers were of one mind and heart, and labored together in love. When they met at their quarterly communions and protracted meetings, they were always glad to see each other and assist each other, consequently there were many additions to the churches. At the conference all seemed desirous for the advancement of the Redeemer's kingdom. We were glad to meet, and sorry to part. Several churches applied for the conference the following year, all anxious to bear the burden for the benefit of the meeting. Thus it was for three or four years. There was always a brotherly contest which church should have the conference the coming year. The decision was by a vote, and all were satisfied. As my health seemed somewhat on the decline, I concluded to take another trip to New York, and arranged matters accordingly.

Third Tour East—1857.—I started a little after the middle of August, 1857, going the same route as in my former visits. Through the protection of divine Providence, I reached there again without any of those disastrous accidents which so often occur on railroads and steam-boats. After tarrying among my relatives and friends about four weeks, being treated with uniform kindness, and preaching several times, I again bid my friends farewell, and my cousin, Mr. Rose, conveyed me in his carriage about twenty miles, to the city of Troy, on the Hudson River. The same afternoon, at four o'clock, I took a steamer for the city of New York, where I arrived before sunrise the next morning. I then visited and made a short stay in New Jersey, and then passed through to Philadelphia. After a brief visit to that city, I took the cars, which go through and over the mountains, to Pittsburg, starting in the morning and arriving at midnight. It was there that my father stopped in 1800, on our journey West. It was then a small village; it was now a large city. Then I was in the tenth year of my age; I was now in my sixty-seventh. Though I had been absent near fifty-seven years, and the village had become a city, I well remembered its location by the junction of the Alleghany and Monongahela rivers, where the Ohio is formed. My stay in Pittsburg was short; after which I engaged my passage on a small steam-boat, and embarked for Ripley, Ohio. This having been an unusually dry season, the river was very low, and we had a tedious trip. I was on the boat one Lord's-day, perhaps the first in October, and preached to the passengers. I felt anxious to get home in time to meet with our conference in October, 1857. I arrived just one day before it met, and by going right on I got there the first day, before the hour for business, with my health and strength greatly improved.

Southern Ohio Conference of 1857.—We were thankful to our heavenly Father that through his tender mercy we had the privilege of meeting with our brethren in conference. It was sweet to enjoy each others' society. The reports of the churches were favorable. The business was conducted in peace and harmony, as it had been for the past four or five years. One matter caused sadness in every heart; that was the condition of Antioch College. It had spent a great deal of money. It had paid none of its debts. Its liabilities were still increasing. Money was borrowed to pay the president and professors. The

Hon. Horace Mann, the president, attended this conference for the purpose of raising money, but I do not recollect any thing being done. The session continued three days. All the business was transacted in the spirit of love and union; and we adjourned in the same spirit, and in the same spirit the ministers returned to their various fields of labor. The spirit of union continued till the next conference. My health having improved during my eastern trip, I was able, in 1858, as before, to preach regularly to the churches of my charge, by being assisted, at my large meetings, by my brethren in the ministry. This favor was reciprocated by me. Many were added to the church, and harmony prevailed during the year. The conference of 1858 met in October. The reports from the churches, as for years past, showed continued prosperity. Conference business went on in love and union, until the invitation was given for members.

Garoutte and Michael.—Then two men came forward to unite, both of whom belonged to secret societies. One was Elder Noah Michael, a Freemason preacher, who belonged to the Miami Conference. He had lived for several years in the bounds of this conference, but had not offered to unite, understanding that he would be objected to as a Mason. The other was a brother, Charles W. Garoutte, an excellent young man, who desired to enter the ministry. He belonged to the Odd-Fellows. The coming forward of these men, who knew that there would be objections, was, of course, unexpected by all, except some who, it was clear, had invited or advised them to do so. Being asked whether they designed to continue to attend these lodges, they answered in the affirmative. I, of course, objected to their reception, and others agreed with me. Then the subject was open for discussion. It was now ascertained that two or three who, a few years before, were opposed to the reception of members of secret societies, had changed, and now favored the reception of these applicants. Here was a striking demonstration of the fickleness of poor human nature, and I said, "Who can be depended upon?" They repeated the old saying, "Wise men change often; fools never do." I replied that there was no such Scripture, but one in the Apocrypha says, "The fool changeth as the moon." And Solomon says, "Meddle not with them that are given to change." Prov. xxiv. 21. I said, if wisdom dwells with the changing, then God, "who changeth not," is not wise, but the weathercock is wisest of all. These men had also formerly opposed receiving members on a party majority vote, as contrary to the gospel, but now argued for such reception. It was manifest, however, that the majority would vote in the negative, and so the applicants withdrew. Elder Michael said that he should never again offer to join that conference. I then looked upon the young man, Brother Charles W. Garoutte, and loved him. I sought a private inter-

view in relation to his feelings and prospects. He manifested
a Christian spirit, assuring me that he should act for the glory
of God and the good of the Redeemer's cause, and intended to
discontinue meeting with the lodge as soon as circumstances
would permit or demand. Consequently, as I made the objection, I went into the conference and stated that my objections
were now removed. As no one else objected, he was received
by a unanimous vote. Soon after this the conference adjourned,
but not in the spirit of harmony and good feeling, which had
characterized it the six former years. Confidence in the stability of men was shaken. Personal allusions marred the spirit
of kindness. Wounds were made not easily healed. After
some months all, for the sake of doing good, ceased to talk of
our differences, and we had peace.

Antioch College.—Early in 1859 an arrangement was made by
the managers of the college to let the mortgage be closed, and
to let the college be sold, that its friends might buy it in at a
fraction over two-thirds its appraised value, and thus free it of
its debts. The Christian denomination, according to the report
of the treasurer, Mr. Palmer, of New York, had already paid
into the college treasury over $100,000 in money. This $100,-
000 was raised as follows: Fifty thousand in donations were
subscribed, paid in, and expended on the building, and
current expenses; and perhaps over fifty thousand were
paid on scholarships. Elder John Phillips, the principal agent,
and others, sold about one hundred thousand dollars' worth of
scholarships, at one hundred dollars each. Where the purchaser desired, he could retain his hundred dollars, at the dis-
cretion of the trustees, by paying the interest, six per cent.
yearly, in advance. This was to secure to the holder free tuition
for one student forever. But soon the resources began to fail.
Then payment was pleaded, and many paid their notes. This
gave only temporary relief. Next, under the pressure of coming ruin, suits were entered and payments were forced, so that
over fifty thousand dollars, perhaps, were collected on scholarships. This one hundred thousand dollars was all gone, and
the college still over sixty thousand dollars in debt. Before the
coming sale, special agents went among both the Christians and
Unitarians to solicit funds to buy in the college. These gave
the Unitarians to understand that they were to become joint
owners. One of these agents, Elder Eli Fay, came to me, perhaps in February, 1859, and asked me to subscribe. This I
consented to do conditionally, that the college should be held
on the joint-stock company plan, in which all the scholarship
holders, who had paid, should be equal shareholders with others,
in proportion to the amounts paid. Elder Fay said that he did
not doubt that this condition would be accepted, but objected
to my writing it in my subscription, as others might also make

such conditions. I said if agreed to the writing would do no
harm, and I would not subscribe without it. So he took my
subscription for one thousand dollars, with this special condition.
I understood that the same condition was made in all the subscriptions in our conference. A meeting was appointed in College
Hall, for April 19, 1859, to arrange matters preparatory to the
purchase of the college, at the approaching sale. I attended.
The scholarship stock plan was repudiated. A close corporation was adopted. The college was made over to twenty
trustees, of whom eight were Unitarians and twelve Christians—
of course, friendly to the Unitarians. This gave the Unitarians
entire control without remedy, for there was no regular election :
but the twenty were appointed to hold their office during life,
and to fill all vacancies as often as they occur in their body,
thus preventing any change! Such were the conditions of the
new college charter after the sale and purchase. Fay and
Phillips were appointed two of the during-life trustees to represent the Christians!!! The holders of scholarships retained
no interest and the Christians no ownership. The college belongs to the twenty trustees, and to no one else. The trustees
are neither elected by the people or responsible to them. In
the meeting in College Hall, before mentioned, when the agents
were called to report the amounts raised, Elder Fay reported
that about three thousand dollars in southern Ohio was keyed
up by Elder Gardner. This brought a call for me to speak, in
opposition to Dr. Bellows and many other able Unitarian and
Christian ministers, who all favored the close corporation plan.
I said in substance, "I am too much of a democrat to have any
interest in the trustee-aristocracy plan which you have adopted.
I labor for the people, and for the rights of the scholarship
holders. These are sacrificed, and the conditions of my subscription are in no part complied with." I could not give
money to purchase the college, to be controlled under the
charter they proposed. I called on Elder Fay for my subscription, and he returned it to me. Antioch College cost the Christians over *one hundred thousand dollars.* In order to its sale it
was appraised at sixty thousand dollars. Eli Fay was one of
the appraisers. The next day, viz: April 20, 1859, it was sold
for forty thousand two hundred dollars, with the understanding
that all claims were to be paid except those of the scholarship
holders; that is, all except those of the Christians. Thus the
college changed ownership, and the first owners, the scholarship
holders, were turned out without consideration. Elder Fay,
after saying that all the subscriptions in southern Ohio were on
the same conditions as my own, yet as soon as the college was
sold and bought, he hastened to southern Ohio, and before the
subscribers could see me, he told them that the college was
bought by its friends, and all was right, and collected all the

money he could. He was called upon by some to pay the money back. He promised to do so, but never did.

Church Divided.—In August following the sale of the college, the Miami Conference met in College Hall. The church at Yellow Springs was "divided. The pastor, Elder Eli Fay, was a party actor, and his party occupied the college hall. The other party owned the church building. Elder Fay, according to usage, arranged for visitors and preaching. His unkindness toward me was noticed, and spoken of by a number. The brethren generally manifested a Christian spirit, and seemed glad of the privilege of meeting once more. I was kindly invited to preach in the church by the party which owned it, but declined. I stated in the conference that there is more affinity between the Christians and the Baptists, Methodists or Presbyterians, on the doctrine of the new birth, and the influence of the Holy Spirit, than there is between us and the Unitarians. It was evident that this offended the two agents, who were two of the during-life trustees, and perhaps one or two others, who desired to lead the Christians into Unitarianism. Elder *Fay* published in our *paper* a number of successive articles in favor of union with the Unitarians, which I answered from time to time as his productions appeared. I stated clearly the marked difference on the vital principles of Christianity; hence he failed in his design. I did not suppose, until our conference in October, 1859, that this man was so greatly offended because I could not be led by him.

Southern Ohio Conference, October, 1859.—Elders John Phillips and Eli Fay were present. Elder Phillips had been a member for several years, but seldom attended. He was there in 1857, when complaints were made of the violation of his promises made in selling scholarships. A number said that he had wronged them. The evidence was positive. He explained, or apologized, with tears. I pitied him, and moved for the conference to accept his explanation, which they did. Sympathy caused me to commit an error. No man's tears should prevent justice. I was told that he was talking, at recess, of preferring charges against me; but he gave me no such notice. A resolution was offered to limit the discussion of questions to perhaps fifteen minutes to a *side*, until all desiring to speak had spoken. I feared unfairness, and offered to amend by granting each *side* equal time. They objected, pleading for fairness and peace, saying, "We can trust each other." I did not insist. Business progressed as usual till the time for new members to be received. Elder Noah Michael, who had said in 1858 that he would never again offer to join, had come near to me. I said to him, "Do you intend to come forward?" He replied, "I have not made up my mind. Some advise me to." He came forward with the others. The others were received, but his case was held for advisement.

Discussion on Masonry.—At two P. M., Fay, Phillips, and others in favor of receiving Noah Michael on a party majority vote, opened their argument, and, excepting about twenty-five minutes granted to the negative, they continued their argument till five o'clock—the time to adjourn.

What Fay Said.—Fay said, "The objection to receiving Freemasons is an incubus on this conference, and prevents its prosperity." I had already spoken, and could not reply. The next morning I spoke about as follows:

Gardner's Reply.—If opposition to receiving Freemasons is an incubus preventing the prosperity of this conference, why has it prospered? Why is its prosperity greater than that of the Miami and other conferences? I challenged them to name one conference whose prosperity equaled ours. I said, "Masonry has its priesthood, its deacons, its altars, songs of devotion, prayers, and its service for worship and burial of the dead. Therefore it is a religious denomination. Religious or sacreligious, their members have no claim to be received as members of other religious bodies until they renounce their own. Asa Coan belonged to the conference, and gave aid to the Fay faction. The parents of that young man, and a number of the family, I had baptized, and they were members of a church which I had organized years before, at Stout's Run, in Adams County, Ohio. It is a mountainous section of poor land. Many of the people follow the lumber business, and the preparing of bark for the tannery, as did the Coan family. Young Asa had been brought up there, and professed religion when about seventeen years old. When about eighteen he began to speak publicly. The youth possessed a mind which, with cultivation, might render him useful; so I took him with me. The pulpit I occupied was the first which he entered. His education was little, and I instructed him; and he soon entered the ministry. I assisted at his ordination, and gave him his charge. I introduced him to a church where there was an academy, which he attended and improved his education, and became popular. In 1858 he was opposed to receiving Masons; this year he favored it. He had become a Freemason! What Elder Coan said had not much weight; but Fay used him to give force to his argument. I said, "When that young man started—then a boy—I took him by the hand; I led him; I instructed him; I nursed him as a father would a son. I was told that he would one day turn upon me. And to-day he has opposed the man who taught him how to preach." He looked down, and made no reply. I insisted that the principle that "the majority must rule," in the reception of members, is contrary to the gospel, which teaches that nothing shall be done tending to the division of the body of Christ. I alluded to the condition of the church at Yellow Springs, the seat of Antioch College, where a small majority with whom Elder Fay acted caused a division. St. Paul says, "Let there be no divisions among you." God and his Word must be the ruling majority in his church. Majorities of poor erring men have slain the prophets, crucified the Savior, and burned the martyrs. Elder Michael knew he would be objected to, and at best be received on a party majority vote, while, in his lodge, no one is received to whom there is one objecting. Elder Michael told me that he had been advised to come forward. Those who so advised knew that it would produce this difficulty. He said that I misunderstood him in regard to "their advising him." Phillips then said, "I did advise him to come forward, and told him that I would see him out in it." The question was taken. A majority voted for Michael's reception. Elder Fay exclaimed, "Elder Gardner is in the minority, as he generally is." So there was great exultation over the result by Fay, Phillips, and others. Some considered Michael's reception an indirect vote for the objectors to leave, but I did not. I had often known persons to leave the church or conference when unkindly treated, as they supposed; but I never approved of such a course. There were many good brethren in the conference with whom I had long labored. We loved each other, and desired to remain. Thus the designs of the Fay faction failed. Had I then left the conference, the little influence which I had acquired by almost fifty years' labor, raising and organizing through divine grace between twenty and thirty churches, would have been neutralized in this conference, and to some extent among the Christians abroad, and Fay could have gone on with his articles, leading the Christians into Unitarianism, regardless of my feeble replies. Elder Phillips intimated that he had a charge against me. I at once demanded of him to make it known. This he refused to do. I had through grace borne all, and the people seeing their antagonistic spirit, sympathized with me. Then Elder Phillips desired a letter of dismission. This he was informed could not be granted until those charges were produced. He confessed that he had none. The vote was then taken on his letter, and lost; but, on reconsideration, it was granted. Fay was not a member. Both were, "during life," trustees of Antioch. Phillips purchased a large farm in Indiana, and went there. Fay went to the Unitarians.

Garoutte Ordained, 1859.—By the special request of Brother Charles Garoutte, I was appointed on the committee to attend to his ordination. He was ordained accordingly, and I gave him his charge as a minister of the Lord Jesus Christ, after which the conference adjourned, but not in the spirit of harmony and love, as in former years. There was party feeling, though no division, and those ministers associated in the following protracted meetings whose feelings harmonized. My communions are generally half-yearly, in May and October, on a uniform Lord's-day, and the meeting lasts three or four days.

The Great Storm of 1860.—The third Lord's-day in May, 1860, was our communion meeting at the Bethlehem church, which I organized, and to which I had preached nearly forty years. I was assisted at that communion meeting by Brother William Pangburn and Brother Charles W. Garoutte, whose labors were blessed, and quite a number turned to the Lord. We continued the meeting on Monday, at ten A. M., and met again at three P. M. The congregation was large. The house was of brick. It was thirty-five by fifty feet in size, and was nearly full. A few minutes before the hour for preaching, a heavy cloud appeared in the west, of a dark-green color, attended with a loud roaring sound. The ministers had ascended the pulpit, which was at the side of the house, and I was sitting on a chair, leaning back against the pulpit. The men occupied the west end of the house. As the cloud approached, the storm gathered strength, the roaring becoming louder and louder. Trees were swept down, limbs and brush were driven along, all accompanied by deafening thunder. Great drops of rain began to fall. The preachers waited, for almost utter darkness prevailed. Suddenly a crash was heard; then cries and screems could be heard above the roaring of the storm. Half of the roof, commencing at the west end, had blown to a great distance. The west gable had blown in, down to the square, and came crashing through the ceiling upon the men closely seated below. Then distinctly above all the din of the storm was heard the cry, "What shall I do to be saved? What shall I do to be saved?" I did not at first leave my seat. Having my trust in God, I felt as safe there as anywhere else, and I knew not yet the end of the calamity. I supposed that a shaft of lightning had struck the house; and as I saw the mass that had fallen upon the men, I said to myself, "There are six men killed." -None were killed. The rubbish was quickly removed, and the men were assisted out, bruised, but all living. A young man who had run from the house got out in time to be struck by a falling rafter, which broke his arm. His was the most serious injury. This was the great storm which swept across the great West in 1860, blowing down forests, churches, houses, barns, etc. The Bethlehem church was destroyed May 21, 1860. All started home with sad hearts. My home being twelve miles away, I went three miles, and tarried all night with Brother Hiram McDaniel, the church chorister. I awoke before day, and prayerfully considered the condition of the church. There were nearly four hundred members, without a house to worship in. The church would soon be scattered, unless the house was rebuilt. To build that summer required immediate action. There was a great conflict in my mind whether to go on home, to learn the injury there, or to remain, and repair the damage here. Duty said, Remain. I arose early, and said to Brother McDaniel, "What are your arrangements for the day?" "I have none in particular," he replied, "excepting to repair the blown-down fences. The hand perhaps can do that." Said I, "Will you go with me to-day to raise money to rebuild Bethlehem chapel?" I gave him my reasons. After a few moments' consideration, he said, "I will go with you." I wrote a subscription, and headed it with $125, and started. We soon met with two or three other brethren, who joined us in the work. We divided the country, and took different routes. Before sunset we had enough subscribed to insure the undertaking. We appointed the next Saturday for the subscribers to meet and appoint a building committee. The committee appointed a day some ten days ahead, to sell the old house, and receive bids for the lowest responsible builder to put up a new house forty-one by sixty feet, to be completed by the middle of October. Thus the building was sold, and the work of a new house went on immediately.

The Pamphlet.—During the spring and summer of 1860 I wrote and published a pamphlet on "Facts for the Churches, Elders, and Brethren of the Southern Ohio Christian Conference," etc. It contained, in brief, historical facts of the conference of 1858 and 1859, giving the names of the prominent actors, and an account of the things which they said and did. It gave also a concise account of the sale and transfer of Antioch College, and the manner in which the scholarship holders were first deceived by the agents, then forced to pay by the trustees, then deprived of their scholarships, not by any natural course of events, but by a cunningly-contrived plan of the "during-life trustees" and their abettors, who seized the college for themselves and their successors forever. *In this work are arguments against the reception of members of secret societies into the Christian denomination.* I proved by the "Masonic Monitor" that "the name of Jesus Christ is not in the whole system of Masonry;"—how could it be when their boast is, that the order is universal, existing among pagans and Jews as well as Christians? It gives the names of perhaps two-thirds of the denominations professing the Christian religion in the United States, all of whom object to their ministers being connected with secret societies. The names also are given of the greatest men in the United States who have and do oppose secret societies; as John Quincy Adams, Horace Mann, etc. It has also arguments against the reception of members into church or conference by a party majority vote. While preparing this work, the question arose, "Is it best to publish all this?" I considered it prayerfully. The Savior opposed sin. God's prophets and apostles gave the names of those who erred. Saint Paul even names Peter as wrong in some things. I decided that it was my duty to lay these abuses before the people for their benefit. After the publication, some objected to it. They did not deny the facts, but doubted the expediency of the work. It was published about three months before conference. In 1860 the conference met at Russellville in October. The party had all prepared, and soon after the opening, Elhanan Devore, a delegate, who was a deacon in the Ripley Church, and one of the "during-life trustees" of Antioch College, after the reading of my pamphlet, offered the following: " *Whereas*, The publication of Elder Gardner, which has just been read, is incendiary in its tendency and bearing, calculated rather to divide than to unite, to scatter than gather, to promote strife rather than harmony, hatred than love, war than peace; therefore, *Resolved*, That the author be requested to take the same back; that it be as though it had never been published; otherwise, that he be considered a mover of sedition, contention, a stirrer up of strife, a sower of discord." " A true copy from the original of the resolution passed by the Southern Ohio Christian Conference at its session in Russellville, Brown County, Ohio, October 5, 1860." The mover of the resolution did not charge me with falsehood, but indiscretion. I said, " I do not think that any man should be condemned for speaking the truth. If any misrepresentation is shown, I will gladly correct it." I asked that if there was any thing false it might be specified, according to the laws of our country and church usage, that I might make my defense. This they refused, but still garbled the work, misconstruing parts of sentences. I corrected their misconstructions, that the people might not be misled by them. They dwelt upon my rebuke of Fay and his faction in the conference of 1859. When Fay said, " Gardner is in the minority," etc., and they seemed uproarious in exultation, I compared it to a "grog-shop" scene. The language, I willingly admitted, was too harsh, though applied only to the Fay faction. Some brethren justified the comparison. Two Freemason preachers, who were visitors, objected most to my statement, that "the name of Jesus Christ is not in the whole system of Masonry." Elder James Maple, a popular preacher from the Miami Conference, and a Freemason, who doubtless came to advocate their cause, admitted that the name of Jesus Christ is not " in or any component part of the system of Freemasonry." Elder John Phillips appeared again, but objections being raised to granting him a seat, on account of his conduct in 1859, he only obtained it by a second vote. He was, of course, boisterous to have the pamphlet " nullified," as it exposed his Antioch agency. Antioch and Masonry were alike alarmed, and brought out their united forces. Masons, acting in confidence, secured the appointment of partizan delegates, and other Masons rushed in from abroad, so that the assembly seemed like a convention of secret society advocates, selected or sent up to advocate the very evils which I had exposed. These were trying times. Even some of those who mourned, as I did, over the inroads of Masonry and the corrupt conduct of the college, were wearied with strife, and preferred uniting with the guilty, to cover up the scandal and bury the heart-sickening corruption out of sight; and disgusted with the discussion, which continued a day and a half, these peace-loving members left for their homes. The Lord gave me patience to bear abuse from some who should have covered their faces for shame. Some of my friends advised me to leave, with such ministers and churches as chose to go with me. This I could easily have done, and I could have organized a strong conference; but, prayerfully considering it, I could not feel it to be my duty to divide the conference. I preferred suffering for Christ's sake.

High-Handed Measures!—Every moment's delay strengthened their party, as they held on, while those who were not partisans left, and some said that they would not vote. So after a day and a half the vote was taken, and declared carried. Then I was called upon to comply. This I could not do; so these men withheld my letter. But as our own, and the people of all denominations and of no denomination were with me, this would not do! So a brother kindly offered a resolution to refer the case to the standing committee. When this business was through, it was near the time to adjourn. The inquiry was made as to which church desired the conference. None responded. At length, after several had declined, one consented to take it "if they would be at peace." The close was not in peace and love, as in former years, when we all loved one another. Happy days were those! When will they return? Not long after the close of the conference, I received intelligence that the standing committee desired to see me. I met with them and received the following decision: Report of the Standing Committee in the case of Elder M. Gardner: "*Whereas*, We, the Standing Committee of the Southern Ohio Christian Conference, to whom was referred the case of Elder M. Gardner, in relation to a resolution that was passed by said conference concerning a late publication of his, requiring him to take said publication back, and that it be as though it had never been published; and inasmuch as Elder M. Gardner could not comply with the aforesaid request, his letter of commendation was withheld; and as it is not charged that said publication contains either falsehood or slander; and as we believe that no man ought to be condemned for speaking or writing the truth; and as we do believe that the aforesaid resolution contains more than Elder M. Gardner or any other man can possibly do; and as it contains language which charges him with things which they did not attempt to prove; and having conversed with Elder Gardner, and he saying that he did not design to include, with Fay and Phillips, any but those who justify their actions and identify themselves with them; and as he says that he is sorry, as there seems to be a misunderstanding in the matter alluded to; there-fore, "*Resolved*, That we request the clerk of said conference to issue Elder M. Gardner his letter of commendation, and re-store his name to its former position on the conference records; and it is further *Resolved*, That we recommend to said conference to strike off the resolution censuring Elder M. Gardner from its journal at the next session of said conference. All of which is respectfully submitted by the Standing Committee—A. P. Thompson, E. K. Davidson, Samuel Shannon. October 29, 1860."

A few weeks after conference adjourned at Russellville, the Christian Church of that town met in their regular church meeting, having a large attendance, and passed direct and pos-itive resolutions protesting against the aforesaid conference resolution, and the actors in the scheme by which it was passed. Also, about twenty respectable citizens, not belonging to the church, who had witnessed the proceedings of the conference, got up a protest among themselves, and signed their individual names, condemning the conduct of the party and the actors in it as unjust and tyranical. The extraordinary proceedings of that conference, and some leaders in our own churches at home, in encouraging popular Freemason speakers and Antioch parti-sans from abroad, as well as others, both at home and from abroad, who had no character for truth, usefulness, and stability, to abuse me, and, above all, enact the high-handed farce of withholding my letter, nearly destroyed the church at Russell-ville, and in that section of country. Bethlehem and some other churches resented the action of that conference as Rus-sellville did. But the report of the committee, when published in the Christian and other papers, gave very general satisfac-tion, except to the leaders who attacked the report in the "Herald."

Domestic Matters.—Being nearly "three score and ten" years old, I desired relief from worldly care. Our youngest son being now of age, I made a sale on the 18th of October of all my personal property, such as horses, cattle, farming utensils, etc., retaining only my own riding horse, and one belonging to my wife. The household goods I left entirely to the disposal of my wife. I was now relieved of much care that old men gen-erally retain.

The Dear Old Man.—I had observed the condition of the old man generally. It is about as follows: In his declining years he gives up the control of his property; others come in to take care of the old folks. The youngest son, or whoever it may be, gives little or no attention to the old utensils which the old man had labored to obtain. When he uses them they are not returned to their places. When broken, they are not repaired. Those who now use them did not purchase them. They will not labor to preserve what they did not labor to obtain. They regard them as of little worth, and prefer them out of the way, that the young man may procure others of later style and fashion. The dear old man sees his tools out of place, and gathers them up and puts them back. He next finds them broken, and goes upon his staff and carefully gathers up the pieces of the old implements, and takes them to the shop, and has them repaired, and puts them back in their place again. This he repeats from time to time, and from year to year, all the time fretting and worrying. His untimely care and unnecessary anxiety makes him and all about him miserable, not considering that the time is past when he has any use for them, or that they do not want them. He thus makes the evening of his life, when he needs rest, a time of toil and care; and instead of repose and quiet, he has torment and vexation. Having seen this, I determined, with the Lord's help, to avoid it, and sold every thing off for what it would bring. The farm contained three hundred and forty acres, and was a little over one mile long and half a mile wide. The original one hundred acres we had moved onto January 1, 1814, and still live there in 1865. I had bought other farms and added to it, all joining it, except about ten acres, one and a half miles distant. These lands I now divided equally between our two youngest sons, John Wickliffe Gardner and Elnathan Matthew Gardner, binding them to pay to me or to my estate a sum defined and understood, which will make their portion about equal to the other children. I thus, almost in a single day, freed myself from the great burden and care which had so long been upon me. After doing this, I felt, for a time, almost like a stranger to myself and my surroundings; as if I had entered into something like a new state of existence; perhaps something as a slave feels when he has obtained his freedom. It was but a short time until those cares began to seem repugnant, and it seemed to me that no earthly reward could induce me to take such a burden of cares upon me again. Bethlehem chapel being completed, the church requested me to preach the dedication on Lord's-day, November 4, 1860. The chapel was one of the best in the county, and my fear was that the church might become vain and prayerless, trusting in their house more than in God. The day came in pleasant and delightful. No day could be more beautiful. The house was filled to overflowing. The text: "And are built upon the foundation of the apostles and prophets, Jesus Christ himself being the chief corner-stone." Ephesians II. 20. The Lord blessed the word. The church was greatly revived. We rejoiced that we had a house in which we could meet together to worship God, built within six months from the destruction of the other, large, beautiful, and free of debt. The meeting continued over Monday. Elder William Pangburn was with us, and his labors were greatly blessed. On Monday this church, consisting of nearly four hundred members, by the vote of a large number present, without a dissenting voice, passed the resolution before named, protesting against the acts of the party majority in the conference at Russellville in 1860. A few weeks after the dedication, my seventieth year, like all other years measured by time, came to its end. It closed December 5, 1860.

> The days of my years are three score and ten,
> If by reason of strength they come to four score,
> Yet is their strength sorrow, and labor and pain,
> Till cut off; I shall be here no more. Psalm xc. 10.

CHAPTER VIII.

PHYSICAL STRENGTH FAILING—DESIRE NOT TO CONTINUE THE PASTORAL CHARGE OF ANY CHURCH—DEATH OF OUR DAUGHTER, LOUISA MARIA—MINISTERIAL LABOR IN 1860—DIFFICULTIES SETTLED IN CONFERENCE IN 1861—IN 1862 PROPOSE TO GIVE ONE THOUSAND DOLLARS TO ENDOW ANTIOCH COLLEGE—CONTINUED LABORS IN THE MINISTRY, AS THE LORD GIVES ME STRENGTH.

December 5, 1860, began the seventy-first year of my life. On the next day we were called to mourn the death of our third daughter, Louisa Maria, wife of Abner Devore, after only four days' illness. We had not heard of her sickness. She died in the thirty-fifth year of her life, and left seven children. She lived in Georgetown, about twelve miles from us. It was a little after sunset, when all was quiet;—suddenly the messenger rode up in haste with the sad and unexpected intelligence. We went quickly to the house of death, to mingle our tears with those of the children. Shortly before she died, she called her husband and children to her and kissed them, and bid them farewell; and near the close she repeated the following lines:

> "Jesus can make a dying bed
> Feel soft as downy pillows are;
> While on his breast I lean my head,
> And breath my life out sweetly there."

She professed religion, and was baptized when about fifteen years old. Lovely child! Louisa Maria is gone! No more

to return to this world of sorrow and care. Her toils and
troubles are over. Although gone, yet I see her pleasant smile,
as of old, when she came home and I met her at the carriage
to help her and the children out. I can yet hear her loving
voice saying, "How do you do, papa?" Oh, the blessed hope
of meeting our children and friends where partings are no
more! I now felt more sensibly than before that my physical
strength was failing. For several years the vitality of my
system had been diminishing. I could not endure the inclem-
ency of the weather as formerly. My health was yet generally quite good, for a man of my age. I had long determined
that if the Lord continued my life beyond seventy years, I
would discontinue the pastoral charge of any church after that
time. I decided to take this course, from my long standing belief that a pastor should never fail to fill his appointments.
This I knew must occur in declining age or subject me to great
affliction and suffering. I had previously resigned the charge
of all the churches under my care, excepting Bethlehem, to
other ministers, promising to visit them as often as possible.
Bethlehem was still under my care. I had preached there
nearly forty years. Elder William Pangburn, who had labored
there from time to time with me for years, consented to take
the charge, and with him the church seemed well pleased.
But when they came together, Elder Pangburn being present,
they were so positive for me to remain that he, seeing their
unwillingness, refused to serve; so the responsibility of continuing or leaving the church without a pastor; I agreed to
continue. The church is twelve miles from my home, which
is too far for me to ride in bad weather. In January of
1861 the Lord poured out his spirit, and we enjoyed a glorious
revival in the Bethlehem church. The meeting continued two
weeks, and there were over sixty added to the church. Elder
Thomas Sheldon and Elder William Pangburn were with us
part of the time, and a young minister of that church assisted
us in the good work. The ministers in this conference during
1861 chose those to labor with them whose feelings harmonized
with their own, so that, notwithstanding the trouble in
conference, the work of the Lord still went on in the church of
my charge, and other churches where I assisted. In
1861 the conference met with the Boat Run church, in
Clermont County. The unusual number of messengers
present, and the manifest understanding among those who
had been instrumental in passing the high-handed resolution
against me, the former year, made it evident that there was a
determined plan to reject the report of the standing committee.
It was manifest that they had predetermined this, by the unusual number of messengers from the churches. The debate
lasted through nearly two days. Some, disapproving of the

proceedings, left, and this strengthened the other side. The report was finally rejected. The committee then gave notice that, on account of words before written to the "Gospel Herald," and now spoken at the conference, together with its present action in confirming the same spirit, they should withdraw from conference. One or more of the deacons of the Boat Run church gave notice that, unless the wrangling ceased, the house would be closed, as the course pursued was contrary to the conditions on which the conference was accepted at the church. Counter charges came up against the leaders for misstatements. A storm seemed gathering. Fears were felt. Unforseen trouble was discovered. Increasing difficulties appeared, and a compromise was proposed in which all grievances should be referred to a committee of nine, chosen as follows: the party first accused to choose the first man; the opposite party the next; and so on, alternating in choice, until the number was filled, none being accepted to which either side objected. The decision of five of this committee was to be final. Bystanders regarded this as fair, and it was entered upon the journal. Then, on motion, a committee of three was appointed by the chair on grievances, to whom I had the privilege of explaining. The committee consisted of Elder Thomas Sheldon, Elder O. J. Wait, and Elder Asa Coan, the first being clerk of the conference, and the two others Freemasons. The pamphlet was read; explanations were made. The principal objection was to my using the word grog-shop in speaking of the Fay faction. I acknowledged that the comparison was severe, and the language too tart; and that there were other things which I would prefer not having written, and would not were it to do again. Elders Wait and Coan desired me to recall my charge, that "the name of Jesus Christ is not in the whole system of Masonry." Elder Coan positively declared that he had a late work, "The Craftsman," which made it clear that the name of Christ belonged to the system. I asked for the book. It was not present, but he would bring it to me the next morning. So I, resting on his assertion, admitted that point also. Other differences were arranged, and we returned to the open conference, where I stated that "*when that publication was written I believed it to be true, and so regarded it still; but if any thing therein had wounded innocent brethren, I was sorry for it, as I would have willingly stated at the conference in 1860, but such an explanation from me could not then be accepted.*" No objection was raised at that time. The resolution passed against me in 1860 was then, without a dissenting voice, ordered to be expunged from the journal of the conference. I had retracted on the word of Asa Coan. He was to bring the book. Elder Coan forgot the book. His statement proved incorrect. The committee were pressed for time, and did not make a written report. To Elder Sheldon's report they took exceptions, and each gave his own version to the "Herald." None was exactly accurate, but Elder Sheldon's, the clerk, was nearest correct. All make me say some things which I did not, though the difference is not important. Elders Wait and Coan should not have been on that committee. Still the settlement was made and remains. But the standing committee, not being all present, nor yet Elder C. S. Manchester, one who had censured them most, no corrections were made for the censorious publications, and no reconciliation took place. And contrary to my advice, for I am opposed to leaving the church or conference, the committee, for these and other causes, all eventually withdrew from the conference. Elder Alexander P. Thompson, the chairman of the standing committee, was then about seventy years old, and for forty years had been a member of that conference. He was an honest man, regarded by all who knew him as one of the best of men. He died two years afterward, without having a membership with us in any conference! All these evils arose out of the efforts of the agents and the "during-life trustees" of Antioch College to run Masons into our conference, over my head, in order to drive me to leave the the conference. In this they were deceived. The difficulties were settled and reasonable harmony prevailed, though it was evident that the great Redeemer's cause was wounded in southern Ohio.

The Aged Pastor.—It was my intention, early resolved upon, not to continue in the pastorate of any church after becoming seventy years old. But so urgent were the requests it seemed impossible to refuse. In October of 1861, a committee, sent by the Union church, visited me, earnestly soliciting me to become its pastor. This was the first church I ever organized, in 1818. I had preached to it twenty-eight years, and gave up from temporary loss of health. I could not comply; but finally consented to visit them the second Lord's-day in November, and preach on the Saturday before also. Elder G. W. Mefford was to be with me. Union church was situated in the lower part of Brown County, sixteen miles from my home. I had left it in a prosperous state, with about three hundred members. The first chapel, of stone, had given place to a good brick house; but strife arose. Three parties shared mutual jealousies. Preachers had been imprudent. The church was divided. Only tens instead of hundreds met to hear any one of the ministers who generally preached there. The great house seemed useless and deserted. Brother Mefford and I arrived; and the people, having learned who were to preach, assembled in large numbers and with good order. The Lord blessed our feeble efforts, and we had a pleasant time, and good attended our labors. I had determed not to take the charge, but had not positively said that "I would not," and I was urged to decide before leaving. The people were more urgent, if possible, than the committee had been. I consulted Brother Mefford, who promised to assist me, as he lived much nearer, and in the inclement weather of winter to attend for me; and then, in view of the feeble state of the church, I yielded to a sense of duty and consented, trusting in God for help. The following January we held a protracted meeting for two weeks. Over forty were added to the church. With a peaceful gospel, harmony and union was generally restored.

Bethlehem Church.—A. D. 1861, my last engagement with the Bethlehem church having expired, I requested permission to retire. This they refused. They would call no other pastor. They constrained me to continue, by promising to engage for me a substitute to preach in the inclement winter weather. So I continued my labors. The Lord continued to bless, and the church continued to prosper. Thus, instead of having no pastorates, two were thrust upon me.

The Great Rebellion.—A. D. 1861, the rebellion of the Southern States against the government of the United States began, caused by "Negro slavery." The official heads of the government said that this rebellion would be put down in sixty days. It was still raging in 1862, and the excitement caused by the war was destructive to religion. In 1862 the first great draft was made. It took to the bloody field, with others, many fine young men, members of the churches of my charge. Some were killed on the various battle-fields; others died in the hospitals; others perished by slow starvation in rebel prisons; and some returned with joy, bringing their religion home with them. But the dearth in religion was general. The churches were divided on political issues. But through it all, by divine grace, there were unceasing additions to the churches of my charge. For I did not preach the war or its causes; but Christ and him crucified. While other preachers pointed to present troubles, I pointed out "the Way, the Truth, and the Life." The members, though divided in politics, were united in religion, and continued in harmony and peace in the church. There was, and had been for some time, a growing dissatisfaction with the management of the "Gospel Herald," by Elder John Ellis, who published articles opposed to me, but refused my rejoinders. The result of this was that many of my friends refused to take the paper. Some brethren in Indiana desired to start a paper there, which I encouraged by giving one hundred dollars to help forward that enterprise, and "The Christian Banner" was started in Indianapolis, edited by Elder H. T. Buff. The "Banner" was well liked by all who subscribed for it in the bounds of my acquaintance. But the "Banner" had a limited circulation, and after a few months was bought out or united to the "Gospel Herald," Buff to be associate editor. The unfortunate organization of Ellis, which will not let him see any side of a question except that where his own interest is hid, soon developed itself, and the brotherhood was broken, and the " Banner" was started again to the joy of its friends. The war, however, increased expenses and decreased subscribers, so that the "Banner" subscription list was soon transferred to the " Herald of Gospel Liberty," published by our brethren in the East. This paper was, in turn, furnished to the subscribers to the " Banner." The " Gospel Herald" soon after this passed out of the hands of John Ellis, and Elder E. W. Humphreys became its editor, and made it an impartial paper.

Conference of 1862.—When I attended conference in 1862 I had with me "The Craftsman" book, which Elder Asa Coan said, in 1861, proved the name of Jesus Christ to be in the "System of Masonry." I had examined the book, and found that I had been deceived by said statement. So I made this known to conference, and desired to recall my former admission, that my publication was wrong in this respect. Elder O. J. Wait objected. Elder Coan reaffirmed. He was positive that there was a book on Masonry in which the name of Jesus Christ is found, in the "System of Masonry." I exhibited the book to which they had appealed in 1861. They had then asserted that this very book contained the name, and, on that assertion, caused me to apologize. Now "it was in some other work!" I demanded the book. It was not there! I demanded its name! They could not tell it! Of course there is no such book.

Woman!—I read from "The Craftsman" this rule: "No woman can be a Freemason." Then I asked, "Can the name of Jesus Christ be a component part of a system which, like Mohammedanism, excludes women? Have not women souls? Shall I indorse such a corporation as a system of Christianity? How can a system be Christian which they boast embraces Jews and pagans, but rejects women?" I insisted that I must recall my admission. The vote was called and carried, and I withdrew my admission; and my publication stood not canceled, but confirmed. I agreed that if they found any standard work indorsed by the Grand Lodge, proving that the name of Christ belonged in the "System of Masonry," and would bring it with them the following year, I would then, in 1863, give up my correction of 1862, and let my admission of 1861 stand. Elder Coan was clerk *pro tempore*. He promised to make the correction and publish it with the minutes, as part thereof. Then he wrote me that he would not. He did not. The correction never appeared! Promises were not kept. 1863 came; another year had passed; but no book was brought to prove what was not proveable. I had been deceived into a public admission, and denied public reparation.

Erects an Office.—Having freed myself from the care of the farm and such business, I erected, in 1862, a small building, to which I could retire with my books, writing-desk, papers, etc., and study undisturbed. This I found very convenient and comfortable. I also erected a separate stable near by for my horse, where I could feed and attend to him myself, and take him out and saddle him, without asking others to do it. This gave me agreeable employment, also I was thus less trouble to others.

Antioch Convention.—In December of 1862 a great convention met in Antioch College Hall, to endow the college. I attended, and offered to give $1,000, if $50,000 were raised. This offer was published in the "Herald of Gospel Liberty," our eastern paper; but Ellis, a during-life trustee of Antioch, who was then editor of the "Gospel Herald," omitted to name my offer for months, and then only alluded to it as not "worth a bill of beans," doubtless because I did not pay it to be used by the during-life trustees, though no more was raised. The college was not endowed! The two churches, Bethlehem and Union, positively refusing to relieve me in 1862, I continued the charge another year, Elder G. W. Mefford assisting me as before at the Union church.

The War.—In 1863 the war still continued, and still heavier drafts were made to extinguish the rebellion. Religious interest was hard to maintain, but by preaching, as before stated, peace, not war, pointing the people to Christ, not to men, and from troubles here to triumph there the Lord blessed his word and I kept my congregations, and additions to the church continued.

Discipleism Again.—In the early part of 1863 a Disciple preacher was introduced into the Christian chapel at Ripley, five miles from my home. His name was James Z. Taylor. He had been taught in Bethany College, Virginia, by Alexander Campbell himself. He was introduced there in the following manner: Ripley is a town of about three thousand inhabitants; but as yet the Disciples had no church there. The Christians, as in every place, were much in favor of charity and union, and had long borne with a disputing layman, who was always advocating Campbell's views, though he had joined the Christian Church. The Christian minister in charge was Elder J. P. Daugherty, a well-meaning man, though supposed to be a little inclined toward Campbellism. Elder Daugherty was induced to invite this Elder Taylor to hold a protracted meeting with him. As the meeting went on, Elder Daugherty being very kind-hearted, stood back, permitting Elder Taylor to take the entire lead and control of the meeting. Some came forward and professed faith in Christ, and were baptized by Elder Taylor. But they did not join the church, the understanding, doubtless, being to use our house to build up a Disciples' church, by either proselyting the Christians or organizing a separate society, as the Disciples had no church there. After the meeting continued about a week, there was an appointment made for the Christians and the Disciples to meet in the Christian chapel, to unite. The time came. Three or four Campbellite preachers attended, to add influences to their cause by their presence. I happened to be in Ripley on that day, and heard of the great union meeting. Being solicited to attend, I did so. The three or four Disciple preachers talked much about the advantages of union, in all of which Elder Daugherty acquiesced. After they had talked on for two hours or more, I rose and remarked that, not being disposed to make a speech, I would only state a few well-known facts, as follows: "To say nothing of doctrine or belief, there are great differences between the Christians and the Disciples in practice. First: Disciples do not permit women to enjoy privileges in the church equal with those of the men. The Christians do. Second: Disciples do not receive into full church fellowship any believers who are not immersed. Christians do. Third: Disciples eat bread and drink wine for the Lord's Supper, every first day of the week. Christians do not. Christians can not find any Scripture authority for it, and think that such frequent taking of the Lord's Supper destroys its utility, as it was established for a memorial not to be used every day, though the disciples broke bread daily. Acts II. 46." I then advised the Christian Church to take time to consider the matter, and appoint a future day to meet again and hear the Disciples' propositions, and then give them an answer. This they concluded to do. When they met at the appointed time, the Christians refused to go into union with the Disciples on the grounds proposed by them, and thus that effort ended.

Union.—There has never been a so-called union of Disciples and Christians, except where the Christians adopted the Disciples' peculiar doctrines, and practices; that is uniting with Disciples to exclude all other Christians. So this union failed. Had it prevailed, the Christians would have gone over to the narrow system of Discipleism, church, chapel, and all. Elder Taylor, being foiled in this, went on and organized a Disciples church in the Christian chapel; and he and Elder Daugherty preached, time about, each twice a month, in the Christian chapel. After a few months Elder Daugherty quit, thus leaving the Christian church without a pastor, and giving the whole field up to Elder Taylor and his Disciples. The Christians had by this time learned the short but expressive system of Campbellism, and could not be moved from their gospel liberty.

Sad Memories.—March of 1863 came in with the cruel war still raging. I felt melancholy as I thought of the tens of thousands of husbands and sons who had hurried to the battlefield to return no more. I thought of the thousands of widows

and orphans. Thus meditating, I heard of the death of an
aged man; an old and highly esteemed friend. Then I thought
of those dear brethren with whom I was associated in my early
ministry. Gone! All gone! The following lines then came
to my mind, and I published them in the "Herald of Gospel
Liberty," of March 26, 1863:

DEPARTED FRIENDS.

BY M. GARDNER.

*Expressive of his sorrow in the memory of the past. Written in 1863, the seventy-third
year of his life, and the fifty-third of his ministry.*

My early companions are gone,
 The friends of my youth are no more;
I wander a stranger, alone,
 And sigh on this desolate shore.
With sorrow, still mingled with joy,
 I think of my labor with those
In union, in Jesus' employ,
 Now gone to reward and repose.

My three-score and ten years are past,
 I linger and wait for the word,
When Jesus shall call me at last
 Away from this sin-ruined world.
Oh! what can this world give to me?
 Here, why should I wish to remain?
Where pleasures, like phantoms, all flee
 And leave me in sorrow and pain?

My journey I'll try to pursue,
 And hope to meet death without fear;
Through grace I'll then bid earth adieu,
 To meet with the friends still so dear.
For he who once died, but now lives,
 Destroyed death's power o'er me;
His grace to his children he gives,
 From sorrow and pain sets them free.

My labor on earth will soon end,
 Aggressors afflict me no more;
Still trusting in Jesus, my friend,
 To bear me to that happy shore.
And as he forgiveth my sins,
 I all sin forgive against me;
This grace, which my glory begins,
 Prepares me his glory to see.

This desert I traversed now long,
 Still seeking that country above;
My faith in my Savior is strong,
 Perfect me for mansions of love.
Oh help me to reach the bright plain
 Where no tears of mothers shall fall
For sons on the battle-field slain,
 Nor death for our loved ones shall call.

My loved ones and friends I'll meet there,
  Where sighing and death can not come :
Tho joys of that paradise share
  With Jesus in heaven my home.
Oh ! land of sweet peace and of rest,
  Where war-whoops will never be heard ;
I'll join in the songs of the blest,
  And sing with the angels of God.

After Elder Daugherty discontinued his pastorate of the church in Ripley, in the summer of 1863, they requested me to preach there. I spoke there first on the fifth Lord's-day in August. The text: "Behold, a King shall reign in righteousness, and princes shall rule in judgment. And a man shall be as an hiding-place from the wind, and a covert from the tempest; as rivers of water in a dry place, as the shadow of a great rock in a weary land." Isaiah xxxii. 1, 2. First: Jesus was born this king. The wise men came, "Saying, Where is he that is born King of the Jews? for we have seen his star in the east, and are come to worship him." Matthew ii. 2. Second: He was to appear as king before his crucifixion, while yet meek and lowly. "Rejoice greatly, O daughter of Zion; shout, O daughter of Jerusalem: behold, thy King cometh unto thee: he is just, and having salvation: lowly, and riding upon an ass, and upon a colt the foal of an ass." Zechariah ix. 9. This was fulfilled before his crucifixion, "as it is written, Fear not, daughter of Sion : behold, thy King cometh, sitting on an ass's colt." John xii. 14, 15. These facts have a "thus saith the Lord," but they reject them to adopt Mr. Campbell's system, which denies the crown to Jesus till his word can not gainsay their system. Fourth : Not so with Jesus' true disciples. They joyfully proclaimed him, saying, "Blessed be the King that cometh in the name of the Lord: Peace in heaven, and glory in the highest." Luke xix. 38. Fifth, I gave a sketch of the rise of the Christians in America (1795 to 1804) and their views. Likewise I gave the rise of the Disciples in 1823, and their peculiar doctrine, and dwelt upon their leading tenet, viz, "immersion in order to obtain the remission of sins;" stating positively that there is not a single passage in the Scriptures which reads so, and that no man could come forward and sustain that doctrine. I remarked that Elder J. B. Lucas, a debator equal to any that the Disciples ever had, had tried with me and failed. In a few days I received a letter from an elder of the newly organized Disciples church in Ripley, a lay elder, proposing a discussion in writing. He did not assume that I had not stated their doctrines fairly. Being well acquainted with the man, I knew his self-esteem to be quite largely developed, so I wrote him that I was not disposed to enter into a controversy with him, but would through him say to the whole denomination of which he was a member, that I stood ready, as heretofore, through divine grace, to discuss their doctrine before the people with any respectable preacher of their order, who would come indorsed as to ability, etc. He then wrote me, doubtless by the direction of Elder Taylor, "that if the Christian church in Ripley would indorse me, they would find a man to meet me." This was, of course, intended as an insult and evasion, as they had their meetings in the chapel, and the Christian church was without pastor or church meetings for business. The deacons and leaders expressed a willingness to indorse me, and said that the church would if they had meetings. We well knew that at any called meeting the Disciples would rush in and make disturbance.

Conference of 1863.—In the meantime conference met. But the unknown book, by which it was to be shown that the name of Jesus' Christ was in the system of Masonry, which book the Masons had promised to produce, was not there; an admission by them that my publication was true, and their denial of my statement was incorrect. A resolution was passed, by a unanimous vote, fully indorsing me, and entered upon the journal of the conference, to be published in the minutes. A copy, signed by the clerk and moderator, was given to me then, in view of the discussion at Ripley. After conference my next appointment in the Christian chapel in Ripley was for the Lord's-day, the 29th of November. The appointment was noticed in the "Ripley Bee," the newspaper of the place, in which paper the subject was announced as follows: "Does the gospel teach remission of sins by immersion?" The congregation was large. I first, of course, named the discussion proposed by the "Campbellites," provided I could be "indorsed." I then read the indorsement of the whole conference. I next proceeded with my subject. The text was, "The beginning of the gospel of Jesus Christ, the Son of God." Mark I. 1. The gospel began with the preaching of the Son of God. Acts X. 36: Heb. II. 3. I exposed the great absurdity of Campbell's system, that the gospel was not preached till Peter preached it on the day of Pentecost, for which they have no Scripture. For the contrary, see Luke IV. 18 and VII. 22. The life, death, and resurrection were all preached and believed before. See Luke XXIV. 25–27. So Christ's preaching was the gospel as recorded by the evangelists; and his miracles, as healing the sick and raising the dead, were not the gospel, but the manifestations of his power, and the evidence of his mission. See Luke VII. 22 and Acts II. 22. So, by the resurrection, God "hath given assurance unto all men, in that he hath raised him from the dead." Acts XVII. 31. By the commission on which Christ sent out his apostles, they were to preach that "repentance and remission of sins should be preached in his name among all nations, beginning at Jerusalem." Luke XXIV. 47. And so they did preach "repentance to Israel, and forgiveness of sins," but not without prayer and conversion.   he first promise by Peter at Pentecost was to prayer (Acts II. 11); and in Acts III. 19 he explains the necessity of conversion.   I also showed that when Jesus sent out the apostles, after his resurrection, he told them to teach the things which he had taught them (Matt. XXVIII. 20)—"this gospel" (Matt. XXIV. 14), not another—of baptism, in order to remission.   Nor could any man come forward and show that Jesus ever sent men to preach this new gospel.   I illustrated the *absurdity* of the *system* of remission by immersion.   It makes man dependent upon his fellow-man to obtain pardon, and upon water to obtain remission. Without both these, God himself can not remit a man's sins. This deprives God of power to pardon without the presence of water and an administrator, which, in many times and places, are inaccessible.   Can it be thought strange that they shun investigation when confronted with any man well versed in the Scriptures? for no man can sustain such a theory.   I required a man fully indorsed; because there are so many men among that people whose self-esteem is too largely developed.   A number had proposed to debate with me, whom I agreed to meet on condition that they come indorsed as to ability, etc., by their leading ministers, which indorsement they could not obtain, proving that their reputation did not equal their self-esteem. As I granted what I asked, I obtained indorsement, though I knew that their demand was insincere, and that they could find no man of ability who would undertake to defend their *system* in discussion with me.   At the close of the discourse, I laid the matter before the people, and read the indorsement of conference.   They did not produce their man, as they promised, and the community decided that they had acted dishonorably.   It was manifest that they knew that the system could not be defended.   They then laid the blame upon the lay elder, viz., E. McKinley, who had written to me.   They said that he was not authorized to make the proposition.   Thus they made a scapegoat of their friend.

Meets Taylor.—A few weeks after this, sometime in December, 1863, having some business in the clerk's office in Georgetown, the county seat, and learning that this same Elder Taylor was holding a protracted meeting in the Christian meetinghouse there, I went in.   He came to me, appearing to be glad to see me.   He invited me into the pulpit, and to open the meeting with prayer, which I did.   He then read, as is their custom, perhaps, half a chapter, and announced for his subject, "The Spirit itself beareth witness with our spirit, that we are the children of God."   Rom. VIII. 16.   His subject was a gratification to me, as I had been told by some ministers who had heard him, that he said that the written Word was the only Spirit, and that the Spirit of God did not operate or influence any human being in any way except by words spoken or written. Thinking there must be some mistake, I was glad to hear for myself. He soon convinced me, however; for, being a ready speaker, he soon launched forth in a strain of ridicule against the generally received doctrine of the Spirit's work, declaring "that the Holy Spirit never operated in any other way than by words spoken or written" I meditated whether I should, by my silence, consent to the doctrine, and thus deceive the people, or make known my objections. I decided to take the latter course. He closed the sermon, extended an invitation for members; and, descending from the pulpit, he stood upon the platform while the congregation arose and sang. No converts came forward; and at the close of the singing, he turned to me and said, "Dismiss." I then arose and requested the people to be seated a few minutes, after which I remarked about as follows:

Elder Gardner's Remarks.—I have often been asked why the Christians and the Disciples are not united as one people, as both accept the Scriptures as their only rule of faith and practice. One of the reasons has just been stated in the discourse to which you have listened, namely, that "the written word is God's Spirit, and there is no other spirit of God, or Holy Ghost, to operate upon the human heart; to reprove the sinner, or to comfort the Christian." This I do not believe. When Jesus said that God would "give his Holy Spirit to them that ask him," he did not mean to be understood that God will give us another written Bible, or even speak words vocally to us. He made no attempt to prove his doctrine, or justify his rejection of the Holy Spirit's gracious work, but took the easier labor of personal abuse, falling into the current course of Campbell and his disciples in slandering me, as they had done for fifty years.

Elder Taylor's Rejoinder.—He said, "He wants me to debate with him," and intimated that he would do it but for my character. This was personal abuse, and I replied:

The Aged Minister's Reply.—"Fellow citizens: I am an aged man. I am now seventy-three years old. You knew me when I was young. I have lived in this county sixty-three years. I have grown old among you. I have preached in this county over fifty years. You know me. Your father's knew me. I have been your neighbor while generations have been born, and have passed away! I am no adventurer. I have now charge of two churches in this county, one of which I have been in the pastoral charge of over forty years. It has now over four hundred members. This house, where Elder Taylor has preached to-night, was built under my labors. These hands of mine performed work upon this building. I helped to erect it, and it belongs to the Christians. We have the deed for it, as the records will show. And now this man (pointing toward him with my finger), who has been but a few months in the state or county, makes a public attack upon my character!" The people had by this time become very indignant toward him, as was plainly evident. Elder Taylor exclaimed, "I have heard something said against your character." Gardner replied, "So I have heard something said against your character, too, sir!" At this there was a general clapping of hands. (He did not ask me to be more specific. It was hinted that he was a little too familiar with certain females in Ripley, and, as will be seen, he did not care to provoke investigation.) As my papers were in my pocket, I read my letter of commendation. I then stated that the conference numbered about three thousand church-members and over thirty ministers, and, said I, "This individual attacks my character!" He wilted. Then one of his brethren whispered to him to dismiss, which he did. He left the town the next morning. He left the county and state in a few days.

Ripley Chapel.—By some arrangement with the trustees, the Disciples continued to occupy the Christian chapel for nearly or quite a year. So, when my engagements closed with the churches of my charge, that is, Union and Bethlehem, as they would not consent for me to leave them, I continued my engagement with them for 1864.

Revival in Bethlehem.—In February of 1864, the Lord blessed us with a glorious revival in the Bethlehem church. Between forty and fifty were converted, and united with the church.

The War.—There were calls for troops now by the government every year from 1862 to 1865, requiring from three to seven hundred thousand men each year. The draft for 1864 came in February, for five hundred thousand men. New recruits were called for, to serve in the great campaigns under Generals Grant and Sherman. Great numbers of fine young men, and many in middle age, responded to their country's call, and went to the battle-field. Some of these had enlisted under the King of Saints, and now left us, never to return. Numbers, while home on furlough, united with the church, and returned to the army with confiding trust in Christ and his divine protection.

Extraordinary Incident—There was in the Bethlehem church an elderly sister, rising seventy years of age, whose youngest son was in the army. She had little or no education, having come to the country in childhood, before schools were established. When letters came from her darling son, she had some one read and answer them for her. When calling upon her, she desired me to set her a copy that she might write to her child. I did so. First I made for her all the letters of the alphabet separately. Then on another line I joined them into syllables and words. I had no faith that she would ever learn to write, but did it to oblige her. To my astonishment, when I called a few weeks after, she handed me a tolerably intelligent letter that she had written to her son, and from this time corresponded with the loved one independently. What a beautiful lesson of the power of motherly tenderness and love.

Churches.—Amid the general dearth in 1864, the churches of my charge continued to prosper. General religious interest was sadly paralyzed in all denominations by the great war excitement and the patriotic desire to put down the rebellion. By grace I was able to meet nearly all my appointments regularly. I missed but one or two days during the winter; then a substitute preached for me. I preach, as usual, many funerals —some for soldiers, who were killed far away in the army, or in rebel prisons, or in hospitals.

Autobiography.—All the time not employed in preaching, from May, 1864, and on, was closely occupied in writing this work.

Conference of 1864.—At this conference all was peace. The reports from the churches did not represent them in a prosperous condition. Some ministers had gone to the war. Others were preaching but little, discouraged in their efforts to do good on account of the prevailing war excitement. A. D. 1865, at the close of 1864, I again requested the Union and Bethlehem churches to release me. Bethlehem would not hear to my leaving, and persuaded me to continue my labors with them during 1865, by permitting me to have a substitute during the inclement winter weather. I failed, however, to obtain a substitute. Union church, having had the labors of Elder Mefford since 1861 laboring in union with me, now consented to have him take the pastoral charge by my consenting to attend with him as often as possible, agreeable to his request.

Begins to Fail.—The disagreeable weather of January and February of 1865 confined me so much to my home that I preached little, except at my regular monthly appointments at Bethlehem. The vitality of my constitution became so much diminished that I could not endure the cold as heretofore. But while confined to my house I could not feel satisfied. My desire was to preach Christ and him crucified to lost sinners. I did get out to a few protracted meetings that winter, and saw some sinners bow to the scepter of love and mercy. Indeed, while earnestly engaged in this writing, I was dissatisfied, as though it were a waste of time. It seemed to me that I should be preaching, and as soon as spring opened I went into the work.

The War Closing.—During the forepart of April of this year (1865), Richmond, the capital of the rebel states, was captured by General Grant, to whom General Lee, the commander-in-chief of the rebel forces, being unable to escape, surrendered in a few days, with all his army. Then there was great rejoicing all over the country, and all with joy anticipated a speedy peace. This, indeed, was the first ray of light, as to our coun-

try's prospects, that had come to give real joy to my mind for
four years.

Assassination of the President.—But the gladness, like all
earthly pleasures, was short lived, for in a few days there came
an overwhelming wave of sorrow, in the sad intelligence that
Abraham Lincoln, the President of the United States, had been
assassinated. The murder was perpetrated in a theater in
Washington City, by a rebel-sympathizing desperado named
Booth. The death of Lincoln filled the land with universal
gloom, dissipating all the former joy and gladness on account of
the wonderful victories which were won by our armies. Old
men wept like children, and the voice of mirth was hushed in
the young. Churches were draped in mourning, and a nation
mourned the death of its chief. Our communion meetings during 1865 with the Union and Bethlehem churches were very
interesting, there being some additions to the former, and some
ten or twelve to the latter.

July 4, 1865.—This is the seventy-fifth "Fourth of July"
which I have lived to see—three quarters of a century! Upon
this day I am at work upon this sketch of my eventful life, preparatory to starting East in a few weeks, to see the land of my
birth once more. My health is good, for a man of my years.

Mrs. Gardner.—The wife of my one and only marriage is still
living, and is in as good health as can be expected, for a woman
of her age. I am seventy-five years old, lacking five months,
and she is seventy-two years old, lacking two months.

Voice, Etc.—My voice is yet good. I can preach twice a day.
I can sing almost as well as ever, for a few verses at a time.
My hearing is yet good. For all these, and the manifold mercies constantly continued unto me, I thank my heavenly Father
every day. I have not lived a day for the past near forty-five
years without offering prayer and thanksgiving to God.

Past Life Reviewed.—In looking over my past life, I can see
some missteps; but I do not think, if I had it to live over again,
that, taking it "for all in all," I could make much if any improvement upon it. I have had to bear a great deal from jealousy and envy, even of preachers from whom I expected aid
and sympathy in my efforts to make mankind better, by preaching the gospel of peace and love to them. My aim in all my
transactions has been to do unto all men as I would have them
do unto me. I remember but one or two instances where I ever
made a misrepresentation in my business transactions. These
were where the amounts involved were of little value; but they
caused me sincere repentance and a willingness to restore four-
fold, if it could have been done. I have been much calumni-
ated, and have always, perhaps too often, when the originators
or actors could be found, proved, by investigation, the accusations to be false and malicious slanders. There were two kinds

of detraction which could not be reached, one being that I had once proposed to unite with the Masons, but, being rejected, I had then and for that cause opposed these secret conclaves being amalgamated with the church by joint membership, that is, by having their members for our preachers. This I have openly and often pronounced false. I never proposed my name to a Masonic lodge; but still the lower class of dishonorable Masons continued to propagate the detraction, solely to injure me. The more honorable Masons and Odd-Fellows would not do so. Many of them were and are my friends, and confess that, though I oppose them, they believe me to be an honest man. The other detraction which could not be readily repelled because of the impropriety of alluding to such things in public, was that propagated clandestinely by Campbellites and other enemies to me or to the church, and regarded obscene talk about women. The defamers would not commit themselves, but pretend that they had heard something, and thus persevere in scandals most damaging to a minister's character, until time would prove all to be false, and make them ashamed. I, in the meantime, knowing my innocence, and understanding their motive, disappointed their intentions by putting my trust in God's divine protection, and keeping straight along laboring for the Lord. I do not deny that from the time I was conscious of a mother's gentle love, respectable female society has been pleasant to me, except when, for study, writing, or other causes, I desired to be alone. But, with the following advice from high authority in my mind, "Converse sparingly, and conduct thyself prudently with women," there have been but few instances in my life where sociability has been permitted by me to go beyond the bounds of Christian propriety, and then with no evil intentions. But where I have discovered any sign of evil, it has caused me repentance and future watchfulness and prayer. Thus it has been, as I believe, divine protection that has preserved me in the hour of temptation, and enabled me to avoid that great wickedness which too many fall into. The story of Genesis xxxix. 10 will bear repeating. Others erring, have been reproved, and become the enemies of those who cautioned them; but ingratitude can never force a true man to be unkind or unmerciful. I have been greatly deceived by my fellow-men. Friendship has been often proved to be limited to self-interest; therefore, the following lines have been truly applicable to the friendship of many for me :

"And friendship—rarest gem of earth!—
Who e'er hath found the jewel his?
Frail, false, and fickle! little worth!
Who asks for friendship as it is?"

Twenty-two churches have been, through divine grace, organized by my labors. Having not kept a particular account of all those who embraced religion under my ministry, I can only state the result of subsequent calculations, which is as follows: *About five thousand* have been received into the church under my preaching.

Union Church.—Of this number over one thousand were received into the Union Church, as shown by the records, during my first twenty-eight years' pastorate, not including those received into other churches where I labored.

Bethlehem Church.—Into the Bethlehem Church, during my pastorate of over forty years, upward of thirteen hundred members were received. This leaves only one-half of the five thousand to be made up from the numbers received into the twenty other churches raised by my labors, and elsewhere. Therefore, it is certain that the number exceeds five thousand.

Disappointments.—During my forty years' pastorate of the Bethlehem Church, I have made but two disappointments: one occurred when I was sick; the other, when high water rendered the streams impassable, before bridges were built.

Denominationalism.—It has often been a question in my mind whether my labors might not have been more useful had I united with some popular denomination, instead of laboring with what was then the new, small, weak, and much persecuted Christian Church. It is probable that I would have avoided much persecution; but would I have done more good? I could not have been sentimentally honest, as I do not regard their position scriptural. I have preached as I believed. The Lord has blessed me in it; and, was it to do again, I can not see how I could do otherwise.

Consolation.—One of the greatest consolations now is, that hundreds who had embraced religion under my ministry have died happy, leaving evidence that they have gone to peace and rest. This itself is more than full reward for all my toil in fifty-four years preaching. I forgive all who have harmed or injured me.

Will.—I have for several years past been determined to re-write my will, which was written several years ago, as I desired to make some small alterations therein. One of these changes is to make a bequest for the publishing of my life. On the 18th of July, 1865, I wrote a new will, in which I made said bequest. After signing the will and having it witnessed, on the 19th of July, 1865, I took the steam-boat for Cincinnati, where, according to previous arrangement, I met Elder N. Summerbell, President of Union Christian College. He at once kindly consented to publish the work if he survived me. After a very interesting and agreeable interview with Elder Summerbell, whom I had not seen for about four years, I returned by steamer to Higginsport, below Ripley, where I preached a funeral discourse on the following Lord's-day (July 23, 1865).

I reached home on the 25th. On the 27th I received official notice from the secretary of Union Christian College, Merom, Indiana, that I had been elected a trustee of that institution, which is a burden I am sorry that they laid upon me. On Lord's-day, the 30th, I preached at eleven o'clock in the court-house in Georgetown, the county seat of Brown County, in which I live. It being what is called "court times," the judges and members of the bar attended, and all gave profound attention to the things spoken. On the 31st I returned home.

The Fourth Trip East.—Having made previous preparation I left my home in Ohio on the first day of August for my fourth trip East. I took the steamer at Ripley for Cincinnati, where, after one day devoted to business, I took the cars on the 3d of August for Cleveland, Ohio, where we arrived after four P. M. My tickets were purchased to Troy by railroad. But the evening being fair, and being very tired and anticipating a pleasant night, I gave my Lake Shore Railroad tickets, from Cleveland to Buffalo, for a passage on the lake steamer. By this change I gained a good night's rest, with supper and breakfast; at the same price as a simple passage on the cars, where I would have spent the night without rest or any thing to eat. The night proved delightfully pleasant. The moonlight was beautiful. The breeze was cool, making even the warm night of August refreshing. Of the thousands traveling on the steamers on these great lakes, comparatively few contemplate the beauties of nature and the wonders of creation, in the formation of these inland seas of pure limpid water, uniting countries hundreds of miles distant, by a common commerce, and supplying millions of people with fish of the finest flavor. When all is calm it is delightful to view the broad and beautiful waters, and behold the glorious sun rising majestically as if out of the waters, or at the close of his daily course sink into the crystal flood, all aglow by the reflection of his own glory. But a storm on the lakes is said to be more fearful than a storm on the ocean. After returning to God thanks for his protecting care, and asking for his mercy to be continued, I retired to my pleasant room and enjoyed a good night's rest. In the morning I arose much refreshed, and after my breakfast landed at the city of Buffalo, in New York, at eight o'clock, August 4. 1865, in time for the cars to Albany and Troy. Albany and Troy are cities lying near each other, at the head of navigation, on the Hudson River. Albany is on the east and Troy on the west side of the river, a little to the north. I took passage to Troy, the county seat of Rensselaer County. I arrived there about six o'clock P. M., after leaving Buffalo in the morning, and the next morning (August 5th) I took the stage-coach at eight o'clock for Stephentown, the place of my birth, in Rensselaer County, New York. I arrived there at the house of my cousin,

Mr. Orlando Rose, about six P. M. I had informed them by letter of my coming, hence they were expecting and awaiting my arrival. I was very tired, being more wearied with that day's stage ride, than with all the former part of my long journey. Otherwise my health was good, for which I gave thanks to God. We were, of course, glad to meet each other after the eventful eight years since my former visit. For during this eight years the great southern rebellion, organized and established by the sword, after a war of four years had been extinguished by the sword, and now peace was restored. The cordial welcome extended to me made me feel at home. The weather was dry, the sun hot, and the roads dusty. I had eaten little during the past thirty-six hours, and was hungry and thirsty. I took a drink of the pure water, which flows clear and cold from the free-stone soil of this mountainous country. I ate a hearty supper, principally of bread and milk, and cheese, the bread being made of rye flour and corn meal mixed. I then, after prayer and thanksgiving to God, retired, and was so refreshed by an excellent night's rest, that I felt almost like a young man again. August 6, 1865, on the Lord's-day morning, I arose in time to view the sun arise in the east, coming up, in all his glory and majesty, from beyond the high mountain of Massachusetts, just over the line, a short distance from Stephentown. It was a beautiful scene on a beautiful morning. I wrote a letter to my family, informing them of my safe arrival. I then sent a note to the Baptist minister, requesting him to announce that I would preach the next Lord's-day at the Christian chapel in Stephentown. The Baptist church was about a mile distant. At eleven o'clock I attended church in the chapel in South Berlin, about three miles north of my cousin's. Elder Olin was then the pastor of the Christian Church. I was kindly welcomed by pastor and people. They insisted upon my preaching, but I declined, it being contrary to my custom to preach at another man's appointment. I consented to an appointment to preach there at eleven o'clock in two weeks, viz., the third Sabbath in August. I followed the minister with some remarks, and went to dine with another of my cousins near by. There I spent a pleasant afternoon, returning to my transient home, three miles distant, about sundown. I spent the week in visiting a few relatives and friends, from whom I heard of the death of numbers who had departed to the spirit world since my visit eight years ago, in 1857. Inanimate things remain. They do not die. The mountains and valleys, brooks and meadows, hills and plains remain as I saw them in my childhood. But the people! Where are they? Gone! Gone to return no more forever! How great the change in eight years? Lonely, I visited the place of my birth. Sadly I entered the house built by my father when I was a little boy, seven or eight years old; then a child, now an old man of seventy-five! I drank of the well that my father dug with his own hands, and I remembered from my earliest recollections. I stood upon the ground where I took my first steps in trying to walk, and where I afterward ran, leaped, and played when a small child. I meditated as I lingered on the ground where I once so much loved to be with my mother, then my only trust. I thought of her kind hand, which so often wiped away my tears. Mournfully solemn were my heartfelt contemplations. I said to myself, "Is it possible that seventy-five years have intervened since those days? that I have lived three quarters of a century, while generation after generation has been born, matured, married, and passed away, leaving children to mourn for them, while I am here, healthy and comparatively strong, viewing again the scenes where my earthly life began?" With these meditations I returned to my transient home; and thus closed the first week of my visit. The second Lord's-day in August, 1865, was a delightful day. I preached, as appointed, at the Christian chapel in Stephentown The house was respectably full, and the congregation was well pleased. The church being at that time without a pastor, expressed a desire for me to take the charge for one year, at least. This I was compelled to decline, as quite inconsistent with my other duties. The second week I spent much as I had the first, visiting the friends of former generations, and calling up interesting reminiscences. I visited this week an aged aunt. She had been the third wife of my uncle, Samuel Gardner, my father's eldest brother, but was now a widow near ninety years old. Like very old people, generally, she had become a child again, but still retained a lively hope of heaven. August 13, 1865, was a fair and beautiful day. My appointment was in the school-house in South Berlin, as the Christian chapel there was being repaired. The house could not contain the people. The word was received with gladness. In the afternoon I accompanied Elder Olin to his appointment from seven to eight miles distant. By his conversation on the way I was confirmed in the truth of reports which I had heard, that he was a preacher of Mr. Alexander Campbell's "system." He said that his parents were Quakers, and that he had been thus brought up, but he had subsequently joined the Methodist Church, and finally the Christians, where he still had a standing. He endeavored to infect me with his Campbellism. "The order of God is," said he, "that immersion must be added to faith and repentance in order to obtain remission of sins; and without immersion sins can not be pardoned." Elder Olin confessed to me that his mother had lived and died a pious Quaker woman, and he doubted not she had gone to heaven. Yet he confessed that she had not been immersed. On meditation, considering that the people to whom he was preaching were not acquainted with "Discipleism," I, after a day or two, concluded to preach on the subject. I then sent Elder Olin a note, that if agreeable to him I would preach in South Berlin the first Sunday in September, on "God's uniform and universal order of remitting sins," and for him to so announce at his next appointment, on the fourth Sunday in August. He replied that he would do so. I continued my visits the third week, as the two former, in interesting social visits with friends and relatives.

Meditations.—Often, walking for meditation to places where my little feet had trod when in childhood's innocence, I thought of the child then and the aged man now! Then a child without the knowledge of guilt or sin, or the experience of sorrow or care; now, with the long experience of life, and a knowledge of the deceitfulness of men!

My first Thoughts about God.—I thought, in my early childhood, that God wanted me to be good; that I must be good, or I never could be happy, and I even then had faith that if I would be good God would take care of me. The philosophy of innocent childhood is more honorable to God, and more useful to men, than the best of the cunning "systems" of men. To be good, I thought, was to be happy. These reflections on my early meditations were as deeply melancholy as strangely pleasant.

The Shaker Meeting.—Having a desire to attend the Shaker meeting, we fixed upon the fourth Lord's-day in August for that purpose. The Shaker village is called Lebanon. It is in Rensselaer County, New York, about eleven miles from my cousin's, where I stopped. This society is probably over one hundred years old. It was perhaps the first Shaker organization on this continent. I had visited the Shakers at their farm in Ohio about sixty years before. That was when I was about sixteen years old. They then had a small society about three miles from my father's, in Brown County, Ohio. They subsequently moved to, and united with, the Shakers at Union Village, in Warren County, Ohio. The day came, and we found ourselves at the Shaker meeting, as proposed. A Shaker man spoke vehemently for about an hour, against what he termed the sins of the world, and in favor of Shakerism. He was particularly zealous in his opposition to men and women living together as husband and wife. "The whole nation," said he, "is a nation of adulterers and adulteresses." Such are the systems of men! I had heard the same idle things said by the Shakers in Ohio when I was a boy. Their worship consisted in singing light tunes, to which they accompanied a rocking motion of the body, and a continued stepping forward and backward, and much walking round and round. These bodily exercises were conducted in their large house by part of the devotees, while a large portion of them, perhaps half, sit quietly as spectators, or sing for those thus exercising. They frequently pause in their singing; then a man or woman will speak a few minutes, after which they commence singing and moving as before. More than half of the male members are boys between ten and fifteen years old. These, being poor, the Shakers gather up wherever they can find them. From the age of twenty-one to forty-five the men almost universally leave them, and go to "the world," as the Shakers call it; but some men are brought in, generally in advanced age. I was quite disappointed in their strength and numbers. From the age of the organization, I expected to see at least a thousand worshipers; but there were but about one hundred and seventy, all told, including men, women, and children. I was informed by a gentleman whose residence is near there, and who frequently counts them, that this is their usual number. There were present about six hundred spectators. My fourth week was spent as the former, in visits, walks, and meditation, except that I made some little preparation for the coming discourse on Campbellism, and made some preparation for my return to Ohio, designing to start on the following Monday. The first Lord's-day in September was pleasant. The morning was fair. The congregation was large. The pastor, Elder Olin, was present.

The Subject.—The subject was "God's uniform and universal order of remission of sins." I announced two texts, one in the Old Testament and one in the New, as follows: Text: "And the Lord descended in the cloud, and stood with him there, and proclaimed the name of the Lord. And the Lord passed by before him, and proclaimed, The Lord, The Lord God, merciful and gracious, long-suffering, and abundant in goodness and truth, keeping mercy for thousands, forgiving iniquity and transgression and sin, and that will by no means clear the guilty; visiting the iniquity of the father upon the children, and upon the children's children, unto the third and to the fourth generation." Exodus xxxiv. 5–7. "Then opened he their understanding, that they might understand the scriptures, and said unto them, Thus it is written, and thus it behooved Christ to suffer, and to rise from the dead the third day: and that repentance and remission of sins should be preached in his name among all nations, beginning at Jerusalem." Luke xxiv. 45–47.

Sermon—A Sketch.—First: As God is one and unchangeable, so his order of pardon and remission of sins is one and unchangeable. The necessities of the human family for mercy are the same; hence God's order of pardon has been the same in all ages. That order is, and always has been, to pardon on repentance and to save by faith; that is, God's order is faith and repentance. The first covenant was given to the Jews.

It was a covenant of works. Its order of life is thus stated: "For Moses describeth the righteousness which is of the law, That the man which doeth those things shall live by them." Romans x. 5. But the law of pardon then, as now, was by repentance and faith. "Even as David also describeth the blessedness of the man unto whom God imputeth righteousness without works, saying, Blessed are they whose iniquities are forgiven, and whose sins are covered. Blessed is the man to whom the Lord will not impute sin." Romans iv. 6–8. David, and all others who sought pardon, found remission then as we do now, by repentance and the prayer of faith. Second: In the new covenant, given by and through Jesus Christ, the one uniform and universal order of God by which sins are remitted, was and is fully made known to be repentance and faith. Christ came fully invested with "power on earth to forgive the sins of all who believe in him, and truly repent." The blessings of the new covenant are not to the Jews only, but to all mankind. "To him give all the prophets witness, that through his name whosoever believeth in him shall receive remission of sins." Acts x. 43. Third: The doctrine of remission of sins by immersion after faith and repentance, as taught by the "Disciples," is not contained in the new covenant which Christ himself instituted and confirmed by his death and resurrection. After he arose from the dead, he gave the apostles their commission, saying, "That repentance and remission of sins should be preached in his name among all nations, beginning at Jerusalem." Luke xxiv. 46; and "teaching them to observe all things whatsoever I have commanded you." But Christ never taught or commanded them to teach "immersion in order to the remission of sins" after faith and repentance. "If he repent, forgive him," is the universal law of pardon with God and man. The doctrine of immersion in order to remission is unscriptural in words, and without authority or command by Christ or his apostles. All who came to Christ by faith repenting, received instant remission. None of the apostles ever taught or practiced immersion in order to remission. Peter on the day of Pentecost did not so teach, as I proved by his words. If he had so taught it was not by the authority of the Lord of glory. Fourth: I contrasted the narrow theory of Campbellism with God's one uniform and universal order of remission of sins to all who repent and believe. "That system," said I, "makes man dependent upon his fellow-man for pardon. He can not immerse himself, or obtain pardon without immersion; but in God's great, universal, and uniform and reasonable order of remission, the truly penitent believer can obtain the remission of his sins in the most lonely place with his God, in the desert most distant from water." Baptism is a commandment for God's children. So Jesus, God's holy Son, was baptized, not to make him a Son, but because he was a Son. Thus we obey our Father in heaven as children, not to make us children. I exhorted all true believers to be baptized as Jesus was, and thus closed.

The Return.—On Monday morning, September 4, 1865, I bade farewell to my friends, and my cousins, Orlando Rose and his wife, took me seven miles, to Berlin, where the stage starts for the city of Troy, twenty-two miles west, over the mountains. There are three Berlins, viz., South Berlin, Center Berlin, and Berlin—called North Berlin. I started with the stage from North Berlin. My feelings, on bidding my cousins farewell, are expressed in the following lines:

> Sweet vales and hills—my native land,
> Where dwell the kindred dear to me—
> I leave. With farewell, parting hand,
> I look on forms no more I'll see.

We reached Troy at three P. M., and the next morning, at six o'clock, took the cars for Buffalo, where we arrived at nine P. M. I had tickets by the Lake Shore Railroad to Cleveland; but no cars would start till twelve o'clock. The steamer was ready to start then. By it we would get rest and a good breakfast next morning. The steamer would accept our tickets. The prospect for a pleasant night on the water was not very favorable; but, anxious to go on, several of us took the steamer. Our worst fears were soon realized. During the night there arose a heavy storm of wind and rain, which caused a number on board to be very sea-sick. We arrived at Cleveland the next day, September 6th, about eleven, and at two P. M. took the cars for Cincinnati, where we arrived the next morning, September 7th, about four o'clock. Being wearied with my all-night travel, and having some business in the city, I tarried there till the next day, September 8th, when I took the river steam-boat for my home, at Ripley, up the Ohio, fifty-five miles above Cincinnati. I arrived home the next day, September 9, 1865, though I was wearied with my journey. I soon recovered from my fatigue, and, after resting, felt that my health had been improved by my fourth trip East.

Home.—I found my family at home, all well, and went, the next day after my return, to fill the appointment of the second Lord's-day in August, made before leaving for the East. By a misunderstanding, the appointment had been announced for another day, so I did not preach. When the days of my other appointments, made previous to my departure, came, I found large congregations assembled, glad to see me, and to hear the word of the Lord. It was a great joy for me to meet with people to whom I had preached for more than fifty years, and clasp hands with old and well-tried soldiers of Christ.

11

Conference.—On the 18th of October, 1865. I attended the Southern Ohio Christian Conference. This was the forty-sixth annual session of that conference which I had, by divine grace, attended, without missing one. The meeting was very precious. I was chosen to preside over the body. We had some trouble. The Mount Pleasant church had become divided on politics, or patriotism. Two sets of messengers claimed seats. The church contained one hundred and thirty members. The preacher and a majority of three were Democrats, in favor of slavery in the Southern States, and opposed to putting down the rebellion by force. The other portion of the church, of nearly equal numbers, constituting the strength of the church, with nearly all its officers, were charged with being Abolitionists. They were at least opposed to slavery, and in favor of the Union, and desired to put down the rebellion. So the preacher and his party had excluded the Union party in mass, without notice, regular charges, hearing, or trial, or even announcing their names; and the same meeting which excluded them chose other officers, instead of those excluded, including deacons, etc. My decision was that neither party should take seats in conference before an investigation. The committee on credentials reported the same. Their case was then referred to the committee on grievances, which recommended that the present pastor should discontinue his labors, and the church submit their difficulties to settlement by a committee appointed by conference to visit it for that purpose. This was approved; and after the adjournment of conference, the committee attended, and the church was blessed with peace and future prosperity. The conference, after doing much business, closed in great harmony.

Photograph.—My children and others desiring to have my likeness correctly taken, I next visited Cincinnati for that purpose, on the 25th of November, 1865. The next day being Lord's-day I, by the pressing request of Elder N. Summerbell, preached at eleven o'clock in the "First Christian Church" of that city. On Monday Elder Summerbell went with me to an excellent artist, Mr. Winder, who took my photograph correctly, which a number had failed to do after repeated trials. On Tuesday we took it to Mr. Stillman's and contracted to have it engraved, including my signature, age, and the number of the years of my ministry—the work to be completed in three or four weeks. After preaching on the first Lord's-day in December, I delayed my return home to stop and preach a funeral on the way, and reached home on my birthday, on Tuesday the 5th of December. I had now lived in this sin-ruined world seventy-five years.

> The rolling years! how swift they fly!
>   May Jesus' grace be given
> By which to live, that when I die
>   My home may be in heaven.

Divine Meditations.—Having entered my seventy-sixth year, I now, more than ever before, thank and adore my heavenly Father for his manifold mercies, and the continued grace which, during three-score and fifteen years, he has bestowed upon me, a poor unworthy creature. I am humbled in view of my failings, and the little that I have done for my blessed Savior who has done so much for me. O, blessed Jesus, continue thy mercies, and help me, for help can come from none other than thee. I thank God that my health is good. My voice is still strong and clear, and I can preach and sing almost as well as in my younger days, though I can not continue to speak or sing so long at a time. One thing is remarkable; that is, that now in my advanced age I am treated with such marked respect by all religious denominations. Now they welcome me into their pulpits, and the ministers of other denominations invite me to preach for them. This seems strange, when I remember that these same denominations in former years so uniformly persecuted me, and also the Christians with which church I have my standing.

The Divided Church.—The committee appointed to settle the difficulties in the Mount Pleasant church consisted of myself as chairman, and Elder N. Dawson, M. D., and Elder William Pangburn, as associate members. We appointed to hold meeting with the church on the 10th of December, 1865, on Saturday night, and to continue the meeting over the Lord's-day following. Elder Dawson met me. Elder Pangburn being absent, we chose Deacon Joseph Bolender in his stead. As Elder Dawson preached on Saturday night, it fell to my lot to preach on the Lord's-day at eleven o'clock. Text: "Have peace one with another." Mark IX. 50. "And when ye stand praying, forgive, if ye have aught against any: that your Father also which is heaven may forgive you your trespasses." Mark XI. 25. Elder Dawson preached at night. The congregations were large and attentive. On Monday morning, at ten o'clock, according to previous notice, the church came together, including both parties, with a large congregation of spectators. The preacher who had been instrumental in causing the division was there also, and he seemed to be exerting all his influence with his party to prevent union. He wrote out eight objections to the committee acting in the premises. This paper he sent to the committee by the hand of one of his party. As he was not a member of the church, we paid no attention to his objections. Oh, that all preachers were peace-makers!

The Proposition.—After prayer, the committee, in a kind spirit, proposed to both parties to cease all unkind feelings toward each other, and to unite in the spirit of Christ, and work together for the advancement of the Redeemer's cause! Discussion was freely participated in by all who desired. There was much talk, but mostly of a pacific nature. When the question was proposed, all agreed to work in union, except ten or twelve, who were seated near the opposing preacher, and were doubtless influenced by him. The rest then gave each other the hand of fellowship in pledge of their sincerity, while tears flowed in confirmation of the deep feelings of their hearts.

The New Pastor.—The church being now united, proceeded to unite on a pastor. This they did in the unanimous choice of the young and talented minister, Elder S. S. Newhouse, to whom there was no objection. We then exhorted them to live in peace, and so bade them farewell. This church at Mount Pleasant, in Clermont County, had been organized by me, through divine grace, near thirty years before. It now commenced a new era of usefulness and prosperity.

Bethlehem Church.—As my engagement for the year 1865 with the Bethlehem church, which I had organized more than forty years before, was about to expire, the church met on Saturday before my meeting on the third Lord's-day in December, and so urgently requested it, that I consented to labor with them another year. This church numbers over four hundred members, and has elected me for its pastor every year for forty years. Christmas-day of 1865 has come. It is a clear, pleasant, beautiful day. This is the seventy-fifth Christmas-day seen by me! Will I ever see another? O Lord. Thou knowest! Elder G. W. Mefford and I agreed to hold a meeting of days, the Lord willing, at the Union church near Higginsport, commencing on Saturday before the fifth Lord's-day in December. This church I, through divine grace, organized near fifty years ago.

Ordination.—On my way to this meeting I took a letter from the post-office from Elder N. Summerbell, pastor of the Christian Church in Cincinnati, urgently requesting me to come to the city on said Lord's-day to assist in the ordination of his son, Joseph J. Summerbell, who had been a student, and afterward professor in, Union Christian College. He had now taken charge of the Christian Church at Blackberry, Illinois. On Saturday, at eleven o'clock, I attended the meeting at Union church, and in the afternoon took the river steamer for Cincinnati, and assisted in the ordination of the first graduate of Union Christian College. The ordination sermon was preached by Austin Craig, D. D., then the acting president of Antioch College. I presented the Bible to the young brother as the guide of his faith and life. The charge was given by Professor J. B. Weston, of Antioch College. The right hand of fellowship was given by Elder A. R. Heath, agent of Union Christian College. Elder Hiram Simonton, Elder Asa Coan, Elder J. B. Rogers, and others, assisted in the exercises. On Monday I returned to the meeting at Union chapel. This was New Year's day,

1866. The meeting continued over ten days, during which time there were, by divine grace, fifty-three additions to the church. After a few days' rest, which was very much needed by me, Elder Mefford and I commenced a meeting with the Bethlehem church, which lasted seventeen days. We commenced on Saturday, at eleven o'clock, before the fourth Sunday in January, 1866. During this meeting one hundred and thirty-five, the most of whom were youths or men, confessed the Lord Jesus Christ before men and angels, and united with the church. Quite a large number of soldiers, after fighting the battles of their country till the rebellion was subdued, being honorably discharged, now enlisted under the blood-stained banner of the Prince of Peace. The converting power of God was manifest in a wonderful manner. Sometimes sixteen or eighteen would come forward on one invitation. One mute, a man who could neither hear or speak, felt the Spirit, and came forward and united with the church. This was the largest number uniting at one meeting that I had ever known. Some years before, one hundred and three or four united with the church of my charge at one meeting. That was the greatest number until this of one hundred and thirty-five.

Revival of Principle as well as Interest.—Since the aforesaid meeting, the Bethlehem Christian Church desires preaching twice a month (two Sabbaths and Saturdays previous), and has raised two hundred dollars by subscription for that purpose, for this year, 1866, and I, in my seventy-sixth year, have agreed to preach for them twice a month instead of once a month, as heretofore. As I could not set a price on my own labors, they gave me what they pleased; that was fifty or sixty dollars a year, formerly, for a two days' meeting once a month. Later, the annual sum was increased a little. The last year, 1865, it was fixed at ninety dollars. Now it arose to two hundred for two visits per month.

The Largest Church.—Bethlehem has received, since I first organized it, as shown by the records, about fifteen hundred members. Besides deaths and removals, it has been reduced by the organization of some four churches within its bounds, from its members, yet the Bethlehem Church now numbers over five hundred members. There were great revivals in a number of the churches in Brown County during January, and up to February 22, 1866. By too much labor during these two months my strength was exhausted, and my voice was so greatly injured that I could speak but little above a whisper; a condition of my voice that I do not remember of ever having experienced before. My general health was also much impaired. I felt feeble. It seemed as if my work was nearly closed. I still endeavored to do a little, so great was my desire to advance the Redeemer's cause. A primary convention was called to meet at Franklin,

Ohio, on the last day of February, 1866. Franklin is near seventy miles from Cincinnati; but as this convention was preparatory to a general convention of all Christians in Ohio who accept the Bible as their all-sufficient and only creed, and are willing to receive into church fellowship all believers in Christ, although I was in poor health, I attended. I was chosen chairman of the convention, feeble as I was. I was requested to preach, but was not able. Arrangements were made for a general convention, to be held on the 22d of the May following.

Boat Run Church.—On my return from the convention at Franklin I stopped at Boat Run, on the Ohio River, about twenty-two miles above Cincinnati, to assist the church there. They were divided on politics, and I desired to get them united on religion. Without previous notice a protracted meeting was commenced the day I landed, and there being but one minister there, I was persuaded to preach. The church had been organized by me nearly thirty years before. I preached a number of days, including the first Lord's-day in March. My labors were blest abundantly. The church became united in the bonds of peace. Nearly thirty converts professed religion. I returned home worn down, my health not being as good as when I left. During the remainder of March and April I continued so feeble as to be barely able to fill my appointments at Bethlehem twice a month, but in May my voice began to improve.

Kicked by a Horse.—On Friday afternoon, before the second Lord's-day in May, as I was going to a communion meeting of Union Church, our son, G. W. Gardner, met me in Higginsport, near where he lives; and as we rode along side by side, his horse kicked at mine and hit my left leg, making a severe wound. I, however, succeeded in going on to the meeting, nearly three miles distant. I tarried that night at my daughter's, Sally A. Shinkle's. She is the wife of Michael Shinkle. She did all that she could for my comfort. The next day I attended meeting. Elder Mefford insisted on my preaching, there being no other visiting minister present. Though my wound gave me great pain, I preached every day, standing with one foot resting upon a chair. The meeting closed on Monday. I was quite sick on Monday night, but started for home, some seventeen miles distant, on Tuesday morning. I was compelled to stop at Higginsport. There I tarried all night with my grandson, Walter Shinkle. On Wednesday, feeling a little better, I started on and reached home about five P. M., suffering great pain in my leg, and being quite feeble. Though improved but little, yet I rode twelve miles to attend my appointment at Bethlehem the third Lord's-day and Saturday before. I was very glad to meet Elders Mefford and Pangburn who, knowing my feeble state, came to assist me, as this was the spring communion—the regular annual meeting. I was with them on Saturday, but being worse on Saturday night, I was unable to be there on the Lord's-day. On Monday I was just able to be there, but not being able to baptize, Elder Mefford baptized twenty of those who had professed religion some time before. My arrangements were made to attend the State General Convention to meet at Columbus, Ohio, May 22, 1866, but my feeble state of health, and the effects of the kick of the horse, prevented my going. Had I been there I should have protested against the resolution approving of our Congress. My views were in favor of Congress, and therefore in sympathy with the spirit of the resolution; but I am opposed to introducing such questions into religious conventions, conferences, or churches. The case was this: Abraham Lincoln was elected President of the United States a second term in 1864. He was assassinated in April, 1865, consequently Andrew Johnson, the Vice President, became President of the United States *ex-officio*. President Johnson's policy seemed to favor the states lately in rebellion, and to oppose Congress. Though favoring Congress, yet I should have entered my protest against the resolution passed by the convention approving Congress.

Baptizing.—By the last Lord's-day in May my health was so much improved that I was able to baptize ten at Bethlehem that day. It was four weeks and four days, from the time I was hurt by the horse, until the wound was healed entirely. Nearly two weeks of that time I was confined to the house.

Union Christian College.—On the 18th of June, 1866, I took the steam-boat at Ripley, about eight o'clock P. M., to attend the meeting of the Trustees of Union Christian College, located at Merom, Indiana, about two hundred and seventy miles from where I live in Ohio. The trustees, of whom I was one, were to meet on the 20th of June. Duty seemed to require my presence. I arrived at Cincinnati the first night, and in the morning took the cars for Indianapolis, and from there to Terre Haute, and thence to Sullivan, the nearest railroad station, to Merom, and the county seat of Sullivan County. Elder E. W. Humphreys went with me. At Sullivan we took the stage-coach for Merom, nine miles west, where we arrived just at sun-down on the 19th. I was very weary. Brother Thomas Kearns, with whom I had some little acquaintance, met me at the coach, and took me to his house, where I felt at home. On the 20th the trustees met, and continued their meetings two days and a half, and part of one night. There was a large amount of business transacted. Finding the fatigue of traveling and attendance too much for my age, I therefore, near the close of the session, after giving my reasons, tendered my resignation. They urged me to continue, but finally saw the propriety of releasing me. Merom is situated on a high and beautiful bluff on

the east shore of the Wabash River, about midway between
Terre Haute and Vincennes. The bluff rising abruptly from
the river, descends in a beautiful inclined plane toward the east,
where the town is built. A little south of the village the bluff
winds round to the east, still gently descending toward the village. On its highest point south of the town stands the fine
college building. The bluff then falls off gently, descending
toward the east, forming the natural surface of the college park.
The college thus stands on a natural mount of almost imper-
ceptible ascent, yet occupying the highest ground along the
Wabash, and presenting a view which for beauty can hardly be
surpassed.

The Return.—As Elder E. W. Humphreys, who was still with
me, desired to return by Vincennes, we took the cars at New
Carlisle, some miles south of Sullivan. This caused a wagon
ride thirteen miles to New Carlisle, the railroad station. To
make our change of cars, we stopped at the crossing, from one
to two miles from the main depot at Vincennes, which distance
we were obliged to walk, carrying our baggage, on a warm
afternoon near the last of June. Then we had to wait for the
St. Louis train for Cincinnati, which arrived about eleven at
night. The sleeping-cars being all full, we were compelled to
sit up all night while running two hundred miles. We reached
Cincinnati about seven on Saturday morning, weary and worn
out. I tarried with Elder N. Summerbell till Monday, when I
took the steamer for Ripley, and came home. The Fourth of
July, 1866, is here! This is the seventy-sixth Independence-
day that I have lived to see, and I thank God that my voice is
almost restored, and my general health is greatly improved.

Salem Church on Big Indian Creek.—On the 8th of July, by
the strong solicitation of the family, I preached the funeral sermon of two children of Brother James Trees, in the stone chapel
of the Salem Christian Church, on Big Indian Creek. One of
the children was a young woman, the other was younger. It
was a sad loss to the parents. I could not refuse them the comfort of my attendance, though it was forty miles distant from
my home, for I had received the grandparents into the Salem
Church among the first members after I organized it, nearly
fifty years before.

Old People.—There was a greater number of aged men and
women at this funeral than I remember ever having seen in a
congregation before. The chapel would not hold all the people who assembled. Twenty-five years had passed since I had
preached there, so that I remembered but few faces, while
many remembered me. We were glad to meet each other, and
to grasp the friendly hand; but there was sorrow when we
came to say farewell. They are building a new frame chapel
at Point Isabel, about a mile and a half from the old stone

house. They requested me to preach the dedication of the
new house when completed. I promised to do so if the Lord
continued my strength. I had an appointment to preach at
night at New Richmond, eleven miles from my morning meeting. New Richmond is about twenty miles above Cincinnati.
Brother Friedman, of Boat Run Church, came with his carriage
and conveyed me for dinner to his house, eight miles on my
way. About three o'clock, and a few minutes before we arrived
at his house, a terrible storm arose. The sky became dark;
the thunder roared, and the rain fell in torrents. The small
creeks through Brother Friedman's farm swept off the fences,
and between his house and New Richmond the creeks swept
the bridges from the turnpike. It was said to be the greatest
fall of rain ever known in that section, during so short a time.

The Meeting.—My subject for the meeting that night had
been announced, but it seemed impossible to get there as the
rain continued. I gave a man fifty cents to take a note to the
Methodist preacher postponing my meeting to the night of the
fifth Lord's-day, viz: July 29, 1866. On going there to take
the steamer the next day, the Methodist minister seemed quite
dissatisfied. He said that a large congregation assembled, and
all were much disappointed; he, most of all, as instead of hearing
me, he was forced to preach without preparation. Circumstances
seemed to demand a sermon on Mr. Alexander Campbell's
"system." The final time arrived and I was there in time, and
so was the congregation. It was a beautiful moonlight night.
When the last bell rung, the house was already about full.
Soon it was crowded to excess, and numbers went away unable
to get in. By divine grace my health and voice had greatly
improved. I felt young again. After singing by the congregation, I called on the Lord for help and proceeded. The text:
"Testifying both to the Jews, and also to the Greeks, repentance toward God, and faith toward our Lord Jesus Christ."
Acts xx. 21. First: I stated that the text presents God's uniform and universal order for the remission of sins. Second: I
clearly presented the new system of Mr. Campbell, for remission in contrast. Third: I gave a brief history of Mr. Campbell and his changes, and his last doctrine. I showed the
contrast between his doctrine and the doctrine of others. They
boast that they are right, and denounce all others as wrong.
Would it not be strange if found that the Bible has always
taught that "immersion in water is the only way to obtain pardon," and yet none of the hosts of the God-loving, and Bible-
reading, and praying people had found it, but only a few, who,
denying any inward work of grace, are driven to this as their
only hope? I made this point also, not before made by
me, namely: The "Disciples" of Mr. Campbell admit that
during the whole time under the law sinners obtained remission

through faith and repentance, and that Jesus so taught while
here on earth. This, then, is sufficient proof of the correct-
ness of that order. God's order for four thousand years must
have been correct. Jesus' order must have been perfect. Many
were saved then, like the thief who could not be immersed.
Had they lived under the gospel, as Mr. Campbell interprets
it, they must have been lost. His gospel places salvation too
far off. He makes it to depend, first, on man's understanding
of the word baptize; next, on water to be immersed in; then
on a minister to immerse him, and on time to be immersed;
and finally on ability to get to the water. If any of these fails,
he must be lost, however honest or good. Would it not then
have been better for the world if such a gospel had never been
heard of? If it be true, more honest, good people, who die
without immersion, are lost yearly than the whole of Mr.
Campbell's church combined; lost not because of any thing
necessary as proved by their admission that it was not required
for remission by Christ, or till Peter preached at Pentecost,
then it was, of course, unnecessarily added, if added at
all, and if added it has been the means of condemning
far more than it saves, and has thus rendered the gospel an
entire failure. But it is not gospel. Peter never preached it.
Its only possible benefit is to increase the desire for immersion,
and the number baptized. It leads to the neglect of true conversion, and lowers the standard of piety, rendering final salvation uncertain. This discourse was about one hour and a
half long. I learned that it gave general satisfaction. In conclusion, I stated that if the points made by me were objected to,
and a preacher of the Disciples would come forward, I was willing to discuss the matter with him. The Methodist preacher
was present; also the Rev. John Rankin, a Presbyterian minister, formerly of Ripley, and before alluded to in these pages,
was present, and at the close led in prayer. I returned home
the following day, feeling that I had done my duty. The Quadrennial Convention of the Christians was appointed to meet this
year on the 2d day of October, in Marshall, Michigan, near the
center of that state. I was appointed to represent the Southern
Ohio Christian Conference in that convention. As the distance
was great, nearly four hundred miles, and the convention was
to meet on Tuesday morning, I was compelled to start the previous week. So, notwithstanding my feeble health, my trust
being in God's protecting care, I took the steamer at Ripley and
went to Cincinnati, and preached to Elder Summerbell's congregation, on the last Lord's-day of September. I took the cars
with him on Monday morning at six o'clock for Toledo. We
arrived at Toledo, on Lake Erie, at four o'clock, P. M., and at
seven took the cars for Marshall, about one hundred miles from
Toledo. Being detained for connections, and delayed by ob-

structions, we were up all night without sleep, and reached Marshall about five o'clock on Tuesday morning, quite weary and exhausted from loss of sleep. The convention met at ten o'clock, October 2, 1866, in the Christian church in Marshall. Representatives and ministers were present from almost all parts of the United States and Canada, except the Southern States lately in rebellion against the United States Government. The body was respectable, both in numbers and talents. The session continued three days and part of one night. The most important business was the founding of a biblical school in the State of New York. Some of the ministers seemed wanting the deep piety and prayerful devotion which characterized our former ministers. This I was sorry to see, as no people can prosper if the ministry is not godly, pious, and prayerful. Elder N. Summerbell went from the convention to visit his mother in New York, leaving me with his son Joseph, a noble young man, to accompany me homeward as far as Cincinnati. On our return, we were again obliged to be up all night without sleep. At Elder Summerbell's I found rest, and remained there from Friday till the following Monday, when I took the steamer for Ripley. and arrived home on the 8th of October, with my health and strength,somewhat improved.

Conference.—The annual session of the Southern Ohio Christian Conference met, in 1866, with the Christian church in Higginsport, on the seventeenth day of October. By divine grace I was able to attend this gathering also, making the forty-sixth annual meeting with this conference, without one case of absence. Being president of the conference, we opened with the usual religious services, after which the reports from the churches were received, showing over twelve hundred additions during the past year. This caused me joy, but the joy was mingled with fear that we might be forgetful and boast, instead of remembering to give thanks and praise to the God of all grace, and to his Son Jesus Christ, to whom all praise is due.

Dedication.—The dedication of the new chapel at Point Isabel was appointed by the church on the 25th of November, of which I received notice at conference. Elder William Pangburn and Elder G. W. Mefford met me there. The building committee informed us that there was a balance of $700 to be raised, to clear the house of debt. The congregation was so large that nearly half the people were forced to remain outside. Elder William Pangburn opened the services, at eleven o'clock, with singing and prayer, after which, as both he and Mefford declined going forward to raise the money, and as I was not willing to dedicate the house until it was clear of debt, the question arose, Who shall do the work? If done at all, I saw that I must do it. I accordingly went to work. First, I called upon all who were willing to give twenty-five dollars each to arise.

After this effort was exhausted, I called for twenty, then fifteen, ten, five, etc., down to one dollar, until the $700 were signed. Nearly two hours were spent in soliciting, after which I preached a sermon of over one hour's length, making three hours' continued work. Of course I was much exhausted. Elders Mefford and Pangburn assisted in the dedication service.

The Revival.—Elder Pangburn left on Monday morning, but Elder Mefford and I continued the meeting several days, and, by divine grace, received eleven members into the church, of whom five were heads of families. Though the weather was very disagreeable, yet, to all appearance, the meeting exerted great influence for good both in the village and in the surrounding neighborhood.

Home.—Although the distance to this dedication was near forty miles, yet, having returned to my home and rested, I found my health about as good as before I performed this labor.

December 5, 1866.—My birthday has come, and finds me at home. It tells me that I am seventy-six years old to-day, having been born in 1790. I thank God for his abundant mercies in the past, and ask him, in the name of his Son Jesus Christ, for a continuation of his protecting care and many blessings unto unworthy me for the future. If I am called to leave this world before my next birthday, do thou, O God, help me to possess that faith which makes a "dying bed feel soft as downy pillows are!" Old Time, in her faithful revolutions, brings us to another Christmas. It is a beautiful clear day, with a light snow covering the ground. An idea prevails in the West that a black Christmas marks a sickly summer. A black Christmas is a Christmas without snow to cover the black ground.

December 30, 1866.—Yesterday, the fifth Lord's-day in this month, I rode about seven miles and preached a funeral, and returned without stopping for dinner. The weather was cold—forty degrees below the freezing point—eight degrees below zero. I was almost chilled through when I reached home.

New Year, 1867.—This New Year's day finds me at home. Through divine goodness, for which I am thankful, it finds myself and family in reasonable health, except my aged companion, the companion of my youth and age. She is much afflicted with the asthma, and has been, during the winter, for several years past.

Bethlehem.—Three months previous to the expiration of 1866, I announced to the Bethlehem church, twelve miles distant, where I have preached for over forty years, that, on account of my age, the distance, and cold weather, I desired to discontinue my labors, and I requested them to choose a pastor to succeed me for the coming year, 1867. As the church made no effort to secure a pastor, but the principal members insisted upon my continuing, I requested Elder George W. Brittingham, whose residence is near there, to assist me, especially to preach for me during the cold weather, if I should continue. I understood him to assent. He is a respectable ordained minister. He embraced religion under my ministry, and is a member of the Bethlehem Church. On my last day there the attendance was very large. The church informed me that they desired me to continue, and that they had not looked for any successor for me, and said that they would leave the responsibility upon me to supply the preaching, or leave the pulpit vacant.

The Salary.—By a unanimous vote, they proposed to give me $200 for preaching for them semi-monthly during 1867, as they had done the year before. Brother Brittingham being present, I asked him whether he would preach for me during the cold weather, and was disappointed when he declined to do so. After considering the matter, I agreed to try, with the help of the Lord, to continue my labors for the coming year. The first appointment came early in January. It was a protracted meeting. Elder William Pangburn and Elder George W. Mefford assisted. I soon saw that there was something wrong, and, on inquiry, learned that Brother Brittingham understood my proposal to him, at first, to be for him to preach half the time, that is, once a month during the whole year, and that, had I proposed this at the meeting, he would have accepted. I replied that I would have been glad to have accepted such a proposal, though that was not what I had proposed. I took the earliest opportunity to see Brother Brittingham by going to his house between meetings. I made the proposal to him to preach half the time, if the church would agree to it, and, if not, I should resign, and leave the responsibility upon him. He promised to give me his answer before the meeting closed, but did not. At the last meeting, I announced that the next regular church meeting, on Saturday before the third Sabbath in January, 1867, I expected to resign my charge, for reasons which would satisfy all who came to hear them. The day came. The congregation was large. Elder Brittingham was in attendance. After stating the facts, I requested the contract for the present year, between the church and myself, to be rescinded. This was done by a unanimous vote. By another unanimous vote I was chosen pastor, and Brother Brittingham assistant, to preach with me alternately, each once a month, the church agreeing to pay $200 for our joint labors, all of which was done in the best of Christian feeling, and with entire satisfaction to all, except the elders laboring with me in the protracted meeting. They, when they heard it, were humiliated, that such an aged minister as I should go to see one so young in the ministry, whose duty it was to have come to me. I replied, "I am nothing; the cause of Christ is every thing." I could have proved what my proposal originally was. But what of that? He had friends

who desired to have him preach part of the time, and by my
allowing his understanding to prevail, we continued in peace
and harmony, with no sacrifice of right. Elder Brittingham,
though young in the ministry, having been ordained but about
eight months, was already pastor of the Enon Church. This
church I had organized some twelve years before, of members
of the Bethlehem Church. It was five miles from Bethlehem,
and numbered about two hundred members. He was a man of
influence in the church. The unhappy jealousies and divisions
which too often take place among preachers and people may be
avoided by humbly obeying the directions of the Lord of glory.
I continued my visits to Bethlehem once a month, during the
coldest weather, though my feeble strength seemed to forbid it.
It was almost beyond my power of endurance. After April,
when the weather became mild, I preached regularly almost
every Sunday. In the latter part of the winter of 1867, the
bank at Ripley was burned, and with it the copperplate engraving of my likeness, which was deposited in it. It was a good
likeness, and impressions from it, suitable for framing, had been
sent by the desire of friends to many parts of the United States.
On the 29th of April, on my way to Cincinnati, on business, a
part of which was to get a new likeness correctly taken, to be
engraved on steel for this work, I was taken suddenly ill with
diarrhea, on the steamer. The attack was very severe. It was
with great difficulty that I was able to reach the house of
Brother Summerbell. There, by the blessing of God and the
kind, Christian attention of Brother and Sister Summerbell,
which I never can forget, I soon recovered. The attack resembled cholera. My photograph for this work was taken on the
first day of May, 1867. In a few days I was able to reach home.

May, 1867.—Beautiful May has come in all its vernal glory,
but I am weak and failing; hence I look forward to a paradise
home that has charms for me which far exceed the charms of
nature; to a glory which far exceeds the May flowers. Though
feeble, I labor on.

The Deceiver.—My general health is somewhat improved,
though I am weak. At my four o'clock appointment on the
third Sunday in June, one of Elder Alexander Campbell's Disciple preachers was present. He had been preaching at the
place of my appointment, the school-house, for several days and
nights, and designed to continue. He had an appointment for
that night, but none at four o'clock, so he came to my meeting.
The following article, afterward published in "The Gospel Herald," our paper, explains his mission, and my course with him:

"JESUS SAID, 'TAKE HEED THAT YE BE NOT DECEIVED.'

"Ever since creation's dawn, when in Eden's garden Satan deceived our first parents, there have been deceivers, and there are

deceivers still. It is known that there exists in many places men of Alexander Campbell's faith. The fundamental tenets of that sect is, that 'no person's sins can be remitted or pardoned, according to the gospel, without immersion in water.' These men sometimes, for effect's sake, assume the name 'Christians.' One of this caste came into Brown County a few weeks ago, pretending to be a Christian minister; he called himself James L. Thornbury, a missionary. He commenced a meeting of days at a school-house about four miles from the Bethlehem church, of nearly five hundred members, of which I have the pastoral charge, and nearly an equal distance from the Fellowship church, of which Elder J. P. Daugherty has the charge, consequently in a neighborhood where numbers of the members of these Christian churches reside. This man claimed exclusive right to the name Christians for his sect, because, as he said, Elder Barton W. Stone took that name, and he was immersed by Stone. Some of the people becoming wearied with his harrangues of 'remission of sins by immersion,' sent to me on Saturday before the third Sunday in June, at my regular appointment at Bethlehem, requesting me to preach at the school-house at four o'clock on Sunday, as he had no appointment at that hour. At the close of his eleven o'clock meeting, he refused to give out my appointment, saying that he was not sure that I would be there; but the people got the word, and they were there, and he was there, and I was there. He introduced himself to me as a Christian minister. I said, 'To what conference do you belong?' Then he seemed confused, and answered, 'I do not belong to any.' I asked, 'Why, then, do you call yourself a Christian minister?' Then he replid, 'Elder Barton W. Stone immersed me, and he never belonged to any conference.' I asked, 'When did Stone immerse you?' He answered, 'In 1833.' I replied, 'Yes, in 1833. Before 1833 Elder Stone had left us and gone over to Mr. Campbell's system of remission of sins by immersion, after faith and repentance.' I said to him, also, 'Your statement, that Elder Stone never belonged to any conference, is destitute of truth. I first united with the Kentucky Christian Conference, of which Elder Stone was then a member. I was ordained by order of that conference, and remained a member of it until the Southern Ohio Christian Conference was organized, in 1820. From and after Elder Stone's adoption of Mr. Campbell's system he never belonged to, or had any standing in, any Christian conference to the time of his death. And we Christians occupy the ground upon which he first came out from sectarianism, and which he left when he adopted Mr. Campbell's system.' He said that Elder Stone told him that he preached immersion in order to remission of sins before Campbell did. I told him that my association with Elder Stone was of twenty years' duration, viz, from A. D. 1810 to A. D. 1830, and during all that time Elder Stone never preached or wrote a word favoring that doctrine. In the discourse I stated clearly the difference between the gospel of the Lord of glory and the system of 'immersion for remission' preached by this pretended missionary. I said to the people, 'Here are two men holding opposite views, both professing to be Christian ministers. Both can not be true Christian ministers. You must view one of us as an impostor. You know me; I have preached for you almost fifty years.' The next day Dr. N. Summerbell called on his way to Adams County, and at eleven o'clock preached an excellent sermon on the true nature of conversion. Elder J. P. Daugherty came also, and preached. Several united with the Christians proper, and eight were baptized by Elder Daugherty. The Disciple preacher soon left, and thus ended the effort to make division in the Christian Church. This 'missionary' is perhaps fifty years old, five feet ten inches high, and, as the counterfeit detecter says, 'well calculated to deceive.' M. GARDNER.

"July 3, 1867."

Fourth of July, 1867, is here, and I am thankful that I am able to record it. There are many of my age who by reason of their trembling can not write. This is the seventy-seventh American Independence-day that I have seen. The people are gathered about two miles from here. They have public speaking, but I am not interested. I feel no inclination to mingle with the crowd, therefore I remain at home. At my regular appointment at the Bethlehem church I informed them that I should close my labors with them by the 1st of October, instead of as formerly the 1st of January. I made this change to enable them to secure a pastor at conference. The church urged me to hold the charge as pastor, and they would secure a supply for the winter. (The church is twelve miles from my home). But my observation of men and things for many years convinced me that there are few men, if any, who can feel a pastor's responsibility when preaching only as a supply. The pastor of a church should be with his charge. I could not, therefore, accede to their request. They must, therefore, procure a pastor to take my place at the end of three months.

Unitarianism.—The General Convention, which met in Marshall, in 1866, appointed Elder D. W. Moore to attend the convention of the "General Baptists" in London, England, in May, 1867. Elder Moore having communicated to the "Gospel Herald" that the leading "General Baptist" ministers in England complained that their people had been injured, and in the vital and spiritual interests of their religion, ruined by their union with Unitarians, and Elder Moore having warned the Christians accordingly, the Unitarians published, in September, 1867, in "The Christian Register," their paper, some very unkind statements concerning Elder Moore and the Christians. The Unitarians published that the Christians are narrow and selfish in their feelings, but intensely Unitarian in their theology. This caused me to reply to the statement, in "The Gospel Herald" in October, 1867. I copy the part alluding to the Christians as "Unitarian in their theology:" "Are the Christians Unitarians." Is the assertion in the Unitarian paper true which states that "the Christians are essentially Unitarian, indeed intensely Unitarian in their theology?"— [Unitarian Paper.] The distinguishing feature of Unitarian theology is their peculiar views of Christ. Is, then, the faith of the Christians, in regard to Christ, identical with the faith of the Unitarians? The extreme Unitarian theology embraces the speculations of Theodore Parker, Dr. Priestly, Collyer, and others, who teach that Jesus was simply a man. In the "address before the (Unitarian) Ministerial Union, by Rev. Robert Collyer," published in the "Unitarian Monthly Journal" of September, 1867, pp. 352-363, notwithstanding the ingenuity of the theologian, the miraculous conception of Christ is ignored; the native, personal, inherent divinity of Christ is repudiated. He compares the blessed Son of God to Luther and to Washington. As they outgrew self, so did Christ. He says, "Christ grew to be Christ by casting aside the old true self." "The false Christs who came before the true," might have become true Christs, "only the task was too painful," etc. He holds forth that as Washington and Lincoln became saviors of their country, by being true to the calls of their country's need, so Christ became Savior by being true to the calls of the Spirit. This Unitarian theology teaches that Christ was simply a good man, a moral hero, endued with the Holy Spirit, and was true and faithful, and others might be equally good. This address is by Rev. Robert Collyer, of high standing with the Unitarians, and is published in their "Monthly Journal" and other denominational papers, and may be considered choice Unitarian theology, agreeing in the main with the views of Doctor Priestly and Theodore Parker. This is intense Unitarian theology.

Christian Theology.—Contrary to this, it is well known that the Christians, as a people, have ever, and do now, believe and maintain the truth of the miraculous conception of Jesus Christ the Son of God. They believe in his native, inherent, personal divinity. Therefore, the writer having been a Christian minister over fifty-seven years, feels it to be his duty, in behalf of his brethren, to contradict and to positively deny that detracting Unitarian statement, to-wit: "The Christians are intensely Unitarian in their theology." It is void of truth. May God deliver us from "the body of this death." I esteem, respect, and thank Brother Moore for his faithful warning.

Ripley, Ohio, October, 1867.   M. GARDNER.

The Pastor's Solemn Reflections.—The time approaches when I am to finally close my pastoral labors, which have continued for over fifty years, much of the time with the care of from two to four churches. The faithful pastor's charge has its weight of cares, trials, and sorrows, mingled with the general sunshine and joys, from witnessing that his labor in his Master's vineyard is not in vain. I have proved this by fifty years' experience, and would continue the charge if my strength would permit. It is a joy to save poor sinners, to comfort believers, and glorify God through our Lord Jesus Christ. The strong ties of my pastoral relation with the Bethlehem Church have grown with the love of Christ during forty-five years, strengthening with its growth. To consider that, during a ministry of forty-five years, I disappointed them but twice, will give the reader some idea of my attachment. How little can those who change the pastoral relation every year or two appreciate my feeling! My long relationship with that church has been as harmonious and agreeable as it could possibly be expected in this world. I was re-elected every year by a unanimous vote each year, except one; then the brother who objected had a wrong spirit, and gave up his objection as soon as he got right himself. He became one of my warmest friends, and died happy a few months since. Though this church has, for many years, had a large membership, they have lived in peace and union, without those divisions which are too common in churches. If any evil arose, it was overcome by Scripture authority, with reason, kindness, and prayer. Thus, while other churches were divided, this church had union. Both the contending parties in politics were largely represented in the church; but the threshold of the church was the line of peace, and they met at the altar in Christian charity. Thus we lived in peace, never permitting politics to disturb our fellowship. One reason was this: The pastor never took politics into the pulpit. He did not preach politics, but piety. While the storm raged, he endeavored to keep the church on the rock of safety. As the wrecked strangers floated by, he gathered all that he could into the haven of peace. Over sixty members of the church went into the United States army to put down the rebellion. Some fell in battle; some were starved to death in rebel prisons; some died in hospitals; others returned after the war, still loving Christ and beloved by the church. Nearly fifteen hundred members have been received into this church from its organization up to October 21, 1867. Nearly forty-five years they have been going home to Jesus, yet the church is large. Four other churches have been organized of its members, still it is the largest church in the conference. I have given the parting hand to many to whom the Master said, "Come up higher," but now they must give to me the parting hand while I, like Elijah, wait for the chariot to take me home.

The Old Man Closing his Pastoral Labors.—The time had now come for me to close my labors with the Bethlehem Church. It was the time of the half-yearly communion. While writing, the tears start unbidden to my eyes. The meeting commenced on Saturday, October 19, 1867. Elder William Pangburn was with me. It was reported that I would preach my farewell sermon on the Lord's-day, at eleven o'clock, and the congregation was very large. Elder Pangburn preached; I could not. I never preached a formal farewell sermon. The churches of which I have been pastor were raised by my labors. The relation has always been cordial. As pastor I have generally served for many years, and the relation has been uniformly harmonious and agreeable, causing increasing attachment. The church has seemed to me as my children, and, in consequence, my feelings of sympathy forbid formality, and prevented formal farewell sermons. After the sermon, I administered the Lord's Supper. There was the largest number of communicants that I remember having ever seen at one time. While the communicants were taking their seats, the following lines were sung:

Jesus is gone above the skies,
 Where our weak senses reach him not
And carnal objects court our eyes,
 To thrust our Savior from our thought

He knows what wandering hearts we have—
 Apt to forget his lovely face;
And to refresh our minds, he gave
 These kind memorials of his grace.

The Lord of life this table spread
 With his own flesh and dying blood;
We on the rich provision feed,
 And drink the wine, and bless our God.

Let sinful sweets be all forgot,
 And earth grow less in our esteem;
Christ and his love fill every thought,
 And faith and hope be fixed on him.

While he is absent from our sight,
 'Tis to prepare our souls a place,
That we may dwell in heavenly light,
 And live forever near his face.

Our eyes look upward to the hills
 Whence our returning Lord shall come;
We wait thy chariot's awful wheels,
 To fetch our longing spirits home.

Next, thanks were given to God for these memorials of his love. It was a time of great solemnity. This was the last time that my hands would ever break the emblematical bread to those whom I had so long served. This was the last time that I would pour out to them the symbolical cup as their pastor, after having administered to them the ordinances of the Lord's house for nearly forty-five years. All, including myself, felt that it was like a father and children parting without hope of the relationship ever being restored in this world. There was much weeping. My own tears mingled with those of the people. While the deacons were passing the bread, I could not refrain from some words of sympathy. It was the last communion we would have together as pastor and people; the last time that I would be the administrator and they the communicants; the last time we would break bread together on earth. I alluded to the loved ones in heaven. Once they too were with us; now they are numbered with the dead. We shall see them on earth no more; but soon we shall see them in heaven. We will meet them up there at the great communion, where Jesus will administer, where sickness and sorrow shall never come, sighing and death shall be known no more. I paused. The emblems had been passed; the vessels were returned to the table; the deacons had resumed their seats. I would have said more; but my heart filled, and choked my utterance. The scene closed as Christ closed the first communion: "They sang a hymn, and went out." But this was not the end. Elder Pangburn preached at night; and though no appointment was made for me, on Monday morning the congregation was again large, many supposing that I would finally preach my farewell sermon, although I had not so intimated. Elder Pangburn and others urged me to do so; but knowing that my feelings would overcome my strength, I declined. Elder Pangburn preached an excellent sermon. Then I felt constrained to speak, if only a few words. The time had come for the pastor to give up his people, for the father to say farewell to his children, the shepherd to resign his flock. I stepped down from the pulpit to the platform, and kneeling, with tears supplicated a throne of grace for God's mercy and protection upon his people; for the light of his love and the glory of his grace to abide with that church forever. I then arose and spoke. I referred to my first visits among them nearly fifty years before. Then the country was wild; now it is cultivated. Then the roads were by mountain paths and the meandering valley brooks. Then they lived in log cabins, where they have now fine residences. I threaded my way over the hills and through the hollows, boldly fording the mountain streams, and searching out their rudest homes. Then the people had little culture, where now they are educated. Then they were without hope and without God in the world. I took them by the hand and led them to God. I was inexperienced, but earnest. I preached in their rudest cabins. I led them in prayer at there fireside altars. I baptized in their woodland streams; I kneeled at the dying pillows of their parents, and preached the funerals of their children. God blessed my labors, and changed the lion to a lamb, the raven to a dove, and made the desert to blossom as the rose. My eyes could see but few present who were living in the country at the beginning of my ministry there. Then I was young and strong, but now I am old and feeble; too old to serve you; and they to whom I then preached are gone—gone, no more to return. I tried to say that this was the last day of my pastorate, the day of final separation as pastor and people, but I could not. I tried to say farewell, but there was so much weeping that utterance was choked, and tears blinded my eyes. Some kind brother started a farewell hymn, and while singing they gave me the parting hand. Then I bowed and bid them farewell! and the labors of forty-five years in that church were closed.

> Farewell, farewell, dear Bethlehem,
> For my down-going sun
> Tells me my day is nearly closed,
> My life's work nearly done;
> Leave me! My steps are growing slow;
> I'll linger near the shore,
> And cross, when Jesus calls, to where .
> We'll meet to part no more.

I shall still preach as opportunity offers and circumstances justify, and I shall try to write some things to speak when I am gone.

Wages for Preaching.—When my ministry began, there were no Christian churches to support ministers. I therefore received little compensation for many years. When the churches grew, my conscience compelled me to decline putting a price on my preaching the gospel. I could find no "thus saith the Lord" for it. I do not reprove those who do, however. I therefore left it with the churches to say how much they would give. This was commonly a mere trifle, about fifty or sixty dollars a year for monthly preaching. Thus it was with the Bethlehem Church till the last few years. That church, possessing a good deal of wealth, proposed to give me one hundred dollars a year, and in 1866 they gave me two hundred dollars a year for semi-monthly preaching on Saturday and Sabbath, and attending their communion and protracted meetings, etc. This was by far the largest salary, if it may be so called, that I ever received; and this was paid for only one or two years out of forty-five.

Southern Ohio Christian Conference.—The forty-eighth annual session of the Southern Ohio Christian Conference met in 1867 at Bentonville, in Adams County, on the 2d day of November. Through divine grace my health was continued so that I could be present. This was the forty-eighth successive annual meeting of this conference that I had attended; that is, I have attended, without one failure, every year since its organization in 1820. There was a large attendance this year. The reports from the churches were reasonably good, without quite so many additions as were reported the previous year. The meetings for business were very pleasant, only marred by "Young America," offensively developed in one or two young preachers, and cropping out in the form of that self-conceit called "brass," which knows no reverence for age. The experience of increasing years, however, will work their cure if they practice prayer, and look to Jesus as their example.

December 5, 1867.—My birthday comes again and finds me at home. I am seventy-seven years old to-day. I heartily thank God, my heavenly Father, that my health has improved of late, and is good for a man of my age.

Voice.—I have not lost my voice, as many ministers have when much younger. I can yet sing tolerably well, considering how many years' vocal labor I have done. For this I render humble thanks, and praise my Lord and Savior.

Prayer.—O God! as I now enter upon my seventy-eighth year, I pray thee in the name of Jesus Christ, thy Son, to let thy mercy still continue with me. Let thy protecting care be over me. Regard the low estate of thy poor unworthy servant. In this, the evening of my life, my trust is in thee alone. Thou art my help and my consolation. The joys of earth could never offer perfect peace. But even their transient joys have long since passed away. Be thou, O God, my fortress, my strong tower, my joy in peace, and comfort in the day of trouble. Thou art my rock; thou art my strength and my salvation.

Christmas, December 25, 1867.—Old faithful Time does not grow weary, but hurrying on, like an ever-rolling stream, brings us our longed-for Christmas. Seventy-eight of these blessed days have dawned on me. This day is dark; I can hardly see to write. There is no snow on the ground. I would that I could be out to protracted meetings, as in days and nights of old, for fifty years; but I can not endure the cold, and am therefore confined at home. Even the remembrance of those meetings, where hundreds found Jesus' pardoning grace through my labors, now gives me joy, while many of these, I trust, are at home in glory, and others are on their way. For continued health I continue thankful, and through faith and prayer enjoy God's love.

New Year's.—Here is New Year's day, of 1868. My God, I thank thee for thy protecting care, which has been over me through the year which has passed. I entreat thee, in the name of Jesus Christ, thy Son, to continue thy mercies toward me, thy poor unworthy servant, through the year that is now begun. If it be thy will that I shall abide in this tabernacle, be thou with me. If I go hence, take me to thyself, to be with thee, to rest in peace, through thy dear Son. The following lines have been proved true to me by long experience and observation:

" 'Time is winging us away
To our eternal home;
Life is but a winter's day,
A journey to the tomb.
Youth and vigor soon will flee,
Blooming beauty lose its charms;
All that's mortal soon shall be
Inclosed in death's cold arms."

At Work in his Study.—Being confined to my room by the infirmities of age and winter weather; after January 1, 1868, I
employed my time in writing a brief work, containing the
scriptural platform of the Christians, clearly showing the difference between the views of the Christians and the system of
Alexander Campbell. Having lived cotemporary with Mr.
Campbell, who originated that system and founded the sect
with which his name is connected, I had investigated it and
observed its effects, and believed that I understood it in all its
parts better than any man now living. It seemed evident to
me that the people needed information on that system, and it
was, therefore, from a sense of duty that I undertook the work.
It was completed about April 1, 1868, and in the hands of the
people. It contained my investigations of Campbellism from
its origin, in 1823, to the present time, 1868; therefore, over
forty years. Though Mr. Campbell's system has often been alluded to, it has not yet been considered as a whole, nor have the
few texts adduced by the Campbellites, to prove that system,
been heretofore examined. It is here clearly demonstrated
that their rendering is a perversion of gospel truth that does
violence alike to reason and revelation, and is in opposition to
the preaching of the Lord of life and glory. So after revising
said work by and with the advice of Elder N. Summerbell, the
only man informed by me of my writing this narrative of
my life, thinking that it may be useful to some when I am
gone, I direct that after correcting the typographical errors
therein, he will give it a place among the doings and events of
my life as a component part thereof, as follows:

*The Pamphlet of 1868 Revised—Sect Defined—Unsectarian
People—Rise of Campbellism—A New Sect.*—Webster says:
"A sect is a body or number of persons united in tenets (tenets written or unwritten); chiefly in philosophy or
religion, but constituting a distinct party by holding sentiments
different from those of other men;" and that sectarianism is
"the disposition to dissent," and "to form new sects;" a
sectary is "a follower, a disciple, an adherent to a sect."
Christians is a generic name. It applies to all sects, churches,
or persons, that profess the Christian religion, however designated by other sectarian prefixes to the name Christian. All
nations that admit the divinity of Christ's mission are termed
Christian nations, in which are the numerous sects distinguished

by the names of their founders, leaders, tenets, forms of worship, church government, creeds, etc. Hebrews, Jews, or Israel are all generic names, designating all the descendants of Abraham, Isaac, and Jacob. This nation and people were divided into a number of sects when Christ came. Three of these sects are mentioned in the New Testament, and others by Josephus. All believed in the law given by Moses, and worshiped together at the temple. The largest sect, and the one having the greatest influence among the people, was the Pharisees. This name is derived from the Hebrew word *pharis*, which signifies to separate, as they separated themselves from others, as more holy. Paul confessed that he was of that sect. The Sadducees, the next largest sect, took the name from their founder and leader, Sadoc. They denied the resurrection, angels, and spirits, but the Pharisees confessed both. The third sect mentioned in the New Testament was the Herodians, so called from their being in favor of the policy of Herod, the Roman governor. (See Matt. xxii. 16–18). Would it have been proper for one of these sects, while rejecting all the Hebrews who could not adopt its peculiar opinions, to term itself "the Hebrews" or "the Jews," discarding its own peculiar name as Pharisees, Sadducees, etc? Certainly not; for how then could it have been known what sect of the Jews they were? Names should designate, not deceive. If said sect retained, in purity, the fundamental principles of Judaism, and received all Hebrews, then their being generic might entitle them to the generic name of Hebrews. But if they received only those Hebrews which adopted the opinions of some man, then common honesty would require the prefix of his name. This rule applies to the sects of Christendom at this day. Therefore, we have Calvinists, Lutherans, Wesleyans or Presbyterians, Methodists, Baptists; that is, Presbyterian (Christians), Methodist (Christians), etc. Mohammedans, in like manner, are divided into sects, all of which believe in Mohammed and hold to the religion instituted by him. These sects took their names from their founders or leaders, as did the Jews and Christians. Walker says that a "sect is a body of men following some peculiar master or united in some tenets." Webster says "sect from Latin sectum, to cut off, to separate, a part cut off, a body of persons separated from, in virtue of some especial doctrine or set of doctrines which they hold in common." And it is, therefore, understood that Christian sects reject other Christians who do not adopt their peculiar tenets. These opposition sects can not be justified. But such is the sect united on Mr. Campbell's tenets. Sects sprang up among the Christians while the apostles were yet living. The first, perhaps, were the Nicolaitans, who took their name from Nicholas, of Antioch, who founded that sect, and was their leader or master. Revelation ii. 6.

The Sabellians of the third century were so called from Sabellius, who denied the personality of the Son of God, and taught that the Father, Son, and Holy Ghost are only three offices, as some trinitarians now teach. When the Roman government banished Arius, those who held his opinion about Christ being only a created Son of God, were called Arians. We pass almost myriads of sects taking the name of their founders, and come down to the sixteenth century, and to the great reformation by Luther. He being a bold, energetic leader, shook the Roman Catholic Church to its center and caused the pope to tremble upon his throne. A great sect arose, taking his name as their founder and master, namely, the Lutherans. Near that time John Calvin founded a sect upon the tenets of unconditional election and reprobation, which took his name, as Calvinists. James Arminius taught the opposite doctrine to that of Calvin, to-wit: man's voluntary agency and God's free grace, and those who thus hold are called Arminians. The sects founded by Luther and Calvin were soon productive of other sects, taking the names of their founders, but all confessing the name Christian, with their sectarian names prefixed, as Lutheran Christians, Calvinist Christians, etc., called briefly Calvinists, Lutherans, Wesleyans, etc.,—the term Christians being understood. Is it not evident, therefore, that sects and doctrines founded by or on the peculiar doctrines of men have been, in all ages, designated by names of their founders? Those, therefore, who claim to be known only by the generic name of Christians should hold only the "common salvation and faith once delivered to the saints (Jude 3), avoiding the minutest variation from the word of God:" but they must fellowship all Christians, and not confine their fellowship to a few bigoted disciples of their own opinions. Such a people has arisen.

The Unsectarian People and Christian Platform.—Near the beginning of this century (1800), an unsectarian people arose in the United States, as no other people ever arose since Christ preached the gospel. There were great revivals of religion in a number of the states, in which the saving power of God was wonderfully manifested. Many who were the subjects of that revival and that spirit, in different states, simultaneously, without any leader other than Jesus, came to the same views at the same time, namely, that the time had come for the followers of Christ to be united according to his prayer, "Father, that they all may be one" (John XVII. 21), although it was years before those in different states, who were of the same views, had any knowledge of each other. Thus, though it is impossible for all God's people to be united upon any man-made creed and sectarian name, they, without knowledge of each other's actions, and with no human leader, took the Scriptures for their rule of faith and practice, and the name Christian by which to be known, as did Christ's followers in the beginning, without any sectarian name being prefixed, and thus formed the true basis by which parties, distant in locality, differing in sentiment, as Baptists, Methodists, and Presbyterians, immersed and sprinkled, Calvinist and Arminian, all came into harmonious union without constraint. No dogmas were to be imposed on any, but all were to form their own opinions from reading the word of divine love, the only test of fellowship being a life and conduct in conformity with the gospel. Nor was baptism in any form, nor is it now, made a test of church fellowship; hence a pious Friend Quaker is not rejected, though believing in the baptism of the Holy Spirit without water.

In What They Agreed.—Agreement on the following points, clearly expressed and defined in God's word, were uniformly received as fundamental principles:

I. Belief in the Father, Son, and Holy Spirit, and that Jesus Christ, the Son of God, is the mediator between God and man, and that the Son is divine.

II. The atonement or reconciliation made by Christ for all.

III. The new birth, by and through the influence of the Holy Spirit.

IV. The resurrection, both of the just and of the unjust.

V. "That God has appointed a day in which he will judge the world in righteousness," and that all will be rewarded or punished, "according to the deeds done in the body."

Christ, having commanded his apostles to teach and baptize, Christian ministers obey that injunction of the Savior. As the primitive baptism was immersion, according to the original Greek, as admitted by Luther, Calvin, Wesley, and others of the learned, it was and is the way in which the Christian ministers, who were formerly Presbyterians and Methodists, as well as Baptists, soon began to baptize. Some at first baptized three ways. It is not a test of fellowship. All live in union. Some Christian ministers did go to an extreme in speculations about the trinity, but without making their views a test of fellowship. It is now spoken of in Scripture language. The views of Christians on the design of baptism are about with the Baptists, except in not making it a test of fellowship. Every one decides for himself. Thus, after pardon and peace are obtained by faith, prayer, and repentance, we are "buried with Christ by baptism," in likeness of his burial and resurrection. Romans VI. 4. In church government the Christians are congregational, as the primitive churches were. Every church does its own business, subject to no higher power. In this Baptists and Christians are about the same, and Christian conferences answer to Baptist associations, to which the churches send messengers to meet with the ministers. Every church is left free in property, faith, and fellowship. Is not this unsectarian platform broad enough, and long enough, and straight enough for all the followers of the Redeemer to unite upon? If Christ's church is ever united it can not be upon any human creed, either oral or written (all differing), but the union must be upon the Bible. Must it not? Some of the largest Protestant denominations are now moving in that direction.

Testimony.—The writer, having been laboring with and observing the Christian ministers for more than fifty-seven years (sixty years now, A. D. 1871), and having been cotemporary with the first ministers of that people, knows that the things here stated are correct and true as to Christians' views, etc.

A. D. 1823—*A Modern Sect.*—There being no religion established by law in the United States, all believe and worship as they please; hence it is the most fruitful field for sects of any country on the globe. In 1823 a sect arose in this country in the following manner: Shortly before that time Alexander Campbell came from Ireland, having been educated for a Presbyterian minister; but, changing his views on baptism, he joined the Baptists, and by his debates on the mode of baptism soon became popular among the people. He then began to propagate the theory that it is the order of God, according to the gospel, that there can be no remission of sin without immersion in water being added to faith and repentance. This differed so widely from the Baptists' faith that they disowned him. But Mr. Campbell, having gained much influence, divided their churches and founded a sect of Disciples for himself upon the tenets aforesaid, taking the Scriptures, as he said, for his rule of faith and practice. He spoke of taking the name Christians, but said, as that name had already been taken by another people who were widely known by it, he would adopt the name "Disciples of Christ," which he did. As Mr. Campbell possessed the great boldness and the assurance common to his nation, he acted with energy. He soon started a paper at Bethany, his residence in Western Virginia; next a college, by which, with his debates and preaching, he propagated his new system, and preachers of different denominations joined him. Among his leading topics in preaching and writing were ridicule and burlesque of a called and sent ministry, and prayer for mourners: he immersing them instead to get the remission of sins. In like manner he poured contempt upon the commonly received views of experimental religion, saying, "It is all delusion. Faith, repentance, and immersion secure the remission of sins, and are the sum total of experimental religion. There is no Holy Spirit to operate on mankind other than the written word, nor any influence of it in the new birth, except by the word, and sinners are not required to pray before immersion," etc. (See "Christian Baptist," Vol. 1. p. 186, and Vol. II. p. 171, Vol. V. p. 223, 132. Also his two standard works, "Christianity restored" and the "Christian

System)." All know, who have heard the preachers of that sect, that these are their themes, almost without an exception. The teachers of that system partake of the spirit of the founder of the sect. Mr. Campbell, hence make their declarations with the great boldness, assurance, and seeming confidence of all errorists. Thus Shakers say that Christ did come the second time in Ann Lee; and the Millerites said that Christ *would* come in 1843; and the Mormons that they *know* they are right and all others wrong; captivating the uninformed by their very assurance. The writer, having been a cotemporary with Mr. Campbell, having heard him preach, and having conversed with him, and read his first religious publications, and, having examined that system for more than forty years, can there be a doubt of his understanding it? All of that sect, from its founder, Mr. Campbell, down, are ever crying out against sects and sectarianism, but we have shown by undeniable proofs that *they are a sect*, according to all the meanings of that word.

First: They, like all sects, had a human founder and leader, Mr. Campbell. He organized that sect, making the fundamental tenets or dogmas thereof. (He states in the "Encyclopedia of Religious Knowledge)" that they are "sometimes called *Campbellites*, or *Reformers*." "As is usual in similar cases, the brethren who unite under the name of *Disciples of Christ*, or Christians, are nicknamed after those who have been prominent in *gathering* them."—*Alexander Campbell.*

Second: They say that sin can be remitted only by immersion after faith and repentance, upon which tenet there never had been a sect founded before. Mr. Campbell and his party, as a sect, separate from others, are united upon the aforesaid tenet. Hence they are a sect.

Third: They will not receive any who do not agree with them in the aforesaid dogma on immersion. Hence they are a sect, as is uniformly understood. So, though they make a show of liberality, and talk about union upon their oral creed, are they not one of the most intolerant, proscriptive sects in Christendom, rejecting all but immersionists? Were they not sectarian they would not seek to build up their sect. For more than twenty years before said sect existed there was a people known by the name "Christian;" therefore, in assuming that name while rejecting Christians, they are also guilty of plagiary, and condemned by the laws of literature, and prove themselves opposed to union on the Bible. No people having a creed or platform, oral or written, which has not length enough and breadth enough for all of Christ's people to unite upon, have a right to the generic name Christian, without their sectarian mark prefixed to it. They have the same right to the name "Christian" that any other sect has; no less, no more. As there were Sadducees, Jews and Platonic philosophers, and as there are Roman

Catholic Christians, and Calvinistic Christians, so they are "Campbellite" Christians, or Campbellites; nothing less, nothing more. Their professing to take the Bible alone, and assuming the sanctified family name of Christians as peculiarly theirs, while having a proscriptive platform and an oral creed on immersion, which dooms to perdition nearly nine hundred and ninety-nine out of every thousand of all professed Christians, is out of character, and indefensible. Why should that sect object (as they do) to being called Campbellites? Mr. Campbell does not deny being their founder; why are they ashamed of him? Do they who believe in the system of Calvin object to the name of Calvinists? Not they; nor do any other sects object to being known by the names of their founders. Was not Mr. Campbell as really the founder of that system known by his name as John Calvin was of the one with which his name is connected? They are parallel cases. Therefore if we hereafter call the followers of Mr. Campbell Campbellites, it will be correct, this being their proper sectarian name. (See Ency. Rel. Kowledge p. 462).

The Union.—About 1830, when Mr. Campbell was on one of his tours in Kentucky, he went to the house of Barton W. Stone, a Christian minister, and proposed that, as they had both taken the Scriptures, they ought to be in union. Elder Stone admitted Mr. Campbell's theory of remission of sin by immersion, but refused to make immersion a test of fellowship. Elder Stone was a great and good man, but he had been an extremist against the doctrine of the trinity. I could not receive all his views. But they went on forming a union, in which Mr. Campbell's system was uniformly received. A hymn-book was soon published by Campbell and Stone, entitled "*Christian Hymn-book.*" Elder Stone and myself had formerly been members of the Kentucky Christian Conference, and had been a great deal in each other's company—had traveled and preached together every year, more or less, for twenty years. Hence, to leave him was like a son being separated from his father, no more to be united. Consequently I carefully examined that system with a *desire* to believe it, but found it to be of man's invention, and not of God. In 1835 I published my objections, entitled, "Twelve Years' Observation of Mr. Campbell's Theory and Practice," etc., which they never answered or denied, but contented themselves with slandering the author, Mr. Campbell himself taking a leading part in his paper, but not permitting me to defend myself. After Elder Stone formed said union, he was never again a member of any Christian conference; but he and those who went with him, though they had left that platform, retained the name Christians, and Mr. Campbell's followers are now adopting it, calling themselves the Christian Church, yet excluding all Christians who do not adopt their opinions on immersion. .

God's One Order of Remission of Sin.—Let us take a concise view of God's one uniform and universal order of remission of sins: "Moses returned unto the Lord, and said, Oh, this people have sinned a great sin, and have made them gods of gold. Yet now, if thou wilt forgive their sin; and if not, blot me, I pray thee, out of thy book which thou hast written." Exodus xxxii. 32. God proclaimed his name to Moses, saying, "I am the Lord God, merciful, forgiving iniquity and transgression and sin," etc. | Exodus xxxiv. 5, 6, 7. "When Moses prayed unto the Lord, the fire was quenched." Numbers xi. 2. This one order of God is like its author, unchangeable, ever the same, suited to the wants and needs of sinful man in every condition, every age, clime, and country. It requires on man's part true faith, repentance, and prayer. Upon these God has promised forgiveness, without the uncertain aid of man to immerse. This was God's one order, "as it was in the beginning, is now, and ever shall be." The law could not shut man out from access to God by prayer; the prophets would not. God said, "He is a prophet, and he shall pray for thee." Genesis xx. 7. Samuel said, "God forbid that I should sin against the Lord in ceasing to pray for you." I. Samuel xii. 23. The righteous man makes his offering, but the sinner prays for pardon. This is the order practiced alike in Eden and Jerusalem.

Abel.—"By faith Abel offered unto God a more excellent sacrifice than Cain, by which he obtained witness that he was righteous." Hebrews xi. 5.

Cain.—And Cain said unto the Lord, "My punishment is greater than I can bear." "And the Lord set a mark upon Cain, lest any finding him should kill him." Genesis iii. 15. "Then began men to call upon the name of the Lord." Genesis iv. 26. Abraham prayed for Abimelech, and he was healed (Genesis xx. 7), and for Sodom, and was heard. The Ninevites repented, and were pardoned. The Publican said, "God be merciful to me, a sinner!" and was justified. God gave to his "Son power on earth to forgive sins." Mark ii. 10; Luke v. 24; John v. 27. God never invested any being with power to forgive sin, except his Son, nor can we suppose that he ever will. Of course the Son forgives sin according to the one order of God, the same as God himself. The repentant sinner, having returned to his Father, as the prodigal son, is pardoned and received into the family, and will obey Christ in baptism, not to make him a child, but because he is a child. Likewise he obeys all other commandments of the Lord. If he is not obedient, Jesus will disown him. The Lord of the universe has but one plan of remission of sins, I think, can not be denied; and that he has always remitted sins in the same way is equally clear. That sect (Mr. Campbell's) denies this one order of God, and says the gospel was never preached, not even by Christ himself, till Peter preached it at Pentecost. But even here they carefully omit Acts II. 21, where Peter proves that we are saved by prayer, saying, "And it shall come to pass, that whosoever shall call on the name of the Lord, shall be saved." This promise they do not regard, but direct all their effort to calling attention to the thirty-eighth verse, so changing it as to make it to mean, "Be immersed *in order to* the remission of sins." Dr. Clarke, and others of the most learned critics, do not render *eis,* the Greek preposition in that text, translated *for,* "in order to." Even Peter positively contradicts them in reference to his words at Pentecost. He says, Baptism is "not the putting away of the *filth of the flesh,* but the answer of a *good conscience* toward God." I. Peter III. 21. Can the conscience be made good without the remission of sins? This is before "baptism." Paul says, "Having our hearts sprinkled from an evil conscience, and our bodies washed with pure water." Heb. X. 22. Then must not sin be remitted according to the one order of God, and the hearts be made pure before baptism? After Jesus had cleansed the leper he said: "Go and make an offering for thy cleansing." Mark I. 44. Was the leper to offer *for* his cleansing *in order to* get cleansed when he was already cleansed, or was he to make the offering for having been cleansed? Which was it? Then were not their sins at Pentecost remitted through faith and repentance, for which Peter commanded them to be baptized? Is not the leper's and that parallel cases? "For," in Acts II. 38, does not mean in order to, but is to be understood as in parallel texts. Take Hebrews, the tenth chapter, for an example: "Sacrifices for sin" (v. 6); "offerings for sin" (v. 8); "once for all" (v. 10); "sacrifice for sins" (v. 12); "offering for sin" (v. 18); "sacrifice for sins" (v. 26). Not in one case here can for mean "in order to." There is not one text in the Bible that plainly states their doctrine. In Acts II. 38, their favorite texts, they have to supply, by their own opinion, the words *water, immersion,* and in *order to,* none of which are stated; and even then it is through repentance, faith, and prayer that remission comes, baptism being the answer of a good conscience (I. Peter III. 21), the offering of the good (Matt. III. 15). They deny too much. They say that Christ did not preach the gospel in full, for he could not preach his own resurrection. Jesus thus reproves them: "O fools, and slow of heart to believe all that the prophets have spoken! Then opened he their understanding, that they might understand the Scriptures, and said unto them, Thus it is written and thus it behooved Christ to suffer, and to rise from the dead the third day: and that repentance and remission of sins should be preached in his name among all nations, beginning at Jerusalem." Luke XXIV. 24–48. But Mr. Campbell's preachers deny these things. Did not Christ preach the resurrection and say that he would rise the third day? Did he not preach his own resurrection when he said to Mary: "Go and tell my brethren that I am risen." Matt. XXVIII. 6, 7; Mark XVI. 6, 7, 8; Luke XXIV. 23, 24, 25; John XX. 15, 16, 17. Paul says Christ's resurrection is the confirmation and "assurance" of the gospel. Acts XVII. 31; I. Corinthians XV. 14, 15. Christ's resurrection is connected with the gospel, proving it true, as testimony proves a case in court. Paul said "if Christ be not risen, then is our preaching vain, and your faith is also vain." What right have they to say that Jesus' preaching was in vain as he preached only part of the gospel, and so contradict God's word? That *system* is based upon the denial of the four plain gospel truths: First: They say that Christ was not king while upon earth. Second: They deny that Christ preached the gospel. Third: They say that Christ was not priest while on earth. Fourth: They deny that there was any kingdom of heaven upon earth while Jesus, the lord of glory, was here. Let us look at a brief contrast between God's word and that system. Jesus says, "He (God) hath anointed me to preach the gospel." Luke IV. 18. They say God never anointed his Son to preach the gospel. "Jesus went about all Galilee preaching the gospel." Matt IV. 23. They say Christ did not preach the gospel in Galilee. "Jesus went about all the cities preaching the gospel," etc. Matt. IX. 25; Mark I. 14. They say it was not the gospel he preached. Jesus said, "To the poor the gospel is preached." Matt. XI. 5; Luke VII. 22. They say the gospel was not preached to the poor nor to any body else till Peter preached it at Pentecost. Of the many passages that might be adduced we quote one more. Jesus says, "This gospel of the kingdom shall be preached in all the world, and then shall the end come." Matt. XXIV. 14. Is not "this gospel," then, that Jesus himself preached (not Peter), the one and only gospel ever to be preached? Peter never preached any other gospel; hence he is slandered by them. That sect, to sustain their system, also denies that there was any kingdom of heaven on earth while Christ was here, or that he was then priest or king. Said Christ "The kingdom of heaven *is* (now) like a grain of mustard-seed." It *is* like leaven." "It *is* like a net cast into the sea." "It *is* like a sower." "It *is* like a householder," etc. They say, not so; there was then no kingdom of heaven in the likeness of any thing. Jesus said, "Woe unto you, Pharisees, for you shut up the kingdom of heaven." Matt. XXIII. 13. They say there was no kingdom of heaven to shut up. Jesus said, "Publicans and harlots go into the kingdom of God before you, Pharisees." Matt. XXI. 31. They say there was then no kingdom of heaven to go into. Jesus said, "The law and the prophets were until John; since that time the kingdom of God is preached, and every man presseth into it." Luke XVI. 16. Campbellites say, not so; Peter first preached that kingdom at Pentecost. How could every man press into the kingdom of heaven if there were no kingdom set up? Do not all evangelical denominations agree that Jesus was anointed prophet, priest, and king, by the Holy Spirit immediately after his baptism? If he was not priest, how could he make the offering for man's sins and the atonement, when he "offered himself without spot to God?" (Hebrews IX. 14), and "by one offering perfected forever them that are satctified?" Hebrews X. 14. If, as they say, he was not priest, he had no more right to offer sacrifice than Ahab. Was he king? Let us see. When he rode into Jerusalem the multitude shouted, saying, "Rejoice greatly, O daughter of Zion; behold, thy King cometh unto thee," etc. Zechariah X. 9; Matt. XXI. 1–6. Ah, say that sect, they were all deluded fanatics. He was not king. That system, founded upon a fancy, requires the denial of these facts and texts. Like the "living child," it dies if divided, and the word of God, the sword of the Spirit, would divide and destroy it if believed. Therefore, as the Four Gospels condemn their system, they condemn the gospel of Christ, and deny his authority. Their first effort, when they begin at a place, is to prove that immersion is the only mode of baptism, thus enlisting baptist sympathy; next, they teach that as three acts broke the union between Adam and God, the last one being his ejection from the garden, which changed his state, so three acts reunite man and God, to-wit: faith, repentance, and immersion; by the last one—immersion—his state being changed. In this they pervert the Scriptures. Adam's state was changed before he was driven from Eden. Webster says, "State, as to men and things, is situation, condition," as the state of the mind, health, etc. So Adam's state or condition was changed when he disobeyed God and hid himself, before he left the garden. An infidel's state is changed as soon as he believes on the Lord Jesus Christ with all his "heart unto righteousness." Their reasoning, like the whole system, is false. They quote: "He that believeth and is baptized (immersed) shall be saved, but he that believeth not shall be damned" (Mark XVI. 16); from which they infer that all will be damned who are not immersed in water. Jesus knew that every man could believe, while the condition of some might prevent their being baptized; hence he did not say that believers are damned if not baptized. They connect with the above text John III. 5: "Except a man be born of water and of the Spirit, he can not enter into the kingdom of God." If born here means immerse, then woo to the Campbellites! for they are not immersed in the Spirit, and are thus condemned by the text they quote to con-

13

demn others. "Happy is he that condemneth not himself in that thing which he alloweth." Romans XIV. 22. They quote the text to prove that none can enter the kingdom of heaven except the immersed, which is, however, such a horrible doc-trine, that they abandon it while trying to prove it, and fall back on the subterfuge that it is only the earthly kingdom that is meant. This shows that they are ashamed or afraid of their own doctrine, and hence do not believe it. Christ's kingdom is one in earth or heaven. And it is pitiable to see ministers try to prove that men can enter God's church, above whom they keep out of their church below. None can hope to enter there who are unprepared for membership here. There must be a "new birth." This birth presupposes remission. "This is the cove-nant that I will make with them after those days, saith the Lord; I will put my laws into their hearts, and in their minds will I write them." "And their sins and iniquities will I re-member no more." "Now where remission of these is, there is no more offering for sin." Heb. x. 16–18. It is evident, there-fore, that Christ did not mean baptism, as there is no text which calls baptism a birth, nor is it literal water, but the gospel of which the prophet says, "Ho, every one that thirsteth, come ye to the waters." Isaiah LV. 1. Jesus told the Samaritan woman if she had asked of him, he would have given her living water. John IV. 10, 15. "Jesus cried, If any man thirst, let him come unto me and drink." John VII. 37. Peter says that we are "born again, not of corruptible seed, but of incorrupti-ble, by the word of God (the gospel), which liveth and abideth forever" (I. Peter I. 23), i. e., not by the corruptible element of water, but through faith in the gospel, and the influence of the Holy Spirit. The word of God has simplified the new birth, and made it plain, by assuring us that "whosoever loveth God is born of God." I. John IV. 7. Hence, if we love God before immersion, and so are born of God before immersion, our sins are forgiven before immersion. Some plead that if a person can not be immersed, God will pardon without it. This yields the question, for they thus admit the truth that conversion is the point of pardon. No one can believe that God forgives one immediately because he can never be baptized, but keeps the other in his sins because he can be baptized in an hour, next day, or next week or year. They who love God keep his "commandments." Because they are born again, and hence children, and love their Father, they keep his commandments, not to make them children. According to that system, sinners are immersed before they love God, to make them love him. That sect repeats, "Arise and be baptized, and wash away thy sins," as equivalent to remit thy sins. So they teach that Paul was commanded to pardon himself, that is, to "wash

away" (remit) his own internal sins and corruption. What are
the facts? Paul was blind, believing, repenting, and praying,
being already an ordained minister of the gospel. Three days
before his baptism, Jesus ordained him to the ministry, saying,
"NOW I send thee." "I have appeared unto thee for this purpose, to make thee a minister and a witness both of these
things which thou hast seen, and of those things in the which
I will appear unto thee, delivering thee from the people and
from the Gentiles, unto whom now I send thee, to open their
eyes, and to turn them from darkness to light, and from the
power of Satan unto God, that they may receive forgiveness of
sins, and inheritance among them which are sanctified by faith
that is in me." Acts XXVI. 16–18. When any believed in Jesus,
he, at that time, immediately owned them as his disciples, without commanding them to be first immersed. When Ananias, a
disciple of the Lord Jesus, entered into the house where Saul
lay, he, putting his hands on him, said, "Brother Saul, the Lord
(even Jesus that appeared unto thee in the way as thou camest)
hath sent me, that thou mightest receive thy sight, and be filled
with the Holy Ghost. And immediately there fell from his eyes
as it had been scales: and he received sight." Acts IX. 17. The
natural inference is that he received the Holy Ghost at the same
time that he received his sight, the Holy Ghost restoring him to
sight. As Paul's eyes were opened and he was filled with the
Holy Ghost, so his sins were pardoned before he was commanded
to "wash away his sins." The only sins that Paul could or did
"wash away" by being baptized, were his external sins or character of persecutor. By baptism he put on a new character,
being no longer Saul the persecutor, but Paul the Christian. Is
that not plain? Who can deny it? I said to a preacher of that
system a few weeks ago: Do you believe that during the law
and the prophets it was the one order of God to grant remission
of sins through faith and repentance? He answered yes. Do
you believe that Christ practiced the same during his ministry
while here on earth? He answered yes. Do you believe that
since Peter preached the gospel on the day of Pentecost it is the
one order of God, and the only one, that sin can be remitted
only in immersion? He answered yes. Said I, is not such a
gospel almost an entire failure as to man's salvation, for there
are nearly nine hundred and ninety-nine out of every thousand
professed Christians who do not believe it, and never were im-
messed? If it is true, they are eternally lost who might have
been saved before Christ died. Would it not have been better
to let the order of remission of sins as under the law and the
prophets, and the teaching of Christ, continue? Would not
man's condition be far better without such a gospel as you say
Peter preached? Or had it never been heard of? He looked
thoughtful, but there was no reply. A few admit that some are

saved without immersion. I ask them, how can they get to
heaven unpardoned? No answer. As an objection to that
system, I have alluded to the condition of the hundreds of our
poor Union soldiers, who, far away from home and friends, were
starved to death in rebel prisons. Many of them believed, prayed,
and repented before death, and said they obtained pardon and
peace, and sent this word home to their connections and friends
to console them. But, according to that system, they were
deceived, and are all eternally lost because they could not be
immersed. A preacher told his confiding hearers, it is said, that
there was plenty of water in the rebel prisons, and all could
have been immersed! They have frequently proposed a union
with the Christians, but the proscriptive platform of their oral
creed is quite too narrow. Intelligent Christians desire no platform too narrow for all God's children, hence there is no probability of the two people uniting, unless they enlarge their
platform. Is it not well known that Christians have more affinity
of feeling and harmony of views with the Baptists, Presbyterians, or Methodists, than with them? Can it be believed that
the God of infinite love and tender mercy is the author of a
system by which man's condition is such that he can not get
remission of sins without being dependent on his fellow-man to
immerse him, or be eternally lost? Never, never! The elements of that system were arranged by Mr. A. Campbell, and
he founded that sect upon them. He was a man of some learning and greatness, but, like others of that kind, he made a great
mistake, such as none but great men can make. *Small* men can
not make *great* mistakes. "A little learning is a dangerous
thing" in sect-building, without humility. Mr. Campbell's system dooms to perdition all mankind except his own sect, and
Mormons, and such Catholics as may be immersed. For the
Baptists, though immersed, not being immersed in order to
remission of sins, their baptism avails nothing for pardon, and
they must abide their fate with the rest. As Christ, our pattern,
when baptized, had no sin to remit, but was the holy Son of
God before baptism, we should be holy, and, having our sins
remitted, go to the water as his followers and as children of
God. Baptism can not make us children, for we are "born, not
of blood, nor of the will of the flesh, nor of the will of man,
but of God." John i. 13. If their system is true, the Mormons,
who immerse as often as they sin, take the safe course. Immersion in order to remission was introduced among them by
Sydney Rigdon, the first Baptist preacher who followed Mr.
Campbell. He did not stop, like Mr. Campbell, but went on to
the Mormons, and went on immersing for remission. And why
not? There is no Scripture which says that baptism is only for
our first or past sins and not for the sins of all our life. Having carefully investigated Mr. Campbell's system for more than

forty years, and having had discussions with one of their ablest debaters (Elder John B. Lucas), we know that the foregoing statements are correct, and can not be answered or denied with truth.

"*Fullness of the Gospel of Christ*"—*Conclusion*.—Paul said in the gospel "the righteousness of God is revealed from faith to faith," etc. Romans I. 17. That is, God's righteous plan of salvation is proposed and offered to all mankind in the "gospel of Christ." As the gospel was preached to Abraham, he believed, and was justified by faith, so all who now believe the "gospel of Christ" are justified with faithful Abraham. Thus it is from Abraham to Christ, "from faith to faith." "If ye are Christ's followers by faith, then are ye Abraham's seed and heirs, according to the promise." Galatians III. 6, 28. "The fullness of the gospel of Christ" is as high as the throne of the universe, deep as the woes and sorrows of sin, and broad as earth's remotest bounds. The most lonely, wretched condition in which fallen man can be situated in this dark, friendless world of affliction and tears, is not beyond its fullness. The boundlessness of "the gospel of Christ" interests the angels so much, that "there is joy in the presence of the angels of God over one sinner that repenteth." This proves that the sinner is pardoned when he repents, and before immersion. Would the angels rejoice over an unpardoned sinner—a child of the devil? Behold that young man! Years before becoming of age, he longed for the time to come when he should be free from parental restraint! The day long desired has come. The world's wealth, long glittering in his view, he is determined to possess. He undertakes an enterprise in a far country. He has many friends till all his money is gone. Most of his fortune is spent in reveling and vain amusements. His enterprises all fail, and he is in a distant land, without money or friends. He remembers home, thinks of his mother and her kindness, recollects father and the family prayers. His early convictions are awakened anew. The gospel invites him to come to Jesus. He resolves to try. He goes out alone to pray. He fears and trembles. The tempter says, "You are too great a sinner to pray." He hesitates, but finally says, "If I perish, it shall be at Jesus' feet." He kneels down and says, "Oh, God, be merciful to me, a poor sinner! Save, Lord, or I perish!" He finds peace in believing the gospel, and says, "Jesus, thou art the sinner's friend! thou art my friend!" See the tender, affectionate mother! She has watched days and nights, without sleep, at the cradle of her sick babe. Great has been the conflict between her hopes and fears; but the angel of death came. The lovely child is cold in death's arms. That mother has pressed her darling to her bosom for the last time, and now prints the last kiss upon its death-chilled lips, while crystal tear-drops bid the long farewell. She says, "My child is no more mine, it has gone to Jesus." "How do you know, mother?" "The gospel of Christ tells me so." Jesus took little children in his arms and blessed them, and said, "Of such is the kingdom of heaven." We visit the graves of departed children and friends, and, lingering there, call to recollection their looks, their smiles, and their last words. But, ah! they are gone. Where are they? The gospel tells us that they are beyond the reach of pain, sickness, sorrow, and death, and that, after a few more sighs have heaved our bosoms, and a few more sorrows wrung our hearts, we will join their society, where Jesus is. While writing, "tears unbidden start." Children and friends are gone. The gospel has set a lighted lamp at the entrance of "the dark valley of the shadow of death," which shines all the way through. Many friends and brethren will doubtless read the foregoing remarks who have never seen the writer, and many others with whom he has bowed at the altar of prayer, but whom he will meet no more in this world. May the Lord help us so to live that we will have a tranquil hour in which to die, and afterward meet in heaven. Farewell, in bonds of love, and in "fullness of the gospel of Christ." Both pamphlets on Campbellism, as republished in one, may be obtained, with the observations, in the unabridged form, at the Christian Publishing House, at Dayton, Ohio.

The Effect.—Soon after the publication of this pamphlet, as I was returning to my home through Ripley, my attention was called to an article in the paper, professing to be a review or correction of my statements. It was signed by Elder H. T. Buff, the Campbellite preacher of that town. He represented that my statements were misrepresentations; my remarks abusive; my object being to make money in the sale of the pamphlet; and he appealed to the people whom he excludes from the name of Christians, for sympathy. Of course I replied. He tried to enlist the people's sympathy by the pretense that by my publication I persecuted them. To this I answered about as follows: The Campbellites doom all the Christian world to eternal perdition, except the few who are of their own faith; and because we object to being lost, they cry out that we persecute them. They pretend to rely on a thus saith the Lord, and when we bring the "thus saith the Lord" and prove their system to be wrong, and reverse their decision, they raise the cry of persecution.

Money-Making.—He represented that I published the work to make money. I replied that I sold them for fifty cents per dozen, and five cents each, post-paid, which would hardly pay for the paper and printing. I might have offered them free; but then the Campbellites would have procured all that they could and would have burned them. That same preacher had borrowed fifty dollars of me more than seven years before, and I had not seen or heard of him for over five years. When I learned that he had come to Ripley I presented the note, amounting, with interest at six per cent, to over seventy-one dollars. I gave him twenty-one dollars off of his lawful debt. If I loved money so much, why did I give him twenty-one dollars? Of Elder H. T. Buff's pretended "review" I said, "We wish it distinctly understood that he does not deny a single one of the five fundamental tenets of the Campbellite sect, which I presented, to-wit:

"*First:* Jesus Christ never preached the gospel contrary to the thus saith the Lord; 'Jesus came into Galilee, preaching the gospel of the kingdom of God.' Mark 1. 14; Luke iv. 18.

"*Second:* The kingdom of heaven was not set up while Christ was here contrary to the thus saith the Lord; 'The kingdom of God is come unto you.' Matt. xii. 28; Luke xvi. 16.

"*Third:* Christ was not king while in this world; contradicting the thus saith the Lord; 'Where is he that is born king of the Jews.' Matt. ii. 2; John xii. 13.

"*Fourth:* Christ was not priest while here; contrary to the thus saith the Lord; 'Christ being come an high priest.' Heb. ix. 11.

"*Fifth:* There can be no remission of sins without immersion; contrary to the thus saith the Lord; 'Whosoever believeth in him shall receive remission of sins.'" Acts x. 43.

Although he has not denied that these are their fundamental tenets, he makes the sweeping charge that both my publications in reference to Mr. Campbell are a "mass of misrepresentation" and abuse. This accusation could not be decided by arguments between gentlemen, not to say Christians, so I made the following proposition: I will submit Mr. Campbell's works and my two publications to three disinterested ministers—to be agreed upon—not of the Campbellites or Christians. And if they decide as he has asserted, I will confess that I have been mistaken, and I will pay the referees for their time. If they do not so decide, the opposite party shall do the same. If that accuser will not accept this equitable proposition, will not all honorable people view him as a false accuser and defamer? I wrote these publications in view of the judgment-day. I know them to be true, hence make this proposition. That has been before the people for several weeks, and there is no word of Elder H. T. Buff or any one else accepting it. Of course they never will.

Labors at Seventy-seven!—While engaged during the winter of 1868 in writing my pamphlet on Campbellism, I felt the same anxiety to preach as formerly, and had appointments made for every Sabbath in April and May. On one Lord's-day in April I preached three times and rode fifteen miles, which was going beyond my strength, and laid me up for some days. The second Lord's-day I preached in the Christian chapel in Ripley. Soon after the publication of my pamphlet, an appointment had been published in the Ripley papers for me to preach there on the subject of "justification by faith." It rained very hard that day and without intermission. The congregation was large for such a day, but as many were prevented coming by the rain, I acceded to the request of the friends, and took a vote of the congregation whether I should preach on the above subject then or defer it. The vote decided for a future day; so I appointed the fourth Sunday in May to speak on justification, and took up another subject at this time.

Union Christian College.—I had subscribed one thousand dollars to the endowment fund of Union Christian College, on condition that sixty thousand dollars were raised. On being informed that the condition was fulfilled, I, according to previous arrangement, went to Cincinnati, and there at the house of Elder N. Summerbell I met the treasurer of said college, on the 30th day of April, 1868, and paid to the college, as a donation, one thousand dollars. The sixty thousand now made up, of which my one thousand was a part, made the endowment one hundred thousand dollars, forty thousand having been raised during the first years of the college. I had before taken a share of stock for one hundred dollars; which makes eleven hundred dollars that I have given in all to Union Christian College.

Our Son is Dead!—May has come with its usual beauty, but it brings deep gloom to our house, sorrow to my heart, and mourning to all our family. Our son, George Washington Gardner, died on the 7th day of May, 1868, aged fifty years, three months, and seven days. He was a deacon in the Christian Church, and was considered by all who knew him a very correct and upright man. He was a farmer, and by industry and frugality he had increased in property so that his income in 1867 amounted to over four thousand dollars. I greatly miss him. I can hardly think him dead, but must believe it. Of all our sons, there remains not one whose counsel I preferred in my secular affairs to his. Washington, our son, is gone, and can not return. My heart swells, and my tears flow. Oh, blessed hope of immortality! We shall meet again; meet our loved ones, to part no more, in that world where "there shall be no more death." The 1st day of June, 1868, is here, and I have been able, through grace, to preach every Lord's-day since the 1st of April. Yesterday, the 31st day of May, 1868, I preached twice to quite large congregations at different places, and rode about twelve miles, reaching home a little after sundown, quite weary.

Sunstroke.—It is July. The weather is warmer than I ever remember it to have been in this climate. Every day of the first part of this month it ranged from 95° to 100° Farenheit, in the shade, and to-day, the 14th, the mercury stands at 102°.

As I was riding along the bank of the Ohio River, returning from visiting three of our children who live about eighteen miles down the river, I was on the north side of the river, exposed to the burning rays of the sun from above, and its powerful reflection from the water, when I was sun-struck. I was about falling from my horse, but a house was near and a friend helped me down from my horse and administered to my recovery. After an hour or so, I ventured to proceed on my journey, but I had not gone far till the effects returned. Happily I was near a covered bridge, where I sought shelter. Here it seemed as if I must die. However, after a time, I started again. Ripley was near, and by great resolution I reached it. There I obtained medical aid, and finally reached home; but I still feel the effect of that "sun-stroke." My adjourned appointment to preach on "justification by faith" at Ripley, on the fourth Lord's-day in May, was recalled on account of the repairing of the chapel at that time. The appointment was not renewed during the warm weather, on account of my feeble health and other labors; but the people still kept requesting it, and I at length consented to speak there on the first Lord's-day in September, at half-past three. This time was chosen, when other churches had no services, that both preachers and people might attend.

Rain—New Moon and Old Tradition.—About two weeks or more before the Ripley appointment, it rained on the first Sunday of the new moon. I have long observed that, if it rains on the first Sunday of the new moon, it will generally rain on every Sunday of that moon. The second Sunday of the moon came. It rained again. It was a wet spell of weather. I then prayed to the Lord that it might not rain on that day. I believe that this prayer was heard and answered in effect.

The Meeting.—I requested the first bell to be rung a little before half-past three. By that hour a large congregation was present. As is my custom, I arose at exactly the time, and began to read the first hymn. I had read a few lines when the sexton began to ring the second bell. I paused, and requested him to stop ringing that bell, which he did. I then proceeded, and opened the service in the usual way. Text—"Therefore being justified by faith, we have peace with God, through our Lord Jesus Christ." Romans v. 1. To illustrate the apostle's meaning, I read the fourth chapter, to which the text refers, showing how Abraham was justified by faith: "For if Abraham were justified by works, he hath whereof to glory, but not before God. For what saith the scripture? Abraham believed God, and it was counted unto him for righteousness. Now to him that worketh, is the reward not reckoned of grace, but of debt. But to him that worketh not, but believeth on Him that justifieth the ungodly his faith is counted for righteousness.

"Even as David also describeth the blessedness of the man unto whom God imputeth righteousness without works." Romans IV. verses 2, 3, 4, 5, 6. Thus proving that as Abraham and David were, so all that believe, both Jews and Gentiles. are "justified by faith." I read the part of the tenth chapter of Genesis, where it is recorded that God brought Abraham "forth abroad, and said, Look now toward heaven, and tell the stars, if thou be able to number them: and he said unto him, So shall thy seed be. And he believed in the Lord; and he counted it to him for righteousness." Then Abraham was justified while alone with his God; but now, according to Mr. Campbell, God alone could not forgive or justify a believer, but must have a man with him to immerse. But God's way with Abraham is the true gospel plan, for "it was not written for his sake alone, that it was imputed to him; but for us also, to whom it shall be imputed, if we believe on him that raised up Jesus our Lord from the dead" (Romans IV. 25), as witnessed by "all the prophets." Acts x. 43. The large congregation gave profound attention. There was no rain on that day, except a short sprinkle during service; but the next Sunday, which was the fourth Sabbath of that moon, and the second in the month, it rained incessantly nearly all day. Summer is gone, and Autumn has come. It is now September the 24th. The "farewell summer" flower, the last flower of the season, stands near the door of my study, and is now in full bloom. It looks to me mournfully beautiful. It calls to memory scenes of the past—past, never to return, and foretells winter, dreary winter, coming. I have been able to preach almost every Lord's-day during the past summer, except on the extremely hot days. During the past week I have been so very sick as to require help to get out of bed. I attribute this to the effects, in part, of the sun-stroke in July. I am now able to sit up and write a little.

Conference of 1868.—The forty-ninth annual session of the Southern Ohio Christian Conference met at Pisgah, October 24, 1868. There was a large attendance. The reports showed general peace and prosperity. Ten ministers united with the conference. Three of them were ordained elders who had previously belonged elsewhere. Two were young men who had embraced religion in this conference and preached some. One belonged to the Freemasons and the other to the Odd-Fellows, and neither would agree to discontinue meeting with these secret societies. I objected, therefore, to their reception. Among other objections, I urged that ministers could not have full and confiding faith in God and his promises for support and protection who belonged to these secret conclaves, as they admit that they belong there to obtain support in time of need. Therefore, they do not put their trust in God. No man can be unreservedly consecrated to God, whose trust is in these secret combinations. The minister of our Lord Jesus Christ, who goes forth to preach his gospel, should trust in the living God, who taketh care of the falling sparrow, they were received by a majority vote, which all acquainted with the New Testament know is contrary to the gospel of Christ, which teaches that the church is to act with one accord. It is also contrary to the rules of the Masonic order, and the order of Odd-Fellows, both of which require the vote to be unanimous. My objections were offered in a spirit of kindness; and when the candidates were received I gave them the hand, requesting them in the name of the Lord to forsake these societies, and to be faithful and trust in God. Their tears seemed to promise compliance.

The Ordination. There were two ministers ordained during the conference, by whose request I officiated, and gave them their charge as elders and ministers of the gospel of our Lord Jesus Christ. I, among other things, charged them that they should make their whole lives living, practical sermons. When the business was through, it was voted that I should give the closing address. This I did in a few remarks upon the uncertainty of our ever meeting again in this world. I then turned to our hope of a glorious meeting above, and so bid them farewell. This conference was first organized in October, 1820. This was its forty-ninth annual session, every one of which, by divine grace, I have been able to attend. December 5, 1868, is here, and with it the dreary cold winter has come again. This is my birthday. I am now seventy-eight years old.

> Three-score and eighteen years have flown,
> And I am here a pilgrim still;
> Two-score and eighteen years are gone
> Since I began to do God's will.

Thanks.—I thank God for his boundless grace, his loving kindness and tender mercy toward unworthy me. My health is better than is common for men of my age. My voice is but little impaired; I can speak and sing, friends tell me, nearly as well as ever. My hearing is good; my eyesight has returned, and I can see to read without glasses; for all of which, and abundance of grace, I thank my heavenly Father, nor can I praise his holy name enough.

Prayer.—O God, I pray and beseech thee, in the name of Jesus Christ, thy Son, do not take thy loving kindness from me in my declining years. Let thy Holy Spirit guide me. O blessed Savior, when it is thy will to take me hence, let my sun go down in peace, without an intervening cloud. And O my only God and Father, do give me an easy transit through the valley and shadow of death, into thine everlasting kingdom of peace and glory. And "all honor and praise be unto Him that sitteth upon the throne, and unto the Lamb, forever and ever." Amen.

A Funeral.—A pious sister of the Bethlehem Church, when upon her dying bed, requested that I should preach her funeral sermon, before her burial, and I was sent for; but on account of the great fall of rain on that day, and it being twelve miles, it seemed imprudent to expose myself in my feeble state of health, so I gave an appointment to preach the funeral at the chapel on the 6th of December, at eleven o'clock, which I did. My text was Job XVI. 22. After the sermon I rode twelve miles to my home, to be with my aged companion, the wife of my youth, my helpmeet in my eventful life. She is nigh unto death with asthma and dropsy. I found her about as she was when I left home—fast declining, with no hope of long remaining with us.

Christmas, 1868.—We once more behold the returning Christmas morning. This is my seventy-ninth Christmas. It is a clear day, with bright sunshine, and the ground covered with snow. The weather is cold for this climate; the mercury stands ten degrees above zero, but it is not so cold as it was a few days ago. The mercury has been below zero. I thank God for peace of mind, and as good health as I do enjoy, though I am mostly confined to my room.

New Year's, 1869.—The old year is gone, never to return, and the first day of another year has come. It is a dark, rainy day. A dark New Year's day is said to signify that the coldest part of the winter is past. Oh, how many have wept at the dying pillows and the graves of loved ones that have departed during the past year; and I with others! One year ago my beloved son, Washington, was alive. Now he is gone; gone, never to return. There is not another thing that should interest us more than death with its solemnities! What numbers on their dying beds have mourned for misspent lives! How many would have given worlds, if theirs to give, for the privilege of living their lives over again, to be prepared for death? But time, once gone, is gone forever.

> Millions of sighs, and floods of tears,
>   Can not recall time past,
> Nor stem the tide of rolling years.
>   Yet time we vainly waste.

How He Became Wealthy.—Having begun the world comparatively poor, I was under the necessity of adopting a system of rigid economy and frugality, which became so habitual as to be like a second nature to me. Consequently, when I had accumulated property, it seemed impossible to depart from my old habits, even in regard to time and apparel; in taking care of my clothing and shoes, being careful to make every thing last and do service as long as possible.

Four Pairs of Old Shoes.—I have now a pair of old coarse

leather shoes that I have worn more or less every year for twenty years. Five or six years they were the only shoes I wore at all when about home. I wear them yet in the house at times, but not out-doors, as for several years past they could not keep out the water. I have thought of throwing them aside, but am unwilling, and feel almost sorry to part with them. It seems like parting with old friends. I have had but four pairs of shoes in twenty years, and no boots at all. These four pairs of shoes—two pairs of coarse leather and two of calf-skin—have lasted me, and are lasting yet. The coarse pair first named are about worn out. The second coarse pair are about two-thirds worn. The first calfskin-pair are about three-fourths worn, while the other pair are not yet quite half-worn out. I wear shoes all the time, both winter and summer. I never wore out but one pair of boots in my life. When our grandsons—now young men—one after another, come to see us I show them these four pairs of shoes, particularly the twenty-year-old pair, and inquire the cost of their boots and shoes during one year. None give the cost less than from fifteen to twenty dollars. One said, "Twenty-five dollars a year." Said I, "The whole cost of my shoes has not been more than from ten to twelve dollars in twenty years, while yours, at the rate you say, must cost you five hundred dollars for the same time." Then I tell them that it was the aforesaid economy and frugality that enabled me to give any thing to their parents or to them. I do this to teach them that economy is the road to wealth, while extravagance is the road to ruin. My clothing of all kinds, including shoes, etc., has not cost me more than ten or twelve dollars a year. The old overcoat I now have, though I have traveled much, is the only one that I have had or worn during twenty years. It was a remarkable piece of cloth, and has never been wet through, though I have worn it in many heavy rains. It is not yet half-worn out. My other clothing has lasted about as proportionately long. These facts may seem strange to some, in the present age of extravagance and pride, yet they are true.

The old Pocket-Knife.—I have in my pocket now a small, two-bladed pocket-knife, which I have carried more than thirty-five years. The first blade I wore out and got another put in, which I broke, and then had another put in, which is in use now, and not very much worn. The small blade that was in it when I bought it is in it yet. When a boy, there was hardly an article which I prized more than a pocket-knife. It was hard for me to get one. They were high in price, and there were none near for sale, and I had little money to buy with; hence if I lost my knife, which was seldom, I was so greatly troubled that I could hardly sleep at night. I finally adopted the plan, that when I used my knife never to lay it down, but put

it carefully into my pocket; and, if I lent it, to keep my eye upon
the person till he was done with it, and if he did not seem to
think to return it, remind him of it. So I have not lost my
knife in either of these ways, since I have adopted said plan.
Another part of the system is to be always certain that my
pocket has no hole in it. Thus I have kept one and the same
knife for thirty-five years. Why could not every man do the
same if careful? The buckhorn handle of this knife is now
nearly worn off. It may be said that a pocket-knife is of too
little value to keep with such care—to preserve so long. I reply: the same care that will prevent its loss a month, will a
year; or a year, ten years, and so on, till the knife is worn out.
Is not this true? Let it it be borne in mind, that small savings
have made great estates, and that the old adage is true: "Take
care of the pennies and the pounds will take care of themselves."

The Old Umbrella.—I have an umbrella that I have carried
for more than twenty-five years. It has sheltered me in many
heavy storms of rain and hail and snow. When the first cover
was worn out I had a new one put on, and it is now nearly worn
out.

Fruits of Economy.—It was this rigid system of economy that
enabled me, without salary from the churches, and dependent
almost wholly upon my own resources, with God's blessing, to
spend half of all my time in traveling and preaching during
fifty-eight years, up to this time, and to support my family, and
to give hundreds upon hundreds of dollars to aid in building
Christian chapels, and to sustain the cause of religion in southern Ohio and elsewhere, and to give a great deal to the needy,
and to give eleven hundred dollars to the endowment of Union
Christian College.

What He Had Left.—I have given to our children, eleven in
number, dividing it equally among them, sixty thousand dollars,
while I have nearly that amount yet left. My own wisdom and
economy could not have accomplished all this. It has been
done through and by the mercies and blessings of my heavenly
Father.

Disappointment.—We had five daughters. Four are yet living.
One, Louisa Maria Devore, died in 1860, leaving seven children.
As I was some time ago giving to each of my living children
nearly four thousand dollars, and two of Louisa Maria Devore's
children had come of age, I, as was right, proposed to give
them their part of their mother's portion. The son is a little
past twenty-one years of age, and has been married more than
a year. He has no other means, and promised me a short time
ago that when he got this he would put it in land to make him
a home. On the 10th of this month, March, 1869, he, being the
oldest of the two first coming of age, came to receive his part,

it being a little over seven hundred dollars that he expected to receive. I now asked him what he intended to do with the money he expected to get. He answered, "I have been selling furniture during the last year on commission, and have used two hundred dollars of the owner's money. This I shall pay out of it first." I told him that he had promised me to put that money into land, and as he, a stout, hearty young man, had, without sickness, got in debt two hundred dollars in one year, he had better first pay that debt by his own industry and economy, and after he did that I would give him the money with the interest. Like the young man in the gospel, "He went away sorrowful." There being few young men in the present day who know the worth of money by having earned it themselves, they need lessons in economy. I considered it better for him to pay his debts from his own resources than to pay them from the money of his deceased mother. His case is one of many in our day and country, and is recorded for a lesson.

Death of Elder John Phillips, March 16, 1869.—Elder Phillips, styled "Antioch John," from his active agency for Antioch College, is dead! In the "Herald of Gospel Liberty" of March 13th, I see several biographical sketches of him. Soon after he got through with his agency he left Ohio and moved to Sullivan County, Indiana, where he purchased a large farm within three or four miles of Merom, on which he resided up to the time of his death. He had been on horseback to a county fair, and on his return home, when near his own house, his horse becoming frightened, sprang suddenly to one side and threw him. He was so greatly injured by the fall that he died in a few hours. He was buried by the Freemasons, whom he had joined a few years before, after having long been an extreme Antimason. That Elder Phillips possessed many traits of character worthy of approval, is admitted by all; but that he had others quite as objectionable, few will deny. The sketches of Elder Phillips are not like the biographies of the Bible. They give what is favorable and unfavorable in men's character; but these, like the popular biographies of men, present only what is favorable; a character without blemish; a life without deviation from the rule of right. Nearly all who knew Elder Phillips are willing to award to him honesty of purpose; but he had his troubles, as other men. He had *his* suits at law, and an orphan boy obtained judgment against him in the court of Brown County, Ohio. He had his weaknesses, and was carried away with the delusions of Millerism. The college of which he was agent was lost, and the people lost their money; but he got rich on the percentage. This is excused in the sketches, and charity forbids me to judge him. I freely forgive him all, and hope that the Lord has forgiven him. I can not decide that Elder John Phillips was either a wicked or a dishonest man. I, as well as he, have imperfections, and I leave his case, with mine, to the Judge of all the earth, who will do right.

May, 1869.—Having urgent business in Cincinnati, I went down to the city the first of this month, and spent a short time very pleasantly with Elder N. Summerbell, whose company is always an intellectual feast to me.

The Birds.—May is here, with its green fields, verdant foliage, singing birds, and blooming flowers. After the cold, rainy months of March and April, the spring blossoms and verdure make May seem like a new world. In the trees near our house the feathered songsters are now warbling their sweetest notes. I never look at or listen with pleasure to birds deprived of their liberty. I love to see them, like these, uncaged and free. Oh, how delightful are their carroling songs to me! They sing the same songs in the shade-trees now which they once sung in the dense, dark forest, when I was a boy not yet in my teens. They bring to my recollection the years when I was growing up, and my lonely wanderings then in the woods in search of straggling stock. They revive the emotions of sweet pleasure of returning home where my mother was. But soon stern reality disturbs the pleasing reverie. That kind mother was laid in the silent grave near thirty years ago, and I, her little boy, am now in my seventy-ninth year, and must soon follow her and the dear children gone before. They, the few, and only they who have lived through the experience of a long life, can realize the almost superhuman sensations which I feel in contemplating the past events of my life, and calling up the countless tokens of a mother's tenderness, and reviewing the fading forms of friends of by-gone years. They are gone; but the birds sing on as they did when those were here. When health permits, I yet follow my practice, once uniform in earlier years, of rising before the sun. But the birds are up before me, singing their morning songs long before my rising time. At the first dawn of the morning, I listen to their clear, shrill songs, welcoming the coming day. These early singers come near my windows. They seem to praise God without our intervening, cumbrous cares, troubles, and sorrows. They seem to call me to arise and join in their devotions, which I try to do. I usually sit out on the portico a long time every morning, to hear the birds sing, and meditate on the marvelous works of the great Creator. In a measure estranged from human society, I enjoy the company of birds. I now personally experience that which I have long made the subject of meditation, that, with mankind in general, the young shun the society of the aged, while nearly all who study wisdom seek it. Nearly every young man who associates uniformly with aged men becomes noted for knowledge. Such seem to feel that there is something yet to learn, and desire the benefit of the long experience of the aged. But the young in general prefer the thoughtless mood, the careless way, the unreserved and reckless risk, the laugh, and cheerful talk, and merry pastime. They seem to think themselves arrived at the zenith of knowledge, or at least that there is nothing more worth knowing. From these circumstances, I listen much to the warbling birds, which, with varied notes, continue all day long their cheerful songs, for my eyes will not permit continued writing, or even reading, and there are, with rare exceptions, no aged people near, and I am almost without human society, except when watching by my afflicted wife, the companion of my youth, whose recovery is hopeless, and whose departure seems near. So, when wearied with watching, I listen to the birds' unwearied songs, to enliven my passing hours of contemplation and thoughts of God.

Man's Best Companion.—Though deprived of human society, I am not alone. One friend, who was the guide of my youth, is the comfort of my age. The associate of former years does not fail me in my declining life. This friend took me while young, and introduced me into the society of Moses and the prophets, and apostles, and even to the Lord of glory, by whose instruction I learned that there is one supreme, infinitely good, and holy God, the Creator of the universe, and of angels and men, and in him we can trust. True, man sinned; but God is merciful! Man was lost; but God loved him, and sent his beloved Son to save him; and all who will believe his words, and repent of their sins, and obey him, shall have eternal life. They taught me that beyond this world there is a heaven, a home of peace and happiness, for all the righteous, and that God will never leave nor forsake those who love and obey him, but will ever be with them. How could I be lonely with such company, or sad with such a hope? Their instructions lead to hope in heaven, and direct me to many great and precious promises of my heavenly Father, which constantly inspire me with the blessed hope that, after I have put off this dull mortality, I shall join the general assembly and church of the first-born in heaven, and enjoy the harmonious society of loved ones who have gone before, in a world where sickness and sorrow, pain and death, are felt and feared no more. This faithful companion has always been with me in all my conflicts to comfort me, in all my trials to strengthen me. Even when earthly friends failed me; when many were false, and others were fearful; when envy rose up, and jealousy was fierce; when floods of calumny came, and persecution threatened to overwhelm me; when earthly friends faltered, turned against me, and stood aloof to see what would become of me, or left me to struggle alone or sink in the storm, —this friend assured me by many immutable promises, and encouraged me by many examples of faithful endurance, and moral triumphs over wicked combinations. This ever reliable

14

companion is the word of God, which introduces us to the society of all the good in earth and heaven. Reader, I heartily recommend this friend to you. A man's best companion is the Bible!

Preaching.—Since spring has opened and summer has come, I have preached a number of times, feeling a pressing duty to work in my Master's vineyard. My stays from home are short, owing to the great affliction of my wife. From day to day and hour to hour it has seemed that she must depart; and thus she lingers, with no hope of recovery, and she desires me to be with her all the time, or within call.

An Incident.—During this time I concluded to attend the regular communion meeting at Bethlehem, where I preached so long; where I was treated more uncourteously by a brother in the ministry than I had ever been before by a true brother in my ministry of nearly sixty years. I mention it hoping that it may save other old ministers from being treated so. Yet if any minister, especially any aged pilgrim, should meet with similar treatment, I advise him to bear it with Christian fortitude and resignation, remembering what Jesus bore, and his example. The communions were twice a year—spring and fall. The communion in the Bethlehem Church, where I preached nearly forty-five years, came on the third Sabbath in May. It was half a year since my last visit. I left my afflicted companion, and went to the meeting. The pastor was friendly with me, and ever had been. For several years he had, from time to time, attended protracted meetings there with me; and being a good man I had introduced him to this large church of between four and five hundred members, and their new fine chapel, to succeed me. The pastor came, and a preacher of this conference with him, who preached twice on Sabbath, then again on Monday, the last meeting. I was there, but during the three days was not consulted or asked by the pastor to preach, or to take any part in the meeting. A number of people asked me to preach. So on Monday, at the close of the meeting, I made a few remarks; and feeling that the people (?) ought to know why I had not preached, I told them in a kind spirit that I had not been asked by the pastor. I then kneeled and prayed with the people, after which the pastor told me to dismiss. I replied, "Not yet. Let us sing a farewell hymn first, as we used to do." The pastor did not signify his assent. So I put it to vote, and the people did. We then sung, but the pastor took no part, apparently. At a brother's house, where we went to dine, I said to the pastor, "Were you hurt with me because I sung to-day?" He answered, "No, not particularly; but I would have preferred you to have spoken to me first." He seemed to think that I should have asked of him the privilege to sing in the church which I had organized and preached to near forty-five years, and in the chapel built under my labors and in part with my money, and in the church where I am still a member. I am not offended at the pastor, Elder William Pangburn. I do not view him as a bad man. I retain him in the bonds of Christian charity. He gave no explanation after my remarks to the people in his presence, nor any reason for doing as he did. And I can give none. Nearly two months after this Elder Pangburn met me in Ripley, and introduced the subject of not asking me to preach, and excused himself by saying that he supposed that I had come simply to attend the meeting. He did not remember saying to me that he would not have been hurt if I had spoken to him about it before singing. I told him that it is the pastor's privilege to choose the man to preach for him, and that I was not offended with him or I should have said so to him. Thus, if his explanation satisfied him it did me, and so I let the matter pass.

Eclipse, August 7, 1869.—On this day there was, though not total here, a total eclipse of the sun. It was almost total at our place. It commenced at 4:46 P. M., and lasted one hour and fifty-two minutes. By looking through smoked glass we saw the form of the moon distinctly as it passed before the face of the sun. This makes three of these phenomena that I have witnessed. The first was in June, 1806, when in my sixteenth year; the second in May, 1854, and the third August 7, 1869. The two former were followed by dry weather and cold winters. What will follow this, time will soon determine.

Mrs. Gardner's Sickness, September 2, 1869.—Swift-winged Time has carried the summer away, and with it have gone the sweet-singing birds, and I am alone in my study. I have been mostly at home since April, waiting upon my dear afflicted wife, the companion of my youth and age. For nearly four months, so intense has been her illness, by asthma and dropsy, that her death would not have been unexpected at almost any hour. It was her request that I would not leave her to go away to preach, but remain by her, or at least within call, which I did. She frequently calls for me. During August I was quite ill myself; and, though not confined to my bed, I and others thought it probable that I would go first. As September wears away I am better.

September 18, 1869.—Sally Shinkle, our eldest daughter, who lives about seventeen miles away, came home to see her mother. As there is no apparent change, and Sally will remain, so I concluded to go to the communion meeting, twelve miles away. I requested my daughter to send for me if she saw any change. She was sleeping when I left, so I did not speak to her, but told my daughter to tell her, which she did. She did not call for me as she usually did during my absence. I preached on Sunday and returned early on Monday. I talked with her, and

she seemed about as when I left her on Saturday. She shouted
the praise of God aloud, as she had often done before, during
her illness.

Her Death.—About one o'clock she desired her favorite hymn
sung. It had often been sung by her request during her illness. The hymn begins thus:

> " What's this that steals, that steals upon my frame?
> Is it death ? Is it death ?
> That soon will quench, will quench this vital flame,
> Is it death? Is it death?
> If this be death I soon shall be
> From every pain and sorrow free,
> I shall the King of Glory see.
> All is well ! All is well !"

It will be noticed that each verse ends with the words, "All
is well! All is well!" These words truly and fully expressed
her feelings. A little before two P. M. she called me. I was
standing by her, and I said to her, "Sally, I am here," and took
her hand in mine. She said, "Call them all," meaning the children, and in a moment said, "It is too late now;" meaning that
she could not live till they came. "It is too late now" were
her last words, spoken with almost the last breath. I felt for
her pulse, but it had ceased to beat. When I let go her hand
it was the long farewell parting hand! I realized that the
hand that I had clasped so often would never, living, be taken
in mine again. Thus did Sally calmly fall asleep in Jesus. She
was one of the best wives that ever a man was blessed with.
Gone, gone, gone! Farewell, farewell, dear Sally! Never can
I forget thee. I hope, through Jesus' grace, to meet thee again,
where there shall be no death or tears. Dear reader, wilt thou
think it strange, when I tell thee that tears have often caused
me to lay down my pen while writing this narrative?

Lamentations—September 20, 1869.—With a sad heart and a
tearful eye, I minute the death of my wife on this date. At two
o'clock in the afternoon her affliction, sorrow, suffering, pain,
and anguish were ended. She died in the triumphs of faith ;
in the hope of immortality and eternal life. She was born in
Spottsylvania County, Virginia, September 12, 1794. She embraced religion when about seventeen. She was married on the
20th of May, a little before she was nineteen. We lived in
wedlock fifty-six years and four months. She died September
20, 1869. Oh, how lonely and desolate the house and every
thing in it and about it looked when I this day, the 21st, returned to it near sundown, after leaving her in the grave!
Fifty-six years she had been here; now she is gone forever.
She came in the freshness of youth. Here she lived to grow
old, and is now gone, never to return to it, or to be seen

here again. All here seems blank to me. I have no home here now. In this melancholy state of mind, after prayer, I went to bed at a late hour that night. But I could not sleep; my thoughts wandered back, from year to year, to our first acquaintance, when she was a little turned of sixteen. I could, in my mind, plainly see her as Sally Beasly, when she was a damsel. I could see her again when, past eighteen, she stood at my side on that day and that moment while our marriage was being solemnized, and Sally Beasly was my wife. I fancied her again, as I saw her slender, lovely form by my side, while with other young people we took a walk, rambling among the beautiful flowers and green shrubbery, on that delightful afternoon of our marriage, May 20, 1813. Two months after this, viz, July 13th, the government called for all the men in Ohio able to bear arms to go to the war, to defend the northern frontier of the state. I went, of course. I thought of her then as she appeared before my mind as I saw her on the day of our parting, when I bade her farewell to go to the army. I saw her again as she stood weeping and looking after me till quite out of each other's sight. Having been sick before that call, and unwell when I left home, I became sick again after going, and in about a month I hired a substitute and returned home. While in the army she was always present in my mind. I could see her again; as when I returned home sick and we met, embracing each other with tears of joy, in her father's house, that time when gladness and thanksgiving filled our hearts for God's protecting care in bringing us to meet once more. Now, in my mind, these scenes transpired again. We lived in her father's family till New Year's day, 1814, when we moved into our cabin on land little improved. The land had to be cleared. Necessity seemed to require work, not only during the day, but by night. Not by my desire, but by her own will, she would come out and help me to burn brush and logs till she thought it time to quit. Then she would say in a soft, kind tone, "You have worked long enough to-night; come, go to the house with me." I could hear her kind voice as she cheered me when cast down, and encouraged me when in trouble. I could see her again as when I was sick she stood at my bedside. Time would fail me to tell all my thoughts, or to give but a mere outline of our eventful pilgrimage of life together, as all passed before my mind that night. She was sick a number of times during her life, and seemed near unto death, but at none of these times did she request me to stay with her and not fill my appointments. She never complained of being left alone. When ready to start, whether my absence was to be long or short, she always asked, "When will you come home?" I would set the time, and seldom disappointed her. I seldom left the house without telling her where I was going, though it were only to a neighbor's, or out on the farm, that if I should be needed she could know where to find me. When I returned from preaching, weary and tired, she tried to make me comfortable. Never more will she ask, "When will you come home?" That kind voice I shall hear no more. There was born to us a large family of eleven children—six sons and five daughters. All lived to be men and women. They were all married and settled in life before her departure, which was the first and is yet the only death that has ever occurred in our house. But three of our beloved children —two sons and one daughter—died before their mother. The dear mother and her three children are now where "sickness and sorrow, pain and death are felt and feared no more," and are doubtless happy together in the bright realms of peace and glory.

Sunday, November 21, 1869—*Past Events.*—Yesterday, two months ago, death took from me the companion of my youth, and left me alone; yet not alone, for I trust the Lord is with me. The house and place looked, when she was gone, so lonely and forsaken, that it did not seem to me like home, so I remained there but one day after she was buried. On the 23d I left home, to visit a church about seventeen miles distant, where our oldest daughter and two of our sons live. As the pulpit seemed more like home to me than any other place, the desire renewed to entreat my fellow-mortals to prepare for death and judgment. I have been preaching every Sunday, except one, since my companion's death, until to-day. To-day I am at the place so long my home while she was here. I have only stopped here a few times since leaving, till about a week ago, when the cold, stormy weather came on. Although it does not seem like home, yet, having here my warm room, and library in it, and my good bed, I must stay here during the coming winter, if it be God's will to continue my life.

Conference of 1869.—The Southern Ohio Conference met this year, on the 16th of October, with the Mount Pleasant church, in Clermont County. This is the fiftieth annual session, all of which, through God's grace, I have been able to attend. There was the usual gathering of ministers and messengers. They reported the churches to be in a prosperous condition. The ordinary business was transacted in harmony, with the exception of one incident, which I will name. The "Herald of Gospel Liberty" is controlled by an executive committee, chosen by a biennial convention, who employ the editor, who uses his judgment about what shall or shall not be published. Last March, when the biographical sketches of Elder John Phillips appeared, picturing him in almost superhuman perfection, I sent my sketch of Elder Phillips, which the editor objected to, and returned. He was present at this conference, with others connected with the paper; and when the report on our publishing interests was read, I offered this amendment, viz.: "We think that there is need of improvement in both the financial and editorial departments." This brought the whole matter before conference; and the editor said, in his haste, that he would "suffer his right arm to be cut off rather than to publish that article." This caused the conference to suppose that there was something dreadful in the article; and when I offered to read it, the president said a majority were opposed. This I cared little for, as the amendment was passed almost unanimously. Elder E. W. Humphreys, former editor, and other ministers, were in favor of publishing my article; not that there was any thing of great consequence in the article, but out of respect for my age and experience. The article read about as follows, some corrections being made, as it remained so long in my possession:

Biographies.—"Dear Editor:—On this day, March 16, 1869, I see in the "Herald of Gospel Liberty," of the 13th instant, some biographical sketches of Elder John Phillips. These sketches are not like the biographies in the Bible, which give both the favorable and the unfavorable traits in men's character, but they are too much like nearly all the biographies of the present day, which represent the men as having possessed and practiced almost angelic purity, without a single blemish, or one deviation from the rule of right. As the house of the writer was the first house at which Elder Phillips stopped when he came to Ohio, the last of December, 1837, or perhaps early in January, and where he remained with his family for several weeks, till he found a place elsewhere; and as I have been well acquainted with him ever since that time, during thirty years, till he died, therefore I knew his virtues and imperfections, and will say, all who were acquainted with Elder John Phillips agree that he possessed some traits of character worthy of approval, and others quite objectionable; yet, perhaps nearly all who knew him are willing to award to him honesty of purpose.

"M. GARDNER.

"Ripley, March 16, 1869."

The above, except a few words to make my meaning more plain, is the article before alluded to, which the editor preferred to lose his right arm rather than publish. I do not record these troubles to reflect on persons, but policy. I was an aged man. I had been long in the ministry. I had been successful in raising churches, and was well acquainted with financial affairs. In short, I had been successful both in religion and business. I was responsible and safe. Yet the words of such men as Fay and Phillips, who were adventurers in business, and unstable in religion, had more weight with many people than mine; and I had been held back and my council unheeded during all the wild speculations about Antioch, and even when ruin came and

we lost the college, and lost $100,000, and, worse than that, lost
self-respect and confidence in our people. Such men could still
be believed when they would say, "We still own the college;"
and my articles were regarded as unfriendly because I could
not indorse their mistakes.

"*The Unincumbered Gift.*"—That is Antioch College, given to
the Unitarians. The following article, republished August 11,
1864, is from "The Christian Register," from the pen of the intensely Unitarian editor, and the most prominent Unitarian
paper. It boasts that they have the college under their "entire
control," and in effect name the Christian "during-life trustees,"
whom they also had under their "entire control," giving the
Unitarians "*seventeen* votes out of the *twenty.*" (The italics are
theirs). Yet these men, who thus gave them the college as "an
unincumbered gift," are the men who opposed and abused me
because I could not approve their course. True, the Unitarians
say that they are to endow it as a condition. They have not yet
fulfilled that condition; but they have it. They say also that it is
not to be sectarian. If one sect, and that the Unitarians, have
the "entire control" does not make it sectarian, what could? It
is thus proved that the Christians gave the college away, as the
following from "The Christian Register" will show:

Antioch College.—"The name of this institution will, we trust,
occasion unpleasant reflections no longer. Instead of fearing,
as the Unitarians have done, very generally, that the money
they had given to it was lost, they may rejoice that the opportunity is now offered to them of taking entire control of it.
The charter was so amended, at the recent meeting of the trustees, as to take the college out of the hands of the "Christians,"
and the board of trustees, a close corporation, so modified by
the election of new members, as to secure its administration to
the Unitarians. The opinions, frequently expressed, of Messrs.
Craig, Weston, Phillips, Devore, Stanton, and Birch, with regard to the unsectarian position the college should assume, the
high rank it should take among the colleges of the West, and
the necessity of employing the ablest teachers that could be
procured, whether they belonged to the "Christians" or not, together with their former action as members of the board, when-
ever catholic measures for conducting the college have been
under discussion, make it as certain that upon every question, in-
volving a principle which the Unitarians would regard as vital to
the interests of the college, they could command at least *seventeen* votes of the *twenty,* as it is that they could rely upon Drs. Hill
and Hosmer or Messrs. Low and Kidder to represent their
views and wishes. Though the Unitarians will never make it
a denominational or sectarian college, yet, as *they* must endow
it, if it is ever endowed, it is well to assure them, that it is now
so completely in their hands, that if they shall raise $100,000

within one year, which is the condition of retaining it in their hands perpetually, they can do with it in all respects as they may choose. They may make other alterations in the charter, and reorganize the school to suit themselves. By endowing it with $100,000, within one year, Antioch will be more fully under the control of the Unitarians than Harvard College, upon which they have lavished their wealth, ever was. In the very heart of the great section of our country, whither the most enterprising young men have been flocking, and to which they must flock for a long time to come—in the very heart of the great north Mississippi Valley, that has done its duty so nobly in our country's crisis, and which will contain, in fifty years, a population greater than the republic now contains, the Unitarians have a transcendent opportunity of establishing a great institution of learning, that shall illustrate their own cardinal principles of mental and spiritual freedom. It is certainly an opportunity for which they could well afford to *pay* very *liberally* if they could avail themselves of it on no other condition, and yet they are now importuned to *accept* it ·as an *unincumbered gift*, on the sole condition that they shall endow and administer it in their own way as a first-class college.''

Hence, Antioch College was a gift from the Christians to the Unitarians, and was lost to us more from want of principle than from want ·of money. They took it from us because we had not endowed it; and secured it while they had not. Near the close of the conference of 1869, I stated that, as my advanced years would not permit me to be out much in the winter, I did not now hold the pastoral charge of any church, but that during the warm weather I could preach every Sunday, and if the conference would give me the liberty, I would make appointments in its bounds, to preach without pay, as my feelings might dictate, without fear of offending the pastors. I had hardly closed my remarks, when the following was offered : ''*Resolved*, That the ministers and messengers from the churches of this conference (and other conferences present) invite Elder Gardner to visit and preach to our churches as he may be able during his remaining years.'' The words (and other conferences present) were added by the request of several ministers present from other conferences. Elder Charles Garoutte, pastor of the Ripley Church, spoke against it, but no one replied, only visiting ministers as above, desiring to have the privilege of uniting in the invitation. It was passed unanimously, except said preacher and Brother Robert Stephenson, a messenger from the same church. On October 29, 1869, I went to Cincinnati. I had a little business there, and in my melancholy state of mind I greatly desired to see and converse with Elder N. Summerbell. The interview with him and his dear companion greatly revived my drooping spirits. On Sunday night, October 31st, I preached to Elder Summerbell's congregation. On Monday, November 1, 1869, I parted with Brother Summerbell and his kind family. It seemed like leaving home. I took the steamer up the Ohio, and stopped where my home had formerly been, and went on and preached at Bethlehem chapel, as I had previously appointed, to a large congregation, on the next Sunday.

Sunday, December 5, 1869.—This is my birthday. To-day I am seventy-nine years old. I can say with the patriarch Jacob, few and evil have the days of the years of my pilgrimage been. On my birthday a year ago the companion of my long life was with me, and had been for fifty-six of my birthdays. But she will be with me no more in this world. The winter days being short, though confined mostly to my room, which is my study, I can find something to do—reading, writing, etc. But oh, the nights, these long, long winter nights of fifteen hours! I can not sleep more than about six hours out of the twenty-four, and never could. How dismally lonesome these long, tedious nights are without her company who was so long the comfort of my life, none can realize but those who are brought to a kindred experience. My chief society now is with the spirit world; in the contemplation of God and his love, his boundless mercy and his grace. I have delight in singing his praise, and thanking him for enabling me to do so.

> Lonely and silent is my room,
> No voice I hear, no face I see
> For she is silent in the tomb
> Who once was here to speak to me.
> Her voice once cheered me in my gloom,
> Her face I always loved to see;
> Companions when in youthful bloom,
> And when in age's infirmity.

Dream—December 8th.—Last night I saw her sitting on a chair in the room she usually occupied. She was beautifully attired, and looked and seemed as in the days of her youth. While I saw her I knew that she had come from the spirit world and was immortal. She said but few words, and these I do not remember. She was not in haste, though she soon intimated that she must go. I exclaimed, "Oh, do not leave us! Do stay with us!" Seeing that she would leave, I wept. Our youngest son, Elnathan Matthew, who lives in the house, has a little son in his fourth year. His grandmother greatly loved him, and he loved her. When she was leaving, she seemed to move toward the door; the little boy followed crying and begging her to remain. As she passed out I took hold of her arm, but she passed away from me. I looked to see which way she went, but could not. This was a dream.

Christmas, 1869.—Feeling quite lonesome, I started on the

day before Christmas to visit three of my children about seventeen miles distant. Christmas day is here again, according to our reckoning, on the 25th of December. There is no snow. It is a dark, rainy day. New Year's day, 1870, has come. I am still with my children. The old year is gone, and hundreds of thousands are gone with it. Like it, they will never return. My thoughts are on my dear companion who was with me last New Year's; but she is now gone, gone, never to return.

> "How swiftly fly the rolling years
> That take our friends away,
> And leave us here in grief and tears,
> While the short time we stay."

Health.—My health is good for a man of my age. My memory and my voice are both good, for which I thank God, with all my heart.

Prayer.—If it be thy will, O God, to call me away from this world during this incoming year, I pray thee, in the name of Jesus Christ, thy well-beloved Son, to give me a tranquil hour in which to die. During the two weeks that I remained with our children there was a protracted meeting at the church, and I preached several sermons. I have now returned to the lonely abode, once my home, when she was here who made it home.

Winter.—Here I am, passing the cold winter, leaving home but seldom.

May 1, 1870.—The lonely, disagreeable winter is past, and beautiful May has come with its sweet-singing birds and full-blown flowers. My health is as good as I may expect. My intellectual faculties are good. I can make calculations in figures about as readily as I ever could. Oh, for a heart and tongue adequate to thank and praise God for his boundless goodness, and the grace bestowed upon me. I thank and praise God every day, with my poor imperfect powers and heart and tongue, for all his daily mercies.

May 20th.—Fifty-seven years ago this day I was married to my now-departed wife, the choice of my heart. It seems but as yesterday; but she is gone. When I was from home, while she was here, I always thought of her welcoming me home on my return. Now, when away, those scenes come to my mind; but there are none to so look for my coming, and welcome me now.

June, 1870.—My health continues good, considering my age. I have preached every Sunday, with few exceptions, since the opening of spring.

The Triennial Convention.—The Triennial Convention of the Christian Publishing Association is announced in the "Herald" to meet in Marion, Grant County, Indiana, June 21, 1870. Desiring to attend, "if the Lord will," I arranged matters accordingly. My will having been written by myself, nearly five years ago (July, 1865), and quite a change having taken place in the matter of my estate, therefore justice to my heirs, and other causes, required some changes in that instrument. After a careful and prayerful consideration of the whole matter, I have rewritten my will, finishing it on the 15th of June, 1870. I have bequeathed $1,000 for the purpose of publishing my life, written by myself. After procuring a steel-plate engraving of my likeness, and having the whole work stereotyped, and furnishing two hundred copies, which I bequeath to my children and grandchildren; all the profits from the sale thereof are given to Union Christian College. I have appointed Elder N. Summerbell to attend to the publication thereof, and its distribution, with provision for another to do the work, in the event of his failing to do it. June 16th I start for the convention, some three hundred miles, taking the will with me to Ripley, where, having signed it, it was witnessed and deposited. About one P. M., June 18th, I took the packet for, Cincinnati, where I arrived at Brother Summerbell's, and remained over Sunday, the 19th, and preached to Elder N. Summerbell's congregation. Monday morning, June 20th, 1, with Brother Summerbell, took the cars, and reached Marion a little before sundown. The kind reception I there met with, and the respect shown to me for my age and long labor, was greater than I could expect. Elder Rush, the editor before alluded to, conversed with me a few minutes, agreeing to publish the article on biography of March 16th, and all our differences were settled. I met here many dear brethren, who were little children when they first heard me preach, and are now able ministers of the New Testament. As there were many preachers in attendance, I preached but once. The Lord helped me; and, as I was subsequently informed, the people were much pleased with what I said. The convention closed on the 24th. This meeting was one of the most pleasant events of my life. The following extract is from a letter afterward received from the man with whom I put up, one of the most respectable citizens of that place, and a deacon in the Christian Church.

"Elder Gardner: * * * You will excuse me when I say to you that your visit to our place has awakened a deep interest in your welfare, on account of your age and long service in the ministry. You have the prayers and best wishes of this entire community. We have no house in this city that would hold the congregation should you make another visit. Mrs. Webster unites with me in sending you our best regards.

"G. W. Webster."

July 4, 1870.—This makes eighty Independence days that I have seen. After resting since my return from Marion, I am refreshed and as well as usual.

Sudden Death—July 13, 1870.—This is a day of alarm and great consternation in our house. Elizabeth, my son's wife, fell dead from her chair, at the sewing machine, about nine o'clock this morning. She was the wife of Elnathan Matthew Gardner. She leaves two children, the eldest four years old. She ate her breakfast and seemed in as good health, and as hearty as usual. How uncertain is life and all our earthly future!

Epitaph.—July 17, 1870. This day I write my epitaph, as follows:

EPITAPH:

ELDER MATTHEW GARDNER,

A CHRISTIAN MINISTER.

Born in New York State, December 5, 1790.
Died

He claimed no merit of his own,
His trust was all in Christ alone.

My ministry began in 1810, from which the number of years to my death, or when I cease preaching, can be ascertained.

Long Labors.—I have now preached over sixty years. I have lived on this farm fifty-seven years, and in this one section and the same neighborhood seventy years.

Goes East.—This day, August 9, 1870, I start to visit the land of my birth—Rensselaer County, New York. I took the packet steamer St. James, at Ripley, and arrived in Cincinnati about nine P. M. I remained at Brother Summerbell's over the 10th, as I had business in the city. I took the cars on the 11th, and reached Stephentown, New York, the place of my birth, on the 13th, at six o'clock P. M. Having traveled nearly one thousand miles I felt weary, went to bed early, and had a good night's rest, which revived me greatly. August 14th being Sunday, I went with my cousin to hear Elder Sweet, a Particular Baptist. The church numbers nearly two hundred. There were from thirty to forty to hear him preach. The church is in the very neighborhood where I was born. He kindly asked me to preach. I declined, but said, "As the Christian chapel (only a few rods distant) is out of repair, I will preach here next Sunday, if agreeable to you and the people." He consented, and requested me to speak after him then. He announced my appointment, and the meeting closed with a good state of feeling. I spent the week in pleasant and interesting visits among my relatives. I went to see the old house again that we moved out of September 1, 1800. It was in a state of dilapidation. Nobody lives in it. I looked into the well. I went all through the house. I remembered it all distinctly, though seventy years have passed since we left it. No language can express my feelings when in view of these

places so sacred to me as the home of my parents. I thought
of my childhood days, and that dear kind mother who once
lived in that house. My heart——! Sunday, August 21, 1870, I
met a large congregation. The Lord helped me to preach.
Many wept. It was communion day. After preaching I took a
chair on the floor, front of the pulpit. They passed the bread
and wine by me, offering me none. The meeting closed. The
pastor complimented me on the sermon. The people apoligized.
They had "never seen the abomination" of "close communion"
as at that day, when it was passed by me, as though the bread
and wine were more than man. I continued to visit. During
the week I attended the Methodist camp-meeting, held three-
fourths of a mile from the spot where I was born. On Sunday, the 28th, I preached at South Berlin, New York, about six
miles north of Stephentown. Since my former visit there has
been a railroad built, running north and south through this
valley, near the thirty acres of land that my father sold to go
to Ohio, on the first of September, 1800. This railroad connects
south at Chatham Corners with lines to New York City, and
Albany, and Boston, and at its northern terminus in Vermont,
with the road to Montreal. By this road it is over sixty miles
from Stephentown to Albany, while it is only eighteen miles by
stage over the mountains.

Return to Ohio.—On Tuesday, August 30th, I took the cars on
this new road at two P. M. for Albany, where I tarried over
night, and on the 31st, at twenty minutes after two P. M., took
the cars for Cincinnati. On the sleeping car, the night after
leaving Albany, a pickpocket took my pocket-book and about
twenty dollars. As I had my money in different pockets, he
did not get it all. I thank God that I met with no greater misfortune. I had heretofore taken a lake steamer from Buffalo to
Cleveland. This trip was all by railroad. I reached Cincinnati
the next day, Thursday, September 1, 1870, about six P. M., and
on Friday, the 2d, I took the steamer for Ripley, in company
with Elder N. Summerbell, on his way to the dedication of the
Hiatt Christian chapel, which is five or six miles beyond my
home. This chapel was thus named for John Hiatt, the man
who gave half the money to build it. We reached Ripley about
eight P. M., where my son, Elnathan, met me with a carriage
and took me home. Thus, through divine protection, I safely
returned from my fifth visit to the land of my birth, with my
health much improved, though I was quite weary with my
journey. Before I left for the East a committee waited upon
me, requesting me to participate in the dedication of Hiatt
Christian chapel. On Sunday, September 4th, I took part in
the dedication, and preached at three P. M.

Southern Ohio Christian Conference.—The Southern Ohio Christian Conference of 1870 met this year in Ripley, on the 1st day

of October. It is the fifty-first annual session, each of which the Lord has enabled me to attend. There was the usual attendance of ministers and messengers, and the churches were reported in usual prosperity. It was quite a short session. It continued little over two days, and but little business was done.

General Convention of 1870.—At the close, I started to the Quadrennial Christian Convention, to meet at Oshawa, Canada, on the 11th of October. Oshawa is nearly seven hundred miles from Ripley. It was appointed there by the request of the Christians in Canada. I went to Cincinnati by the steamer, and by railroad to Detroit. About sixty miles from Detroit we crossed the river that connects Lake Huron with Lake Erie, and took the Grand Trunk Railway in Canada, to Oshawa. The convention was largely attended, and in all its business peace and harmony prevailed. Through divine grace and protection I stood the journey quite well, both going and returning, and reached home on the 22d in good health, my age considered; for all of which I thank God with all my heart. November 7, 1870, is here, and a delightful day it is. Nature has put off its beautiful attire for the mourning apparel for departed summer. The beautiful blossoms and verdure are laid aside for the sombre dress of autumn, suited to the dreary cold that is approaching. The sweet singing of birds has given place to the whispering winds which tell of coming winter. Yesterday, the first Sunday in November, I preached the funeral of an aged sister in Christ, in the Fellowship Christian chapel, seven miles from my residence, as requested by her before her death. She was seventy-five years old. There was a large congregation, and many mourners. The Lord helped me to preach in the spirit. The last month of the year is here. This has been the most delightful fall I ever saw, except the fall of 1800, the year my father moved to this country, which this resembles.

December 5, 1870.—Here is a day which in my youth I did not expect ever to see. Being born on the 5th of December, 1790, I am this day eighty years old. It seems strange to me. I never expected to live to reach this age, yet my general health is better than usual. My voice is good. I have often heard aged people say, that in looking back over their past life it looks short. Not so with me. When I retrospect my past life, the strange events and many dangers through which the Lord has safely conducted me, while all the companions of my youth have fallen, the way seems long.

Prayer.—O God, accept my heartfelt thanks, in the name of thy Son Jesus Christ, for all thy past mercies. And do thou still guide me by thy counsel through all my remaining days in this world, and afterward receive me to glory, through Jesus Christ.

Alone at Eighty.—Being alone in my room the nights seem very long and dreary, and pass tediously.

CHAPTER IX.

My eighty-first year has begun. I am still confined to my
room by the winter weather. My enjoyment is in the continued
contemplation of God's boundless goodness.

Christmas, 1870.—Here is Christmas day on Sunday, making
eighty-one Christmas days seen by me. It is cold, but pleasant.
The mercury is only two degrees above zero. A light snow
covers the ground. Being alone in my room, the days are
pleasant enough, but the nights are long and lonesome.

> My lonely room, how sad to me,
>   No voice to break the gloom ;
> No human face for me to see,
>   While here alone — alone.
> " Sweet star of hope, with ray to shine
>   In every lone, sad breast
> 'Tis only thee gives cheer to mine,
>   Man's first, last friend, and best."

A. D. 1871.—The year 1870 has passed and gone, never to return. The first day of 1871 comes in on Sunday, and a clear,
beautiful, sunny day it is.

> Oh, hallowed day! thy light proclaims
>   Afar the dawn of the new year!
> Lord, tune my heart with thankful strains
>   For mercies past, and mercies here!
> O Jesus! let thy guardian care
>   Still guide me to my journey's end!
> Oh, bow thine ear and hear my prayer,
>   In life, and, dying, be my friend!

Memories of the Dead.—Many to-day, like myself, doubtless
think of loved ones who were with them on past New Year's
days. Oh, how impressive are the reminiscences of my dear
wife! How dear the memory of our three children that are
gone! and keen thought adds to these my daughter-in-law,
Elizabeth, who was last year one of the family with us, who
died so suddenly as she sat at the sewing machine, on the 13th
of July last. She was always kind to me. Oh, how I do miss
her! Memory causes the tears to fall while writing.

May, 1871.—I have passed through the dreary winter. It
seemed long and lonely to me. While so greatly afflicted with
congestion of the lungs and inflammation of the throat, I have,
by God's mercy, yet lived to see this fourth day of May. My

224

health is now much improved, though I am quite feeble yet. The congestion of the lungs caused such protracted hoarseness that I sometimes feared that my voice would not return; but it improved slowly, so that I was able to preach the last Sunday in April. I am now able to sing again. May comes in young again with freshness and beauty, not old like me. The flowers are blooming as they did when I was young; the birds are singing just as they did then. The crystal dew-drops on the grass shine the same as in my youthful days. Yet I know, I feel, that there has been a great change in me. May always possesses charms for me. In the month of May I was married to my dear departed wife. My life has had its joys, but most of them were mingled with sorrow and tears. I thank God with all my heart for the hope of a higher life, where death can not take away those we love; "where everlasting spring abides, and never-fading flowers."

May 30, 1871.—I to-day preached the funeral of Nancy Lake, my sister-in-law, my wife's sister. She embraced religion under my ministry, when about sixteen, and lived a pious, praying, exemplary Christian life forty years, that is, until she died, in the fifty-eighth year of her life. She was born September 20, 1813. A few days before she died, at one of the times I visited her, to pray for her, she told me the place she had for secret prayer, when yet a girl, and of her chosen places for secret prayer since her marriage. She left an affectionate husband and four sons, all grown to manhood but one, to mourn the loss of a wife and mother, among the best that ever lived. Reader, if you want to die happy, neglect not secret prayer.

Going East—June 27, 1871.—Having again written my will, and made all necessary arrangements for the trip, I this day started, for the sixth time, to visit my native state. I went down the river to Cincinnati on the steam-boat, and then by railway, and reached Stephentown on the 30th of June, thanking God for his protecting care over me, and my safe arrival. The journey or change of living improved my health. But death has been here; and though the mountains, brooks, and valleys look just as they did when my father left here for the West, seventy-one years ago, the inhabitants have changed. Year by year my relatives have dropped off, till few even of my cousins remain. The *religious* interest seems now quite low in this country. I preached in South Berlin, and tarried in and about Stephentown nearly three weeks, and then took the cars, July 20th, for Boston, about two hundred miles, and reached there at six P. M. the same day. July 21st I took the cars for Exeter, New Hampshire, fifty miles, where I was met by Brother Mark Roberts, whose acquaintance I formed at the General Convention at Oshawa, in 1870. He took me to his house, where I was kindly received by his family. I re-

15

mained a little over a week, and preached twice on the fifth
Sunday in July, in Stratham, near Brother Roberts'; and
he took me the next day to the sea-shore, at North Hampton Beach—a ride of ten miles or more, where I was
kindly received by Elder N. T. Ridlon and his accomplished
lady. Elder Ridlon is pastor of the Christian Church at
North Hampton. This place is a great summer resort.
Thousands of visitors are here. Among the notable women
here is Harriet Beecher Stowe, best known as the author of
Uncle Tom's Cabin, who is here spending the summer. On
the 2d day of August I walked about two miles to see her.
On the third day of this month Elder Ridlon and Sister Ridlon
and myself went on the cars to Portsmouth, in the north-east
part of the State of Maine, and there took a steamer to the Isles
of Shoals, about fifteen miles on the ocean. There are ten or
twelve of these barren islands in sight of each other, all covered with rocks of great size. I did not see a green shrub upon
them. Yet fine hotels and large boarding-houses are plenty,
where people go for a summer resort. We returned about sundown the same day, quite tired. Here we have fresh fish from
the ocean at almost every meal. On the first Lord's-day in
August (6th) I preached twice to Elder Ridlon's congregation,
and the next day I returned to Brother Roberts', expecting to
start homeward soon. I had written to Elder Edmunds, of
Boston, that I expected to pass through that city on the 10th,
and desired to see him. He answered my letter and requested
me to preach in Boston that night, and to prolong my stay
there. On the 10th I bid farewell to Brother Roberts' dear,
kind family, and others who came to take the parting hand, and
he took me to Exeter, where I bid him farewell and took the
cars at about 8:30 A. M., and reached Boston by eleven A. M.

The Infidel.—Soon after my arrival in Boston I was introduced
to a converted infidel. His name was Southmade. He was
about fifty years old. He had for twenty-five years denied the
being of a God, and cursed the Bible. He was then an atheist.
For the last four years he had believed in God, but denied Christ
and the Bible. He was then a deist. He had lately been converted to the Christian religion. He related to me his experience. He said, a few weeks ago, in the night, between midnight
and morning, the Holy Spirit came to him, and said, "Southmade, what harm has Jesus ever done to you that you so revile
him and persecute him, and that you will not believe in him?"
This melted his heart. The tears flowed; and he said, "O Lord,
I do believe." And in the morning he arose rejoicing. He
then went to his former infidel companions and exhorted them
and others to believe on the Lord Jesus Christ. He continued
this till he became so hoarse that he could scarcely speak. The
doctors told him that he must cease or it would cause his death.

He could scarcely speak aloud when talking to me. I preached at night to an attentive and intelligent congregation. I felt the spirit of the subject myself, and after I closed quite a number arose and spoke in approval of the discourse. Southmade, being a hearer, arose also. Being very hoarse, he said: "The doctors have forbidden me to talk, but I must speak of the love of the Savior." He did so, and his words had great effect. Elder Edmunds and others urgently requested me to remain longer, but having appointments in eastern New York, I could not comply. I promised, if health and circumstances would permit, the Lord willing, I would visit Boston previous to going home. So I bid them farewell, and the next morning took the express train for eastern New York. I wrote from there to Elder Edmunds, that if he desired it, I would return to Boston and preach two or three weeks, asking no reward other than a hard bed to sleep on, and brown bread and milk to eat. He answered, "Come; it is of the Lord," etc. Having filled my appointments in Berlin and Petersburg, New York, on the 7th of September I took the cars at North Stephentown, and arrived at Boston about five P. M. On the Lord's-day, the 10th of September, I preached to a respectable congregation as to numbers and intelligence, and the word spoken seemed to gladden many hearts. On Monday, 11th instant, I went to New Bedford, about sixty miles south of Boston, and there on the 12th instant attended a very interesting session of the Rhode Island and Massachusetts Christian Conference. It was published in the papers of New Bedford that a man of over four-score years would preach, and the congregation was large. I gave the scriptural view of the elevated character of the Son of God, the Lord of life and glory, and real divinity. As such he is worthy to be honored and worshiped. And as he has power on earth to forgive sins, it is right and proper to pray to him, as did the first Christians, and as Stephen did while being stoned to death. I have no recollection that any discourse of mine was ever received with such great expressions of joy and gladness as this was. I returned to Boston, and on Sabbath, the 17th, preached again to Elder Edmunds' people—the congregation being much larger than before. The word was again well received. Elder Edmunds was not with us at either of these meetings, being absent on missionary service. I complied with the urgent request of Brother Edmunds and the people to remain over one more Sabbath. These three months' sojourn in New York and New England have been among the most agreeable and pleasant of my long life. I have been courteously and kindly received by Christian ministers and people, without exception; and in every place I have been urged to remain longer. The Christians are not the only people who have kindly received me, and desired to hear the words of an aged man. All denominations that I have met with have been equally kind and courteous. Congregationalists, Presbyterians, and others invite me to preach, and desire to hear the man who has seen more than eighty and preached more than sixty years. A learned and popular Presbyterian minister said to me, "My congregation have heard of you, and they want to hear you preach; and so do I. Will you preach for me?" I complied; and after the sermon he commended it to his people very highly. The courtesy of Elder Edmunds and his people, and that of his good lady to me, can never be forgotten. My health is so much improved that I feel almost like a young man again. I have gained twenty pounds in weight since leaving home in the latter part of June last. During the past week I have walked to meeting seven times. To go and return is one mile and a half; this makes ten miles and a half walking, not including my rambles and visits in the city. This is Saturday, September 23d. The next day I attended meeting four times, including my own "last-sermon" meeting. The Lord was with me. The congregation was large. The Spirit helped me to preach. The people wept, and so did I. Monday morning, September 25, 1871, I bade Elder Edmunds' dear family, and friends there, farewell. He and Elder Thomas accompanied me to the depot, and there, before 8:30, having taken the parting hand with them and the friends at the depot, the words were soon heard, "All aboard," and in a few seconds I was on my way home at the rate of thirty miles an hour. We were detained six or eight hours on the way by the breaking of an axle. No one was injured, though some were much frightened. I stopped four days on the way, and arrived home on the 2d day of October, 1871. I found all well. Thank God for his protecting care.

The Conference of 1871.—This conference of 1871 met on the 21st day of October, in the chapel of the Rockyfork Church, in Highland County, about six miles east of Hillsboro'. This was the fifty-second annual session, all of which the Lord had enabled me to attend. Soon after the conference assembled a number of brethren said to me, "Will you serve as president if elected?" I replied, "If such be the desire of the conference, I will try to serve them." I was chosen accordingly. The number in attendance was larger than usual, not only of people, but of ministers and messengers from the churches. The churches were reported to be in general prosperity and peace. The conference continued four days, including the Sabbath. It was one of the most pleasant that I ever attended.

Eighty-first Birthday—December 5, 1871.—This is my birthday. To-day I am eighty-one years old. My health is much better than it was on my birthday one year ago. Thank God for all his tender mercies unmerited by me. "O, God, be thou my portion in the land of the living." I will soon be gone.

My pilgrimage is nearly done,
Lord, fit me for thy heavenly home.

My life seems long, as I contemplate the astonishing changes which have been made, a few of which I record. *Progress of Science.*—Four great advancements have been made in human progress since I was born. Few, like myself, have lived to see their commencement and consummation. First: The application of steam for propelling boats on the rivers, ships on the ocean, cars on the land, and numberless kinds of machinery. Second: The electric telegraph, by which persons, thousands of miles apart, can talk to each other as though face to face, and the submarine telegraph, uniting distant continents, so that Americans can talk, without loss of time, with the people of Europe or Asia. Third: The construction of railroads across the states and across the continent, from ocean to ocean, thus uniting the Atlantic and Pacific oceans by railroads, as well as the Old and the New World by the electric cable. Fourth: The liberation of four millions of slaves of the African race, in these United States, all of whom are enfranchised and made American citizens with the same right to vote as white people.

THE HONOR AND GLORY OF THE SON OF GOD.

December 21, 1871.—I will here record the argumentative part of a third article, which includes all important matters contained in two former articles, and others on the subject, published in the "Herald of Gospel Liberty," maintaining the exalted honor and glory of the Son of God. The following views were not learned from the teaching of men. While contemplating the glory of the Son of God, I prayed to Jesus for light and understanding, and a glory and a beauty pertaining to the Son of God were manifested to my mind, such as I never saw before. My views are that the Son of God is worthy of higher honor than is ascribed to him. Let us go back to the beginning. In Genesis I. 26 God said, "Let *us* make man in *our* image, after *our* likeness." Here God speaks to some one. In the next verse God alone is spoken of, and there the plural form of the pronoun is not used, but it reads, "God created man in *his* own image." Genesis I. 27. But in Genesis III. 22 God says, "The man is become as one of *us*." The plural pronoun is thus used four times, as follows: "Let *us* (1) make man in *our* (2) image, after *our* (3) likeness," and "the man has become as one of *us* (4)." I am aware that some contend that the plural form of the pronouns "us" and "our" is frequently used to signify one speaker or writer. But that reasoning will not apply to the phrase "us" in Genesis III. 22, as no writer calls himself "us" in the phrase "one of us." Who, then, was this person associated with God in creation? Let Saint John, the beloved disciple, answer.

"In the beginning was the Word, and the Word was with God, and the Word was God. The same was in the beginning with God. All things were made by him; and without him was not any thing made that was made. And the Word was made flesh, and dwelt among us (and we beheld his glory, the glory as of the only-begotten of the Father), full of grace and truth." John I. 1–14. This Word was the Son of God who was with God and was God. Now turn to the Revelations.

"He was clothed with a vesture dipped in blood: and his name is called The Word of God. And he hath on his vesture and on his thigh a name written, King of kings, and Lord of lords." Rev. XIX. 12–20. If you wish it made plainer, turn to the great apostle. Saint Paul says:

"God, who at sundry times and in divers manners spake in time past unto the fathers by the prophets, hath in these last days spoken unto us by his Son, whom he hath appointed heir of all things, by whom also he made the worlds." Heb. I. 1, 2. Will any one who believes the Bible reject this undeniable evidence of the honor and glory of the Son of God, the testimony being in the words of him who said, "Let there be light, and there was light?" "All men should honor the Son even as they honor the Father." John v. 23. Webster defines honor to be worship, and gives this text (John v. 23) as an illustration.

"Who, being in the form of God, thought it not robbery to be equal with God." Phil. II. 6. I can not comprehend how the Son is equal with God his Father; yet I believe it because the word of God says so.

"For it pleased the Father that in him should all fullness dwell." Col. I. 19. This harmonizes with the former texts in establishing the glory of the Son of God.

"In whom are hid all the treasures of wisdom and knowledge." Col. II. 3. In maintaining the honor and glory of the Son of God, we quote these records of the treasures of wisdom and knowledge from the word.

"For in him dwelleth all the fullness of the Godhead bodily." Col. II. 9. Is this a mystery? I grant it. The great apostle said:

"Without controversy, great is the mystery of godliness: God was manifest in the flesh, justified in the Spirit, seen of angels, preached unto the Gentiles, believed on in the world, received up into glory." I. Tim. III. 16. God was manifest in the flesh in Jesus Christ. God was justified in the Spirit of Jesus Christ. God was thus seen in the flesh "which things the angels desire to look into." I. Peter I. 12. God was preached unto the Gentiles; for "God was in Christ reconciling the world unto himself." This was Jesus the Son of God. He suffered; he died; he arose from the dead; he ascended upon high, leading captivity captive; received up into glory, while saints and angels sang:

"Lift up your heads, O ye gates; and be ye lifted up, ye everlasting doors; and the King of glory shall come in. Who is this King of glory? The Lord strong and mighty, the Lord mighty in battle. Lift up your heads, O ye gates; even lift them up, ye everlasting doors; and the King of glory shall come in." Psalms xxiv. 7–10. Some think that they know all about God and his Son! This immortal theme is no mystery to them! I say with Saint Paul, "Great is the mystery." Yet I believe it. Is it not strange that man will object to believing a mystery concerning God and Christ, the Son of God, while they do not understand their own organization, or how, or why the hair grows upon their own heads? If they do not know themselves, how can they know all about God? Now read again:

"And again' when he bringeth in the first-begotten into the world, he saith, And let all the angels of God worship him. But unto the Son, he saith, Thy throne, O God, is for ever and ever: a scepter of righteousness is the scepter of thy kingdom." Heb. i. 6–8. The very next verse explains this. Read verse 9:

"Thou hast loved righteousness, and hated iniquity; therefore God, even thy God, hath anointed thee with the oil of gladness above thy fellows." Heb. i. 9. Saint Paul explains further, saying:

"He humbled himself, and became obedient unto death, even the death of the cross. Wherefore God also hath highly exalted him, and given him a name which is above every name." Phil. ii. 8, 9. It is to be noticed that after God said, "Thy throne, O God, is for ever and ever," he adds:

"And, thou, Lord, in the beginning hast laid the foundation of the earth; and the heavens are the works of thine hands." Heb. i. 10. Thus he is our Emmanuel as it is written:

"They shall call his name Emmanuel, which being interpreted is, God with us." Matt. i. 23. Such is the glory of the Son of God.

> "Never does truth more shine,
>   With beams of heavenly light,
> Than when the Scriptures join
>   To prove it plain and right:
> Than when each text doth each explain,
> And all unite to speak the same.

The Three Orders.—There are three orders of intelligent beings—God, angels, and men. To one of these orders every intelligent being belongs. Of which order is the Son of God? Is he not of the highest order? There are many dear brethren who talk quite fluently about the divinity of Christ who hold that Jesus, the Son of God, is neither *God, angel, or man!* They think that he is called man because the Word was made flesh, and came in the form of a man. They think that he is called an angel because he is "the messenger of the covenant" to us. Malachi III. 1. They think that he is called God because of "being made so much better than the angels, as he hath by inheritance obtained a more excellent name than they." This name can be none other than the name of God, his Father. Therefore he is called "Emmanuel, God with us." I ask, to which order does the Son of God belong? Which was he related to when he had glory with the Father "before the world was?" John XVII. 5. Could he be truly the Son of God, and be of any order below God? He could not. It being admitted that the Lord of life and glory is of the same order of being as God his Father, and truly related to him as the only-begotten Son of God, his Father, can it be denied that the Son of God is properly God, as the Bible says he is? Yet, when this is said, men will cry out, "Two Gods!" I believe no more in two Gods than they do, and I can not comprehend how the Son of God can be equal with God his Father. Yet, though our limited capacity can not comprehend the being and existing relation between the Father and the Son, let us humbly worship and "honor the Son, even as we honor the Father." O Jesus! give us of thy spirit, by which to worship thee aright.

Timid Brethren.—Many fear to call Jesus God lest they should seem to have two Gods. But we should not fear to do whatever the Bible teaches us to do. Who will deny that there are two together in heaven, exalted above all creatures? See the following Scriptures:

"The Lord said unto my Lord, Sit thou on my right hand." Matt. XXII. 44.

"The Word was with God, and the Word was God." John I. 1.

"Unto the Son he saith, Thy throne, O God, is for ever and ever." Heb. I. 8.

"Blessing, and honor, and glory, and power, be unto him that sitteth upon the throne, and unto the Lamb." Rev. V. 13.

"And now, O Father, glorify thou me with thine own self, with the glory which I had with thee before the world was." John XVII. 5. Here are two, exalted, above all creatures.

Shall we deny the word of God, or be afraid to say what the Bible says? The Christians receive the whole word of God. They do not deny it because they can not explain it, but leave the mysteries with God. The great apostle plainly states all these facts in a brief history of Christ, recorded in his letter to the Philippians.

Divine History of the Son of God.—"Who, being in the form of God, thought it not robbery to be equal with God: but made himself of no reputation, and took upon him the form of a servant, and was made in the likeness of men: and being found in fashion as a man, he humbled himself, and became obedient unto death, even the death of the cross. Wherefore God also hath highly exalted him, and given him a name which is above every name: that at the name of Jesus every knee should bow, of things in heaven, and things in earth, and things under the earth; and that every tongue should confess that Jesus Christ is Lord, to the glory of God the Father." Was he in the form of God? I believe it. Did he not think it robbery to be equal with God? I shall not deny it. Did he make himself of no reputation? I accept it. Did he die for me? I am thankful for it. Did God highly exalt him? Then I will try to exalt him also. Did God call him by a name which is above every name? There is no name above every name but the name God; so I will give it to him. Shall every knee bow to him? So shall mine; and I will confess the Son of God to be Lord, to the glory of God the Father.

Humanitarians.—Some people think that Jesus was a proper man, exalted to be called God, and to be worshiped. But I answer, would God exalt a mere man to be called the only-begotten Son of God, and call him God? Did God ever command the angels to worship a proper man? Did God ever say to a mere man, "Thou, Lord, in the beginning hast laid the foundation of the earth; and the heavens are the works of thine hands?" Could a mere man lay the foundation of the earth or the heavens? Could a finite spark be the brightness of infinite glory? Could one less than omnipotent possess all power? Could one less than infinite put all things under him, God only excepted? Could one of yesterday have had glory with God before the world was? Would God *make* an image of himself to be worshiped, and then forbid the worship of images? No; Jesus is truly God, though I can not comprehend it.

A comparison.—All the truth of both Unitarians and Trinitarians is mine, though I am of neither sect. Without deciding which is nearest right, where both are in error, do we not see how much more Trinitarians, who exalt the Son of God, whatever may be their errors, are doing for the conversion of the wicked, than Unitarians are doing, who do not so exalt the Lord of life and glory? Who will attempt to deny this? Here I rest my argument. Will they now cry out, "Two Gods, two equal Gods, a second deity;" things which I have said nothing about? I shall not answer such insinuations, but leave them to contend with the fearful odds of omnipotence, and the eternal truth of the great I AM! Will they say to Jehovah, "In proclaiming to thy Son, 'Thy throne, O God, is forever and ever,' thou makest two Gods?" Will they? I believe no more in two Gods than they do. I only contend that we are to give to

Jesus the honor which the Bible gives to him. This I will do,
and I am willing to trust the consequences to God. I do not
agree with either Unitarians or trinitarians who say that "a
derived God is no God at all" (Moses Stuart). Jesus is God
because he is the Son of God. This is the word of God.

Has Not Changed.—The doctrine which I preached at first
does not conflict with the views I now entertain. More than
forty years ago (1830) a learned Presbyterian preacher, Rev.
John Rankin, of Ripley, Brown County, Ohio, published a work
accusing Christians of believing that Jesus is an inferior being.
I answered that publication, denying the said accusation, a copy
of which answer is now before me, which does not conflict with
the views I now entertain. The preface to said reply says
[Here the copy is from an old pamphlet] : "These views are
my own, and I alone am accountable for them. In 1830 Rev.
John Rankin, a Presbyterian minister in Ripley, Ohio, published a pamphlet to sustain the trinitarian doctrine that the
Father is God, the Son Jesus Christ is self-existent, co-equal
God with the Father; and the Holy Ghost is self-existent, co-
equal God with the Father and the Son; and these three are all
co-essential, co-existent, and co-eternal, one God." The Christian doctrine, which was spreading in southern Ohio, was the
doctrine which was first preached by Christ and his apostles,
viz: "There is one God, the Father, and one Lord Jesus Christ,
the Son of God, his Father, and one Holy Ghost, the Comforter."
I thank God that this said work has been preserved, or mistaken
accusations might be believed, that I had changed. When this
bounding heart has ceased to beat, and this trembling hand,
which now holds this pen, is cold in death, I want my children
and my grandchildren and my great-grandchildren to know and
to understand, and to tell it abroad, that it was not by preaching
Christ as an inferior being, the creature of creeds, that caused
between six and seven thousand to embrace religion under my
ministry during sixty years' preaching.

Sister Lansdown.—The death-bed words of Sister Lansdown,
published in the "Herald of Gospel Liberty," a few weeks since,
seem appropriate for a place in this article on the glory of the
Son of God. She said: "Most of the preaching concerning the
Savior is too light. It does not properly represent him. He is
high—above all principality and power. Sing to me of Jesus."
If I remember rightly, Sister Lansdown and nearly all her
father's family embraced religion and united with the church
under my ministry.

Praying to Jesus.—"And they stoned Stephen, calling upon
God, and saying, Lord Jesus, receive my spirit." Acts VII. 59.
O, blessed Jesus, how many millions, when upon their dying
pillow, has thy dear name comforted and made rejoice in the
hope of future glory, immortality, and life eternal in a world

beyond this world of sorrow, sin and death? O, thou Lamb of God, let thy dear name give joy to me—unworthy me—as it has to others, when on my dying pillow I lay my head.

> "Dear Jesus, be my guide and friend,
> Unto my weary journey's end."

The following article of mine, which was first published in the "Herald of Gospel Liberty," fully sets forth my views of the way that we should preach on disputed doctrines: "*Thy Word Is Truth.* (John XVII. 17). Dear Editors: It is not my design to expatiate upon the text referred to, but merely to call attention to the fundamental teaching of Christ and the apostles. It is to be distinctly understood that the word of divine truth, and human renderings or explanations of that word, are different things. Will it not be admitted that the human definitions of the word of life have caused all the jargon and divisions now in Christendom? Can it be denied that said definitions are all false, in a greater or less degree, while 'the word is truth?' Now, let us look at a few items pertaining to this matter. A year or so ago a western Christian conference received a minister who said he believed in the trinity, and in the sprinkling of water on men, women, and infants, for baptism. A number of writers in our paper stated their objections to the reception of a man with such a faith and practice. What then? Of course, if we believe him to be a Christian, are we not bound to receive him? 'But not to doubtful disputations,' said Paul. Let such agree to use no words as to their belief, other than are in God's word. There will then be no trouble about differences in faith. Do not Father, Son, and Holy Ghost, as found in God's word, express enough to be believed in order to salvation? For several months past there have been lengthy essays in our paper, for and against the trinity. Why all this? Is it not because men do not state and express their faith by using the inspired words of truth, saying no more nor less than God's word says? Do any pretend that the word trinity is in the Bible? Surely not. Do not nearly all trinitarians define trinity thus: 'The Father is God, the Son is equally God, and the Holy Ghost is equally God with the Father and Son; and all these three are co-equal, co-essential, and co-eternal—all three of whom constitute or make one God?' Are not the Unitarian doctrines, that the Son of God is mere man, likewise not in the Bible? Now, without contending about the truth or falsehood of these theories, ought they not to be rejected for the plain reason that Jesus did not design that his followers should so believe, or the Holy Spirit would have indited the language or words of said system, or that phraseology; and it would have been recorded and contained in God's word, which it is not? I have preached in the same section of country, and among the same people, for more than half a century, and have often expressed my faith relative to the Father, Son, and Holy Spirit, using Scripture language, and I have never heard of one trinitarian objecting."

Christmas Comes Again.—This is December 25, 1871. A beautiful day it is. Upon this day millions rejoice and think of Him from whom the day took its name.

New Year's.—Here is New Year's day 1872, making eighty-two New Year's days seen by me. Perhaps not one in a thousand live to see eighty-two New Year's days. Thank God for his care that has been over me through a long life, and for my mental faculties, and for the health which I now enjoy. I am as well as I can expect. My thoughts will wander back over scores of years and to other generations, to the days of my youth, when Ohio was little more than a wilderness; to the days when young and strong, I threaded my way through forests to the settlements, and preached during the winter in log school-houses and in log cabin residences, which became temples consecrated by the conversion of souls. And when the warm weather came, then the crowds came. Multitudes would attend, many coming from quite a distance. Then I preached in the forest, and hundreds embraced religion in the shady temples built by nature. Being poor then, and without salary, I supported myself and family with the labor of my hands. It may seem to many now to have been a great sacrifice to me to thus devote one-half my time to preaching; but the labors were pleasant to me, and I felt "woe is me if I preach not the gospel," consequently I did not wait for money to "call" me. Those were happy days, and I now have a reward of more value to me than thousands in gold, namely: hundreds who then embraced religion under my ministry have died in triumphant hope. My memory now calls to mind the companions of my youth in the ministry—those with whom I met to toil and travel, preach and pray. When we met in those days we did not jest and joke, as is too much practiced by ministers now. We felt that we had important work. These pioneers of a free gospel are now gone—all gone—while I alone am left. Again I think of the loved ones of my own family, who were with me on past New Year's days, but are here no more.

April 18, 1872.—I have been quite poorly for nearly two weeks with a distressing cough, for which there seems to be no relief.

May 26, 1872.—The beautiful May month has come, and almost gone again, with all its native charms, while I am here yet, almost deprived of enjoyment of this world by an afflicting cough. Is it not true that we can not properly appreciate the blessings of health till it is gone? During the past five

weeks I have been much confined to my room. I have had
four physicians to see me at different times. Thank God, I am
now improving in health. None can know the true value of
religion till earthly comforts can no longer be enjoyed. I now
think, the Lord willing, that I shall be able to start on my next
preaching tour East in about two weeks.

The Seventh Visit East—June 13, 1872.—I, this morning, start
East, intending to make my seventh visit to the land of my
birth, and then go on to New England. I go first to Troy,
twenty miles above Dayton, to meet there, June 18th, with the
American General Convention, and Christian Publishing Association, which meet at the same time and place, in order to
hold consultation. O Jesus! prosper my journey if it be thy
blessed will. June 18, 1872, I met with the aforesaid conventions. After their close I took the cars for Rensselaer County,
New York. I reached Stephentown, Rensselaer County, New
York, on the 25th instant, during a heavy fall of rain. After
tarrying there two weeks, I took the cars for Boston, Massachusetts, on the 11th of July, where I arrived at five P. M., the
same day, and was kindly received by Elder E. Edmunds, the
Christian minister of that city. I tarried there four days, and
preached on the second Lord's-day of this month to Elder Edmunds' congregation. This was the first time that I had been
able to preach since the fourth Lord's-day of March. On the
16th of July, I took the cars to Cape Cod, Massachusetts, where
I could breathe sea air, and where they were making preparations for the great New England Christian camp-meeting, to
open August 1, 1872. After four days I left for Fall River,
where I spent the third Lord's-day in July, taking part in the
service, but not preaching. Monday, July 26th, I went to New
Bedford, where I spent that week, a part of the time sailing on
the ocean, as far as to the island of "Martha's Vineyard," etc.
On the fourth Lord's-day I preached at New Bedford. On the
first of the week I returned to the Cape Cod camp-ground. The
meeting began on Thursday, the 1st of August, 1872. Not
having a tent of my own, I hired a lodging under a common
"factory muslin" tent, with only a straw mattrass between me
and the ground. There I slept every night during the week,
my health improving all the time. It was truly an interesting
meeting. There was a prayer-meeting for all to meet at every
morning at sunrise, after which they had social meetings of
prayer, speaking, singing, etc., in various tents; for those from
each city, town, or church, had each a large common tabernacle
of wood or canvas, where many meetings were held until the
hour for preaching. They had sermons at ten A. M. and three
P. M., and prayer and social meeting again for all at 7:30 P. M.

He Preaches.—On the 6th of August, the sixth day of the
camp-meeting, at three P. M., by request, I tried to preach.

The report of the sermon I take from the "Christian Herald," of Newburyport, Massachusetts, Elder D. P. Pike, Editor: "At three P. M. Brother Matthew Gardner gave an interesting sermon from the words, 'The Son of man is come to seek and to save that which was lost.' Brother Gardner is one of our oldest ministers from the West. · His sermon was able, and lovingly delivered." On the 7th of August I took the cars to Boston, and thence to Stratham, New Hampshire, almost seventy miles north-east of Boston. I was kindly welcomed to their home by Brother J. B. Severame and his kind lady. I tarried here two weeks, and preached on the third Lord's-day in August (18th), and left on the 22d instant, for Newburyport, Massacusetts, in which city there is a large Christian church, of which Elder D. P. Pike is pastor. In this church there has been a continued revival, yet continued, with meetings for preaching or prayer every night since January 1st. Brother Pike having requested me to visit his church and preach, I spoke for them on Lord's-day, the 25th, to a large congregation. The following is from the "Herald of Gospel Liberty," the first religious newspaper in the world; now published at Dayton, Ohio.

"*Brother Matthew Gardner.*—The following is from the 'Christian Herald,' published in Newburyport, Massachusetts, September 3, 1872, Elder D. P. Pike, Editor: 'We have had the rich pleasure of a visit from this venerable minister of Jesus Christ. He came to us with the blessing of the gospel of Christ. Brother Gardner experienced religion August 10, 1810, at the age of nineteen. He was born in the State of New York; moved into the State of Ohio in 1800. He commenced preaching immediately after his conversion, presenting Christ as the sinners' friend. He was baptized by Archibald Alexander, and was ordained in 1815. He has had a successful ministry. Between six and seven thousand have professed the religion of Christ under his ministry. He was one of the first ministers who formed the Southern Ohio Christian Conference, in 1820, and has not missed a session of that conference since, and is, at the present time, president of that body. It is composed of about thirty ministers, and between four and five thousand members. He is now in his eighty-second year, and of course his ministry extends over sixty years. It spans two generations. His health is good, his mind active, his powers strong and vigorous. He is an able minister of the New Testament, evangelical and orthodox in his doctrine, true to the preciousness of Jesus, holding forth his equality with the Father, and his power to save repenting sinners. It is encouraging to meet with those ministers who have not been carried about by every wind of doctrine. He has walked by the same rule, and attended to the duties of the same gospel. He gave Court Street Church, in this city, a sermon, August 25th, in the afternoon, from Luke VII. 22. It was an impressive sermon, received with devout attention, and will be long remembered. His introduction was appropriate and truthful. The anxiety of John the Baptist, and the kindness of Jesus, was feelingly presented. The miracles of Christ were ably set forth, admitted, and defended, the gospel correctly defined, and the mission-work of Jesus earnestly commended. 'To the poor the gospel is preached.' Our people will not soon forget Brother Gardner nor his sermon. Many manifested their faith in Christ, showing that they rejoiced in the pardoning mercy of Jesus Christ. God bless Brother Gardner, making his last days his best, and crowning his sunset with a glorious immortality. He left us August 26th, on his return West. Safely may he reach his home, blessed with improved health and increased encouragement to trust the Master, and honor his own blessed work in saving souls.'" After parting with the kind friends at Newburyport, I took the cars for Boston, where, after tarrying two days, I left for North Stephentown, where I arrived on the 29th, at two P. M. There I remained and visited a little more than two weeks. I preached on the third Lord's-day, September 15th, to a Presbyterian congregation, by the request of their preacher. They were all well pleased. On the 16th instant I bade farewell to my dear friends and relations, and started for home, where I arrived on the 19th, about three A. M., with my health much improved. Thank God, through Jesus Christ, for his boundless mercy and goodness toward unworthy me! At home! yes, I am here at home! Home that was, when the one was here who made it home, who relieved my cares, who shared my toils, my sorrows, and my joys. Yes, home it was then; but now, no home to me!

Conference.—The conference of 1872 met on the twelfth day of October, in its fifty-third annual session. I was there. I have, by divine grace, attended every one of its fifty-three annual sessions. It met at *Point Isabel*, in Clermont County, in the new chapel of the Salem church, which has been erected over three miles from the old house. There was a full attendance. The reports from the churches were favorable. I was nominated for chairman, but declined being a candidate. My health, thank God, continues to improve. I am able to preach every Lord's-day. During the conference I preached in the Methodist church to a large congregation. On the 27th of October, agreeable to the dying request of a deceased sister in the church, I preached a funeral discourse in Hiatt's Christian Chapel, to a large congregation.

Eighth Visit East—November 12, 1872.—On this day I started on my return to the land of my birth, to spend the winter. I had a pleasant journey, and reached my intended home in safety, on the fourteenth day of November, in good health, for a man of my age. I found my relatives in good health generally. The winter weather has commenced early. After freezing weather for a week, it commenced snowing, November 22d, and continued at intervals several days. The snow is ten inches deep. It is beautiful sleighing. The first day of December I went in a sleigh, with my cousin, Mr. Rose, with whom I am stopping, to the Baptist meeting, over three miles. The minister invited me into the pulpit, and requested me to preach. I declined, but followed him with prayer and some remarks, which were well received. The preacher said, "Brother Gardner, come as often as you can."

December 5th.—My birthday has come. It seems interesting to be here where I was born, on the 5th of December, 1790, eighty-two years ago. My health is improving slowly, but steadily. I am quite well, considering my age. Thanks be to God.

December 25, 1872.—This day is regarded as Christmas all over Christendom. The day is cold. The mercury has been ten degrees below zero, or about that for ten or fifteen days. Yet I do not feel the cold much, though I take my sleighride every few days. New Year's day, 1873, is here. This makes eighty-three New Year's days that I have seen. My health is improved. My voice is so far restored that I can sing again as in past years. My transient home is a pleasant place indeed. Every thing is done to make me comfortable—more than I can ask. Mr. Rose is an excellent man. His wife was a Gardner—a second cousin of mine.

Prayer.—O God, as thou hast thus far led me and given me a long life in this world, I humbly beseech thee, in the name of thy dear and well beloved Son Jesus Christ, that thou wilt let thy Holy Spirit and thy fatherly care attend me through this year, the first day of which I have, by thy grace, lived to see. If it be thy will to call me hence during this year, grant me, O Lord, a tranquil hour in which to die, and afterwards give me a humble part with the redeemed, and those saved by grace. O blessed Jesus, thou Lord of life and glory, who hast said that thou wouldst be with all who trust in thee, do grant to guide me by thy counsel during my few remaining days on earth, and then receive me to glory to praise God and the Lamb forever. Amen. Thanks be to God! Let all within me praise his holy name.

The weather is cold. The storms are fearful. They say that in the woods and where drifted the snow is from four to five feet deep. For several hours preceding one of these tremendous storms its approach may be seen by the driving snow and bending trees, as it comes over the great mountains of Massachusetts several miles east of us. It comes with a loud roaring sound like the sea. When this is heard, all prepare for the storm. All stock of every kind must be housed. The roads become filled with snow-drifts. Travel ceases entirely, until men turn out and clear a track. Cold as it is, this "shoveling snow" must be often repeated, for it is common for storm to follow storm, sometimes with only a few day's interval, filling the roads anew. By these storms and drifts the pleasure of sleighriding is often interrupted, to the mortification of many who enjoy it, notwithstanding the cold weather.

February 1, 1873.—The mean temperature of the weather for the past two months has been near zero; sometimes below— seldom above. January 30th it was twenty-three degrees below zero. Much of my time has been employed during the past months in writing and preparing for the press a pamphlet of thirty-five pages, octavo, containing two articles of mine, which were declined by Elder Henry Y. Rush, editor of the "Herald of Gospel Liberty," together with seven letters addressed to him on the subject, and some theological remarks. It will not be inserted in this work, but may be found among my other productions. I negotiated, by letter, with Elder W. A. Gross, the agent of the Christian Publishing Association, at Dayton, Ohio, for the printing, binding, and distribution of said work. So about the last of this month (February, 1873), I mailed the manuscript entitled "THE CHRISTIAN REVIEWER," to be published for gratuitous distribution.

March 10, 1873.—This morning I bade farewell to my dear cousin Rose and his kind companion, and left that pleasant home for Ohio. Cousin took me to the depot, three-fourths of a mile, to take the 6:30 A. M. train, and I was soon on my way. I stopped at the Publishing House at Dayton, Ohio, and found the new pamphlet ready to mail. It cost me one hundred dollars. I arrived home on the 14th of March.

Ministry of the Angels.—This was my eighth journey East since 1851, or during the last twenty-two years, and no accident has occurred. Thanks be to God for his guardian angels, which I believe have attended me since the day when I first gave my heart unto the Lord. The angels are the servants of God.

"The chariots of God are twenty thousand, even thousands of angels: the Lord is among them, as in Sinai, the holy place." Psalm LXVIII. 17.

They all worship the Son of God. "Again, when he bringeth in the first-begotten into the world, he saith, And let all the angels of God worship him." Heb. I. 6.

Angels first appeared as cherubims, guarding the tree of life. Gen. III. 24.

The angel of the Lord took care of Hagar when she was an outcast. "And the angel of the Lord found her by a fountain of water in the wilderness, by the fountain in the way to Shur. And he said, Hagar, Sarai's maid, whence camest thou? and whither wilt thou go? And she called the name of the Lord that spake unto her, Thou God seest me: for she said, Have I also here looked after him that seeth me?" Gen. xvi. 7-13.

Angels visited Abraham to guide him. Gen. xviii. 1.

The angel of the Lord preserved Isaac. "And the angel of the Lord called unto him out of heaven, and said, Abraham, Abraham. And he said, Here am I. And he said, lay not thine hand upon the lad, neither do thou any thing unto him: for now I know that thou fearest God, seeing thou hast not withheld thy son, thine only son, from me." Gen. xxii. 11, 12.

Angels appeared to Jacob, showing him the way to heaven. Gen. xxviii. 12.

The angel of the Lord redeemed Jacob, and Jacob prayed him to bless the sons of Joseph, saying, "The angel which redeemed me from all evil, bless the lads." Gen. xlviii. 16.

An angel appeared to Moses in the burning bush. Ex. iii. 2.

The angel of the Lord accompanied the Israelites in the fiery cloud. Exodus xiv. 19.

The angel shut the lions' mouths. Daniel iii. 28.

Angels announced the Savior's birth, saying, "Glory to God in the highest, and on earth peace, good will toward men. For unto you is born this day, in the city of David, a Savior, which is Christ the Lord." Luke ii. 11-14.

Angels ministered to Jesus in the wilderness. Matt. iv. 11.

An angel strengthened Jesus in the agony of Gethsemane, as we read: "And there appeared an angel unto him from heaven, strengthening him." Luke xxii. 43.

Angels rejoice when sinners repent. Luke xv. 10.

Angels rolled back the stone from the sepulchre. John xx. 12.

Angels conveyed Lazarus to Abraham's bosom. Luke xvi. 22.

An angel delivered Peter from prison. Acts xii. 8.

Angels carried the messages of Jesus to John, when on the Isle of Patmos. Rev. i. 1.

These angels ofted speak as God, and represent the Lord of life and glory; but Saint Paul says: "Are they not all ministering spirits, sent forth to minister for them who shall be heirs of salvation?" Heb. i. 14.

And Jesus says: "They which shall be accounted worthy to obtain that world, and the resurrection from the dead, neither marry, nor are given in marriage: neither can they die any more: for they are equal unto the angels: and are the children of God, being the children of the resurrection." Luke xx. 35, 36.

The visits to the land of my birth were as follows:

The *first* visit was during May and June, of 1852.

The *second* was during August and September, of 1854.

The *third* was during August and September, of 1857.

The *fourth* was during August and September, of 1865.

The *fifth* visit was made during August, in 1870.

The *sixth* was during August and September, of 1871.

The *seventh* visit was from June to September, in 1872.
The *eighth* was from November to March, of 1872–1873.

Another Division of Property.—Two of my sons being in need of pecuniary relief, I felt disposed to divide a part of the means with which God had blessed me, and to be freed from the care of it; and about the last of March or first of April, 1873, I gave $4,500, as follows, to-wit: $1,000 each to my four sons, now living, and $500 to a grandson, whose father is deceased, all of which are advanced legacies, sums having been given to daughters before, as advanced legacies, this being part of $3,640 which each daughter had received more than the sons since both sons and daughters received their first portions. Through divine grace, care, and protection, I have lived to see the beginning of the charming month of May, 1873, this being the sixth day of that month. My health is good for a man of my age; and the delightful scenery, the verdant fields, and blossoming trees, enlivened by sweet-singing birds, make me almost fancy myself back to the days of my boyhood. But those days, with their then precious interests, have long since gone, never to return; but faith and hope look forward to happier hours in a country more beautiful than the May months. "There everlasting spring abides, and never-fading flowers." Thank God, in Christ, for this hope!

May 20, 1813; *May* 20, 1873—*Married Sixty Years Ago.*— The twentieth day of May, which I have lived to see in 1873, is an ever-memorable day to me. The memory of this day is endeared to me because it was the twentieth day of May, 1813, on which I took the hand of Sally Beasly to be my wife. It was on this very day, sixty years ago. Then both were young. We grew old together. She was born on the 12th of September, 1794. We were married on the 20th of May, 1813. She died on the 20th of September, 1869. She is no more here! My heart fills while I write, and my thoughts mournfully wander back to the day of our marriage, and return again, lingering all along the years we lived together. Tears will flow to ease a burdened heart. The beauties of May are charming still; but, ah! they can not cheer this heavy heart of mine! Jesus, I lay myself at thy feet!

Parting with Brethren.—On the 21st of this month I went to Dayton, Ohio, to the Christian Publishing House. I was quite kindly received by Elder Rush, the editor of the "Herald of Gospel Liberty." Our interview was quite friendly indeed, and we so parted. I returned to Cincinnati, and on Lord's-day, the 25th, went to hear Elder N. Summerbell, the pastor of the Christian Church in that city. He kindly requested me to preach, which invitation I declined, preferring to hear him. Our interview was kind and brotherly, and thus we parted.

Returns Home.—On the 26th of this month (May, 1873), I returned to my home.

Things Pleasant.—My visit to Dayton, Ohio, a few days ago, though fatiguing, was quite pleasant, being very kindly received by Brother Rush, the "Herald" editor, and Brother Gross, the publishing agent, and I enjoyed the company of Bro. Byrkit, our blind minister, and several other ministers who happened to call at the Christian Publishing House during my short stay in Dayton, which was on the 22d and 23d days of May, 1873. My interview with Brother Rush was quite pleasant indeed. On the 24th I returned to Cincinnati, and on Lord's-day, the 25th, went to Bible Chapel to hear Elder N. Summerbell, who kindly requested me to preach, which invitation was declined by me, preferring to hear him. The chapel is well fitted up, and looks like prosperity. though the congregation is not large. I saw Sister Summerbell, who does more than the work of one woman. She looks quite feeble. I view her as one of the best of women. I was glad to hear that Elder Joseph J. Summerbell, whom I helped to ordain when perhaps little more than nineteen years of age, is doing well at Spring. Pennsylvania. After a very pleasant interview with Elder N. Summerbell, I took the steamer on the 26th, and reached our daughter's (Sally A. Shinkle), near Higginsport, that night. about nine o'clock, in tolerable health but quite tired.—[Herald of Gospel Liberty.

Ripley, Ohio, May 29, 1873.   M. GARDNER.

Expected Eastern Sojourn.—If the Lord wills, it is my purpose to start East (to spend the summer) about the 10th of June, proximo. Hence, would say to all not to write me at Ripley, Ohio, after the last of this month (May), but after that time direct to North Stephentown, New York.—[Herald of Gospel Liberty.   M. GARDNER.

THE LAST RECORDS.

On Lord's-day, June 1, 1873, I preached to a large congregation in Ripley, the appointment having been published in the newspaper of that town.

End of the Manuscript—June 10, 1873.—This morning I start to make the ninth visit to the land where I was born.

The above is the last line penned by Elder M. Gardner in the manuscript of his autobiography. It is probable that he left it at his home, near Ripley, on the morning of June 10, 1873, and never saw it afterward.

LAST PREACHING TOUR.

"Go preach my gospel," saith the Lord ;
 " Bid the whole earth my grace receive:
He shall be saved that trusts my word,
 And he condemned that won't believe.

"I'll make your great commission known ;
 And ye shall prove my gospel true,
By all the works that I have done,
 By all the wonders ye shall do.

"Teach all the nations my commands ;
 I'm with you till the world shall end :
All power is trusted in my hands ;
 I can destroy, and I defend."

He spake,—and light shone round his head ;
 On a bright cloud to heaven he rode ;
They to the furthest nation spread
 The grace of their ascended Lord.—*Watts*.

The autobiography of Elder Gardner, as written by himself, closed on the former page; but by carefully gathering the future incidents of his life from his articles in the papers, his letters, and his words as reported by friends, the reader will be enabled still to follow him, by his own writings, from step to step, place to place, and sermon to sermon, until the last sermon is preached, and the last farewell is spoken, and the last word is uttered, and until the aged hand has for the last time laid down the pen, at the gates of Paradise.

For he waits, like patriarchs of old, "who confessed that they were strangers and pilgrims on the earth. For they that say such things declare plainly that they seek a country. But now they desire a better country—that is, an heavenly: wherefore God is not ashamed to be called their God, for he hath prepared for them a city."

I shall meanwhile carefully refrain from any comments of my own, or even of others, until his voice is silent. Therefore, the reader will continue to read the words of Matthew Gardner, to the last moments of his life.

N. SUMMERBELL.

LAST GLIMPSES OF HIS LIFE.

Eastern Sojourn—No. 1. After leaving my home, near Ripley, Ohio, on the 10th instant, I reached this place (through divine protection) on the 12th, in the afternoon, having traveled day and night, by taking a sleeping-car—the journey, as a whole, being near one thousand miles. My health (except being tired) is quite good for a man of my age. I found my friends and relations enjoying good health in general. The spring has been quite cold and backward here. Some have not yet planted their corn, while a great deal of what is planted is not up. Religion is quite low all over this country. I expect to leave this section and go into New England (Providence, Rhode Island) about the first of July, if the Lord will. If any write me, they will direct to North Stephentown, New York, and I will leave instructions to remail to me.

When we meet loved brethren in Christ and dear friends and relations, it is a cause of joy and gladness, which seems to give new wings to time; hence the hours pass quickly and pleasantly away. But the parting-time must and will come; thus, in view of the uncertainty of our ever meeting again in this world, we feel sad in our parting, after which there is a lonely melancholy that pervades the heart. Have we not all experienced this? The above were my feelings, and of course those of others, when I preached in Ripley shortly before leaving for this eastern sojourn. The congregation was large, and there were present some of those whom my hands had baptized in the early part of my ministry, when they were young men and young women. Their locks are now white, and their families grown up to be men and women, while some have gone to their graves. It had been a good while since I had preached in Ripley, this appointment being made at the request of the brethren and Elder J. W. Marvin (one of the best of men), who is the pastor of that church. I expect, if the Lord will, to return home about the first of September.   M. GARDNER.

North Stephentown, June 16, 1873.

THE NEW BIRTH.

Ye Must Be Born Again." (John III. 3-7.)—Perhaps there is no part of the Savior's teaching that more directly interests mankind than the above, and no subject in theology about which the views of men more greatly differ. Be this as it may, there is one thing certain, according to the general teachings of the New Testament, namely: that if saved, the heart and the affections must be changed from the love of this world "to love

God because he first loved us," and the character changed from a wicked person to that of a humble follower of the meek and lowly Jesus. This can not be done by the wisdom and power of man; it is the work of the Holy Spirit through faith, prayer, and repentance in us. The way we can know that we are born again is, "that every one that loveth (God) is born of God," etc.; hence, if we love God and his people, we are born again. I. John III. 7. Now, what are we to understand by the words "born of water?" Do not all careful Bible readers know that the prophets spoke of the gospel as a "river of water and a *fountain* for sin?" Zachariah XIII. 1, says: "In that day there shall be a fountain opened to the house of David and to the inhabitants of Jerusalem for sin and for uncleanness." Christ used the figure of water to represent the purifying influence that his word would have upon the hearts of those who hear it. Hence he said, "If any man thirst, let him come unto me and drink." Peter says, "Being born again, not of corruptible seed, but of incorruptible, by the word of God (water) which liveth and abideth forever." I. Peter I. 23. Thus the word enters the heart by faith with its purifying influence, and the word in union with the Spirit transforms the person into "a new creature" in Christ Jesus; hence, "born of water and the Spirit;" who can deny it? [Herald of Gospel of Liberty.

North Stephentown, New York, June 17, 1873.   M. GARDNER.

Eastern Sojourn—No. 2.—The time of my stay in North Stephentown, New York, of about three weeks, including three Lord's-days, was spent as follows: The first Lord's-day after my arrival I was taken to South Berlin to hear Brother Taylor, who has lately come there to preach to the Christian Church of that place. He kindly requested me to preach, which I declined. On the next Lord's-day (fourth Lord's-day in June, 1873), I preached in Petersburg, New York, according to previous appointment, made by the request of Brother J. E. Hays, pastor of the Christian Church of that place. I think Elder Hays is useful and doing good, being well beloved by the church of his charge and the people. I was kindly received and entertained by him and Sister Hays, his excellent lady. On the fifth Lord's-day of said month, I attended the close-communion Baptist meeting. The minister manifested a Christian spirit—inviting me to take part in the service, which I did. On the 3d day of July, 1873, I took the cars, at half-past six o'clock A. M., for Providence, Rhode Island, which place I reached near nine o'clock P. M., and was kindly received by Elder John A. Perry and his excellent lady. Being kindly requested by Elder Asa W. Coan, who is pastor of the Broad Street Christian Church in said city, I preached to the people aforesaid on the first Lord's-day of this month. My father was born in Rhode Island in 1760. On the 10th of July I took the cars with Brother Perry and his family, at seven o'clock A. M., for Cape Cod, Massachusetts, the place of the New England Christian Camp-meeting, which we reached between twelve and one o'clock P. M. of that day. On the second Lord's-day of this month I was taken about a mile and a half in a carriage to a Congregational meeting in the village of Centerville. The minister, having seen me at the camp-meeting last year, knew me, and came to the seat and asked me to preach, which I did, and had a good time, being helped by the Holy Spirit. My health is quite good for a man of my age. After the camp-meeting, which is to begin on the 4th of August, proximo, and to end the 12th of that month, I expect to start homeward and reach there on the 3d of September, if the Lord wills.—[Herald of Gospel Liberty.   M. GARDNER.

Cape Cod, Massachusetts, July 17, 1873.

HOMEWARD BOUND.

When for eternal worlds we steer,
And seas are calm, and skies are clear,
And faith in lively exercise,
Sees distant hills of Canaan rise,
The soul for joy then claps her wings,
And loud her lovely sonnet sings,
Vain world adieu, vain world adieu.

With cheerful hope her eyes explore
Each landmark on the distant shore;
The trees of life, the pastures green,
The golden streets, the crystal stream;
Again for joy she claps her wings,
And loud her lovely sonnet sings,
Vain world adieu

The nearer still she draws to land,
More eager all her powers expand;
With steady helm, and free bent sail,
Her anchor drops within the vail;
Again for joy she claps her wings,
And her celestial sonnet sings,
Glory to God.

July 26, 1874.—From this date the aged pilgrim's bark was visibly turned toward worlds eternal, and pressed hard for the distant shore.

Painful Change in the Narrative.—Elder A. W. Coan wrote: "The numerous friends of the venerable Matthew Gardner, of Ripley, Ohio, will learn, with much regret, that he is now prostrate in his room at the hotel, on the camp-grounds near Hyannis, Massachusetts, from the effects of a fall from the steps of the hotel on the grounds. He fell on Saturday evening of July 26th, breaking the left thigh-bone at the hip-joint. He is re-

markably patient, and appears to suffer as little as could be expected. It is not probable that he will ever be able to walk."—
[Herald of Gospel Liberty.

Elder H. Y. Rush wrote: "The above intelligence will be
received with sorrow throughout the brotherhood. The life of
Elder Gardner has been an eventful one, and the cause of gospel truth has received from him much effectual service. His
mission among us is not without just appreciation, nor will this
sorrowful accident fail to draw toward him the sincere sympathy of his people. We fear that from such a hurt as that
described by Brother Coan, Elder Gardner can hardly recover;
but if his days are thus to be shortened, we can be assured that
he stood till the last on Zion's walls, and that he 'endured as
seeing Him who is invisible.' May God comfort and sustain
him in his suffering."

Elder A. R. Heath responded: "Let us all pray." He said:
"At the Sturgis House we found Elder M. Gardner prostrate,
with the head of the thigh-bone broken off, and the socket it enters bursted, but quite well in other respects, and even cheerful;
and he hopes in God to get up and preach the gospel. Yet he
does not trust in man or nature, but in the power of God. Let
all pray for our aged father in the gospel."

The veranda was broad, without front safety of banister or
balustrade. The steps extended but a portion of the way across
the broad front; and in the dark the aged minister missed the
steps and walked off, falling about three feet. It is supposed
that the sure-footed old man came down upon his feet, the
weight of his body, by the fall, bursting the socket of his thigh.

"*Let All Pray!*"—This was expressive of the general feeling of sympathy throughout the entire brotherhood. C. A.
Tillinghast wrote as follows: "Universal regret and sorrow
were expressed for the sad accident which confined Brother
Matthew Gardner, of Ohio, to his room in the hotel, with a
broken limb. He was often remembered in prayer." "Let us
all pray for this aged father in the gospel," said Elder Heath,
and an audible "amen" went out from a thousand hearts. We
will pray.

The Promises.—"Ask, and it shall be given you." (Jesus).
Matt. VII. 7. "The prayer of faith shall save the sick, and
the Lord shall raise him up. Pray one for another, that
ye may be healed. The effectual, fervent prayer of a righteous man availeth much." James V. XV. If the aged sufferer
may be able to reach his distant home in Ohio, there to be
with and be cared for by his children, and so end his days in
peace, with grace to sustain him, is all that can be asked or
hoped for.

Sunday, August 10th, by the pen of Rev. Austin Craig, D. D.,
Elder Gardner gave the following farewell words, which were

read at the camp-meeting: "I have now been sixty-three years
a Christian minister, and would say with the apostle, 'I have
fought a good fight; I have finished my course; I have kept the
faith.' I was born December 5, 1790, in Rensselaer County, in
the State of New York—near the Massachusetts line. In the
year 1800, my tenth year, my father moved to the then north-
western territory of Ohio, and settled in the wilderness. I
embraced religion in 1810, and began to preach immediately.
There were no schools there at that time, and my education was
limited. All I had I obtained by my own industry, purchasing
books as I earned means to do so. I never would have preached
if I had not thought I would be eternally lost without it; nor
would I ever have preached, if I had not thought sinners would
be eternally lost if they did not repent. When I began in the
world I was poor, with no means except my hands—no churches
there to pay preachers. I believed I could make a living in
one-half of my time; and I promised the Lord, on my knees,
that I would devote the other half of my time to the work of
calling sinners to repentance. I hoped the people would quit
coming to hear me, and then I could be excused from preaching.
But I was disappointed. They still kept coming, and are coming yet. So I never found a place to stop. I never preached
hair-splitting theology; but preached the full gospel to sinners,
and the great plan of salvation. I did not preach Jesus Christ
the Son of God, as an inferior, finite being; but viewed that he
must be infinite and omnipresent, or he could not fulfill his
promise, 'Lo, I am with you alway, even unto the end of the
world,' nor could he say, 'Without me, ye can do nothing.' It
was my uniform practice never to go into the pulpit, nor try to
preach, without first specially asking Christ to help me that one
time. He never did fail to help me when I thus asked him, and
the few times that I did not ask, I failed to have his presence.
I lived a grave and sober life, not because Paul commanded it,
but because of the weight and burden of the cause of Christ,
which I felt. I have ever lived a regular praying life, always
having daily prayers in my house. I never jested nor joked;
and seldom reproved either preachers or people for it, by words;
but when they referred to me, I generally evaded, and would
take no part, that being reproof enough. I have lived and
preached sixty-three years in the same section of country, and
among the same people. The congregations which attend my
ministry are now larger there than anywhere else. I would
tell my hearers first to find Jesus, and then find a church in
which they could live as his followers; hence many of those who
were converted under my ministry, united with churches of
other denominations. As nearly as I can compute, about six
thousand and one hundred persons have embraced religion

under my ministry. Now I bid my brethren and friends a Christian farewell. All is peace! All is well!"

His Son and Grandson, John W. and John F. Gardner, go and bring him home to the house of his Son-in-law, S. H. Hopkins, arriving August 15th.—He writes from Bentonville as follows: "I am now staying, in my affliction, at Bentonville, Adams County, Ohio, which is about twelve miles east of my old home. I reached here on the 15th of August, having left the campground on the 12th of August. We came day and night, making our connections without detention. My friends told me that I would stop at the first station after starting, but, by more than human strength from the Lord, I was enabled to stand the journey through, though very feeble indeed. I am at the house of my daughter, Julia C. Hopkins, and all is done that can be in reason for my welfare.   M. GARDNER."

Elder A. R. Heath wrote: "He stood the trip home well. The route was by Fall River boat to New York; thence by broad guage railroad to Cincinnati, and by Ohio River boat to Manchester Landing, and thence by spring wagon to Bentonville, unto the house of his daughter, Sister Hopkins. He will be kindly and well cared for. Let brethren address him at Bentonville, with words of cheer."

Brother Samuel Hopkins writes as follows from Bentonville, Ohio: "Elder Gardner is here, and there are some hopes of his recovery. He is now able, by a little help, to walk on his crutches. His general health is tolerably good."

H. Y. Rush said in the "Herald:" "Brethren, let us still pray that the life of Elder Gardner may be prolonged, and that his feeble voice may yet bear its unfaltering testimony for the cause of Jesus. Our brethren will be much gratified, and thankful to the kind Father, if Elder Gardner is permitted to attend another session of the Southern Ohio Conference. May it so be."

"Dear Brother N. Summerbell: Yours of the 29th ultimo, containing words of Christian sympathy and advice, is thankfully received. As you advise, so my eventful life has uniformly been, ever remembering, 'Thou, God, seest me.' Life is uncertain and death near. The six questions contained in yours have never troubled me, feeling to put my whole trust in my dear Savior, who will guide me safely through unexplained mysteries. My general health is as good, or perhaps better than could be expected, under the circumstances. The bones that were broken are mending slowly, and are so far improved that I am able to move about the room a little on crutches. I feel calm and composed, trusting in the Lord, knowing that all will work together for good. It is with much difficulty that I am able to sit and write these few lines, therefore you will excuse the shortness of the letter. My Christian regards to Sister Summerbell, and to Joseph and Mary. Yours, in love. From one whom you will perhaps see no more. M. GARDNER.

"Bentonville, Ohio, September 4, 1873."

Soon after this Rev. S. S. Newhouse wrote: "Elder Gardner is still improving in health. The first Sunday of September he was able to be conveyed to the church in a spring wagon, a half mile from the village where he is stopping. Brother Abbott also writes us that he took part in the service, speaking with much earnestness and with good effect upon the hearts of the people. The elder is still in the care of his daughter, Mrs. Hopkins, who is attentive to all his wants. We are yet hoping that he may be able to attend the approaching session of the Southern Ohio Conference."

September 27, 1873.—Elder Gardner writes: "It is now over two months since I received the injury at Hyannis, namely, on the 26th of July; and how I have been able to endure the suffering is truly a mystery to myself. Not that the injury itself gave me such great pain, but the being confined upon my back for four weeks, during which I traveled from Hyannis, Cape Cod, Massachusetts, to this place. My health is as good as could be expected under the circumstances. I move about the house on crutches, and my leg seems to be slowly mending.

"M. GARDNER."

The Conference Notice.—The Southern Ohio Christian Conference will meet, in its fifty-fourth annual session, on Saturday, October 4, 1873, at ten o'clock A. M., at the Bethlehem Christian chapel, Brown County. Ohio. The chapel is about one mile from the Ohio River. Persons coming by way of the river will get off at Aberdeen. THOMAS SHELDON, Clerk.

This conference he had assisted in organizing in the tenth year of his ministry, and had attended for fifty-three years. Bethlehem, where it was appointed to meet, was only ten miles from where he was now lying sick.

The Last Letter (*Unfinished.*)—"Dear Bro. Craig: Yours, of the 15th ultimo, was received a few days ago, after having been lying in the post-office of Ripley, and then remailed to this place, where I am now staying in my affliction, which is about twelve miles, nearly east of my old home residence, near Ripley, Ohio. As to the state of my health now, it is, in the general, as good perhaps as could be expected under the circumstances. I can move about the house upon crutches, and my leg seems to be mending slowly. I would again thank you for preparing and forwarding to the 'Herald' my farewell words read at the camp-meeting. You, of course, have noticed that, in the printed copy, the words, 'I have kept the faith,' are left out, which words I am certain that you read to me from your written copy. I blame no one. In addition to the words, 'I have kept the faith,' there should have been the words, 'All is peace! all is well!' which, though on my mind, I do not remember of speaking, which will appear, with explanation, in my life, if the Lord permits me to write more.

"Bentonville, Adams County, Ohio, September 28, 1873."

Last Writing.—"The events of my life are given as briefly as possible; hence, I would not know what to leave out without injuring the narrative, though perhaps another might.

"M. GARDNER."

"Bentonville, Ohio, September 28, 1873."

October 4, 1873—The Conference.—Saturday morning Elder Matthew Gardner rode, seated in a large chair, in a spring wagon, and was thus conveyed ten miles, to the conference, by his son-in-law, S. H. Hopkins; and thus he returned in the evening to his home, that is, to the house of his son-in-law, where he made his home after his return from the East.

Tuesday Morning, October 7, 1873.—Brother Hopkins, his son-in-law, conveyed him, for the second time, to conference. This was the last conference that he would ever attend, and he went to preach his farewell sermon. He was conveyed, as before, in a spring wagon, sitting in a large chair. It was ten miles—a long ride; but he was inured to hardship.

Elder Thomas Sheldon, the conference clerk, writes: "Elder N. Summerbell:—My Dear Brother—Elder M. Gardner was at the conference on Tuesday, and expected to leave the conference that afternoon, and not to return again during the session. The usual day to deliver the 'letters to the ministers' is Wednesday—the next day; but, considering the circumstances, we concluded to give him his letter before he left. So Brother S. S. Newhouse, the president, signed his letter, and I signed it and presented it to him, saying, 'Brother Gardner, I think, in all probability, this will be the last letter that I shall have the privilege, as clerk of this conference, of handing to you.' He replied, 'Yes, there is no doubt that, before another conference meets, I shall leave you.' I said, 'Brother Gardner, we will miss you very much; at least, I shall.' He replied, 'Brother Sheldon, do you stand firm, and we will meet in a better world.' Elder Gardner remained from eleven A. M. to two P. M.

TO ALL WHOM IT MAY CONCERN:

This is to Certify, That **Elder Matthew Gardner** is a regularly **Ordained Minister,** and a Member in good standing, and in full fellowship, in Southern Ohio Christian Conference, and as such we recommend him to the Christian Community, to administer the Ordinances of the Church, and Solemnize Marriages, etc.

Done by order of the Conference, at Bethlehem Chapel, Brown County, Ohio, the seventh day of October, 1873.

P. P. Newhouse, President.

Thomas Sheldon, Secretary.

P. C. Walden, Assistant.

His Last Sermon.—The hour has come. Here is the church which he had organized half a century before, and of which he had been pastor forty-five years, and was yet a member. Here are the representatives of the churches, many of which he had organized, and to all of which he had preached statedly or at intervals for many years. The aged patriarch could not stand, but sat in his large chair. It was a sermon directed chiefly to the ministers. Before the sermon he sang in a loud, clear voice, that touching hymn :

> " Oh land of rest, for thee I sigh,
> When will the moment come,
> When I shall lay my armor by,
> And dwell with Christ at home ?

> " No tranquil joys on earth I know ;
> No peaceful, sheltering dome :
> This world's a wilderness of woe :
> This world is not my home.

> " To Jesus Christ I sought for rest,
> He bade me cease to roam ;
> And fly for succor to his breast,
> And he'd conduct me home.

> " When, by afflictions sharply tried,
> I view the opening tomb,
> Although I dread death's chilling tide,
> Yet still I sigh for home."

But his utterance was almost stopped when he came to the last verse ·

> " Weary of wandering round and round,
> This vale of sin and gloom,
> I long to quit the unhallowed ground.
> And dwell with Christ at home."

Text.—" Preach unto it the preaching that I bid thee." Jonah III. 2.

Elder Gardner said : " I believe that the Lord has spared me to preach this sermon."

I. He expounded the text, showing the necessity of abiding by the word of God. If it is changed ever so little, it is no longer God's word. The universal command of God to every preacher, sent by him, is, " Preach the preaching that I bid thee." He said :

" 1. This is the last conference that I ever expect to attend." He then alluded to the conference in its rise and history, and of his early labors in this region of country and elsewhere, and said :

" 2. 1 desired to be at this conference, and the Lord has granted my request."

II. He exhorted the preachers to faithfulness, and spoke of the opposition which he had encountered, the persecutions which he had endured, and the long labor which he had performed, and said:

"2. Be faithful. Never preach a doctrine which can not be stated in the exact words of the Scriptures." He then exhorted all to live prayerful lives, and said:

"3. My success in a ministry of over sixty years I attribute to my strict adherence to the word of God. I have preached the preaching that God bid me to preach. This is the last conference that I ever expect to attend. Remember the word, 'preach the preaching that I bid thee.' And now, farewell! farewell!"

Brother Newhouse says: "His sermon consisted in a statement of *his* experience as a minister, and an exhortation to the ministers of the conference to be faithful to God, and 'to preach the preaching' that God commands them; that is, the BIBLE. From the words of the text he spoke of *his* obedience, through his entire ministry, to this command of God. He had preached what God gave him to preach. He spoke of an instance or two in his life when he was reasoned into error, and was thus about to espouse false doctrine; but by obeying the command of God, in the words of the text, he was led to give them up."

Report of Elder Rush, the Editor.—"We made good time to Maysville. Landing there we ferried the river to Aberdeen. It was now eleven o'clock A. M., and the conference nearly two miles away. We heard that Father Gardner was to preach at eleven. So learning, we hastened to a livery stable, determined to hear at least a part of what we feared would be the dear old man's dying discourse. And so it proved! He preached with strength and emphasis; told them it was his last sermon, went home, and two days afterward died, after thirty minutes' sickness. After Elder Gardner's discourse there came a season of farewell handshaking! The crippled and helpless old veteran sat in the chair from which he had preached his sermon. The large congregation came forward, and one by one bid him a final farewell. Ah, who that had tears could not have shed them then? Strong men wept, and from many, many eyes, came these overflowings of grief. It seemed really like a funeral of the living, and such in a sense it proved to be. It was Father Gardner's dying farewell to the people for whom he had been pastor forty years; it was his final farewell to his brethren of the ministry, who shall see his face no more in the flesh."

Elder J. P. Daugherty says: "He gave his last solemn charge to his brethren in the ministry, in the fifty-fourth session of the Southern Ohio Christian Conference, he himself having never failed, in a single instance, to meet the conference in any of its sittings. Every heart was full, and every face bathed in tears, as he bade the conference an affectionate farewell. As he clasped my hand he said, 'My dear brother, I have been anxious to see you. I desire to have a talk with you at some convenient time.' Then the tears of seemingly mingled joy and sorrow flowed freely, and I turned away to make room for others.

The Maysville at which Elder Rush landed on his way to Bethlehem, over a mile distant, to hear Elder Gardner preach, was the 'Lime Stone' village in the fall of 1800, just seventy-three years before, at which Matthew Gardner landed, then a little boy, on his first voyage down the Ohio. How little the boy thought, when standing on the shore in 1800, that in seventy-three years he would be preaching his final farewell to a weeping congregation, within about a mile of where the boy then stood, and that editors and ministers would be hastening over that same Lime Stone landing to hear him! How little we know of the future! The meeting has closed. The pilgrim has bidden farewell to his brethren, the church, and the conference; and under the shadows of the great hills which border the eastern shores of the Ohio River, the aged minister, sitting in the spring wagon, is for the last time returning to his earthly home, then only ten miles; but he will be far, far away in two or three days."

Elder Daugherty further writes: "He said to his son-in-law, on his way home from the conference, 'I am now entirely released from the affairs of this life, and will never again be entangled therein.'"

The Last Day.—The morning before his death he had a talk of about two hours with his daughter, Mrs. Hopkins, in which he said, "If I die soon, all is well; the will of the Lord be done. All I need here is a place to stay a little while."

The Last Night.—"He was well and hearty last night. He ate heartily at supper, and retired as well as usual."

The Last Hour.—He began to complain soon after half-past one o'clock in the morning. He was perfectly sane, but said nothing about dying, except the words, "*I fear that I shall not live till morning.*" His mental powers continued strong to the very last; and his utterance was clear and distinct.

His Last Words.—His son-in-law, Samuel H. Hopkins, wrote, "I was holding him in my arms, when he said: 'LAY ME DOWN.'

"He lived but a few minutes afterward. A more devoted man I have never seen end his days than Father Gardner." The immediate cause of his death was supposed to have been "valvular disease of the heart." He had often prayed, "Lord, give me a tranquil hour in which to die," and the hour was there. The prayer was answered, and he said, "Lay me down." And all the days of Matthew Gardner were eighty and two years, ten months, and five days; and he died.

October 11th his body was conveyed by land, thirty-two miles, for interment; as he had himself directed them to bury him in the burying-ground of the "Union Church," the first church organized by him, in his early ministry, and now commonly called "Shinkle's Ridge," near Higginsport. The body was interred October 12th, after which a funeral discourse was preached by Elder J. P. Daugherty, on the words of Saint Paul (II. Timothy IV. 6–8): "For I am now ready to be offered, and the time of my departure is at hand. I have fought a good fight, I have finished my course, I have kept the faith: henceforth there is laid up for me a crown of righteousness, which the Lord, the righteous Judge, shall give me at that day; and not to me only, but unto all them also that love his appearing." While the minister was proceeding from one to another of the parallels between the deceased and the great apostle, in perseverance, energy, devotion, labor, persecution, suffering, and success, the audience, largely composed of the most prominent citizens and statesmen of the four consecutive counties, was bathed in tears. After reading Elder Gardner's own account of his life, as read to the Hyannis camp-meeting by Dr. Craig, the preacher said:

"As a minister of the gospel, and indeed in every relation of life, he was most scrupulously exact and punctual in his promises, both with regard to time and the thing promised. When he announced preaching at eleven o'clock, he never meant ten minutes after. He was a textual preacher, carefully stating his points in the exact language of the Bible. Though not a learned man, in the common acceptation of the term, yet his knowledge of the Bible and of men made him successful in many theological discussions. He was *practically educated*. He was a man of prompt decision, and seldom, if ever, had occasion to change his first impressions. He was an excellent financier; and by his industry and economy accumulated a large estate. His large compass of mental vision, and far-reaching judgment, enabled him to succeed in almost every thing he undertook. His moral courage enabled him to stand where most of men would have fallen. Having determined his course, he was unmoved by flattery or reproach; hence, while he had many *warm* friends, he also had some *bitter* enemies. These he at last won, and died, so far as I know, without a personal enemy. He was a profound judge of human nature, and hence was seldom deceived in men. He was emphatically the man for the time and place of his ministry, and though it lasted sixty-three years, yet he kept pace with the world's advancement in thought; hence his congregations were large and attentive till the close of his ministry. He was a strong, lion-hearted man—victorious over fear; gathering strength and animation from danger, and bound the faster to duty by its hardships and privations. He was a man of great firmness—his countenance at times wearing the stern decision of unyielding principle. Uninfluenced by numbers, popularity, or power, he seemed almost too tenacious for his own convictions. His heroism had its origin and life in reason; in the sense of justice, and in the disinterested principles of Christianity, which recognize the rights of every man. He had great respect for minds which had been trained in simple habits, and amidst the toils of an industrious life. He despised indolence and lack of economy almost beyond expression. With whatever faults he had, he was a great and good man. His greatness as a minister was immeasurably above the arts by which inferior minds thrust themselves into notice. Surrendering himself wholly to the cause of God and salvation of men, he labored to that end with unfaltering zeal till Jesus called him to his immortal home.   *   *   *   *

"Having timely made his will, and properly adjusted all his earthly business, he now seemed to have nothing to do but to fall asleep in Jesus; hence he calmly sank into the repose of death without a struggle.   *   *   *

"But what shall I say more? The time would fail me to speak of all the interests of so long and eventful a life as that of Elder Matthew Gardner! What I have here said is but the plucking of a little fruit here and there from the wide-spreading branches of a life-tree, bowing under the fullness of more than three-score years. We are only satisfied to pause here, and await the production of some abler pen, and in the expectation that we shall soon be favored with the autobiography of his long and eventful life.

"His remains were interred in the cemetery at Shinkle's Ridge, on the 12th of October, 1873 after which a sermon was delivered with reference to the deceased, by the writer, in the presence of a large and weeping audience. The Lord sanctify this dispensation of his providence to the good of all concerned.

"Georgetown, Ohio, October 18, 1873.

"J. P. DAUGHERTY."

HOPE.

The Christian religion, by the grand assurance of a resurrection to immortality and eternal life which it gives, is adapted to the wants of our nature, and commends itself to the admiration and to the hearts of all people of feeling, judgment, and consideration.

N. SUMMERBELL.

[EPITAPH WRITTEN BY HIMSELF.]

ELDER MATTHEW GARDNER,

A CHRISTIAN MINISTER.

BORN IN THE STATE OF NEW YORK, DECEMBER 5, 1790.
DIED IN THE STATE OF OHIO, OCTOBER 10, 1873.

"He claimed no merit of his own,
His trust was all in Christ alone."

HE PREACHED THE GOSPEL SIXTY-THREE YEARS.

RECOLLECTIONS OF ELDER GARDNER.

BY ELDER H. SIMONTON.

It may be of interest and value to the "Herald" readers to make a brief record of my early recollections of Elder Gardner, who met the adverse and prosperous events of eighty-three years, and has, at a good ripe old age, quietly passed to his reward. The conflict of life with him was long, and, at times, the battle raged fiercely and strong; but with him all is hushed in quiet and retired silence. Now, after life's fitful fever, the once strong man sleeps well. All is quiet in the retired city of the dead, and let us, as we should in all cases, pass over, in the kind spirit of Christian charity, the *errors* and supposed errors of erring humanity, and look at the nobler and finer traits of character.

Our aged ministers are fast passing over the dark, turbid stream, to view the distant, and we trust, better land—the land of which they have so often spoken to us, and the one to which they so often looked with aspiring wings of an inspiring Christian hope. The most of them have gone over into the better land, and doubtless they are at home among the loved ones who passed on before them. They fought the hard battles for Jesus and his blessed truth, and theirs will be the glorious victory; they will be crowned by the Master. Heaven and glory will be their eternal home. Their venerable presence, their rich, ripe experience, and their wisdom in council, will be enjoyed no more in our annual and other meetings. But it is the fortune and end of earth with men, and it is for us to learn to be content. In their day, they did a grand and glorious work for Jesus, truth, and humanity. The world's conference of ministers and others have recently held a grand union jubilee on the basis of the union on which our fathers started, lived, and died, and could their bones be made to *see* and *hear*, they would move in their graves for joy. I thank God that we ever had such fathers, who came out on the only sure and true basis of the word of God and the union of all who love Jesus.

Elder Gardner stood long in our midst as an *able* and *notable* minister of the gospel, and I can remember him as such between forty and fifty years. I have been quite intimate with him ever since I commenced preaching, which has been over thirty-five years. He and my father often met in the work in my younger days. Elder Gardner, when in the prime of life, had a very commanding presence when before a congregation. Even his general appearance itself would demand attention. I remember well before I was a man to have seen and heard him preach Jesus and the resurrection with great power and effect. I can yet see him standing and calling on sinners to come to Jesus. This was in the days of his physical and mental strength, when he stood before the great congregations with his strong, nervous, muscular, and well-built frame, with his strong mental powers in mature vigor, and his fine, strong, full, musical and well-managed voice in good condition for both speaking and singing; always self-possessed, having a complete command and control of his physical and mental powers; often speaking with great energy, and power, and pathetic feeling, and in the deep sympathy of his soul, but never exhausting his physical and mental powers. Hence, in the defense of truth, and in calling sinners to the Lamb of God, having such good command of his physical, mental, and passional powers, to an extent that but few men ever attain, it gave him great power in argument, and in presenting the claims of the gospel. In this there were but few, if any, who were in advance of him. I think I may say, and not use words of adulation, that, in the days of his full manhood, in this light, he had but few equals. In those days, he always had a definite point before him, and that was clearly defined in his own judgment by cautious, deliberate reflection; and, as a general thing, he would make that point. He might not do it at the first effort; if not, he would continue on in the same line. He was a man of great nerve and energy. When duty presented itself, he had no use for the words, "I can not do it;" hence, he worked all his long life, up to almost the day of his death. In the days of his strength, he was a man of remarkably strong, comprehending motive power, with a large and full development of hope, connected with an unbending will, and a large portion of moral courage which gave him great force to stand up for what he believed to be right, and to meet adverse events; hence, what would be great obstructions and hindrances to the most of men in life, to him would be but as small pebbles in his path, and he would move on in life in the way he had marked out for himself with firmness, so far as others could judge, caring but little for the adverse events of life.

Elder Gardner has met with much strong and intensely bitter opposition from different sources, and from different causes; but these he stood until the last day's work was done, like an old weather-beaten oak in the midst of the forest, that had stood many hard and pelting storms, and was prepared to meet others, should they come that way; but the last storm was death, which found the old man standing up, fighting the real battle of life, at the post at which he had stood for about sixty-three years.

Extremes often meet in men, and it was so, in a marked degree, in Brother Gardner. He was a man of strong combative powers, and at one time in his life was fond of debate; and

when this power was fully aroused and called forth in all its
tints of color, in debate, or otherwise in self-defense, he was inclined at times to be severe. His sarcasm was pointed, taunting, bitterly satirical, cutting, withering. Hence, he could do
this with much self-possessed gravity, and often in an indirect
as well as a direct manner, which made it all the more severe.
This was something peculiar to the man. He could use it when
so disposed, or he could dispense with it at his pleasure.

Then, on the other hand, he was a man of more than an ordinary amount of tender feeling, when that part of his nature
was called forth. Let him take for his theme, as I have often
heard him in my younger days, the love of God and the com-
passion of Jesus, and let his strong mind and large soul become
all absorbed in the loving spirit of the man of sorrows, he was
tender, kind, gentle, and full of the loving sympathy of Jesus,
and one could scarcely believe him to be the same man who
was so severe in debate. Both of these conditions of mind I
have seen and heard in Brother Gardner as I have never found
them so strongly developed in any other man.

He was, indeed, a very remarkable man. In many of his
movements he was hard to comprehend. He, as a general
thing, developed his plans in his own mind, and, as a general
thing, you got hold of his intentions by his actions. He was
one among our most independent thinkers. He seldom gave
you to understand fully his main designs in advance. It was
very hard to anticipate him. This gave him an advantage and
strength in debate. When his plans were well matured in his
own mind, then, with his strong, unbending will-power, he
would go to work with a fixed and settled determination to
attain the desired end before his mind. He had many devoted
friends, and many bitter enemies. He was a man of that peculiar tact, that those who were his friends were real, devoted,
and settled in their friendship. But few men, if any, in my
experience, had such bitter enemies as he has had at times in
his life; yet he stood up in the midst of all opposition, and I
think that he lived long enough to soften down very much of
it. Had he been as pure as an angel, he was the sort of a man
to have enemies. He has left us, and left his mark in the world.
He had the imperfections of human nature, in common with
others, to contend with.

A VERSE.

There is no *remedy* for time *misspent*,
  No *healing*—for the waste of *idleness*,
  Whose very *languor*—is a *punishment*
Heavier than *active* souls—can *feel* or *guess*.

A LETTER.

BY ELDER JAMES SUMMERBELL.

Dear Brother:—I had often heard you speak of Elder Matthew Gardner in terms which excited my curiosity. I had also sometimes read his name in such connection as to make me feel an interest in the man; but he being far advanced in years, I had no expectation of ever seeing him. In the spring of 1871, I took my seat in the pulpit of the Christian chapel of South Berlin, New York, and while waiting for the gathering of the congregation, side by side with Brother Philo Hull, entered a tall, straight form, with a head crowned with hair white with age, and a face outside of the range of ordinary aged men. Who can it be? This was Elder Gardner, on a visit to his old friends and home in the East!

Being properly introduced, he, with convincing positiveness, declined my invitation to preach, saying he "was an old friend of Elder N. Summerbell, and purposed to hear his brother preach." I agreed that he should listen at this time, but preach the following Sunday, and the appointment was made accordingly. Many who were personal friends, or who had heard his fame, came at the appointed time to hear him. Prompt at the time, with an almost youthful vigor of step, and a face aglow with the theme which animated his mind, the man of eighty years took his place in the desk. Without the aid of glasses, he read the Scriptures, dropping here and there a pertinent comment; and the hymns, not omitting a well-administered rebuke to the man who, unable to write as well as himself, altered and mutilated such grand and sacred poetry as "Rock of Ages, cleft for me;" or, "My faith looks up to thee, thou Lamb of Calvary;" and then printed their garbled work in hymn-books, confusing and confounding people, who, having learned a part, try to sing together.

His text was Genesis XXII. 2; and his subject grew out of his text as naturally as a tree grows out of its seed, and as majestically. At first the text seemed a crumbling, eliminating germ; then it rooted outward, here and there taking hold, in surprising ways, on Christ. Then did Genesis XXII. 2, as I thought it never did before, "grow up into Christ, the living head." It was an Old Testament gospel sermon, full of Christ, of faith, of love, of obedience, and full of the mountain of the Lord. As he told of Abraham's love for Isaac, and his struggle between love and duty; as he described the mother expecting the return of her son, and then the odium that should come upon him for killing that son, he seemed to stand an Abraham before us, and tears moistened many a dry cheek that day.

The old man lost both age and infirmity in his theme, and we lost the old man in his sermon.

After preaching, he readily accepted an invitation to visit me at my home in Berlin, and preach to my congregation there. When he preached for us, his subject was "the providence of God." His text was: "Behold the fowls of the air: for they sow not, neither do they reap, nor gather into barns; yet your heavenly Father feedeth them. Are ye not much better than they?" Matthew VI. 26.

All were interested in the subject. First: He dwelt on God's love everywhere, always, in all things, culminating all in Christ, and on his people. Then he told us how intimate our heavenly Father is with all our experiences, wants, dangers, sufferings, sins, our very thoughts; and last, he told of his bounteous providences, particular as well as general, running out into his *controlling* providence somewhat peculiarly. Elder Gardner had opinions of his own. They were a part of himself; and on this occasion, as was his wont, he advanced them with great frankness, and I, with equal good-nature, indulged in an agreeable repartee. Being public, it was enjoyed by others as well as ourselves, and gendered no ill feeling. After this, Elder Gardner spent two or three days with me, at my home, and visiting at Elder James Hays', in Petersburg, during which time he was ever ready to discuss all religious subjects with sufficient energy to convince me that—first, any doctrine, once received into his faith, would not be soon forgotten, or die of neglect; second, that he was honest in his convictions, and untiring and fearless in their propagation; third, inside and outside, whether in the field or in the pulpit, that his religious faith was his life, and just what he tried to make it seem to be.

A BEAUTIFUL PARAGRAPH

A Deity—*believ'd*, is joy *begun;*
A Deity *ador'd*, is joy *advanc'd*
A Deity *belov'd*, is joy *matur'd*.
Each branch of piety *delight* inspires:
Faith—builds a bridge from *this* world to the *next,*
O'er *death's* dark gulf, and all it *horror* hides;
Praise the sweet exhalation of our *joy,*
That joy *exalts*, and makes it sweeter *still;*
Pray'r ardent opens *heav'n*, lets down a *stream*
Of glory, on the consecrated hour
Of *man*—in audience with the *Deity.*

ELDER GARDNER.

The candid and thoughtful reader, in tracing the strange life in this book, has formed no exaggerated conception of the man. I knew him intimately nearly a quarter of a century. I am acquainted with those who knew him longer, and am certain that the picture is not overdrawn. He was always associated in my mind with the old Grecian philosophers, Diogenes and even Socrates. I do not mean that he was a cynic, like the first, or as cool a reasoner, as the last; yet I do mean that he resembled both in the peculiarities of character which rescued each from oblivion, and rendered the names of both immortal, and that he, living in their age, would have ranked with them as a wise and great man. His mental powers were strong; his perceptive powers were quick; his judgment was deep; his observation was close; his memory was retentive. He inquired into causes; he perceived consequences; he studied men. I do not regard Elder Gardner as a perfect man, after whom others should pattern their lives, but I do rank him as a great man, from whom all may learn. He resembles Joshua rather than Moses, Elijah rather than Isaiah, and Peter more than John. Powerful himself, it is doubtful if he considered any with whom he associated as his equal, and therefore he feared no one. Persecution only roused his resolution, and his courage rose with the occasion. Difficulties called for increased resources, and obstructions only developed greater exertion. Yet, though strong and confident, he relied not upon himself. He was a man of prayer; but, while praying for help from on high, he prepared to help himself. No recluse was more thoughtful, no ascetic more self-denying, no philosopher more disciplined. Every thing was exact—his dealings, his devotions, his labors, and his rest; his daily walk, and his manner of walking; his daily talk, and his manner of talking; his preaching, his prayers, his food, his drink; every thing was prescribed, defined, restricted, and governed. He was more studious than the student, more laborious than the laborer, more saving than the miser, more devoted than the devotee, more prayerful than the Puritan, and more zealous than the fanatic. He was always punctual to time, always true to his word, always faithful to his promises, always prompt to duty; so that with him, whatever came next in order demanded his next attention. No matter whether it was of much or of little importance; if he had consented to the arrangement he would be found present, prepared, earnest, and all attention.

ELDER GARDNER AS THE YOUNG PREACHER

I have at various times met with aged people who knew Elder Gardner when he was a young minister. They describe him as he appeared in his early days. He was then what the world calls a "fine-looking man." He was tall, but well-proportioned. His hair was as black as the raven, his eyes keen and piercing; his voice was loud, clear, and musical, his disposition kind, his spirit affectionate, his heart full of sympathy and tenderness, and his labor, exposure, and endurance wonderful; his manner was dignified and commanding; his speech was attractive; his spirit was earnest; he spoke right to the people, and made them to feel that he was addressing them. He felt that his mission was important, and his manner gave expression to his feelings. To him it was a message of life or death, heaven or hell; and each sinner saved was a brand plucked from the burning. One of his opponents said to me it was of no use to oppose him, for the crowds would go with him. If he had no house, he would speak in the open air; he would preach and pray and sing anywhere, and the people would always go to hear him. One, speaking of him as a stranger, at an out-door meeting, where many ministers were preaching, said, "When Gardner began to speak, every body was attracted, and pressed up to hear. He wore common clothing, but his appearance was wonderful. The people gazed at him as they would at something strange that had just appeared in the sky." His voice was so clear that all could understand his words, and his words were so plain that all could understand his meaning. Every body was affected by his preaching. He was a power when alone, and poor, and every change increased his power. His studious habits soon made him well-informed. By careful speaking, he soon became widely known as an eloquent orator. His indomitable courage commanded respect, and his unwavering perseverance secured success. His physical strength and unfaltering self-sacrifice won the respect of the rustic, while the soundness of his judgment won the admiration of the refined. By his wonderful success in preaching, he won converts, planted churches, built chapels, secured friends, and his independence excited envy. When young in the ministry, plots were formed against him by opponents, but cautious, politic, and ingenious, he would snatch the victory from his enemies when they were preparing to shout a triumph; and while he went on preaching the gospel, they would meet, like Milton's fiends, to—

"Consult how we may henceforth most offend
Our enemy, our own loss how repair;
How overcome this dire calamity
What reinforcement we can gain from hope;
If not, what resolution from despair."

ELDER GARDNER'S MIDDLE AGE.

As Elder Gardner's ministry and years increased, his troubles also increased. His popularity created fear in the enemies of his faith. His eloquence created envy. His success excited opposition. The crowds attending his ministry spread alarm. Counsel was taken by the opposers of his religious views to destroy his influence. Jealous priests, forgetting that they had no jurisdiction over him, stept out of their own sects to publish defamatory pamphlets concerning him. A new sect arose, with a new way to pardon, and holding that any number of anxious brethren may be organized into a church, and that the church is "the highest tribunal." The adherents of the new sect, finding free chapels built by the Christians, entered into them and organized their highest-tribunal churches; and as Elder Gardner did not regard them or their tribunals, they often tried him without his knowledge, and excommunicated him without informing him of his fate. The waters were troubled; the storms beat upon him; but while he had suits at law, he had success in the gospel. Relieved from court, he labored in revivals. He went from legal battling to baptizing; from court to communion. He turned from law pleadings to pleading with sinners to be reconciled to God, and was everywhere successful. The suits were decided in his favor; converts were multiplied; new churches were planted; new chapels were built, and the cause of truth advanced. Then new trials came. Champions challenged him to debates. But in discussion it was soon found that no ordinary man could cope with him. He was quick to discover the weak points in his opponent's system, and terrible in exposing them. He would keep those weak points constantly before the people. No fear or flattery, no tact or cunning of his adversary could decoy him from his work. He made the weak points the base of all arguments, the butt of all criticisms, the index to all errors, the grounds of repeated appeals, the cause of damaging denunciation. He would stir the assembly by his eloquence, and drown his adversaries in floods of questions, difficulties, and arguments. During the first day they discovered that, right or wrong, he was not a man to be managed; and before noon of the second day they were willing to close the discussion. The feelings of Elder Gardner's friends at such times were never those of care or fear for him, but pity for his unfortunate opponent. His skill in debate kept his opponents in awe, and his success in publishing, widened his reputation. The able management of his home by his wife relieved him of half his cares, and the growth of a large family, instead of encumbering him, gave him a young colony of industrious children for farmers. His rapid accumulation of wealth now made him one of the richest men in the county, and his widely increasing fame for honesty, industry, courage, and success, made many to confide in him. The last time that I saw Elder Gardner was on Monday, May 26, 1873. He came from Dayton the Saturday before, and called at my house. He was at church on Sunday, but declined preaching. He returned to see me on Monday, before leaving for his home, and we talked over matters in general, especially in relation to publishing his life. He requested me to prepare it for the press, as I had his former works; which I assured him that I would do. Though looking well, his spirit seemed more subdued than formerly, and his manner more tenderly affectionate. Tears fell from his furrowed cheeks when he bade us farewell. We all felt sorrowful, thinking it possibly the last meeting, as his solemn partings seemed ominous. The following lines are descriptive of his appearance on this his last visit in Cincinnati, and are recorded here to preserve a last view of him while in the strength of his old age.

THE CHRISTIAN PREACHER—AGED, YET ABLE.

If you would picture to your mind a portrait or a representation of Elder Gardner as he appeared in the spring of 1873, when nearly eighty-three, do not fancy the form of a poor old man, with piping, treble voice, feeble, infirm, and pitiful, bracing his bending body over a staff to stay his tottering form, and turning up a haggard face, sore eyes, thin jaws, sunken cheeks, and drooping chin, to tell over in child-like tones the sad complication of infirmities of mind and body; rheumatic, toothless, sight dim, hearing dull, memory almost gone; life a great burden, yet loth to lay it down; nothing to live for, yet afraid to die;—such a picture is no portrait of Elder Gardner. Though aged, he is yet strong; though tall, he is erect. His body is large, and was once athletic, as his mind is now. His solemn, measured step is slow, but firm. Every move is precise and accurate; every word designed. His self-reliance never falters; his faith never fails. His mind is ever bent on business or devotion. He has no playful mood; no jest; no joke; no nonsense or playful word; no relaxation of mind; no pleasure-seeking; no pandering to appetite or self-indulgence—at least, he approves of none. With him all is earnest effort. Each moment, each opportunity, each material, however small, i made to minister to the wealth of this world, or of that to come His bearing is bold and confident. Once his youthful eye, strong as an eagle's, flashed in preaching with Promethean fire. Even now, its second sight has strange, magnetic power. His face in meditation is placid, calm, and pleasant, but when in the deep study of silent thought, with every fibre drawn, and every muscle strained, its deep furrows and hard ridges show the indelible lines traced by the cares of four-score years. In speaking, all is changed, and it glows with animation, earnest and forcible; expressive of every emotion, and completely chaining attention. His voice is still powerful, and he sings with more ease and accuracy than most people of middle age. His hair, once black as the raven, is now of silvery whiteness, profusely covering his large head, and rising like a snow-tower high above his wrinkled forehead. His address is earnest, his answers ready, his speech positive. He will canvass any question, explain any theorem, solve any problem, extinguish every supposed heresy, and defend every approved principle—battling with opposition as naturally as the sea dashes its force against the island rocks. His whole appearance represents a man of giant frame, vigorous constitution, and determined will, waiting the slow approach of death without awe, resolutely attending to the things of time; unwilling to bow to the infirmities of age, and determined to resist to the last moment all approaches of debility. Though long an octogenarian, he braves any danger, presumes upon the soundness of his own judgment, persists in traveling alone, determines to carry out his own plans, and is in every thing independent.

HIS RELIGION.

Elder Matthew Gardner held to no doubtful faith or uncertain religion. Every thing with him was conformed to the Scriptures with verbal accuracy. Like his brethren of the Christian Church, he held to the Bible as his all-perfect and sufficient heaven-given creed and discipline, such as Jesus left for his church, with nothing purposely added, and nothing designedly omitted. On this he relied. This was the creed of the ancient church, and is the *only* evangelical creed of the church now. He says: "As I found no human system exactly suiting me, I adopted the following platform for myself: *I will use no terms or language in explaining the personality, character, or relation of God and his Son, and the Holy Spirit, but such as are contained in the Scriptures.* This being now the character of my preaching, few were disposed to contradict me. Many of the most talented Christian ministers traveled at large preaching union, in the hope of bringing all the followers of Jesus into union. Regarding this as their mission, some of the first and most able and talented Christian ministers never organized a single church, but seemed opposed to separate church organizations." (See his words on human systems, p. 34).

Confirmed by the Scriptures.—"Search the Scriptures; for in them ye think ye have eternal life: and they are they which testify of me." John v. 39.

"In vain do they worship me, teaching for doctrines the commandments of men." Mark vii. 7.

"If they hear not Moses and the prophets, neither will they be persuaded, though one rose from the dead." Luke XVI. 31.

"Which things also we speak, not in the words which man's wisdom teacheth, but which the Holy Ghost teacheth; comparing spiritual things with spiritual." I. Corinthians II. 13.

"All Scripture is given by inspiration of God, and is profitable for doctrine, for reproof, for correction, for instruction in righteousness: that the man of God may be perfect, thoroughly furnished unto all good works." II. Timothy III. 16, 17.

The Bible was the only creed of the first church; and there need be no better proof that a man is not sound in the faith than is afforded by his not being satisfied with the Bible, the God-given creed.

II. His God was "the God and Father of our Lord Jesus Christ, the God of glory, the Creator of the universe, and of all things seen and unseen, as beautifully stated in his words on the Bible, man's best companion. (See p. 209.)

Confirming Scriptures.—"Hear, O Israel: the Lord our God is one Lord: and thou shalt love the Lord thy God with all thine heart, and with all thy soul, and with all thy might. And these words which I command thee this day, shall be in thine heart: and thou shalt teach them diligently unto thy children, and shalt talk of them when thou sittest in thine house, and when thou walkest by the way, and when thou liest down, and when thou risest up. And thou shalt bind them for a sign upon thine hand, and they shall be as frontlets between thine eyes. And thou shalt write them upon the posts of thy house, and on thy gates." Deuteronomy VI. 4–9.

"Which is the first commandment of all? And Jesus answered him. The first of all the commandments is, Hear, O Israel; the Lord our God is one Lord: and thou shalt love the Lord thy God with all thy heart, and with all thy soul, and with all thy mind, and with all thy strength: this is the first commandment. And the second is like, namely this, Thou shalt love thy neighbor as thyself: there is none other commandment greater than these. And the scribe said unto him, Well, Master, thou hast said the truth: for there is one God; and there is none other but he: and to love him with all the heart, and with all the understanding, and with all the soul, and with all the strength, and to love his neighbor as himself, is more than all whole burnt-offerings and sacrifices. And when Jesus saw that he answered discreetly, he said unto him, Thou art not far from the kingdom of God." Mark XII. 29–34.

"These words spake Jesus, and lifted up his eyes to heaven, and said, Father, the hour is come; glorify thy Son, that thy Son also may glorify thee: as thou hast given him power over all flesh, that he should give eternal life to as many as thou

hast given him. And this is life eternal, that they might know
thee the only true God, and Jesus Christ whom thou hast sent.
I have glorified thee on the earth: I have finished the work
which thou gavest me to do. And now, O Father, glorify thou
me with thine own self, with the glory which I had with thee
before the world was." John XVII. 1–5.

"There is none other God but one. For though there be
that are called gods, whether in heaven or in earth (as there
be gods many, and lords many); but to us there is but one
God, the Father, of whom are all things, and we in him; and
one Lord Jesus Christ, by whom are all things, and we by him.
Howbeit, there is not in every man that knowledge." I. Corinthians VIII. 5–7.

"There is one body, and one Spirit, even as ye are called in
one hope of your calling; one Lord, one faith, one baptism, one
God and Father of all, who is above all, and through all, and in
you all." Ephesians IV. 4–6.   .

III. The Savior he believed to be "the Son of God his Father," and adored him with all his heart. He did not regard
him as an inferior being, but the true and proper Son of God,
inheriting and equally sharing all his Father's greatness, goodness, wisdom, power, and glory; yet, not so as to make two
gods, nor yet make Christ to be God the Father. He held the
highest possible views of the Savior, consistent with the faith
that he is the Son of God. Those who go farther, in effect deny
the Son, as all those do who deny his being a derived being.

Confirming Scriptures.—"God, who at sundry times and in
divers manners spake in time past unto the fathers by the
prophets, hath in these last days spoken unto us by his Son,
whom he hath appointed heir of all things, by whom also he
made the worlds; who being the brightness of his glory, and
the express image of his person, and upholding all things by
the word of his power, when he had himself purged our sins,
sat down on the right hand of the Majesty on high." Hebrews
I. 1–3.

"And Moses verily was faithful in all his house, as a servant,
for a testimony of those things which were to be spoken after:
but Christ as a Son over his own house." Hebrews III. 5, 6.

"In the beginning was the Word, and the Word was with
God, and the Word was God. The same was in the beginning
with God. And the Word was made flesh, and dwelt among
us (and we beheld his glory, the glory as of the only-begotten
of the Father), full of grace and truth." John I. 1–14.

"For God so loved the world, that he gave his only-begotten
Son, that whosoever believeth in him, should not perish, but
have everlasting life." John III. 16.

"For I came down from heaven, not to do mine own will,

but the will of him that sent me. "And this is the Father's will which hath sent me, that of all which he hath given me I should lose nothing, but should raise it up again at the last day." John VI. 38, 39.

Father, I will that they also whom thou hast given me be with me where I am; that they may behold my glory which thou hast given me: for thou lovedst me before the foundation of the world." John XVII. 24.

"If thou believest with all thine heart, thou mayest. And he answered and said, I believe that Jesus Christ is the Son of God." Acts VIII. 37.

"Then was Saul certain days with the disciples which were at Damascus. And straightway he preached Christ in the synagogues, that he is the Son of God." Acts IX. 20.

"Then cometh the end, when he shall have delivered up the kingdom to God, even the Father; when he shall have put down all rule, and all authority, and power. For he must reign, till he hath put all enemies under his feet. The last enemy that shall be destroyed is death. For he hath put all things under his feet. But when he saith all things are put under him, it is manifest that he is excepted which did put all things under him. And when all things shall be subdued unto him, then shall the Son also himself be subject unto him that put all things under him, that God may be all in all. I. Corinthians XV. 24–28.

"And we have seen and do testify, that the Father sent the Son to be the Savior of the world. Whosoever shall confess that Jesus is the Son of God, God dwelleth in him, and he in God." I. John IV. 14.

"And this is the record, that God hath given to us eternal life: and this life is in his Son. He that hath the Son, hath life; and he that hath not the Son of God, hath not life. These things have I written unto you that believe on the name of the Son of God; that ye may know that ye have eternal life, and that ye may believe on the name of the Son of God." I. John V. 11–13.

"And I knew him not; but he that sent me to baptize with water, the same said unto me, Upon whom thou shalt see the Spirit descending and remaining on him, the same is he which baptizeth with the Holy Ghost. And I saw and bare record that this is the Son of God." John I. 33.

IV. He relied upon the Holy Spirit as his comforter, and regarded it as the Spirit of God the Father, and by no means as a separate person from God the Father.

Confirming Scriptures.—"In the beginning God created the heaven and the earth. And the earth was without form, and void; and darkness was upon the face of the deep: and the Spirit of God moved upon the face of the waters." Gen. I. 1, 2.

18

"And the angel answered and said unto her, The Holy Ghost shall come upon thee, and the power of the Highest shall overshadow thee: therefore also that holy thing which shall be born of thee, shall be called the Son of God." Luke I. 35.

"Jesus also being baptized, and praying, the heaven was opened, and the Holy Ghost descended in a bodily shape like a dove upon him, and a voice came from heaven, which said, Thou art my beloved Son; in thee I am well pleased." Luke III. 21, 22.

"He shall baptize you with the Holy Ghost, and with fire." Matt. III. 11.

"And suddenly there came a sound from heaven, as of a rushing mighty wind, and it filled all the house where they were sitting. And there appeared unto them cloven tongues like as of fire, and it sat upon each of them. And they were filled with the Holy Ghost, and began to speak with other tongues, as the Spirit gave them utterance." Acts II. 2–4.

"The Holy Ghost fell on all them which heard the word." Acts X. 44.

"And I will pray the Father, and he shall give you another Comforter, that he may abide with you forever; even the Spirit of truth; whom the world can not receive, because it seeth him not, neither knoweth him: but ye know him; for he dwelleth with you, and shall be in you." John XIV. 16, 17.

V. He contended all his life for the necessity of the "new birth," but considered the love and service of God the best proof that a person had experienced it. He often quoted, "He that loveth is born of God."

Confirming Scriptures.—"Born, not of blood, nor ot the will of the flesh, nor of the will of man, but of God." John I. 13.

"Jesus answered, Verily, verily, I say unto thee, except a man be born of water, and of the Spirit, he can not enter into the kingdom of God. That which is born of the flesh, is flesh; and that which is born of the Spirit is spirit. Marvel not that I said unto thee, Ye must be born again. The wind bloweth where it listeth, and thou hearest the sound thereof, but canst not tell whence it cometh, and whither it goeth: so is every one that is born of the Spirit." John III. 5–8.

"Every one that loveth is born of God, and knoweth God." I. John IV. 7.

"Being born again, not of corruptible seed, but of incorruptible, by the word of God, which liveth and abideth forever." I. Peter I. 23.

VI. The atonement he regarded as the reconciliation of men to God, by the death of him who died for all, that all might live through him. (See p. 34).

Confirming Scriptures.—"The atonement was made, to consecrate and to sanctify them." Exodus xxix. 33.

"And not only so, but we also joy in God, through our Lord Jesus Christ, by whom we have now received the atonement." Romans v. 11.

"If when we were enemies, we were reconciled to God by the death of his Son; much more, being reconciled, we shall be saved by his life." Romans v. 10.

"He was wounded for our transgressions, he was bruised for our iniquities; the chastisement of our peace was upon him; and with his stripes we are healed." Isaiah LIII. 5.

"He died for all, that they which live should not henceforth live unto themselves, but unto him which died for them, and rose again." II. Cor. v. 15.

"But we see Jesus, who was made a little lower than the angels for the suffering of death, crowned with glory and honor; that he by the grace of God should taste death for every man." Hebrews II. 9.

"Who gave himself a ransom for all, to be testified in due time." I. Timothy II. 6.

"He is the propitiation for our sins; and not for ours only but also for the sins of the whole world." I. John II. 2.

VII. He received into full fellowship all who professed to love God and his people, and to believe in the Lord Jesus Christ as the Son of God, who were willing to obey the Bible.

Confirming Scriptures.—"Wherefore receive ye one another, as Christ also received us, to the glory of God." Romans xv. 7.

"By this shall all men know that ye are my disciples, if ye have love one to another." John XIII. 35.

"Then they that gladly received his word, were baptized: and the same day there were added unto them about three thousand souls. And they continued steadfastly in the apostles' doctrine and fellowship, and in breaking of bread, and in prayers." Acts II. 41, 42.

"If thou believest with all thine heart, thou mayest. And he answered and said, I believe that Jesus Christ is the Son of God. And he commanded the chariot to stand still: and they went down both into the water, both Philip and the eunuch; and he baptized him. And when they were come up out of the water, the Spirit of the Lord caught away Philip, that the eunuch saw him no more, and he went on his way rejoicing." Acts VIII. 37–39.

"Him that is weak in the faith receive ye, but not to doubtful disputations." Romans XIV. 1

VIII. He believed in baptism, as the immersion of believers, (but made no form of baptism a test of fellowship).

Confirming Scriptures.—"Then went out to him Jerusalem, and all Judea, and all the region round about Jordan, and were baptized of him in Jordan, confessing their sins." Matthew III. 5, 6.

"And Jesus, when he was baptized, went up straightway out of the water." Matthew III. 16.

"John also was baptizing in Enon, near to Salim, because there was much water there." John III. 23.

"And he commanded the chariot to stand still: and they went down both into the water, both Philip and the eunuch; and he baptized him. And when they were come up out of the water, the Spirit of the Lord caught away Philip, that the eunuch saw him no more: and he went on his way rejoicing" Acts VIII. 38, 39.

"Therefore we are buried with him by baptism into death: that like as Christ was raised up from the dead by the glory of the Father, even so we also should walk in newness of life." Romans VI. 4.

"Buried with him in baptism, wherein also ye are risen with him through the faith of the operation of God, who hath raised him from the dead." Colossians II. 12.

"If ye then be risen with Christ, seek those things which are above, where Christ sitteth on the right hand of God." Colossians III. 1.

"Let us draw near with a true heart, in full assurance of faith, having our hearts sprinkled from an evil conscience, and our bodies washed with pure water." Hebrews X. 22.

¶ IX. Communion he practiced usually semi-annually in the country, but conformed to the custom of the churches where he preached. He invited all Christians to his fellowship, though in the heat of debate he might sometimes seem to excommunicate precious persons; his anathemas were only designed to include impious opinions.

Confirming Scriptures.—"This is my body which is given for you: this do in remembrance of me. Likewise also the cup after supper, saying, This cup is the new testament in my blood, which is shed for you. But behold, the hand of him that betrayeth me is with me on the table. And truly the Son of man goeth as it was determined: and woe unto that man by whom he is betrayed." Luke XXII. 19–22.

"And they, continuing daily with one accord in the temple, and breaking bread from house to house, did eat their meat with gladness and singleness of heart." Acts II. 46.

"And upon the first day of the week, when the disciples came together to break bread, Paul preached unto them (ready to depart on the morrow), and continued his speech until midnight. When he therefore was come up again, and had broken bread, and eaten, and talked a long while, even till break of day, so he departed." Acts xx. 7, 11.

" For as often as ye eat this bread, and drink this cup, ye do show the Lord's death till he come." I. Corinthians xi. 26.

" For ye are yet carnal: for whereas there is among you envying, and strife, and divisions, are ye not carnal, and walk as men? For while one saith, I am of Paul: and another, I am of Apollos; are ye not carnal?" I. Corinthians iii. 3, 4.

X. While teaching the purest piety, and holding ministers to the strictest accountability, he suffered in members the greatest liberty; seldom resorting to expulsion.

Confirming Scriptures.—"Thou thyself art a guide of the blind, a light of them which are in darkness, an instructor of the foolish, a teacher of babes, which hast the form of knowledge, and of the truth in the law: Thou therefore which teachest another, teachest thou not thyself? thou that preachest, a man should not steal, dost thou steal? Thou that sayest, a man should not commit adultery, dost thou commit adultery? thou that abhorrest idols, dost thou commit sacrilege? Thou that makest thy boast of the law, through breaking the law dishonorest thou God?" Romans ii. 19-23.

"Then came Peter to him, and said, Lord, how oft shall my brother sin against me, and I forgive him? till seven times? Jesus saith unto him, I say not unto thee, Until seven times: but, Until seventy times seven." Matthew xviii. 21, 22.

XI. He was circumspect in his conduct, much absorbed in religion, faithful in prayer, seldom visiting a family without worship, strict in the observance of the Sabbath, faithful to his engagements, true to his word, punctual to his promises, but cautious in all his manners and conversation.

Confirming Scriptures.—"These things command and teach. Let no man despise thy youth; but be thou an example of the believers, in word, in conversation, in charity, in spirit, in faith, in purity. Till I come, give attendance to reading, to exhortation, to doctrine. Neglect not the gift that is in thee, which was given thee by prophecy, with the laying on of the hands of the presbytery. Meditate upon these things; give thyself wholly to them; that thy profiting may appear to all. Take heed unto thyself, and unto the doctrine; continue in them; for in doing this thou shalt both save thyself, and them that hear thee." I. Timothy iv. 11-16.

"Neither filthiness, nor foolish talking, nor jesting, which are not convenient: but rather giving of thanks." Ephesians v. 4.

"To them who by patient continuance in well doing seek for glory and honor and immortality, eternal life." Rom. ii. 7.

DEATH OF ELDER GARDNER.

REMARKABLE INCIDENTS AND COINCIDENCES.

July 10, 1873, Elder Gardner arrived at the Hyannis camp-ground, at Cape Cod, Massachusetts. Precisely three months from this date, his spirit arrived at a more coveted country. July 26, 1873, he fell, injuring himself so much that few thought that he could recover. The note of prayer was sounded throughout the whole country—prayer that he might live to return home and die among his friends. He was on the sea-coast a thousand miles away, and, when nearly eighty-three, received injuries regarded as fatal. Then prayer from a thousand fireside altars went up to heaven for him! He gave his farewell address to his brethren there; he lived to get home. His age, the warm weather, and the jolting of travel, were against him, but he lived to get home. He slowly recovered, so as to attend church. His own loved conference was to meet in a few days, under three months from the time he was hurt, and he was able to meet with it. It met in the church, his loved church, of which he was the sole pastor nearly forty-five years; he lived to preach his last sermon to that church and to the conference assembled there, and to visitors from distant states. This took place within two days and a half of his death, yet he lived to see it, and was able to preach. It was recognized as his last sermon. He bade the people "farewell," went home, and died without a murmur. Died after all was done! Died as he desired! Were the prayers answered?

Farewells.—He bade his friends farewell at Dayton, Cincinnati, Ripley, Stephentown New York, Petersburgh New York, Providence Rhode Island, Boston Massachusetts, the Hyannis camp-meeting, the Bentonville congregation, and finally the Southern Ohio Christian Conference, with all its ministers, and the church at Bethlehem. He preached his last sermon, after seventy-three years, within a little over a mile of the place where he waited in 1800 while his father bought his farm in Ohio. He died in 1873 at Bentonville, where he confessed Christ in 1810. His funeral was preached, and his body was buried at the Union Church, the first church organized under his labors when a young minister, in 1819. He had divided his property among his children, he had bidden all farewell, his work was finished, he said, "Lay me down;" and thus closed a life of sixty-three years' labor in the Christian ministry! Were the prayers answered? He often prayed for a tranquil hour in which to die, and he had it! He often prayed for the Lord

Jesus to be with him to the end, and one of the best meetings of his life, one in which he was able to preach, and sing, and pray, and bid farewell to over a score of ministers and hundreds of brethren, where all felt that the presence of God was with them, took place only sixty-two hours before he died.

NORTH STEPHENTOWN, August 14, 1874.

DR. SUMMERBELL: Inclosed find the pay for the biography of Elder M. Gardner. We received a postal card from you asking for some of the last letters of Elder Gardner. Looking them over I find very little that would be of use to you, as his letters were generally confined to business. Elder Gardner spent some of his last summers with us. I can say of him, he possessed an almost inexhaustible fund of knowledge; was a safe counselor, and a true friend. Religiously, I esteemed him one of the best men of the age. I think that he possessed an even devotional frame of mind, such as is seldom found. The Spirit's influence seemed to pervade every prayer, and frequently, when in the desk, while meditating upon the theme of his discourse preparatory to delivering it, I have noticed a change in his countenance that seemed almost divine.

Kindly yours.

ORLANDO ROSE.

APPENDIX.

Some documents of a legal character are preserved by the editor for future reference. They will be deposited with the copyright, only to be published in a future edition, should circumstances demand it. N. SUMMERBELL.

No agents are yet appointed for this book, but to those who buy to sell, a discount is made. N. S.

This book can be obtained by mail, prepaid, of N. SUMMERBELL, 184 Longworth street, Cincinnati, Ohio. Price $1.25.

The minutes of the Oshawa General Convention will be sent, post-paid, on receipt of ten cents, by N. SUMMERBELL, Cincinnati, Ohio.

SUBSCRIBERS' NAMES.

MINISTERS OF THE GOSPEL.

Abbott, Elder A. J.
Addington, Elder Thomas.
Allen, Elder Lyman.

Brandon, Elder Thomas A.

Carroll, Elder Asher W.
Chadwick, Elder Nicholas S.
Chrisman, Elder B. H.
Coburn, Elder Keyes.
Cooper, Elder B. A.
Craig, Elder Austin, D. D.

Dawson, Elder N., M. D.
Dykes, Elder J. P.

Fifer, Elder Joseph.

Hanger, Elder A. C.
Heath, Elder A. R.
Heston, Elder Thomas.
Henry, Elder Thomas.
Holverstott, Elder H. H.
How, Elder Moses.

Kindle, Elder Joseph M
Kirby, Elder Joseph.

Lepley, Elder D.

Morrill, Elder W. S.
Morrill, Elder Alva H.

Orr, Elder W. H.

Pangburn, Elder William.
Phillips, Elder Oliver.
Pittman, Elder William.
Poff, Elder Samuel.

Rapp, Elder E. M.
Rilea, Elder S.
Roberts, Elder Oliver A.
Robinson, Elder J. T., M. D.
Rush, Elder Henry Y.

Searls, Elder George R.
Sheldon, Elder Thomas.
Smith, Elder Jeremiah M.
Summerbell, Elder B. F.
Summerbell, Elder James.
Summerbell, Elder J. J.
Summerbell, Elder M.

Topping, James P.
Trull, Elder W. W.
Tuck, Elder M. W.

Vancamp, Elder Jesse.

Whitney, Elder Joseph.
Winebrenner, Elder Peter.
Wright, Elder R. J.
Wyman, Elder O. T.

SUBSCRIBERS' NAMES.

Abbott, Lou J.
Abbott, Rosana.
Allen, C. B.
Anderson, Lucinda.
Atkins, Almira.

Anderson, R.

Baldwin, D. H.
Bartholomew, Samuel.
Bagby, William.

Banner, Rebecca.
Bellis, John.
Bentley, A. N.
Bodine, H. F.
Bone, Christian.
Briton, Ezra.
Bransion, Martha.
Brownell, Mrs. Isaac.
Brookover, A. J.
Brookover, James.
Brookover, John.
Bugbee, C. A.
Bushnell, S. P.
Bussing, Isaac.

Carter, Rane C.
Chadwick, Elsworth E.
Chase, Willard W.
Chapin, Asa.
Clemons, William M.
Colburn, Harvey.
Cranston, John B.

Daugherty, Jane.
Davis, E. S.
Day, John.
Day, Joseph.
Demint, J.
Deyo, James B.
Dearborn, J. L.
Dillman, W. H.
Dimmit, Joseph.
Dooley, Kirkham.
Dunham, L. C.

Ellis, George, M. D.
Eshelman, Peter.

Falson, Mrs. S. T.
Famous, John.
Farnsworth, H.
Fiefield, J. C.
Finch, Smith.
Flaugher, Jesse.
Forman, Caroline.
Ford, A., M. D.

Gage, Isaac R.

Gamsby, D. A.
Gander, John.
Garvin, Sarah O.
Gordon, James C.
Gotwals, Daniel.
Goldsbery, Mary V.
Greenwalt, Rebecca.
Grout, Benjamin.
Greeley, Mrs. Samuel.
Grove, Reuben P.

Hall, H. C.
Harrington, J. W.
Hatton, Thomas S.
Hale, Mrs. E. A.
Hastings, Henry.
Harris, Cummins O.
Hains, John.
Heath, E. M.
Heath, Mrs. M. S. Harpin.
Helfinstine, S. Q.
Hensley, Martha A.
Hiatt, Aaron.
Hill, J. W.
Hill, George C.
Howard, Titus F.
Howser, J. N.
Hoel, Catharine.
Howard, J. R.
Herman, John H.
Hornbeck, Cyrus.
Hunningham, John.
Hucy, Hannah.
Huff, Peter.

Inst, Dr. D. A.

Jervis, Mrs. C.
Johnson, Herman.
Johns, Esther.
Jolly, Mrs. John.
Jones, Evan.

Kinney, Ellis.
Kitchen, Charles H

Lang, B. S.
Larkin, Amos.

Lawrence, Reuben.
Leedum, Davis.
Leonardson, II., M. D.

Maddon, J. P.
Malory, Ottis.
Mankes, James.
Mann, Davis.
McChesma, Eliza A.
McDaniel, R. H.
McHarman, Lydia.
McKee, R. D.
McHench, James.
Miller, Peter S.
Miller, John II.
Miles, John J.
Moore, T. B.
Moore, H. C.
Moore, Mary.
Mouck, J. W.

Nevers, Joshua U.

O'Daniel, Dennis.
Orr, Elizabeth.

Palin, Exum N.
Patterson, E., M. D.
Parker, Mrs. Lucia.
Parker, Mrs. C.
Paulin, Uriah.
Perry, A. G.
Pettit, Robert.
Phillips, II. II.
Phister, Colonel, Jacob O.
Pierce, Henry P.
Poff, Kate.

Qualks, Joseph.

Randolph, Barbara A.
Reynolds, George A.
Robinson, Jonathan.
Roggers, John.

Rose, N. II.
Rowe, Elizabeth.
Ryan, G. W.

Shinkle, J. T.
Sherman, Nathan.
Shocking, H. A.
Show, Wizziah.
Skinner, Catharine.
Snare, Eliza.
Snider, Caroline.
Sprong, Cornelius.
Starn, John.
Stephenson, F. E.
Stephenson, James.
Stoughton, Maggie.
Stroman, Sarah.
Stuart, Perry.
Stuart, O. N.
Sunday-school Rye, N. II.
Swope, Eliza A.

Tatman, Francis M. II.
Taylor, Daniel W.
Tyler, Franklin.
Thompson, A. C.
Thompson, James II.
Trisler, H. S.

Uhl, George II.

Walker, Alanson.
Waterfield, Samuel.
Waterfield, William.
Watson, John.
Wellman, John R.
Wells, B. F.
Whitcomb, Almore
Wood, Owen.
Worley, T. A.
Wyley, Jane.
Wyman, Emily.

Yetter, Levina.

INDEX.